REVENGE NEVER RESTS

OTHER BOOKS AND AUDIOBOOKS BY LAURIE LEWIS

Unspoken

The Dragons of Alsace Farm

Sweet Water

Love on a Limb

Awakening Avery

Love on the Line

Cross-Country Christmas

Tallie Brown Suspense Series

Secrets Never Die

Revenge Never Rests

HISTORICAL ROMANCE WRITTEN UNDER THE PEN NAME L. C. LEWIS

Free Men and Dreamers series

Dark Sky at Dawn

Twilight's Last Gleaming

Dawn's Early Light

Oh, Say Can You See?

In God is Our Trust

REVENGE NEVER RESTS

A *SECRETS NEVER DIE* SEQUEL

LAURIE LEWIS

Covenant Communications, Inc.

Front cover images: *The Jungle Muse* © Ander5, shutterstock.com; *The Seal of the United States* © Morphart Creation, shutterstock.com; *Rear-View Running Man* © m-imagephotography, istockphoto.com
Back cover image: *US Capitol Building* © orhancam, istockphoto.com

Cover design by Julie Olson

Published by Covenant Communications, Inc.
American Fork, Utah

Library of Congress Cataloging-in-Publication Data

Name: Laurie Lewis
Title: Revenge never rests : a secrets never die sequel / Laurie Lewis
Description: American Fork, UT : Covenant Communications, Inc. [2022]
Identifiers: Library of Congress Control Number 2022941919 | ISBN 978-1-52442-246-2
LC record available at https://lccn.loc.gov/ 2022941919

Printed in the United States of America
First Printing: December 2022

28 27 26 25 24 23 22 10 9 8 7 6 5 4 3 2 1

PRAISE FOR LAURIE LEWIS

REVENGE NEVER RESTS

"I found Laurie Lewis to be an exceptional author that combines action, love, and mystique in her inspiring romance *Revenge Never Rests*. It is a well-written novel that keeps you anticipating the next sinister ambush awaiting Tallie and her inner circle. The setting takes you from a secluded forest to a heavily armed private island. The characters of Tallie and Jackson generate chemistry that confuses Tallie at times. You get wholly involved in how they manage to have each other's backs when they face danger from different parts of the country. The story is memorable, as it is laced with danger, captivating characters, and a riveting storyline that shifts at the whims of a twisted psychopath. I highly recommend this book for those who enjoy a clean romance woven with danger."

—Readers' Favorite five-star review

"What a gripping book! You can't put it down! This book starts off drawing you in with its intensity, and it stays that way to the end. Yet the intensity is never overpowering, as the author weaves other aspects to keep the story from becoming too heavy. A great read."

—NetGalley review

SECRETS NEVER DIE

"*Secrets Never Die* by author Laurie Lewis is one of the most intricately plotted and perfectly executed novels I've ever read. The action and drama hooked me from the first page, and never once did my attention drift. I'm still marveling over how the author was able to keep this very tense, twisty tale on course given all the moving parts. Every character is drawn with a careful hand, bringing a rich texture to this large cast, each with their own mysterious history, adding layer upon layer of intrigue, speculation, and ulterior motives. And in the end, each one of their stories fits together like pieces of a puzzle. But I must warn you—once you get started, you won't want to put this one down! Highly recommend!"

—Cynthia Hamilton, author of the Madeline Dawkins Mystery series

"A powerful, suspenseful Christian novel."

—Michelle Kidwell, author of *The Sky Is Falling*

"This story unravels every hidden detail in an intriguing and fast-paced plot. This suspense-filled tale has a lot of twists and turns, drama, and plenty of interest to hold your attention to the very end."

—Emily Yager, author of the *Mud River Weddings*

Cross-Country Christmas

"Readers will love this tender, thoughtful story."

—*Meridian Magazine*

"*Cross-Country Christmas* by Laurie Lewis is one of the loveliest contemporary Christian romance novels I've ever read! For readers who enjoy wholesome, sweet romances with a bit of grit and complex characters, this is a perfect read."

—Amazing Family Books

"Laurie Lewis has a wonderful, smooth writing style; crisp, clean text; and a perfect-pitch storyteller's voice. She masterfully controls the pace and keeps you turning pages."

—T. N. Traynor, Chick Lit Café Reviews

To Amanda,
who, like Tallie Brown,
has faced hard things
with courage and hope

ACKNOWLEDGMENTS AND AUTHOR'S NOTE

THE FIRST BOOK IN THIS series, *Secrets Never Die*, was by far my most challenging project, and I had major apprehension over attempting a sequel. A conversation with a friend who asked about a sequel set me straight. She told me what readers wanted, and the story came together from there.

This sequel was written during a strange time in American history. The pandemic has continued to rattle our security, but social, political, and economic factors are also straining the nation's foundation. I finished my presubmission edits on this manuscript as Afghanistan fell to the Taliban. All these events impacted me, and I have no doubt that they also influenced this manuscript.

My husband's work selling ruggedized computer hardware to the military has taken us to many military bases and shows along the East Coast. I have the greatest respect and a humble appreciation for our military men and women and their families. I'm awed by what they do and what they're willing to sacrifice. Living in the Northeast Corridor put us in contact with many former military members who'd moved into government service or the private security sector. While the characters in this book are creations of my imagination, I hope I have accurately captured the patriotism, discipline, and personal sacrifice of the courageous men and women I've known. I have raised the issue of the frustrations they must experience over protecting a nation while being subject to ever-changing four-year political currents.

This book came together like a patchwork quilt, and I wasn't sure if I had filled in all the holes. I owe tremendous thanks to my Willowsport Crew of beta readers, whose feedback helped strengthen the story and its flow from book one, *Secrets Never Die*. Special thanks are owed to Bruce F. Morse and Cheri Frazer, whose notes and comments inspired changes that made this book tighter and better.

Finally, many thanks to the Covenant Communications publishing team, the orchestra to my lonely violin. Thank you to their committee for giving the green light to this sequel. This is my third book with awesome editor Kami Hancock, who works her magic, catching silly blunders and seeing the big picture clearly when I get stuck in the weeds. She makes me and my work better, and I'm grateful I've had multiple opportunities to work with her. I'm also grateful to our marketing and sales teams, headed by Jessica Bybee and Amy Parker, respectively, who work long and hard to get our books before readers. Covenant authors get a copy of their book, signed by everyone who worked to bring it to life. It's humbling to see how many hands are involved in the production of a single book. Thank you to everyone who made this manuscript a published work.

And thank you to each reader who opens page one. I hope this book made you consider how fragile freedom is.

All the best,

Laurie Lewis

CHAPTER ONE

Saturday, June 21, 2014
Near Burley, Idaho

Tallie Brown's gaze slipped from the white plaster ceiling of the James family's sunny guest bedroom to the sunflower wall clock for what felt like the thousandth time in the last hour. She pushed back against the music playing in her head . . . a lullaby that made her heart ache and choked her with uncertainty, stealing the peace she'd enjoyed during the early days of her stay at Jackson James's family home. The room had felt like a hug when she arrived a week ago, but no more. The events of the previous evening had stolen that peace and, with it, the hope that she could feel whole and worthy of a man like Jackson. Everything, all her losses, all her doubts, were tied to the cataclysmic shift in her world that had occurred following the death of Julia Brown, the woman who'd raised Tallie.

The loss of Julia had left Tallie reeling, but what she left behind for Tallie to find—a brief note and a photo—was much worse, like the first ball roll in a Rube Goldberg device that had set every other detail in Tallie's world in motion until all that remained were rubble and deceit.

Tallie had always wondered why her mother had insisted on raising her only child in isolated third-world outposts while stressing education in every area from art to combat. Why not a city with people and paved streets and good schools? It was not to be. Julia had been teacher, trainer, and adjudicator, instilling knowledge in Tallie with strict militaristic discipline until, even as a child, she could think like a scientist, track like a predator, and defend herself like a warrior, all while scaling a mountain wall or crossing a plain without leaving a trail. While her successes had won her Julia's respect, questioning the woman's decisions had brought detachment and disappointment, so Tallie had followed directions and obeyed. And then Julia was gone and Tallie was alone, with nothing but a photo and a few ominous words:

> *I wasn't the mother you deserved . . . . my former choices have always placed you in danger, never more than now. . . .*
>
> *You stand at the fork between two lives. One requires you to change your name, but it keeps the memories of our life together intact. Answers lie along the other one, but so does pain. If this is what you choose, start with the photo. You'll figure the rest out.*

Two and a half weeks ago, Tallie had started with the photo, which had led her to a dying coal-mining town in West Virginia named Cutler's Ridge on the day a small private jet fell from the sky in a fireball behind the inn owned by Bodie Glick. A disgraced reporter, Jackson James, had been sent there with a career-saving lead about that flight from the very man he blamed for derailing his career. When it became clear that certain facts in their two quests overlapped, Tallie and Jackson formed an alliance, and with the aid of the seemingly misplaced, highly overqualified local librarian, Marlene Bodine, they uncovered how deeply all three of their lives had been manipulated to bring them together for a cause they could not have foreseen.

Tallie's life had been the most upended, obliterating everything she thought she knew about her identity. She'd discovered that Julia Brown was actually Lieutenant Diana Howard, more accurately Tallie's kidnapper than mother, and that she herself was one of Julia's creations, or at least her persona was. Tallie was actually Molly Kaswell, a twin daughter born to then-Captain Mordecai (Cai) Kaswell and his wife, Deidre.

Tallie drew her arm across her moist eyes and flipped onto her side, away from the clock, trying to end the agonizing recounting of her twenty-plus stolen years.

Sorrow at last gave way to fatigue, but somewhere in the space between sleep and awakening, the music returned, and with it the image she'd happened upon earlier. She had followed the tune and found Jackson's ex-fiancée, Dawn, in his sister, Kelly's, room, rocking her son, Ethan, and singing with him. Tallie had met them earlier in the evening. The James family had hosted an open house to welcome Jackson home after his long estrangement. When Dawn arrived, she had been swept up in Mr. and Mrs. James's love. The woman had looked so at home there in the Jameses' house, singing to her son, like the final puzzle piece Jackson had needed to complete his perfect world.

The sweet music and the tender scene pulled at Tallie's broken, motherless heart and made her want to flee. Her training and wits and intellect, the tools upon which she relied, seemed insignificant gifts to offer Jackson compared to the music and gentleness Dawn and her son offered. Tallie's life was a mess. A disaster. And meeting Dawn had increased those feelings of inadequacy.

The woman was stylish and pretty with curled hair and makeup and painted nails. Before getting ready for bed, Tallie had looked at her own appearance in the mirror. She was tall and strong and dressed for function rather than fashion, in cargo shorts, hiking boots, a T-shirt, and thick socks. She'd never really done anything more with her wheat-colored hair than pass a comb through it and bind it up in a ponytail or braids. Jackson said she was pretty, but if she was, she figured it was a tomboy kind of pretty, not like the loveliness of this woman who sang sweet songs.

Two more tears broke free as her feelings of inadequacy encroached. She flipped over again and was nearly asleep when the disturbing blare of an Amber Alert brought her fully awake. The last threads of her miserable thoughts left her sweat-soaked and shaking, yet she counted the alert a blessing, an answer to a silent prayer for her plaguing reverie to end and take away the swelling self-doubts. *Prayer.* She barely understood such spiritual things or the God to whom they were offered. God and prayer were as foundational to Jackson as home and family, but as delicious as these concepts were to Tallie, they were not as easily mastered as tying off a line. Like the song, they added to her personal struggle to be enough, leaving her feeling more inconsequential than she had since she was a child.

She dressed quickly and grabbed her new phone and the coordinating watch Jackson had helped her pick out before they'd caught their flight to Idaho. She didn't need the ability to talk to someone through her wristwatch, but Jackson had convinced her that she would come to appreciate all its functions. Mostly, she'd agreed it was time to begin anew, and that would be best accomplished by tossing the old phone—Julia's phone—aside, along with all its reminders of their fractured past.

The future was still unclear. She and Jackson had just helped solve the mystery surrounding the murder of Deidre and Meghan Kaswell, her birth mother and twin sister, the passengers killed in a fateful plane crash in Cutler's Ridge along with the pilot. Tallie had never known them and never would. Theirs was a love she had never enjoyed nor would ever enjoy. But out of the ashes had come some hope. Cai Kaswell, now a general, was still alive. He was the father she had never known and a man of power. In return for Tallie's efforts to protect the crash site of his wife and daughter, the general had come to meet Tallie, offering her and Jackson jobs on his security and PR details.

Before she could begin another round of self-examination, the alert sounded again, and she left her self-pity behind to read the accompanying message.

A recently adopted child had become lost after wandering away from her new parents' campsite. It wasn't far from the James family's farm.

So much about the situation picked at the raw wounds still plaguing Tallie—a lost child, lost parents, a lost home, new parents, a new home. She felt the child's fear and pain. She wanted to shout her own story to her father, to tell him, "I'm Molly. I'm your daughter!" But could he believe such a ludicrous tale?

She tried not to hope for such a thing. She'd known enough disappointment. Instead, she would at least get to know him as she worked beside him, even though she might never be able to claim him as her father or be claimed by him. Small dreams . . . small hopes . . . those were safe anchors. Right now, her small dream was to find this lost child and return her to the parents who loved her. Helping her would be a balm to Tallie, a reminder that she was useful and valuable, so without more than a moment's thought, she packed her things.

She had never really unpacked more than the necessities for each day. She was grateful she had resisted Jackson's suggestion to leave her pack behind and bring a small suitcase instead. Julia had taught her to pack for emergencies, so she carried carabiners and ropes, plus a handgun, a medical kit, and other necessities, including her laptop. At times, she wished she could leave the need to prepare for disaster behind and simply relax, feeling comfortable and enough at ease to carry nothing but a lipstick and a brush in a purse. She wondered if Jackson saw her as knotted up or constantly on defense. Was that why he'd urged her to carry a suitcase instead? She set that concern aside and returned her focus to the alert.

She hefted her expedition pack onto her back and headed down the stairs of the James family's quiet, darkened house. After scribbling brief notes to the family and to Jackson on pages torn from a pad of shopping lists magnetically attached to the fridge, she was out the door and into the darkness.

As deficient as she was in social affectations, she still knew her exit was rude and thoughtless, but that concern was less discomfiting than the thought of staying around to face Jackson and his family in the morning.

She caught a ride on a bread truck driven by a man who respected her unwillingness to chat. When Tallie mentioned her destination, the man seemed to understand her urgency. He dropped her off at the turnoff as another car whizzed past. Tallie uttered a terse thank-you and was out of the vehicle before the truck tires stopping rolling. She hurried on in the direction the car went. It led her to the camping area where several sheriff's department vehicles were parked, before disappearing from view.

The smell of the warm woodlands revitalized her. She was back in her element, energized and happy to be useful. She walked up to the man wearing the sheriff's badge and said, "My name's Tallie Brown. I came to help you find that missing little girl."

The sheriff's brow wrinkled as he looked at her. "You did, did you? How'd you even know about her? I just sent the Amber Alert out five minutes ago."

The man was either mistaken about the time frame or simply dismissing Tallie, but she wasn't deterred. She'd met similarly patronizing people when she and Julia had answered distress calls in the past. She'd also seen those people's looks shift to respect and even awe once they saw her determination, strength, and skill, and she hoped it would be so in this case. "All I know is that I received your alert and came as fast as I could. I'm an experienced tracker. I can help."

The sheriff scanned her tall, youthful frame and wrote her off again, calling for assistance. "Deputy Kirkham, would you please escort this young lady away?"

The deputy arrived and took her arm to lead her away, but Tallie tightened every ironlike muscle in her body and anchored her five-foot-seven inches, rendering him unable to move her. When the sheriff teased him over his failure, Tallie pulled out her US Park Service credentials and showed the man.

He turned the credentials over and read every word, then called her bluff and phoned the ranger station at the Gifford Pinchot National Forest in Washington State, where her former boss, Chief Ranger Louis Barber, answered.

Tallie could hear Louis proudly roll off her résumé of degrees and awards, confirming that she was, in very deed, uniquely qualified to head into the forest at night when others dared not, his words assuring Tallie that he still had her back. Until recently, he'd been the closest thing to a father she'd ever known, and the soothing sound of his voice and his words of approval steadied her once again.

She heard him ask to speak to her, and then the sheepish officer extended his phone her way. She took it and said, "Louis?"

"Oh, Tallie. I'm so relieved to finally hear from you. I've been reading a lot of things, and . . . well, let's just say I'm glad to know you're there, using your talents."

"Thanks."

"And, hey, listen to me. Whatever happened between you and Julia, don't discount what she taught you. You're amazing. They're lucky to have you, so go do what you do best."

"Thanks, Louis. I'll call you soon. I promise."

There hadn't been time enough to deal with Julia's death and all the lies she had told, but Tallie swept away the deficiencies in her lie-filled life and embraced the useful lessons Julia had taught her.

When the call ended, the sheriff closed one eye and stared Tallie down with the other, as if he were still skeptical. "If you're what and who you and this ranger fella claim you are, then this is either the uncanniest luck I've ever seen or a miracle." He returned Tallie's credentials to her and added, "You had to have been close by. None of my regular teams of trackers and their dogs have had time to show up yet. Just hold on until we get you some help."

But Tallie wasn't willing to waste anymore time. She strode over to the frantic woman who must be the mother and asked questions about the woman's newly adopted child. The man Tallie presumed to be the newly adoptive father tugged on his beard and paced, offering no constructive information. Emily, their new daughter, had wandered off with their dog, a little terrier named Bristol. The mother seemed to know more about Bristol and his habits than she knew about Emily, so Tallie focused on the pet and headed into the dark forest, once again feeling that her life had value in her world at least, if not in Jackson's.

The child's footprints had become lost in the thick layer of humus, but the dog's frolicking had stirred the leaves and debris, making him easier to track. Tallie called on the skills drilled into her through Julia's militaristic tutelage carried out in lonely, remote locations across the globe. Her fists clenched as the woman's emotionless words returned to her.

"There's no need to whine. Tell me what animal made the tracks."

"A mongoose."

"Is that all those tracks tell you?"

"No. It's a young mongoose."

"And how do you know that?"

"His tracks are tiny, and they barely leave a mark."

"Very good. What else can you read from those tracks?"

"He wasn't running."

"And you know that because?"

"The prints are close together."

"Very good. I'm proud of you, Tallie."

Tallie had lived for such praise that fell as infrequently as desert rain, and though her feelings for Julia now swung between fury and sorrow, she whispered a thank-you to the woman who had stolen her away years ago, for preparing her with the skills she'd need to save Emily this night.

The dog's tracks skittered left and right, around stumps and rock outcroppings. Tallie deduced by the increased depth and pacing of his prints that he'd often meandered away in a run. She figured he kept leaving to chase wildlife but that he was a good and loyal dog who always returned to Emily's side and to her harder-to-trace trail.

The dog's trail eventually led Tallie nearly a mile into the forest to a steep embankment. The ground at the edge was scuffed by the prints of innumerable hikers who paused to check out the view. Tallie's heart thundered as she considered the injury such a fall could inflict on a child. A call to Emily went unanswered, except for a dog's bark from below. Tallie peered past the limbs of scrub brush growing out of the bank and saw purple. She called out again, and again received no response, but the purple spot moved, and a darling face looked up at her. Emily was awake and conscious, but her disturbing lack of responsiveness at the prospect of rescue left Tallie worried she was in shock . . . or worse.

Tallie kept speaking to the child in soft, steady tones as she rigged the gear she'd need to rappel down. Before she made her descent, she heard movement in the brush behind her and wondered if some animal had frightened Emily into leaping off the embankment to that ledge some twenty feet below. The last thing she wanted was to have a bear or a cougar waiting for them when they reached the top, so she told Emily she'd be right back and rummaged in her bag for her gun and another length of rope to rig a snare.

She scouted out the area for sturdy young limbs to use for her traps, keeping her gun ready in case she stumbled upon a wandering animal. She found two good locations that would make powerful snares, one capable of safely entrapping and holding a wild cat while the other delivered a snap that would deter a nosey bear. The two together would safely guard the ridge.

She returned and found Emily as still as she'd been before. Minutes later, tethered to a strong tree growing at the embankment's edge, Tallie rappelled down the bank with a first-aid kit strapped to her back. She found the child and dog huddled together, and amazingly, the child appeared unharmed, with nothing more than dirty clothes and tree litter in her hair as physical evidence of her ordeal.

Soon Emily was strapped to Tallie's back with the little dog resting in her arms. After Tallie explained that they were ready to make the climb up, one possible explanation for the child's failure to reply to her calls became apparent. When Emily finally relinquished a meager smile and uttered something, it came out in a Slavic-sounding tongue. Tallie made a failed attempt at interpreting it by running it through her limited command of Russian, Italian, and Farsi. Her poor interpreting skills rendered a very unlikely translation—something about doing a good skill. She smiled back at Emily, hoping her response was understood if the child was attempting to thank her. Grateful Emily was finally responding, Tallie dug her feet in and climbed back up the embankment.

She heard a snap and a thud above her and knew something too big to capture had wandered into her snare and received a hit from that ricocheted branch. She crested the top and listened for sounds of animals stalking nearby. Hearing none, she assumed the snare had disabled the threat or sent the animal deeper into the woods. She'd tell the sheriff to send a ranger up to check on the animal later.

Emily felt still on her back, and when Tallie turned her head to check on her, she appeared to be peacefully sleeping, her arms still wrapped securely around Bristol. The child's weight was therapeutic to Tallie, who felt the most serene satisfaction zip through her, knowing that tonight's rescue would have a wonderful outcome. This little girl would not suffer what she had suffered.

But each step out of wooded comfort took her closer to the reality she wanted to flee. She struggled to balance her anger at Julia for hijacking her life with her gratitude for the skills the woman had given her that had allowed her to help Emily.

She sensed the increasing excitement in Bristol and knew they were approaching the edge of the forest long before they reached the clearing or heard the cacophony of barking search-and-rescue dogs ahead. Bright lights blinded her as the trio broke through the dark tree line. The gathering crowd of arriving dog handlers and hikers gave a whoop of joy when they appeared, but Tallie stopped short and shrank from the unwanted attention.

She thrust her hand forward and shouted, "Emily's fine, but you're blinding me and frightening her." Her words were lost as Emily's mother and the sheriff rushed forward. Bristol jumped out of Emily's arms to greet them. Some deputies and the father attempted to hold the well-wishers in the crowd back, but they would not be contained. Tallie pulled Emily around in front of her and smiled into the child's dirty, tear-streaked face before the crowd swarmed them. "Your mom and dad are coming."

Emily tightened her arms around Tallie's neck and started to cry over this chaotic welcome. When the mother approached, Tallie loosened Emily's arms and returned her to her parent, hoping to slip away through the crowd. The reporters had different ideas. They chased Tallie down, and she panicked over the thought of being on public display. She remembered the day of Julia's funeral, when news choppers had circled above as she and Louis stood on a cliff to release Julia's ashes. Cameramen had aimed their cameras at her, shooting film and stills of her as if she were a curiosity or a public monument made of stone instead of a private person in pain.

Julia's words returned to her again. *"Keep your head down, and trust no one."*

Tallie shielded her face with her arms, but her unwillingness to answer the press's questions seemed to make them more rabid to follow her. She felt the clamor of people reaching for her, touching her, shouting over one another, asking for her name and details of the rescue. A familiar voice shouted above the crowd, moving them back, and one arm wrapped securely around her while the other served as a battering ram to move people away—Jackson James.

CHAPTER TWO

"How did you find me?" she choked out.

"You didn't make it easy." His reply was terse and clipped.

Her throat tightened. She felt small again. Like a disappointment. Jackson wore the rumpled clothes from the previous day, and his dark hair was tousled, as if he'd dressed straight from bed. Fatigue and worry lined his eyes and brow, leaving him looking much older than his twenty-nine years, and she knew she was the cause.

Jackson kept her tall, thin frame tucked under his protective arm and led her to his father's truck, where he then stood with his arms outstretched, holding the crowd back as she climbed in. The sheriff broke through, demanding answers of his own, but when he saw how upset Tallie was by the throng, he helped Jackson hold the group at bay.

Tallie slid down in her seat, still shielding her face with her arms. Until a few weeks earlier, she'd rarely been in a town or seen more than a dozen people in a day. But as distressing as the crowd was for her personally, she had bigger concerns about maintaining her anonymity—concerns Jackson understood.

She saw a conversation occurring between him and the sheriff. It ended with Jackson's determined voice telling the crowd, "The sheriff will make a complete report of the rescue. Back off and get your story from him."

The sheriff confirmed Jackson's announcement, adding, "These good people are wrung out from this experience. Why don't you folks just celebrate this happy outcome and leave them in peace for now."

The sheriff instructed Jackson to get into the truck, while also ordering a deputy to follow behind to make sure he headed straight for the station. Jackson started the engine without making eye contact with Tallie.

Once the vehicle was on the road with only the deputy behind them, Tallie asked, "What happens now?"

"We drive to the sheriff's office so you can give a statement."

Tallie knew all about the government's love of reports. "No interviews. I just wanted to help that little girl. I don't want my name published."

Jackson finally turned to her and said, "What did you think was going to happen when you ran into the forest ahead of the rescue party to save that child in the middle of the night?"

Tallie's hackles rose. "Would you have preferred I leave her out there, afraid, cold, or maybe worse?"

"Of course not." Jackson's jaw bulged and released the way it did when he was stressed. "Why didn't you ask me to take you to the site instead of sneaking away and hitching a ride on a bread truck?"

"You know that? How?"

"Does it really matter?"

"I just don't want you to think I plotted my exit in advance. I was responding to an emergency."

"So were the people who called us. One of them saw a woman walking down our lane in the dark. He called Dad to see if everything was okay. That's when we found your notes."

She heard the wounded tone in his voice.

"Another friend drives the tank truck that picks up milk from all the local dairies," he said. "Dad called him to ask if he'd seen you along the state road. He said he passed a woman being picked up by a bread truck. I tried to call you and saw the Amber Alert on my phone. I figured that's where you went."

She looked out the window to avoid his disappointed eyes. "I'm sorry. I handled things badly."

From the corner of her eye, she saw Jackson's hands twisting around the steering wheel. She knew he was wrestling over what to say next.

"Sadly . . . I wasn't that surprised that you'd left. Neither was my mom." His voice became subdued. "We were worried sick that we drove you away."

"No, no, no," Tallie raced to assure him. "It wasn't you."

"I haven't helped the situation. I've been thoughtless. You've had so much loss in a few weeks' time, and I dragged you across the country to watch me return to my big happy family. I'm an idiot."

Tallie stared at her hands, feeling the emptiness settle in again.

"How could I have thought that being around a houseful of people, no matter how well-intentioned, could in any way ease what you've been through? It's a wonder you're not curled up in the fetal position, sucking your thumb."

Jackson's concerns for Tallie hit home, but they appeared to only increase his own remorse.

"I'm sorry, Tallie. My whole family is. We hope you can forgive us and that you'll come back home with me and give us a second chance."

So many tender moments returned to her, like Mrs. James's never-ending embrace the day Jackson returned after years of estrangement, with Tallie by his side. She cataloged Mr. James's tearful hug, Kelly's laughter, and Jackson's older brothers' mischievous tales into her memory under a tab called Family. To those preserved memories she added the luscious sights and smells of endless food and the continuous welcome from innumerable smiling neighbors. She could still feel the gentle, reassuring weight of soft hands on her shoulder or in the center of her back as one family member or another guided her from guest to guest, as if she were the honored child, instead of Jackson.

Exquisite sadness rode along on the joy of each memory. His family was everything she dreamed a family could be, and after tasting it, losing it would be unbearable. If a goodbye was coming, better to bring it early.

"No apology is needed. Your family was wonderful." She laid her head against the cool glass. "Too wonderful."

"Meaning what?"

She lifted her head and challenged Jackson. "If I were going to paint the perfect home and family, it would be yours—a home filled with cozy furniture covered in afghans, and generations of family portraits on the walls so you know who you are and where you came from. A home where friends and family rush in with casseroles and cookies to celebrate the return of the prodigal son while swapping old familiar stories everyone knows. How could you have turned your back on all that? On the very life I long for?"

"Wait. What? Yes, I-I-I was wrong. You helped me see that, and now I'm back . . . because of you. But if you loved it there so much, why did you leave?"

She forced a tense smile and dodged the question. "I'm so glad you found your way home, Jackson. All the mistakes that separated you from your family are in the past. And when you return to New York, it'll be with a media position at the UN and an exclusive interview waiting for you. Your career is back on track."

Jackson drove into the sheriff's department parking lot and braked hard, shoving the transmission arm into park as he swung around to face her. "I can't believe you just said that."

She knew why he was upset, and she quickly backtracked. "I'm just saying that you've restored your journalistic credibility."

He gritted his teeth and groaned. "That might have been what I wanted when you met me, but how could you still say that after—"

"I didn't mean it that way. I'm sorry. You sacrificed everything to help me get answers. I'm just glad things worked out well for you. That your future is back on track."

"Today . . . all this . . . it isn't about my future. It's about you avoiding yours." He took Tallie's hand and leaned close, but she closed her eyes and shook her head, willing the conversation to end. "It's just the two of us, Tallie. You can say his name out loud. He's your father."

Her steeled courage failed as tears spilled over. "No, I can't. I don't dare get comfortable saying that. He doesn't even know the truth yet, and I don't know how he'll react when he does. What if he rejects me? I don't think I could survive another loss."

"I understand that. Through no fault of your own, you've had to face more hard things than any person should. But I can't imagine anyone not loving the woman I'm sitting right here with."

Tallie was almost grateful when Deputy Kwiatkowski knocked on the window and gestured for them to follow him into the office. Jackson held up a few fingers to plead for a few more minutes, and the officer reluctantly signaled that he'd give them five as he moved to the building's door to wait.

"If that fear of rejection is what made you run today, then hear me out. I walked away from my family, but they never stopped loving me. You were ripped from your family, and I'm sure they never stopped loving you. Don't repeat my mistakes. Family takes hard work, and yes, it's loaded with challenges and risks, but the rewards are worth it all. So please don't give up on me or my family or yours. Please."

She wanted so desperately to melt into him, to believe everything he said, but there was something else stopping her. A hurdle more terrifying than all the others.

Tallie squeezed his hand and then released it as she turned to face forward, avoiding his eyes. "Okay . . . I'll take my second chance if you take yours."

"I have. I'm home."

"Not completely. What about Dawn?"

"Dawn? What about her?"

His minimization of his former relationship infuriated her. "What do you mean 'what about her?' You were engaged to be married."

"We've already talked about all that. It was over ten years ago, when I made the biggest mistake of my career. And when I needed her love and support the most, she walked out on me and married someone else. I don't know why she showed up at the open house."

"And last night she told me *that* decision was *her* biggest mistake. She's divorced with a child, and she still loves you. And she'd be good for you."

Jackson's brows pinched together. "She loved the man I was, and the man I was loved her, but I'm not that same man anymore, Tallie." He tipped her chin toward him. "I've probably done more growing up since I've met you than in the last ten years on my own. She isn't the woman I need or want anymore. You are."

Jackson James was the first person in Tallie's life to make her feel loved. Whatever she felt for him, infatuation or real love, she wanted it to last forever, but it was impossible. Regardless of what Jackson believed, he had been raised in a rich heritage of love, and that's what he needed. Tallie had been raised in a vacuum, a petri dish of Julia's design, without a normal childhood or a personal history of loving or being loved, except for the limited access she'd had to Louis and his kindness.

"We've known each other two weeks, Jackson. Fifteen days."

"You know me better and you've made me better in fifteen days than anyone else could have in a lifetime."

Tallie swallowed her choking fear and gave it voice. "I don't know any lullabies or bedtime stories."

"What?"

Tallie could tell Jackson was unable to follow the train wreck that was her thoughts. "I heard Dawn with her little boy. I was coming from the bathroom, and she was in your sister's room, singing a lullaby to Ethan. I just stood there, staring at them as they cuddled and laughed and finished one another's rhymes." A flood of tears burst past her dammed lids. "I suddenly realized I'm a completely empty vessel."

"Tallie, how can you say that? You're the most amazing woman I've ever met."

"I have the tools and skills to scale a rock wall or stitch a wound in the field or build a shelter in the wild, but I have zero experience on how to mother or how to love. I've held a bear cub but never a human baby. Who else can say such a thing? I don't remember ever being hugged or held as a child. No one told me things would be all right. I was told not to whine and to work the problem instead." She looked up into Jackson's vacant expression. He appeared as clueless about how to comfort her as she was about how to comfort a child. "I thought I loved Julia, and everything about her relationship to me was a lie."

"What about Louis?"

"He's been kind to me, but what if that was all it was? What if I don't know what love is? Or worse . . . what if I'm just like Julia? Unable to love?"

Jackson took her arms and pulled her close. "None of what you said is true, Tallie. First of all, Julia did love you. It wasn't the kind of love you deserved, but Major Norris told you that you were her last thought. And you're not anything like her. I've seen how you soak up love and how quick you are to give it. Julia's mistakes were hers. Not yours."

"My biology master's program included psychology, remember? I know we imprint on our children."

"Then, the Kaswells' loving imprint is also on you, right? And that's a legacy of great love."

She felt her skin prickle with want. "You can't know how badly I'd like to believe that, but I don't even know who I am without Julia always being in my head. I need some time."

"If you're not able to tell the general who you are, then ask Major Norris to tell him you need a few weeks of rest before you begin serving in his security detail. He understands what you've been through." Jackson took her hand again and went on. "We'll find you a little apartment in D.C. It's a beautiful city, Tallie. And some weeks we'll be working together in New York. Imagine all we can see and do together there. And when you're working in D.C., I'll take the train down so we can be together on the weekends."

He'd hit a nerve, but Tallie didn't know how to explain the problem to him.

"I don't just need time away from work and Julia's influence." She couldn't bear to look him in the eyes. "You've been my support and strength these past few weeks, but I need to know I can stand on my own without you. What I'm saying is . . . I also need time alone, away . . . from you."

Jackson released her hand and slowly dropped back against the seat. "You don't want to see me anymore?"

"I'm not saying that," she rushed. She slumped over her lap. "I don't know who I am or what I want or need. I need time and room to figure all that out."

"I don't want to lose you, Tallie. I have another job offer, one where we wouldn't be working together. I'll take it if it'll save us."

Guilt piled on top of her inadequacies and doubts. "I don't want you to decline General Kaswell's offer for me. It's a once-in-a-lifetime opportunity."

"I don't care. This other opportunity pays more, and it sounds intriguing."

"What job is more intriguing than handling the PR for America's next UN ambassador?"

Tallie's head shot around at the sudden sound of wind and a concussive whir that swirled above the car, but Jackson pulled gently on her chin to bring her back to face him again.

"It's a company called Infinity Brain Trust, and maybe it's not *more* intriguing than working with your father at the UN, but the headhunter said they're a philanthropic organization doing good around the world. I started out looking for redemption a few weeks ago. This job would keep me working for something good, but it would give you the space you need to sort things out."

The wind increased, and debris flew about wildly. "A helicopter is landing," Tallie said as she exited the car. She raised an arm over her eyes to shield them from the swirling dirt and litter. The deputy called out on his walkie-talkie while urging Tallie and Jackson onto the department's porch, and the three watched in wonder as the pilot landed the chopper in the empty lot.

Major Stephen Norris exited the helicopter and bent low until his imposing six-foot, four-inch body was past the whirling blades. His bent position hid his scarred face until he had almost reached Tallie and Jackson. His stern, authoritarian presence no longer terrified her as it once had. He was a close associate of her birth father, General Kaswell, and the man at the center of the secret about her identity and the loss of the life she was meant to have. Tallie wasn't surprised Norris *could* find them—he'd proven on multiple occasions that he could do pretty much anything he wanted, legal or otherwise, and no privacy laws would stop him from tracking her phone if he desired. What worried Tallie was *why* he had come at this moment, to this odd location. Why hadn't he simply called or waited an hour and approached her and Jackson at the James home? Prickles raised on her arms. His arrival could mean only one thing.

"Something's happened to him, hasn't it?" She dared not identify her father with the deputy standing nearby.

Norris pulled her to the side and Jackson followed. "He was in his Kensington home. Not in New York. We don't know what went down, exactly, but he's missing."

Tallie felt as if the very life was ebbing from her at the news. Julia was dead, as were her birth mother and sister. All she had left was a hope of someday being able to tell General Mordecai Kaswell, the next United States Ambassador to the United Nations, that she was his daughter and have him claim her as his own. And now he was missing.

"There's something more, isn't there? What aren't you telling me?"

"We found blood at the scene. It's his."

Tallie took a breath and held it as time slowed, then stopped, and reversed as a whirlpool of emotions pulled her down into the same painful abyss she'd experienced after Julia's death. Each agonizing thought returned—the fear of losing the last family she had left, the urgency to do something, the weight of responsility, as if only she could save them. And then came the accompanying paralysis, followed by Julia's voice in her head from an encounter many years earlier.

"I know you can do this, but you need to know it. What are you afraid of?"

Tallie, ten years old during this confrontation, had been too afraid to answer, knowing the truth would likely aggravate the woman she'd known as Mother more than her own surrender.

"Are you afraid to fail? Is that it?"

Tallie had nodded and wiped her nose.

"If you fail, you learn. Quitting is the only true failure. Work the problem."

She eventually found the solution to the problem she could no longer remember.

"Good girl. See? I knew you could do it."

Tallie didn't hear love in Julia's voice, only pride, and even that was not as much about her own success as it was about Julia's in prodding her along. Later that evening, Tallie had dared approach her mother with a comment, knowing that if she didn't speak it and face the consequences, she'd fear the woman for the rest of her life.

"There is one thing I fear more than failure."

"Really? And what is that?"

"Disappointing you."

That fear of disappointing someone whose opinion of her mattered still petrified Tallie, and she could have drawn upon a dozen similar scenarios. It was why she was willing to walk away from Jackson rather than ever see disillusionment in his eyes, that same disillusionment Julia had shown her from time to time. It was why she'd dedicate the rest of her life, if that's what it took, and every skill she possessed, to finding her father and bringing him home.

She pulled out of her reverie and straightened her shoulders. "Take me to his home so I can search for clues."

Jackson slipped his arm around Tallie and stepped in front of her. "I'm sure the FBI, NSA, and every other three-letter agency in Washington has scoured that place a dozen times."

Tallie shook free. "But it's different with me . . . and you know why."

"I hoped you'd see it that way," Major Norris said. "I'm worried the brass sent the investigators in with some pre-drawn conclusions about what may have happened." He rubbed a scarred hand over his equally scarred face. "We've prepared for the possibility that Somali rebels would come for him and call for an international inquiry into what happened that night in Mogadishu, but before the higher-ups run for their foxholes and start writing their disavowals and denials, I'd like to be sure that's what happened, and I think we have the best chance of knowing that if you come along, Tallie."

"Then, I'm going too," Jackson said.

The major shook his head and eyed Jackson knowingly. "No. Go home and pack your bags." He handed him an envelope. Here's your itinerary to D.C. I need you handling the media on this. We've got to keep it under wraps in the hope that we can find Cai and bring him home quickly and discreetly. Your particular knowledge of his history and past makes you essential on that task."

That *particular knowledge* of the ambassador's history was what prevented Tallie from coming forward as his daughter. She couldn't risk drawing attention to his time in Mogadishu and to the woman who served with him and later took his baby daughter as her own. Keeping those secrets were Tallie's way of protecting her father and his reputation.

Cai Kaswell and teammates then-Captain Stephen Norris and technical-arms expert Diana Howard had been deployed to Mogadishu, Somalia, on an op to take out the rebel leader responsible for killing US citizens and dragging their bodies through the streets. Bad intel had led to tragedy when Cai fired on the rebel holdout. The soldiers were unaware the rebels had filled the building with civilians being held as human shields. Despite the heroic rescue efforts made by Cai and his commander, now Major Stephen Norris, dozens of captive civilians, including innocent children, were badly burned or killed. When Cai's body could not be found, it was presumed that he had also perished during his rescue efforts or that he'd been dragged away. He was labeled as missing and unaccounted for, and while the rest of his company searched for his body, Major Norris and Lieutenant Howard returned home to answer the Pentagon's questions regarding the incident.

The world knew little to nothing about the op that went sideways that night, nor did they know that villagers had dragged Cai's badly burned body from the fire after he'd nearly perished attempting to save rebel-held children from the inferno. Weeks had passed, and while he teetered on the brink of death in a remote village thousands of miles away, all his wife and family were told was that he was missing. When his survival was assured, he was whisked to a hospital and lauded as a hero across the globe.

But the tragedy in Somalia had bled into another. In an effort to cover up the disaster in Mogadishu, the army gave Deidre Kaswell vague answers about her husband's assignment and situation. While driving her sick babies to the doctor, and already in distress over her missing husband, Deidre Kaswell was involved in a car accident that sent her car plummeting down a mountain cliff, throwing one of Deidre's twin toddler girls from the vehicle. The local base sent out a search party that included Diana Howard, but when little Molly wasn't found, she was presumed dead.

She was sick and injured but still alive when she was found and cared for by a couple—Petty and Susan Bodeil. They'd approached Major Norris, offering to return her, but in another ugly twist of fate, when Petty realized the stakes involved in the child's silent return, he asked for leverage of his own. He'd return the child and never speak of the incident to the press in return for forgiveness of the town's debts. An onerous deal was struck, and Molly was placed into Diana's care while Major Norris worked out a way to return her without bringing further scrutiny to her father and the Mogadishu debacle. In Diana's paranoid mind, she saw herself as the most likely scapegoat for the incident, and Molly Kaswell became her protection, proof of a coverup, which she could wield in case her brothers-in-arms threw her under the bus.

Diana laid her plan out to Major Norris, whom she blackmailed into helping her in return for her silence. Her death was faked, her identity and Molly's were changed, visas were issued, and cash was disbursed. Diana had become Julia Brown, a single mother with a toddler named Tallie.

While Cai Kaswell traveled the globe, dedicating the remainder of his career and life to humanitarian causes that crossed tribal and political lines, Diana, thereafter Julia Brown, took her purloined daughter, Tallie, and also traveled the globe, moving frequently from one obscure third-world village to another. And while Cai's work led to his appointment as America's next ambassador to the UN and a reputation for being the world's best hope for the cause of peace, Julia's increasingly bizarre paranoia stole Tallie's true identity and the life and family she was meant to have.

"Tallie needs someone." Jackson's argument with Major Norris brought Tallie's focus back to the present. "She needs me."

"What she needs is for each of us to do what we do best. A chopper is coming to take you to the airport. Don't be late. You don't have any of the necessary credentials to qualify for this assignment, but I've vouched for you personally to people who count on me to have their backs, which means my can is on the line with yours, so don't make me regret this. Do we understand one another?"

The air felt twenty degrees cooler after the major's warning. Tallie read the turmoil in Jackson's face, knowing he likely wanted to crawl away and become invisible, while also knowing he'd take Norris's rebuke before abandoning her. She placed her hands on his chest to calm him, but he straightened and tightened his hold on her as he challenged Norris again. "If they came for Kaswell, they might want Tallie. You could be putting her in danger too."

"That's why I brought Marlene. She's in the chopper. She'll be with Tallie anyplace I can't go. Next to me, she's the one I trust most to have Tallie's back."

As if she'd heard her father, Marlene stepped from the helicopter. Next to Jackson, she was the person Tallie also trusted most.

She loosened Jackson's hold on her. "I'll be okay. You protect my father's good name until I find him, okay?"

"Then, you're okay with me staying on this job?" He drilled his worried gaze deep into Tallie. "What about everything we were discussing? There are so many things I wanted to say to you. Most of all, I want you to know that none of what you said about yourself is true." He pulled her close, and she savored the security of his embrace as he whispered into her ear. "Come back to me, Tallie Brown. Please don't do anything foolish. Promise me."

Her throat felt thick and her skin cool and damp as she realized all she had on the line—her father, Jackson, and perhaps her own safety. "I'll be careful. I promise."

It wasn't the promise to return to him that Jackson had asked for, but it was all she could honestly pledge at this point. Inch by inch, she moved away until they released each other's hands.

"Wait! Wait!" the deputy shouted over the thrum of the chopper's blades. He placed his hand over his holstered weapon to intimidate the group.

Major Norris swung around to face the man. "Do we have a problem, Deputy?"

The man shrank and then straightened an inch. "The sheriff needs her to file a report about the missing child she rescued today."

"Emily Davenport? Age three, blonde hair and blue eyes, last seen wearing a purple jacket and in the company of a terrier named Bristol?"

"Yes, sir," the deputy sputtered.

Norris shifted his weight onto one hip. "Son, tell your sheriff that Tallie Brown's services are needed in D.C. on a matter of national security. That's our priority, but I understand and respect your local concerns. I've been monitoring your transmissions on the missing-child case. Miss Brown'll dictate her report in flight and have it in your departmental inbox in an hour. Understood?"

"Yes, sir."

Tallie heard Major Norris begin to brief Jackson as she slipped away toward Marlene and the chopper.

She was grateful to see Marlene. The gorgeous redhead was Tallie's first friend, and though they'd met only a few weeks earlier, they'd bonded over their mutual aloneness. The women greeted one another and hugged, but the reason for their reunion hung over them like a cloud.

"I'm sorry about your father."

Her honey-sweet Southern accent warmed Tallie's heart. "Thank you. I'm so glad you're here. I've missed our talks. How's Bodie?"

Marlene replied with a head bobble. "Are you referring to our friend Bodie, the sweet innkeeper, or Mr. Glick, the successful graphic novelist who just received an offer to be represented by a big New York literary agency? Because the two are no longer the same."

"I'm sorry. It sounds like we've got some catching up to do."

"There'll be plenty of time for a good ole hen party later, but right now all that matters is you and your father."

A new worry swept over Tallie as her eyes shot to the pilot and copilot. "Does the flight team know *everything*?" She punctuated the last word with scrunched brows and a dubious tone, leaning close to her friend.

"No, but we can speak openly on the flight. Daddy made sure the flight crew is wearing headphones that allow communication only between each other and the tower at the airport. They'd have to remove them to speak with us or hear our conversations."

"Your father is thorough."

"Especially when it comes to protecting people he cares about."

"I appreciate that. He didn't tell me much about what he thinks happened to the ambassador. What can you tell me?"

Marlene's mouth formed a sad smile. "The *ambassador*? You still aren't ready to call him your father yet?"

"How can I? I can't risk letting the wrong people know my ties to him. As long as the Somali rebels who survived that fire are alive, they'll keep searching for evidence to prove the general fired that shot."

"I'm sorry you're a big part of that proof, Tallie."

She shrugged. "Imagine the frenzy the press would be in if they found out the Kaswells' supposedly dead daughter was actually kidnapped and raised by a soldier deployed with him in Mogadishu."

Marlene nodded. "They'd keep digging until they'd pieced it all together."

"And then they'd head straight to the International Criminal Court and put the general on trial. I can't risk that."

Marlene bit her upper lip. "I hope someday he finds out what you're sacrificing to protect him."

"Your sacrifice means more than you realize," Major Norris said as he entered the chopper. He told the pilot to take off and then turned back to Tallie. "Dangerous consequences would follow if the truth about Cai's part in that fire were uncovered. At the very least, his reputation would be destroyed, but if he were brought up on war crimes, dangerous actors like those ruling Afghanistan, Iran, and North Korea would use that as an excuse to opt out of the treaty negotiations Cai's arranged. He's the only man who could get them to the table, and this might be our last chance to broker for peace."

"Because they only trust him," Tallie clarified.

"So long as what happened in Mogadishu remains buried." Major Norris nodded.

"So are you saying we have four possible groups who'd want to capture him? The Somali rebels, the Iranians, the Afghans, and the North Koreans?"

The major's features seemed to slide toward his chin. "Tallie, your father is trying to bring peace to the world. He has far more than four enemies. He has more people trying to kill him than he has friends."

The news was not surprising, but it made her shiver.

"Let me grab you a blanket," Major Norris said as he pulled two from a compartment, handing one to each of the women.

The cold Tallie felt couldn't be eased by a blanket, but she welcomed the comfort it provided. She thanked him and settled into her seat, then pulled her laptop from her bag, both to discourage casual conversation and to prepare her statement to the sheriff as the major had promised the deputy she would. Once she hit Send on the report, she sat back and closed her eyes, suddenly feeling drained and more exhausted than she had since the day Julia died. She tried to blame her fatigue on her early rising and on the hours spent tracking and rescuing Emily and her dog, but she knew this wasn't physical fatigue. This was mental and emotional overload.

She tried to conjure images of her father. If she couldn't publicly acknowledge him, she could at least dream of him and imagine him claiming her as his own. She tried three times to clear her thoughts, but each time, her mind produced only reminders of her time with Julia. The first attempt resurrected memories of Julia challenging Tallie in self-defense and marksmanship. She remembered the blows she'd taken and the bruises they'd left behind until she was every bit as skilled as her teacher. The second effort produced vivid visuals of her sitting in front of her computer and Julia drilling her in science and history and a dozen other topics. The images flew past one another faster and faster, like a movie, reminding Tallie of Julia's crushing expectations, and then she saw the payoff for that instruction—two master's degrees by her twenty-second year. On the third attempt to clear her mind, Tallie recalled herself as a child in the woods while Julia conducted one of her master classes in observation.

She attempted to stop the scene from replaying, but Julia's face and voice soon filled her mind.

"To most people, a room or the woods is like a book written in a foreign language. At best, they can read a few words, but the rest is a page of scribble. You will not be like them, Tallie."

"I don't understand."

"Because your training is just beginning. What do you see right now?"

"Trees, grass, the sky."

In the replay of Tallie's memory, Julia's voice didn't sound as stern as it was determined, leaving her unafraid of revisiting Julia's instruction in her mind.

"Get on your knees and study the world under the grass line. Tell me what you see now."

"Isopods, crickets, ants . . ."

"Better. There's a whole world under there and another above you. What do you hear?"

"Some birds."

"Close your eyes and clear your mind. Listen with your brain, not just your ears. What do you hear?"

Tallie hadn't understood the stern request at the time, but she had tried harder to listen, and she was amazed by all the sounds that suddenly surrounded her. *"I hear leaves rustling."*

"Anyone can hear leaves rustling. What do they tell you?"

It was as if she had been given new ears. The rustling leaves had a dozen different sounds, depending on the direction of the wind, the types and sizes of the leaves, and whether an animal was moving along the branches. She relayed her new findings to Julia, who nodded at her with a new respect.

It was as Julia had promised. Over time, Tallie's surroundings had revealed their secrets to her as plainly as if she were reading them from the pages of a book. She read every change in the ground and the wind, noticed the slightest movement of a twig, and could tell who or what had passed through ahead of her. Julia had taught her all that.

She'd ripped Tallie from the life she was meant to have, and Tallie'd had only two weeks to process that revelation, but it explained so much about her strange life—why Julia had kept them isolated from people, why they'd moved so often, why the woman Tallie had thought was her mother had never seemed able to love her.

Then Tallie remembered Jackson's previous words.

"Julia did love you. It wasn't the kind of love you deserved, but Major Norris told you that you were her last thought. . . . I've seen how you soak up love and how quick you are to give it."

Tallie knew only one thing for sure. In lieu of hugs and songs and sweet words of praise, Julia had made her strong and smart and capable. These gifts might not make her soft and lovely or capable of loving in the way Jackson and his family did, but she'd use everything Julia taught her to find Cai Kaswell.

Maybe that was also a way of loving.

CHAPTER THREE

The pilot announced that they were thirty minutes from landing. Tallie had more questions than answers, so she turned to Major Norris. "Have you spent much time with Ambassador Kaswell since he returned home from Deidre and Meghan's funeral?"

"Some. He hasn't wanted company."

Tallie nodded. She understood that mindset completely. "How was he holding up?"

"Not well." The major set his gaze on the view out his window. "I think their deaths broke him. He paid a generous severance to the maid who had been with his family for years and dismissed her. Then he asked me to leave him. We posted a two-man military detail outside to give him some privacy and keep people away, but we didn't keep eyes on him. I became concerned when he didn't return calls or texts. That's when we went in and found him missing."

"He's the Ambassador of the United States of America to the United Nations. Didn't he have his own protective service detail through the Diplomatic Security Service?"

"He never formally accepted the UN post. He was waiting to talk to Deidre about it."

"He's not the ambassador after all? I didn't know."

The major dropped his gaze again. "I assumed Cai would carry on with the plan to take the UN post, but as I said, the loss of Deidre and Meghan has been devastating to him. The job and the announcement have been put on hold to give Cai time to grieve and decide whether he still wants to pursue that post now that his family is gone."

Tallie sucked in a soft gasp, and the major's head shot around.

"I'm sorry, Tallie. That was . . . I didn't mean to discount or minimize your relationship to him. Of course you're family . . . it's just that . . ."

"He doesn't know it."

"No, he doesn't. What I meant was . . . Cai may not want such a demanding assignment after so much upheaval in his life."

Tallie knew what he meant. She was still a nothing to Cai Kaswell. Not a daughter. Not family. Not a source of comfort of any kind. She felt Marlene's small, gentle hand land on her back, rubbing light circles there.

"I can't imagine being in your position," Marlene said. "We're going to find him, and then you're both going to see that you're not alone."

The sentiment was appreciated, but Tallie needed more assurance now and turned back to Major Norris. "He seemed to recognize my earring when you introduced us back in Cutler's Ridge. Did he . . . did he ever mention it or ask about me?"

The major nodded slowly. "He did."

A thrill zipped through Tallie at that news. Cai Kaswell had had jewelry pieces made from blue tanzanite stones he'd been given by a grateful tribal leader—a necklace for Deidre and earrings for his twin girls, Meghan and Molly. Tallie still couldn't voice her birth name aloud. Even thinking of the name Molly Kaswell caused her heart to race and her breathing to go rogue. "And what did you say?" she pressed.

"I followed the plan we agreed to."

She knew the news would hurt. "But what did you say?"

"I deflected, and when Cai pursued the question about how you had an earring that looked like the ones he designed for his twin baby girls, I convinced him it was understandable that he'd try to find memories of his wife and daughter anywhere he could."

Tallie's heart raced over the first part of the news and nearly stopped beating over the end. She stilled her quivering lips and asked, "And he accepted that?"

Fatigue or the sheer weight of considering the question showed on the major's face. He rubbed a gnarled hand over his face and gazed at Tallie straight on. "At least for a while."

She eased back against her seat and pulled the blanket over her shoulders, ending further conversation as she tried again to clear her mind.

The chopper landed at a military airfield, and the trio boarded a plane for Maryland. Tallie tried to feign sleep, but Marlene struck up a conversation.

"Bodie signed an offer from a publishing company the very day after you left."

Tallie couldn't help but smile at the dramatics behind Marlene's failed attempt to be matter-of-fact. Her Southern drawl was on full display, and her head tilts and eye-rolls were proof that she cared more about their mutual friend than she was willing to admit.

"They set him up with a publicist *and* an editor," she continued with a flip of her long red hair. "The way they fussed on about him over the phone, you'd think he'd written *War and Peace* instead of a bunch of graphic novels about a detective name Dirk Dash." Her eyelashes fluttered like a hummingbird in flight, and her voice rose an octave and took on cartoonlike tones as she reenacted the call. "'We need you in New York ASAP, Mr. Glick. We have signings and public appearances scheduled in major cities for weeks.'" She harumphed.

"What about the inn?"

That question brought a glimpse of fury to Marlene's eyes. "Do you know who he put in charge of the place while he's away?"

"Who?" Tallie knew only one person who could raise Marlene's ire that way.

"Remember that little tart taking classes at the community college?"

"Wendy?"

"Yes, Wendy."

"I thought you made peace over her friendship with Bodie."

"I did too, until she offered to help him pack all his costumes for the PR tour. No *girl* should be helpin' a man pack his spurs and capes when he has an understanding with a *woman*."

Tallie did her best to keep her reaction blank, but the more she allowed the last line to snake through her mind, the more impossible it became to deny the chuckle tickling the back of her throat. She brought her hand to her mouth and pressed it there to camouflage her smile, and then Marlene busted out with a laugh that made her father turn in his seat to see the cause.

"We're fine, Daddy," Marlene said to the major. "I just needed to see if I could make Tallie laugh."

"So none of that was true?" Tallie asked.

"Oh, it was all true. I just left out the part where I showed little Miss Wendy the door and told Bodie Glick we need to take a break while he evaluates his priorities."

"So you left him groveling."

"Of course I did. That's the secret to a good relationship—establish control early."

She was her father's daughter.

"And what about you and Jackson?" Marlene asked.

Tallie leaned her head against the window and pretended to look out at the ground below. "There's nothing to tell."

"It looked like he had plenty to say back there in Idaho this morning."

"We're not right for each other."

"According to you."

Tallie shrugged defensively. "It's obvious."

"Again, according to you, 'cause that man is clearly in love with you."

The observation pleased Tallie, even warmed her, but she quickly returned to her position leaning against the window. "I'd rather not talk about it."

Marlene laid her hand over Tallie's. "I believe that, and I understand it too. You just rest, sugar. I'm sure you need it. But do me a favor and promise to keep the door to your heart cracked a smidge for Jackson, ya hear?"

Tallie didn't want to talk about her insecurities regarding Jackson, but neither could she ignore Marlene's wise advice. Her friend was everything she dreamed of being—not only brilliant and a force to be reckoned with but also beautiful, gentle, compassionate, and humble. Bodie had nailed it when he said she was *"too pretty and sophisticated"* for Cutler's Ridge, *"like a movie star or something."* More importantly, Marlene seemed to know how thoroughly she could disarm a misfit like Tallie, so she downplayed her own intelligence and ramped up her Southern charm when she spoke to Tallie friend to friend.

"I'll try," Tallie conceded before closing her eyes, shutting down the conversation. She finally managed to clear her mind of distractions and catch a few hours of sleep before the jolt of the landing brought her to. A black SUV was waiting for the party on the runway, and soon they were driving through D.C. en route to the bedroom community of Kensington.

Tallie's hands felt sweaty as she mentally prepared to visit the home she was meant to have lived in with the Kaswells. The car moved through quiet, stately neighborhoods lined with grand multimillion-dollar homes partly concealed behind canopies of mature trees, manicured shrubs, and flower beds. Sidewalks were loaded with people walking or jogging, some with pets and some without. Some driveways were gated, but all the properties seemed to have security cameras, which Tallie could easily understand, considering that the community was home to Washington power players and successful business types.

The vehicle passed through a black security gate manned by soldiers guarding a three-story brick colonial. The semicircular driveway ran between a massive flower bed and the front entrance, which was flanked by marble planters trailing colorful vines and flowers. Bright-yellow pillows with white lettering that read *Welcome* sat in the corners of a wrought-iron bench. There was no yellow caution tape or flashing lights indicating a crime scene. The place looked as if the happy family was simply away on a trip, expected home at any time. Instead, the Kaswell women were dead and Cai Kaswell was missing.

Tallie's throat tightened at the sight of the doorknocker the Kaswells had chosen—a Huguenot cross shaped like the earring Tallie wore. Her hand instinctively moved to the piece she had always believed was Julia's until the truth was exposed. The woman's stern voice sounded in her head, calling her back to her task, so she closed her eyes and swallowed her emotions. She'd be no help to anyone, let alone General Kaswell, like this.

"Everything all right?" the major asked in the fatherly tone he generally reserved for Marlene.

"No," she answered as she touched the knocker that suddenly seemed sacred.

"Can you handle it?" His voice took on Julia's emotional detachment. They were so alike, and Tallie understood why. The major had trained Julia, at least at the end of her career. Right now he and Tallie had important work to do, and he needed her laser-focused on the job ahead.

"Yes. I can handle it."

"Good." He offered her a pair of latex gloves. "Put them on and let's go."

She glanced back at Marlene, whose sympathetic expression assured Tallie she understood how hard this task was.

"Did I ever live in this house with them?" Tallie asked.

"No." The major's brows knit together in understanding. "They bought this house a few years after Mogadishu, when your father was promoted to major. They rented it out when they left the states on foreign assignments, but this was the home they always came back to. They accepted the reality of your death publicly, but not here. They held on to the dream that a miracle would bring you back to them, here, to this house."

Duty steeled Tallie, until she entered the lovely home and found herself unprepared for what she felt and smelled and saw. The faint scent of lavender lingered in the air of the foyer that served as a museum-quality patriotic photo gallery. The first piece Tallie's eyes beheld was a beautiful painting of a wind-filled flag with soldiers, sailors, and airmen positioned in front. Across the top waved a ribbonlike banner that read, That We May Be Free.

Next she saw a glorious painting of Cai in full military dress and a photo of Deidre and him in formal attire at the White House. Smaller photos, some in color, some in black and white, showed Cai and/or Deidre and Meghan. Tallie's throat felt thick as she saw the family attending key D.C. events or standing with generals or presidents without her.

When she entered the formal living room, her eyes fell upon the far wall filled with more photos of the Kaswells. She tried not to stare so longingly at them, but she couldn't help imagining herself pictured there between the Kaswells and their dark-haired little girl. Where she belonged.

She studied the mother she couldn't remember and would never know, imagining the songs she had sung to her babies. Tallie closed her eyes to deny the tears that stung behind her lids, and tried to imagine the feel of those arms around her.

"The evidence is in the kitchen," the major said.

"Daddy, give her a moment," Marlene urged.

Tallie silently thanked Marlene for her support and took a deep cleansing breath to refocus her mind. When she opened her eyes, she saw another family picture, but in this one Cai and Deidre held not one but two pink-gowned baby girls. She moved to the photo as if pulled by a tractor beam, and her fingers shook as they hovered over the photo of the lighter-haired child. Another photo of both children sat to the right, but this time the two toddlers, dressed in red Christmas dresses and black patent-leather shoes, were standing by a tree.

Three other photos of the blonde daughter lost to the Kaswells were on display. An inexplicable battle began within Tallie, a battle of relief versus regret, of love versus anger. The back of her throat burned from bile churning inside over the waste and lies and loss. She wanted to run or scream or burn the place down to stop the longing and the pain, but instead she heard the major again, speaking words she could have imagined Julia saying.

"You said you'd be able to handle it."

She tightened her fists, and for a moment, she wanted to plow one into the man's scarred face. He'd had a part in her pain too, and she was not ready to forget that.

Then Julia's voice sounded in her head from a time when Tallie was nine. They had been stationed at Gifford Pinchot National Forest, conducting studies of mountain soil samples to determine the impact the eruption at Mount St. Helens was still having on their park. During the three hours of tromping through the woods, gathering samples, debris had filled one of her loosely tied shoes and caused blisters to form. Her pain evidently showed on her face and in the slowing of her work, and Julia had noticed.

"I didn't bring you out here to pout. You can do that somewhere else. People are counting on us. What's the problem?"

She hadn't dared say.

"Are you tired? Is the work too hard for you?"

"No," she'd replied defensively.

"Then, what is the problem?"

Confirmation of her suspicions about Julia's mental health hadn't reached Tallie until Julia's death, but even then, as a small child, she'd known the woman's reactions weren't what a mother's should be. Mixed with the fear of failing, it had left Tallie unable to express her concerns. Instead, she'd sat down and slowly removed her boot and sock, revealing the open and bloodied blister.

"How long has it been like this?"

"A while."

"Would you hurt yourself on purpose?"

"No!"

"Well, that's exactly what you've done by waiting to fix the problem."

Julia had then gently cleaned and wrapped her foot, replacing Tallie's shoe and pulling the laces tight to keep further debris out. Tallie's expectations of Julia's understanding had been so low that she was nearly moved to tears by the woman's show of concern.

"Don't live with pain, Tallie. Fight through it, fix it, or get away from it. Don't let it control you. You'll become ineffective at best and likely useless to your work."

Today's work was saving Cai Kaswell, but to do that, Tallie needed to turn off her pain. She shut her eyes to the photos of denied blessings, cleared her mind, and followed the major into the kitchen.

On first observation, the large gourmet kitchen had been trashed, with shards of broken crockery and china scattered across the floor, lying atop photos and documents that were strewn everywhere, as if a scuffle had occurred there. Various markers peppered the scene, indicating items marked as evidence by the previous investigators who'd been through.

Tallie saw the smear of blood along the counter and the small, dried pool on the floor. The sight of it wouldn't have frightened her if she hadn't known whose blood it was. She swallowed and asked the major, "Can I walk around and get a closer look?"

He nodded. "Just don't move anything."

Years spent tracking animals in deserts and forests had made her nimble enough to move about the floor without touching a piece of debris. She scanned everything and each item's position to determine what happened and in what order. As important as getting this right was, she allowed herself to imagine what Julia's instructions would be in that moment:

Map the details in your mind, then step back and look at the whole picture.

She began with the details:

Ceramic canisters, including a cookie jar painted by a child, smashed on the floor by a small pool of blood. Blood on the broken jar.

Broken bowls and plates, including a whimsical birthday plate, also on the floor.

Two empty plastic containers, which she assumed had once held the hundreds of loose snapshots that were tossed about as if by a whirlwind.

The contents from an under-counter file drawer were strewn from one end of the room to another.

Chairs and plants had been tipped and tossed about.

Could all this have occurred as Cai Kaswell fought off attackers? Possibly, but the debris field wasn't randomly spread, as if by a scuffle. Something about the entire scene felt painfully familiar, leading Tallie to another possibility.

She knelt to better view the documents scattered on the floor. Paid bills from January to the present lay amid recipes and coupons. Random personal items like a college calendar of events, an advertisement for rain gutters, and a catalog of women's summer clothes had likely flown out of the scattered folders labeled *Cai's Stuff*, *Deidre's Stuff*, and *Meghan's Stuff*.

A colorful receipt caught Tallie's eye. Upon closer inspection, she saw that it was the invoice for a birdhouse called The Pagoda. The delivery date was listed for two days earlier.

"Marlene, could you check outside for a birdhouse?"

"A what?" Marlene sputtered.

Tallie caught the sideways glance Marlene gave her father and his nod indicating for her to proceed.

Marlene nodded agreeably and headed outside.

Tallie moved to the massive fridge, noting the items secured with magnets along the top—a wedding announcement with a couple pictured on the front, an invitation to a summer barbecue, and a to-do list pad with four items written on the front page: *return RSVP*, *order birdhouse*, *pick up dry cleaning*, *ask Cai to install new wall plates in our bathroom.*

Such normal things, Tallie thought, and she had to remind herself that two weeks earlier Cai Kaswell was just retired General Kaswell, not the man invited to be the next United States Ambassador to the United Nations. Everything had changed after that. In all their lives. In such a short time.

Tallie read the to-do list. Her heart hitched as she read the last item. Now she felt more confident about her theory. She turned to the major. "Where's the master suite?"

He cocked his head sideways and seemed tentative as he replied, "Upstairs."

Tallie headed for the staircase with the major hurrying along to cut her off. "Tallie, wait!"

Tallie grabbed the wooden banister and climbed the first step when the major's hand landed softly over hers, his eyes filled with pleading. "Take a minute and ask yourself if you can handle seeing the life they lived without you."

The words *the life they lived without you* burned, but more than merely wanting to see those spaces, Tallie *needed* to see them. "I have a theory. Do you want my help or not?"

"Of course I want it," the major said. "I just hate to see you turn the knife and cause yourself more pain."

She turned without another word and climbed the stairs, needing this singular opportunity to know her parents, to see where they'd dreamed their dreams and grieved their losses. At the top of the stairs stood two doors. She passed them and turned to the right, where instead of the master bedroom, she found two guest rooms and a large bath. She turned back toward the stairs. The next room was clearly Meghan's, decorated in black and dark purple, with posters reflecting the reportedly troubled young woman's mindset. A few items of clothing were piled haphazardly in a rocker. Tallie wondered why her sister had decided not to pack these items for that fateful flight that ended in Cutler's Ridge.

She closed the door and pressed her forehead to the wood while she settled her broken heart once more. When she was ready, she moved down the hall on the left to the next door. As she placed her hand on the knob, the major arrived, again covering her hand with his. "I checked this room myself. There's nothing here that will help us find Cai. Let's move on, please."

His attempt to deter her only strengthened her resolve. She opened the door to another room, this one seeming nursery-like, though the furnishings were for an adult. The walls were striped in pink and white, and a shelf held stuffed animals and photos of the twin baby girls. A white rocker sat in one corner, and four depressions in the carpet formed a rectangle, as if a crib had sat there for many years.

"This was the nursery, wasn't it?"

The major closed his eyes and nodded. "Yes. No matter how many years passed, Deidre kept one crib up as a reminder of the baby she lost."

"You mean me." Tallie noticed that the white queen-sized bed linen was new and unused, and the elegant furniture smelled of new wood. She could barely breathe as the observations came together in a bittersweet truth. "She prepared this room for me to come home to."

"Yes, she did," the major said. "The investigators made quite a fuss over this 'clue'"—he rolled his eyes and formed air quotes to highlight their folly—"assuming this room was prepared for the expected arrival of a guest or a visiting dignitary with whom Cai had close ties. But I knew better—that once Deidre got Julia's text telling her you were alive, she raced to prepare a room perfect for her grown girl."

Tallie's mind returned to that morning, just two weeks earlier, when she'd stood outside Bodie Glick's inn as the Cessna plane fell from the sky. A week later she knew the truth, that Deidre had arranged a secret flight after receiving a text that her missing daughter, Molly, was not only very much alive but that she would be in Cutler's Ridge on a specific date. Tallie didn't know if she'd ever be able to be Molly again, but seeing the other side of the story, the efforts her mother and sister had made to welcome her home, both warmed her and hollowed her. Her eyes burned over more evidence of what she could have had if Deidre and Meghan had survived, but it was not to be.

Instead of realizing a joyful reunion, the women had fallen for a trap intended to hide the secret of Molly's disappearance forever, and that trap had taken their lives. Tallie blinked rapidly to stave the welling tears. "If she and Ambassador—I mean General Kaswell—" The entire situation overwhelmed her fragile nerves, and she dipped her head to hide her frailty until she was back in control.

"I know how hard this is for you, Tallie."

"If they were so close, why didn't she tell him about the text? Why did she arrange a secret flight for herself and Meghan without telling him where or why?"

The major leaned against the doorjamb. "Guilt, I suppose. Your mother never forgave herself for the car accident that threw you into those woods. She blamed herself for your alleged death and the impact it had on Meghan. I suppose she wanted to fix things herself. We'll never know."

Tallie spun on him. "But you know more than anyone, don't you? You were involved in every person's decision. The game master and puppeteer." She had rendered a direct hit that visibly wounded the man. His face went slack and his chin dropped. His next breaths were heavy and drawn through an open mouth.

Tallie tried to convince herself that he deserved every bit of pain she'd inflicted, but her actions wounded her more than they likely harmed him. "I'm sorry. That was cruel of me."

"I deserve it. It's true. No matter why I did what I did, well-intended or not, I am partly to blame for your separation from your family." He moved closer to Tallie. His normally authoritative voice maintained an unusually caring tone. "What you must see from all this is that your family never forgot you. They missed you and loved you and grieved for you every day."

Tallie took a final glimpse around the room and turned for the door. Upon reaching it, she held on to the doorframe, unprepared to let go, and then, micron by micron, her fingers slid past the wood. She heard the major close the door softly, almost reverently, as if he, too, recognized the space as sacred.

The last door on the floor led to the master suite, which was, as she'd suspected, elegant yet cozy, decorated in soft grays and teal. She could imagine her mother reading in the armchair by the window while her father sat at his desk nearby. She wanted to lie on their bed and imagine lying there as a tiny child as they cradled her and comforted her from nightmares.

Work the problem. Julia's training broke her from her reverie.

Tallie saw a screwdriver sitting on one of the dressers. She quickly scanned the suite's sockets and switches to see if any showed signs of recent work. A feeling of contentment warmed her when she entered the master bathroom and found two smudged nickel wall plates, knowing they further confirmed her theory. She smelled the bar of soap and the bottle of aftershave sitting by the sink, breathing in the scents that surrounded her father. She opened his vanity drawer and relished its military order, everything in its rightful place. Three spaces were empty. Tallie closed the drawers, taking care not to move anything from its original position.

Her mother's drawers were a different story. Her toiletry items were haphazardly crammed together, and Tallie could imagine her mother grabbing and tossing needed items into her bag for the surreptitious flight. Tallie's hands began to shake, and she closed the drawer and moved on to the closet.

She ran her fingers over her father's perfectly hung clothes and did the same when she reached her mother's side, trying to learn all she could about the woman who'd raced to claim her mere weeks ago. She leaned close and drew in the scent from her mother's robe, allowing herself to dream of her mother being there.

Work the problem.

Tallie turned back to her father's side of the closet and studied the shoe racks. He'd organized his shoes in a straight row by purpose and color—formal wear, dress shoes, casual dress, sport shoes, hiking boots, and two pairs of military-grade field boots. Three empty spaces hinted that three pairs of shoes were missing. One empty space was situated between two pairs of hiking boots, one space was between two pairs of sport shoes, and the last space was at the end of his field-boot section. She rushed out to the dresser and opened drawers until she found his underwear section. It was stocked low, as was the spot where his T-shirts were stowed.

The major asked, "What are you thinking?"

Tallie rushed around, opening every drawer as she asked the major, "Where are the washer and dryer?"

He pointed to a double set of louvered doors off the bedroom. "Behind them. Why?"

Tallie found the laundry-room closet, and as she'd suspected, there was no pile of unwashed clothes. Everything Cai Kaswell owned had been washed, but it wasn't all in the house.

Marlene called up from the bottom step. "Tallie, I found a birdhouse out back on a pole."

"What did it look like?"

"A pagoda. It looks new. Real new, except the little pointy thing on top is broken."

Tallie nodded and gestured to the major. "Follow me." When they were back in the kitchen, she stopped the major and Marlene in the doorway and said, "This mess wasn't caused by a man in danger. It was caused by a man in grief. The broken things remind him of his loss. The birthday plate, the cookie jar Meghan must have painted, the photos and files representing the normalcy of their perfect life."

"But why would he break precious mementoes?" Marlene asked.

"Exactly," the major said. "They preserved memories of you in the nursery for over twenty years. Why would Cai lash out at these personal items?"

"*They* preserved them—he and Deidre, but now she's lost to him too. When they thought I died, they still had each other and Meghan, but this time, Cai was utterly and completely alone. I think it crushed him."

Tallie moved to the to-do list on the fridge and felt disturbed by the wedding invitation hung there. She quickly dismissed the feeling and pointed to the list. "Is this Cai's or Deidre's handwriting?"

"It's Deidre's." Tallie heard the ache in the major's voice.

"So, after finding out his wife and daughter were dead, he came home and attended to Deidre's list, like a private memorial. His emotions were raw. Deidre would never know whether he attended to those items, but they were critical to him. One of the items is *order birdhouse*. Another is *swap new wall plates*. Remember the screwdriver on the dresser? The master bath has all new nickel wall plates. They're smudged, which tells me they were probably installed after Cai fired the maid, or she would have wiped them clean."

"And you think he just snapped?" Marlene asked.

Tallie pointed to the colorful invoice of the birdhouse. "I suspect item two, this birdhouse, was the catalyst to his breakdown. Deidre ordered it weeks ago, but it just arrived two days ago. Maybe it was a reminder of some wonderful memories or a place they were planning to visit. Marlene said the birdhouse was broken. Imagine how frustrated he would have felt if this special birdhouse his dead wife ordered arrived broken. Maybe he started digging through the files to find the original invoice, and in the process, he came across so many mundane reminders of the life they all shared that his grief overwhelmed him."

Tallie's gaze settled on the broken cookie jar. "I was in shock after Julia's death. Alone, frightened, unsure of what or who I was anymore. And then I found Julia's note to me, and it unleashed all my pent-up fear and pain. I lashed out. I opened every drawer, ransacked every closet. I think that's what happened here." She turned and pointed to the broken dishes and asked the major, "Have you ever seen this cookie jar and plate before?"

"Every time I visited. They were Deidre's countertop decorations."

"I don't think he planned to smash them. My guess is that it was a gut reaction"—Tallie laid her arm on the counter and pretended to sweep everything off—"one he regretted immediately."

"But what about the blood? The investigators listed the cookie jar as the weapon since parts of it had Cai's blood."

"The bloody pieces are on top, indicating that they landed last. He was probably picking the broken pieces off the floor when he cut himself. Then he likely stood over the mess for a time, absorbing what he'd done as blood dripped to the floor, creating that pool of blood there. I think that's when he paused to gather himself and managed to shift gears."

"To what?"

"Next to his family, what did he love most?"

The major moved back to the foyer and pointed to the photos that lined the wall. "His country and his men."

"How does that patriotism translate into this stage of his life?"

The major leaned back against the wall and rubbed a tired hand over his face.

Marlene asked, "What was that story you were telling me, Daddy? About the NSA field officer and others who disappeared recently in Mexico?"

The major turned to Tallie. "Over the last four months, seven North Americans—some civilians and some in government service—have disappeared while traveling to foreign countries. Four others became deathly sick and disoriented and, when interviewed, told stories of awakening on a beautiful island. At first, no one saw a correlation between the two groups, but the similarities in the four cases finally drew attention—debilitating nausea and short-term memory loss resembling amnesia. Both are symptoms of poisoning, but blood tests proved nothing. More disturbing was the fact that each of the eleven missing or ill people were leaders in their respective fields, people whose lives were dedicated to their work, with no family who would notice their absence. The similarities in their cases warranted further investigation, so the NSA sent two agents undercover to a Mexican resort, where the last case occurred, and one of our agents disappeared into thin air."

"How long ago?"

"Less than a week."

"And Cai knew about it?"

"We were fumbling with what to say, trying to fill the silence after the funeral, and I got a text about the missing agents. He asked about it, and I told him. For a while, he was his old self, asking questions about the investigation and laying out plans to storm the resort. I saw hope in his eyes in those moments. I'd give anything to believe he's out there like a one-man army rather than a prisoner somewhere."

"I don't think he's a prisoner. Not unless his captors gave him time to pack."

The major's face brightened. "What do you think happened to him?"

"Three items are missing from his vanity drawer. A toilety bag might fit in one of the spots. One of the other missing items might have been a small first aid kit. I found a bandage wrapper and some blood in the drawer. I don't know what clothes he owns, but most of his underwear and T-shirts are also gone, and three pairs of footwear are missing from his closet—outdoor shoes and field boots. I'd be willing to guess his rucksack is missing as well."

The major checked the garage and confirmed the missing pack. "The feds are following the abduction scenario. Let's see if your theory pans out." He turned to Marlene. "Are you up for a trip to Mexico?"

"I took a leave of absence from the library as soon as I heard about Cai's disappearance."

Tallie smiled, grateful for Marlene, who pulled her back to normal from time to time. "I'll never be able to see you as a mild-mannered librarian again."

Marlene dipped deep into her pool of Southern affectations, her voice dripping with lilt and charm. "You wouldn't want this little ole librarian to stamp your book?"

"I'd rather have you watching my back."

With a wink and a total transformation into a battle-ready pose, Marlene replied, "Anytime, sugar. Anytime."

A worry crossed Tallie's mind. "All I have are fake passports, as you well know, Major."

"They'll pass snuff in any border in the world—I made sure of that—but if it will put your mind at ease, I can order a new legit one to be waiting for you before we reach the airport."

Tallie closed her eyes and shook her head with a smile as she considered the reach of this man's power and network. "I have no doubt."

"So are you ready to go?"

She thought back to the photo on the fridge. "I'd like a minute alone in the house, if you don't mind."

Marlene walked over and gave her a hug. "You take your time, sugar. Daddy and I will be waiting outside in the car."

When the door closed and Tallie was alone, she moved to the kitchen to satisfy the lingering worry nagging at her. Something about that wedding invitation on the fridge picked at her peace and left her unnerved. She studied it and the faces entangled in a kiss on it. It was romantic and alarming at the same time. She didn't recognize the woman's face, and the man's face was partially hidden behind the woman's hair, but the longer she studied it, the more certain she became. He didn't have a beard in this photo, but the angle of his jaw, the dimpled cheeks, and the shape of his eyes and his nose were unmistakable. His name appeared to be Cooper Burke, but Tallie knew him as someone else—the man who'd claimed to be the father of Emily, the little lost girl in Idaho. But that raised other questions. Who was the woman he'd claimed was his wife, and who was Emily?

The child's odd comment returned to Tallie. Something about doing a good skill. She had assumed it was about her own skill, but what if it was about the child's? Had Emily also been playing a part?

Tallie suddenly remembered Julia's primary warning: *Trust no one.* She had felt so safe with Jackson and his family that she had foolishly forgotten about the people who had been chasing Julia and trying to entrap her father for twenty-one years. Was this man one of them? His photo was on her father's fridge. Did that mean he was somehow linked to the people in her circle of trust? Her world was so small. Jackson, Major Norris, Marlene, Louis. Was one of them a danger to her?

She closed her eyes, wishing Julia were there to consult. What would she tell Tallie? The last lines of Julia's final message returned to her.

Trust your instincts . . . I believe in you.

She took three deep breaths and considered everything she knew about each person in her small circle. More importantly, she considered everything she felt in each of their presences. Moment by moment, as memories passed through her mind, she felt her shoulders relax and her breathing steady. One name brought her peace, without question. If she had to trust anyone, she would place her trust with him.

Calmer now, more focused and on full alert, she entered the living room and stood in front of the wall of happy family faces, hoping the God Jackson had testified of would carry her words to the heaven he also believed in and to the ears of her dead mother and sister. Jackson had spoken to her of wonderful promises, like powers stronger than death and promises of life everlasting. She didn't know if what he'd told her was true, but she desperately wanted to believe in those things. To trust in them. She marveled that, while standing amid those photos, remembering the room her mother had hastily prepared to welcome a daughter she had never stopped missing or loving, it all seemed possible, merciful, and even right.

"I love you, Mom and Meghan. And don't worry about Father. I'll find him."

CHAPTER FOUR

As THE MAJOR HAD PROMISED, a chopper came to take Jackson to the airport, where a ticket was waiting. His private plane landed five hours later on a runway at the far end of Baltimore/Washington International Airport and taxied to a remote hangar where an intimidatingly muscular man waited, holding a small sign. Jackson shivered when he read the words on the sign clenched in the man's hands: *Jackson James*. The major hadn't bothered to mention that Jackson's ride to Ambassador Kaswell's office would come via a man who appeared able to singlehandedly push the plane into its parking space.

The man waved as Jackson approached him, and the simple motion caused his bicep to bulge as if he were curling a fifty-pound weight. Jackson was generally comfortable with his lean runner's body, but the ripped bodybuilder standing before him brought a flashback to his mind, of his scrawny twelve-year-old self dressed in his sixth-grade gym uniform for co-ed volleyball.

The driver extended his hand gave Jackson's a firm shake. "Jackson James?"

"Yes," Jackson replied.

"Cool. I'm Makai Kapono, but everyone calls me Mak. Hungry?"

"Very."

"Excellent. We'll hit a drive-through. Are burgers okay?"

"Sure."

"Good deal. Take your seat in back. I'll get these."

Mak tossed Jackson's heavy bags into the back of the vehicle, closed the hatch, and took his seat behind the wheel. Before starting the ignition, he grabbed the phone resting in the console between the front seats and made a quick call.

"Delta five. Package arrived. En route with one stop to refuel. ETA is thirty."

The cloak-and-dagger military vibe creeped Jackson out. "Are you messing with me?" he asked with a nervous chuckle.

Mak stared him down in the rearview mirror until a broad smile turned his cheeks into two happy lumps and segued into an infectious laugh. "Maybe . . . just a little."

Jackson's chuckle thinly guised his trepidation. He instinctively grabbed the door handle in case an escape became necessary. He figured Mak was one of the major's men, or at least a man of similar ilk, but his easygoing manner, ponytail, playful smile, and happy music selections countered Jackson's fear enough to keep him from jumping from the car.

He attempted to call Tallie as they exited the terminal. When the call went unanswered, he texted her, partly to be sure she knew he was thinking about her and partly to leave a record in case Mak drove him to a pier and dropped him into the Chesapeake Bay.

His comfort level didn't increase when their short drive along the highway ended with a turn into a business district of nondescript office buildings, industrial shops, and fast-food places. Mak pulled into an unknown joint's drive-through and ordered without consulting Jackson about his preferences.

"Hey, Reggie. Give me my regular order and toss in a number two with a side order of cheese curds and fries."

A few minutes later, two large bags passed through the window. Mak handed one back to Jackson, along with a bottle of water. "You'll like the number two. I figured you for a bacon-and-cheddar guy."

Jackson didn't confirm the man's eerily accurate assumption. "Did you figure me for a water guy too?"

"Sure, just like me. You look fit, so I assume you're someone who respects his body, understanding the delicate balance between fueling his temple properly and enjoying the pleasure of a good meal."

Jackson wondered if he'd just received a compliment or whether he was the subject of the man's humor. "Thanks . . . I guess."

"You're welcome!" Mak replied with genuineness. "Now, you look like a 2800-calorie-a-day guy." He raised his own bag of food. "I, on the other hand, have to consume as much protein and as many calories as I burn lifting and running."

"Are you in training for something?"

"Always. For hours every day. That's just part of the job."

Jackson clutched his bag against his 2800-calorie-a-day–fed chest and wondered what kind of ambassadorial PR work Cai Kaswell had waiting for him.

They pulled into the small parking area beside a five-story building with the exterior charm of a penitentiary. Jackson assumed they'd pulled into the innocuous building's lot so they could enjoy their lunch, but once he'd parked the vehicle, Mak exited the SUV and opened Jackson's door. "We're here."

The longer Jackson looked at the building, the more certain he became that his previous predictions of doom were correct. The tiny windows were the yellowish block building's anemic but only highlights. No effort had been made to add a single feature of architectural interest, and the tiny plot boasted no landscaping, unless tufts of dead, unmown grass counted as shrubbery.

He swallowed and looked at Mak, remaining firmly in his seat. *"Here?"*

Mak raised his arms and beamed proudly at Jackson. "It doesn't look like much, does it?"

"And that's good because . . . ?"

"Great camo. No one would ever look at this place and think it was anything special."

"You've got that right. And is it . . . special?"

Mak eyed him as if he were daft. "It's the bomb."

Jackson surveyed the building's slightly sooty exterior, most likely stained from the constant exhaust that blew from the highway over the structure in a gray haze, leaving its safflower-colored paint more beige than yellow. "What is this place? I'm supposed to work in Ambassador Kaswell's office."

"*Supposed* is the operative word."

"Wait. What?" Jackson scrambled out of the SUV, but Mak didn't offer any further explanation. Instead, he opened the vehicle's rear doors and handed his food bag to Jackson, who shuffled both bags of burgers while Mak hefted Jackson's luggage as if the two pieces were mere hand weights. Their discussion shifted into a move-in as Mak headed into the building while Jackson puttered along.

Mak positioned his badge over a scanner. An automatic lock clicked, and the aluminum and glass door opened. The men entered and faced a second door. Mak opened his eyes wide and peered into a four-inch-by-six-inch glass window. Fascinated, Jackson watched a light move across Mak's eye. A few seconds later, that door also opened with a heavy click.

"A retinal scanner? What kind of PR do you do here?"

Mak didn't comment as he led Jackson over to a security-check station. "Empty your pockets into a tub. Your cell phone and laptop too," he said as he emptied his own belongings into a tub and set Jackson's luggage on the belt.

While Jackson complied, one of Mak's thick-armed associates entered. The bald man's ebony skin had a sheen of sweat over it, as if he'd just left a workout. Jackson wondered if everyone who worked here had to hit the gym for several hours every day.

“So this is the new grunt?” the man said.

“He’s okay. Rich, meet Jackson. Jackson, Rich is our security specialist.”

As Jackson extended his hand for another firm handshake, he remembered something his father had told him, how some men tried to impress people with their solid grip. Well, two could play that game. “Nice to meet you,” he said, squeezing back against Rich’s hearty shake. “I’m still waiting for answers. I was hired to run interference with the press about Ambassador Kas—”

“We’ll bring you up to speed about the general,” Rich said as he began rifling through Jackson’s luggage.

Frustration rose in Jackson over the personal invasion occurring before his eyes as his skivvies landed outside the suitcase. “Do you mind?” he barked as he bundled his things back up.

“Just cool your jets, newbie,” Rich said with a chuckle as he continued his search. “Security checks of all personnel and packages going in or out are SOP for everyone around here.”

“What the heck is SOP?” Jackson asked as Rich finished excavating through his unmentionables. Jackson zipped his case and straightened.

Rich’s expression twisted in complete disbelief. “Is this a joke, newbie?” He looked at Mak. “Did the major seriously send us a grunt with zero understanding of military protocol or chain of command?”

Mak shot Jackson a look that said “cool it” and answered with a tense smile. “SOP means standard operating procedure. It’s the same for everyone at this installation.”

“I’m here, so you obviously have Major Norris’s personal recommendation of me. That should override SOP and chain of command, shouldn’t it?” Jackson asked. “And this ‘installation’ doesn’t look like any PR office I’ve ever seen. What is it? I think I deserve some answers.”

“You what?” Rich snapped.

Mak shook his head, warning Jackson, but it was too late. Rich was already in Jackson’s face.

“Listen, Pulitzer,” he said with a finger jab to Jackson’s chest. “Mak and I and the rest of the team have spent years crawling through forsaken parts of the world together, so we trust each other. Now, you? You’re an unknown element. All we know is that you’re a has-been writer whose star career crashed and burned until he happened to land in the right place at the right time when the Kaswell women’s plane went down. That sounds a bit questionable, and all we have is Major Norris’s nod that you’re okay. Frankly, that’s not enough for me. The major’s been off his game since the Kaswell women were killed in that crash, so cool your jets and lie low until you've earned our trust around here. Got it?"

Pulitzer. Major Norris had tagged Jackson with that derogatory nickname ten years ago while running the journalism prodigy through secret tests of his journalistic integrity. Jackson had hated the man and the word until a few weeks ago. Now they were both more of an annoyance. Rich's use of the nickname seemed to imply that Norris had been talking about Jackson to these guys.

"Fine. But first, tell me why I'm not working from Ambassador Kaswell's office. Norris said my assignment was to redirect questions about his disappearance."

"The job's the same, but you're doing it for *General* Kaswell. He didn't accept the post yet, and he might not."

Jackson heard the worry and sorrow in Rich's voice and knew he was in the company of people who loved Cai Kaswell. He felt like an idiot. It made total sense. Instead of an ambassadorial-level office decked out to receive endless high-powered visitors, Cai would prefer an obscure special ops office setup for a retired, grieving, special ops general in limbo. Jackson capitulated. "Understood. Where do you want me? Put me to work."

Mak led him to a spartan off-white office in the corner that could have been the interior of a fridge for all the warmth it exuded. A fluorescent light buzzed from the center of the ceiling, and the only natural light came from one of the narrow rectangular windows high on the outside wall.

Answering phones and deflecting questions was not what Jackson had expected when he took the job handling PR for the man he'd thought was America's next Ambassador to the United Nations, but he was delighted by the high-tech furnishings—an ergonomic chair and a desk that converted to a standing workstation. The computer system made his fingers tingle. Three monitors were connected in a semicircle with a camera mounted in the center. The only other visible components were a printer, a sleek keyboard, and a mouse. A compartment under the desk held a central processing unit and a hard drive with a massive memory. And, from what Jackson understood of his new colleagues, he could only imagine the layers of security software installed to ward off cyber threats. He tried to hide his pleasure. "Nice system."

"Nice?" Mak feigned offense. "It's a cutting-edge multilevel security computer with DataVault, all tied into the building's Secutor System network. The entire building is wrapped by an electronic Faraday cage so nothing we don't want gets in or out. We're locked down tighter than the NSA. I told you, man. This place is the bomb!"

"But . . . what exactly do you do here?"

Rich came to the doorway and leaned against the jamb. "We deal in information. Let's just leave it at that for now." His silence on the matter spoke volumes.

Rich left and Mak said, "We should get you settled in, Jackson."

"I gave up my apartment when General Kaswell offered me the new job. I figured I could afford a nicer place with my new salary." He chuckled. "So much for that. I'll have to check into a motel until I find a place."

"No need." Mak's mile-wide smile beamed again. "This place has personnel quarters."

"You sleep here?"

"Not always, but this station has to be manned twenty-four seven by a small and trusted crew. Most days, it's hardly worth leaving. Follow me."

Mak and Jackson each grabbed a suitcase and a bag of cold hamburgers and headed back toward the lobby. They passed an elevator but opted for the stairs instead. An open commons area with a small kitchen setup awaited them at the top of the stairs. Mak led Jackson to the third room on the left, furnished with a twin cot, small dresser, footlocker, and chair. The letters IBT appeared on inconspicuous surfaces of some of the gear.

Jackson pointed to the acronym painted on the bar of the cot. "I've seen that somewhere. What's that stand for?"

Mak looked to where Jackson was pointing. "Some think tank called the Infinity Brain Trust."

"Huh," Jackson grunted. "That's right. They tried to recruit me. IBT was on their letterhead."

"Rethinking your career decision, bro?"

Jackson laughed. "Ask me in a week. So why would a think tank supply the military with hardware?"

"We're not regular military anymore, so the company procures gears from civilian suppliers. Our badged operators—"

"Badged operators?"

"Guys with special ops training who are qualified to go outside the wire, as opposed to members who are hired specifically as support personnel."

"Like me."

"Still important . . . but yes, exactly. Anyway, some of our badged guys have done work for IBT, providing secure transit for some of their people, and in return, they've supplied us with gear."

"So if you're not regular military, what are you?"

"I could tell you, but I'd have to kill you."

The expression on Mak's face brought back all of Jackson's initial fears about this place and these men. "You're kidding, right?" he asked with a slight squeak to his voice.

"No," Mak answered as he raised one eyebrow. Jackson could count the passage of time by the thundering beats of his pounding heart, and then the mood changed as Mak seemed to explode in a volcano of rumbling laughter and dance. "I'm just messing with you, man, but I got you. I totally got you!"

Jackson fell down on the cot and attempted to deny that he'd been "got," until Mak's expression convinced him that confession seemed the best course of action.

"Good times, man. Good times. Let's get you settled in." Mak pointed to a footlocker. "Stow your stuff here. Bedding and towels are in the supply closet, door number three. The bathroom is at the end of the hall. Laundry is across from the latrine. You saw the kitchen. The rules are simple. Wash what you use. Don't eat it if you didn't buy it, unless we're having baseball night."

"Baseball night?"

"That's when we all pitch something in and share."

As weird and scary as this place was, Jackson knew important things happened here, and that completely intrigued him. "Got it."

"Great."

"What's on the upper floor, beyond that heavy door?"

"Security."

"Like Rich?" Jackson asked.

"Yeah, but they aren't *personable* like Rich."

"You call him *personable*?"

"He's the major's second-in-command over this installation. He's been taught to get along with his coworkers. Those other guys? Not so much. Just think of them as Rich on steroids."

"And what goes on in the basement behind that electronically locked metal door?"

Mak puffed up and blew out an exasperated groan. "Stuff that will get you in bigger trouble than if you go snooping around upstairs. All you need to know is that all floors besides this one and the main level are off-limits to you. Don't ask who does what on any of the floors above or below you. And take my word for it; don't go rogue reporter on us and explore the place. Those guys don't play nice with others."

Another cold chill snaked along Jackson's spine, causing him to shiver. "Got it."

"Good, 'cause I like you."

Mak's approval didn't reset Jackson's nerves to normal, especially since he thought he heard a veiled warning of danger if he stepped out of line. Still, Mak liked him, and Jackson decided to capitalize as much as possible on that goodwill. "Now that we're alone, can I ask you what Rich meant when he said you deal in information?"

Mak closed his eyes as his mouth slid left and right. After a dozen seconds, he walked down the hall to a small rectangular window that overlooked a crowded industrial district. "What do you see when you look out this window?"

"Same as you—buildings, a water tower, highway ramps, and cars."

"Some of the buildings you see are carefully created facades that camouflage a powerful antenna system that pulls down feeds from satellites scanning signals around the world. That data is streamed directly here. A team of linguists sort out and translate the conversations from the metadata. Lawyers and computer specialists decide what metadata material we can legally use, and cryptologists analyze the encrypted data in the hopes of breaking down the senders' programmed algorithms. If all those brainiacs do their jobs perfectly, and if they have a little luck, they might just know what our enemies are planning in time for us to thwart an attack."

"Are you messing with me again?"

"I wish I were."

Mak didn't show a hint of a smile, and Jackson knew he was giving it to him straight. His throat tightened, and he almost wished he hadn't asked because—despite the crazy tech and security and all the geniuses purported to be working in the building—American success seemed fragile and failure seemed a real and frightening possibity.

"I guess that explains why Rich is so tense."

A hint of Mak's smile reappeared. "He's a good guy. You'll come to love him. He's just under a lot of stress right now. We all are. There's been a lot of chatter on the airwaves recently."

"More than usual?"

Mak's face slackened. "Yeah."

Jackson felt his arms prickle. "A lot more?"

"More than I've ever known before."

The reporter in Jackson pushed past the fearful innuendos as random information came together. "Do you think it has anything to do with Cai Kaswell's disappearance?"

"Tell me how you and the general got so tight."

Jackson noticed how deftly Mak segued away from his question. As affable as the guy was, he was good at his job and careful with what he said. Jackson respected that.

"A friend and I were on the ground where the plane crashed."

"Tallie Brown."

"Yeah." Jackson was surprised by how quickly Tallie's name rolled off Mak's tongue, and then he smiled, remembering that information was Mak's business. "We had details about the situation that we withheld from the public because they were so personal to the general. I guess we earned his respect and trust."

"Makes sense. I feel bad for that Tallie girl. Her life was so private. Not anymore if the press has its way."

"Wait, what are you talking about?"

"Maybe the Idaho press didn't run the photo, but a picture of her standing guard over that burning fuselage made all the big-city papers."

Jackson barked, "What?" and grabbed Mak's shoulder, but the effort ended up more like a shove. Mak stared at Jackson's hand until he removed it, but he was less afraid of Mak than he was of what Mak had said. He threw his hands to his head. "Just tell me . . . please . . . is she part of that chatter you were talking about?"

Mak gave a hesitant nod. "She's mixed up in the chatter about the general."

"What are they saying?"

"That's above your pay grade, bro."

"Is she in danger?"

"It's just chatter. She's a curiosity to people, but she's in good hands with the major. And even if the chatter escalates, you don't need to worry about her. Operators up and down the line are analyzing everything."

The rogue leaders who wanted to publicly destroy Cai Kaswell by discrediting him had likely put a hefty bounty on his head—perhaps on Tallie's as well. Jackson needed to speak to her to be sure she was okay. And with all he was hearing and learning, he needed her to give him clarity. She had a way of sorting through the muck of things to help him see what was real and true.

He turned toward the hall that led to his assigned room. "Thanks for showing me around and explaining the house rules, Mak. I think I'll unpack and take a nap. Don't worry about me. I promise I'll be good and stay where I'm allowed."

Mak chuckled. "Okay, man. I'll give you some privacy. Your burgers are nasty cold now. I'll head to the kitchen to rustle you up some grub from my stash."

Jackson hurried to his room, closed the door, and dialed Tallie's number. His stress level doubled when she didn't answer. All the reasons she might not pick up ran through his mind, from the fact that they had argued earlier in the morning to thoughts of her being kidnapped and carried to Somalia. He began to dial her number again and stopped before he crossed the line from worried boyfriend to cyber-psycho. He busied his hands by putting his clothes away until the phone rang. He snatched the device, and when he saw Tallie's number appear on the screen, his heart cheered. He sat on the edge of his cot and answered. "Hi. Thanks for returning my call."

"Of course. How are you?"

Her voice sounded tense and on guard. "I'm fine, but how are you? Something's wrong, Tallie. What is it?"

Her voice became muffled as she whispered into the phone. "I'm sorry about this morning."

"Is that why you sound upset?"

"I need to trust someone, Jackson. Please tell me I can still trust you."

Jackson felt his heart split. He rose to his feet and started pacing. "Of course you can. You've got to know that. If you broke my heart and told me to take a hike, I'd still be there for you. What's going on?"

Each second of her pause felt like twenty, and Jackson wanted to jump through the phone to her. "Have you been to the Kaswell home yet?"

"Yes." Her terse delivery was as telling as the answer itself. Jackson knew such a visit would stir up myriad feelings and questions, which she was apparently unwilling or unable to discuss at the moment.

"Do you want to talk about it? How was it to see the life you were supposed to have? Was it healing . . . or just . . . hard?"

She sighed more than answered, and Jackson assumed that meant it was both.

Marlene's sultry drawl could be heard in the background. She sounded close to Tallie, and Jackson wondered if that was what had suddenly made Tallie reluctant to speak candidly.

"How are you and the major and Marlene getting along?" he asked.

"It's hard. He's really depending on me."

"Just do what you can do. Anything you add is a help."

He heard Marlene's voice increase in volume, as if she were drawing nearer. Tallie responded to her with a false cheeriness that made alarms go off in his head. When she returned to the call, she switched topics completely. "There's this math thing."

"*Math* thing?"

"Yeah, similar to the one from last week."

He racked his brain to recall a math thing from last week, and then he remembered their conversation about how some pieces of evidence didn't quite add up. Was that it? But what things weren't adding up now?

In a voice brim with false cheer she asked, "Hey, could you do me a favor?"

Jackson's head spun over the abrupt shift in her mood. "Anything."

"I heard a rustle in the brush this morning when I was getting Emily, so I set a trap to keep any predators from greeting us when we reached the top. I heard it spring, but I didn't have time to check on the animal then, and things got so crazy after the rescue that I forgot to ask the sheriff to send someone up to set the poor thing free. Could you please call the sheriff and ask him to check on that? And could you also get me the name and contact info for Emily's parents? I'd like to see how she's doing."

She uttered the request in a tone that caused the hairs on his arms to rise. "Of course. Tell me what's really worrying you."

In an almost imperceptible whisper, she said, "I can't fail, but I'm not sure I'm strong enough to get through this."

"You are, Tallie."

"I hope so. And please get me Emily's info, okay?"

"I will, I will."

Tallie thanked Marlene for something and returned to the call with that unnatural bouncy cheer again. "By the way, you might not be able to contact me for a few days."

Jackson felt like one of the facility's cryptographers, attempting to decode her words to see if there was some information meant only for him buried in her casual comment. "Where are you headed?"

Her voice returned to a muted whisper. "Mexico. The Grand Blanc Riviera Resort."

"Do you think your father is there?" He realized that he too was whispering.

Her voice became cheery again. "Could be, but thanks for checking in on that bear or whatever I snagged."

Tallie was clearly bringing the conversation to a quick end. The way she was whispering and changing the subject signaled she was on edge. *What is going on?* At the very least, Jackson was desperate to make sure she knew she could trust him. "Call or text me as often as you can. Give me a trail in case I need to follow you. Please."

"Good luck in your new job. The shoe is on the other foot now. Instead of uncovering the truth, you're the one protecting it."

He hadn't thought about it, but Tallie was right. He was protecting Cai's truth and Tallie's too. Maybe telling him that was her way of letting him know she trusted him. Or, perhaps, even in her distress Tallie's final thoughts were intended to do exactly what he'd hoped she'd be able to do for him—help him sort out what mattered.

Or perhaps she was sending him another message. He pulled out his phone and dictated their conversation as perfectly as possible so he could study it. She'd been struggling since being in the Kaswell house. He could hardly imagine what seeing what her life could have been was doing to her. She was clearly afraid Norris would yank her from the case if he thought she was off her game, so she was pretending to be fine. That seemed dangerous.

As if that weren't enough to worry about, a few other things were evident. Something somewhere wasn't adding up; something peculiar had happened in those woods, and there was something odd about the child Tallie had saved.

CHAPTER FIVE

Sunday, June 22, 2014
Grand Blanc Riviera Resort, Mazatlan, Mexico

THE DRIVER DROPPED TALLIE, MARLENE, and Major Norris off at the Grand Blanc Riviera Resort before dawn. The Pacific oceanside location was exquisite, with white sand lying in rippled berms from which palm trees waved, as if paying homage to the crystal-blue waters beyond. The sunrise tinted the sky pink and yellow, and Tallie believed it was the most beautiful place she had ever been. She wondered why, in all their running and moving, Julia had never chosen such a lovely place as this. She soon knew. Mere minutes past sunrise, people began carrying bags, blankets, chairs, and coolers to the shore to stake their claims on a square of white sand.

When Tallie was young, she might have loved the sights and sounds of a thousand strangers, but isolation had changed her. Such crowds unnerved her. She was more like Julia than she preferred to admit.

Marlene was Tallie's complete alter ego. The more people, particularly single men, who walked by, the more she longed to be among them, until she let out a sigh intended for both her companions to hear. "Why didn't you just hang me by my thumbs over smoldering coals, Daddy? It'd be less painful. You actually expect me to work here with that ocean and those beautiful toned and lotioned men, with no time to lie on that beach?"

Major Norris's eyebrows knit together. "Focus, Marlene. We're here to save Cai Kaswell."

She looked at Tallie and quickly sobered. "Sorry, Tallie. Of course we are. The last few weeks have done me in, I'm afraid." She pulled herself up ramrod straight. "All right, Daddy. I'm back to my senses and ready to work. Where do we begin?"

Major Norris pointed to a young man coming their way. "There's a familiar face. My guess is that he's been protecting the room where the last American agent, Agent Gonzales, disappeared for two days and reappeared with no idea what had happened to her. We sent her back to D.C. He'll bring us up to speed on the investigation going on down here."

Marlene curled a strand of red hair around her fingers and smiled encouragingly at the man. Her instant attraction to him was impossible to miss. He was handsome enough, Tallie thought. Six-foot-one, she assessed. Thirtyish and lean with wavy brown hair and a swagger when he walked. But there was something else . . . something familiar about the lines of his cheeks and jaw. She felt every nerve fire as he drew close enough for her to see the dimples in his cheeks and recognize where she'd seen him before. His name was Cooper Burke—the man in the wedding announcement on the Kaswells' fridge.

Her fists curled, and she stepped wider, in a protective stance, in case she needed to defend herself from Burke. But Major Norris knew him. Vouched for him. Something didn't add up.

Major Norris noticed the change in Tallie and placed a hand on her shoulder. "What's wrong? You look as if you're preparing for battle."

Tallie stared Burke down with his every approaching step. He knew her, and she wanted him to be sure she knew him too.

The major called, "Burke."

"Hey, Major," he replied with a lazy salute.

"Let me introduce you to my team on this assignment." He turned to Marlene. "This is my daughter, Marlene, and this young lady is—"

"The amazing Tallie Brown."

The words were disarming, aluding to some familiarity he believed he had with her, and she wondered if that was precisely his intent—to disarm her and get her to lower her guard. Some other emotion was woven into his demeanor. She couldn't read it or him, but that gift for deception would have been part of his training. He was, apparently, one of Norris's men.

She kept her guard up, her eyes fixed on Burke as she watched Major Norris's response from the corner of her eye. He, she was relieved to note, seemed shocked by Burke's reply.

"How . . . have you two met?" he asked.

"We've met," Tallie replied with dripping skepticism. "Only, he wasn't Agent Burke from whatever task force he claims to be a part of. He was at the campsite yesterday morning, during the search for that missing girl. Your agent was posing as the missing child's father."

Burke stepped toward Tallie. She noticed that the dip when he walked appeared to be more of a limp. She also noticed that he kept his left arm close to his body, as if he were protecting his side, and she caught the hint of a wince when he lifted his right arm to wave a scolding finger her way. When he saw her attention drawn to his bruised and bloodied knuckles, Burke quickly lowered his hand and stepped back.

"That was your assumption, Miss Brown. As I recall that interaction, I never said a word. You incorrectly assumed I was Emily's father."

Tallie replayed the moment in her mind—the lone worried man beside the frantic mother, pulling his beard as he paced and muttered under his breath. Had she added up one and one and gotten three this time? "You had a beard then."

"I've shaved. Men do that."

"And your hands. They weren't cut and bruised yesterday."

"Look again, Miss Brown. These are day-old wounds. You're mistaken."

Tallie wondered how much of Burke's arguments were rehearsed, designed to cause her to doubt herself.

"I don't think you care about how I scraped my knuckles on that mountain, do you? The real question you're avoiding asking me is how did I just happen to be there yesterday and now here? You're thinking to yourself that it's just too coincidental to be merely that, so you're wondering why I'm following you. Correct?"

Major Norris stepped protectively in front of Tallie and bore down on Burke. "So am I, Burke. How do you even know Miss Brown, let alone happen to show up at some campsite in Idaho where she's searching for a missing child when you're supposed to be down here, protecting a federal crime scene?"

Burke's bravado melted as his body relaxed and rounded forward. He chuckled. "I'm just messing with all of you, Major." He pulled himself back to his full height and bowed slightly to each of the women before extending his hand to Major Norris. "General Kaswell"—he paused and shook his head—"I haven't wrapped my head around everything that's happened to him lately. About four days ago, he pulled me off the assignment to guard the room where Agent Gonzales was abducted, to serve protective duty on Miss Brown instead. He gave me her cell number and opened authorization for me to track her phone signal. I've been shadowing her since then."

"You what?" Tallie barked. She wasn't buying the man's far-fetched story. "Have you been listening in on my personal calls?"

"No, ma'am. I just get a signal; that's all."

"How dare you—" she started to argue, but Major Norris was already leading the charge against Burke's story. His hands shot to his waist, and he leaned into Burke's face.

"You're saying Cai did what?"

"He said Miss Brown was a personal friend, the one who protected the crash site. He also said the press had been swarming around her then and he wanted me to protect her and keep her from becoming the next story."

Tallie's caution was sidelined by the words *personal friend.* Cai Kaswell had called her a *personal* friend? Had he put the ragged pieces together and figured out he was her father?

Major Norris pulled back and eased his protective stance. "I can see Cai doing that." A new look of worry crossed over his face. He turned to Tallie. "You probably didn't know this because you took off for Idaho so quickly, but some photographer published a photo of you standing at the burning crash site, guarding the perimeter. It was accompanied by a couple of quotes from that dimwit innkeeper Bodie Glick, about how you heard the plane's engine failing before anyone else and how you ran to the crash site as if you knew where it would go down. That photo and caption made a lot of the papers after Deidre's and Meghan's bodies were identified."

Burke pulled the image up on his phone and handed it to Tallie. "You honored the general's family ma'am. He wanted to spare you notoriety for doing such a kindness, so he sent me to ward off any reporters that might come looking for you."

All Tallie saw was her hopes being dashed again. General Kaswell wasn't protecting his daughter. He was merely protecting a stranger who had done a good turn to his family. A family that didn't include her. She bit her bottom lip and handed the phone back.

"So . . ." Norris was on the attack again. "If you've been trailing Tallie, who's been guarding the scene here?"

"I don't know, Major. The general said he'd take care of assigning my replacement."

Major Norris leaned into Burke's face again. "And have you checked in with your *replacement*, Burke?"

Worry darkened Burke's face. "I assumed you knew . . ."

"Knew?" Major Norris drew the syllable out as if it formed a hated curse word. "Knew what?"

"Daddy . . ." Marlene took hold of Major Norris's arm in a failed attempt to calm him.

Tallie studied Burke's reaction to the dressing down he was receiving. Most people, even those trained to respect their superiors, would show some minor betrayal of that training when being verbally flogged, especially in such a public way—an eye twitch, paling skin, a tensing of the lips or jaw—but Burke showed no reaction at all. He didn't lean away or shrink back from the major, whose scarred and angry face was mere inches from his own. It was as if the major were no real threat to him, and Tallie wondered whether they were such close colleagues that Burke knew that was true or he simply felt he was Major Norris's equal.

"Major, I arrived here just a few minutes before you and headed straight up to check on things and make sure the room was secure, but no one was protecting it. According to the housekeeper, it's been released back to the hotel."

"Who authorized the release?"

"No one, officially. She said a tall white-haired man arrived and asked for the key to the room."

"Do you think General Kaswell came to guard the room himself?" Marlene asked.

"Maybe," Burke said. "Whoever it was, the bellman took him up and settled him in his own room and then led him to Agent Gonzales's room so he could do his own search. The maid went in to clean the man's room the next day, but aside from a wrinkle on the edge of the bed, the room appeared as if it hadn't been used. She straightened the duvet and returned the next day, again finding the room unused. After three days had passed with no sign of their guest, the hotel figured we had concluded our investigation and they took possession of both rooms. Maids were up there stripping the beds when I arrived. Whatever evidence was in there is likely gone now, and I haven't been able to reach the general for confirmation on either room's release."

Major Norris stepped back and rubbed a gnarled hand over his stubbled beard. "No one can reach him, Burke. That's why we're here."

Tallie still didn't trust Burke, so she studied his reaction to the major's disclosure. She caught a tiny delay in his response to this news. Also, his response was more curious than concerned, which kept him high on her list of suspicious behavior. Contrary to his previous statement, she now wondered if he had, in fact, been listening to her calls. If not, how had he already known Cai Kaswell was missing, and why had he tried to act as if he wasn't aware of that fact?

"What's the plan?" Burke asked.

"I still want to see those rooms," Tallie tossed out as she made her way into the lobby.

"Hold up, Miss Brown. I have the keys. I'll take you to them."

Nothing added up, and she spun on him. "How do you have working keys? If they've returned the room to the hotel for cleaning, they also would have cleared the old keys' codes from the system."

"I made arrangements a few minutes ago," he replied without skipping a beat.

"You managed to check on the room, talk to the housekeeper, and get new keys after arriving only slightly before us?" It was more of an indictment than a question.

"I know the major well enough to anticipate what he's going to want from me."

Tallie glanced at Major Norris, who showed no reaction to Burke's effort to win points with him. Marlene, however, appeared to be dazzled by the agent's snappy repartee. Maybe he did know the major that well. And maybe that familiarity was exactly why he was able to handle the major's inquisition with ease. Maybe. But Tallie was still not convinced.

She motioned for the man to lead the way, and Major Norris and Marlene followed. "I'd also like to see video footage of the exits and hallway."

Burke jumped in. "I went over every inch of that security footage with our tech guys last week before I headed to Idaho. It was inconclusive."

"Get it for her." Major Norris wasn't making a suggestion.

"Will do, Major."

Tallie sensed that Burke's stiffness signaled he was annoyed with her and her insistence of making her own assessments. *Good*, she thought.

She knew the resort was likely in a constant state of cleaning, but still she scanned every inch of carpet and floor molding, every doorway, and every elevator for signs of scuff marks or damage that could indicate a struggle or the dragging of a body.

A pile of soiled linen lay on the floor outside Gonzales's room. Tallie entered the room, moved to the center of the space, and said, "Tell me again about the field officer who became sick in this room."

Burke and Major Norris played rock paper scissors with their eyes, shooting glances back and forth until the major nodded to Burke to fill Tallie in. He did, with curt military precision.

"NSA agent Esther Gonzales, thirty-five. Former navy IT security specialist. Divorced, no children. She passed her last physical with flying colors and was fine when she arrived here with a second agent to investigate the disappearances of US Citizens. Her partner reported her missing the next morning.

Two nights later, security found her wandering the halls in a panic, so they called the local police, who contacted the American Embassy. Her partner verified her identity, flew her back to D.C., and took her directly to Walter Reed National Military Medical Center for evaluation. The agency dispatched two other agents to investigate what happened to her because the situation was so similar to four other recent cases of North Americans who'd traveled abroad and ended up suffering some sort of amnesia."

"What do we know about her partner?" Marlene said.

"He's stellar, and he submitted to a lie detector test that cleared him."

"Did Agent Gonzales remember anything?" Tallie asked.

"Not really. She said she awoke disoriented and unable to remember where she was or why, so she ran into the hall to see if she'd recognize anything."

"Has her memory improved?" Tallie asked.

"Not as far as I know. The major might have more current information."

Major Norris shook his head. "She still has a two-day hole in her life, just like the others."

"Two days?" Tallie asked. "Is the time lapse exactly the same for the other US citizens who've been abducted and returned?"

"No," Burke said. "Of the twelve we're studying, one person has about thirty-six hours they can't account for. One has more like three days. The rest were two days, like Gonzales."

Tallie pulled the curtain aside and checked all the windows for anything strange. Finding nothing, she started pulling sheets from the pile of soiled linen and examining them as she asked more questions. "You said she was an IT security specialist?"

Marlene piped in. "I can't speak for government security, but in the private sector, that could mean anything from making sure the staff has their passwords up to date to checking firewalls and searching systems for vulnerability and breaches."

"Government specialists do about the same things," Burke said, "except they're the best in the country, tasked with protecting systems through which national and global security information is passed."

"Were the others also security people?"

Major Norris had been examining the door, its knob, and the keycard locking mechanism. Evidently satisfied that no clues would be found there, he turned back to Tallie. "I know where you're going with this, Tallie, but we've already run the security theory and hit a wall. The others' careers are all over the map—a banker, a mathematician, an artist, and leaders of business, the media, and the government. Doctors performed tests and checked every inch of their bodies and couldn't find any IV marks or any drugs in their systems to explain the memory loss."

"And those are just the victims we've identified," Burke said.

"What?" Marlene asked.

Major Norris wove an arm behind his daughter and said, "We can't account for nineteen other US Citizens who are missing."

Marlene gasped. "Nineteen others?"

"And that's just those we've identified as missing in the last six months," Major Norris said. "All professionals in various fields. All traveling internationally for various reasons. All gone without a trace. We're not sure if others began disappearing months or years before that. Other countries are reporting similar disappearances of prominent scientists, artists, and media people. We can't help the missing unless we can solve the mystery here. Where would you like us to begin, Tallie?"

Ideas raced across her mind, ideas she couldn't prove, though the pieces came together the same way no matter how many times she turned them about. "Why don't you three get the camera footage for the days covering Agent Gonzales's stay here and the period when Burke was away. While you set it up for viewing, I'd like to check the other guest's room to see if anything about it seems odd."

"I'll help you," Marlene offered.

"Thanks, but . . ."

A knowing smile crossed Marlene's face. "I understand. You want to be alone. Take your time, and I'll come for you when we're ready."

Tallie entered the room, and once the door shut behind the others, she closed her eyes and tried to picture Cai Kaswell in the space. Had he left his home in Kensington intending to investigate the attacks on American citizens? If so, where was he now? And had he left this hotel of his own volition, as she suspected, or was it possible that he was now among the missing?

"Are you listening, Tallie?"

Julia was in her head again, and Tallie knew why. After being in her real family's home, she kept imagining telling Cai Kaswell who she truly was and having a relationship with him. She daydreamed about him acknowledging her and about living in that house with him someday. But his trail was cold, and emotional whiplash between being in her family home and watching her father slip away again left her feeling hopeless and drained. She'd felt that way on another occasion. The memories of a terrifying conversation she'd had with Julia, when the possibility of being separated from one another had loomed real, returned.

"If there's ever an emergency . . . if, for some reason, I have to leave the cabin unexpectedly, I'll leave you a secret message, a sign."

The thought of Julia leaving her had terrified her, while the prospect of a secret message shared between them had seemed to bind the two loners to one another in a new way.

"What sign?"

Julia had opened her fisted hand, revealing a large coin, not a monetary coin but a piece with an insignia. She'd often pulled it out and flipped it back and forth across her fingers as she sat staring off blankly at the forest.

"This coin will be our sign. If you can't find me, look under the mattress. If you see this coin, you'll know I left it for you. It means you can trust that I'll be back."

"What if you're gone and I don't find a coin?"

Julia had closed her fist. "*Find Louis.*"

Though Tallie had been only twelve at the time, she knew what not finding that coin would mean. Julia was never coming back. The conversation had left a never-ending fear that Julia might abandon her someday. But since Julia's death, when all the lies and secrets of the woman's life were revealed, Tallie had come to a new understanding of what the missing coin could have meant—that Julia simply hadn't had time to leave it because she'd been found by the people she'd spent her life running from.

Julia left more times than Tallie could count. When Tallie went back to their mountain cabin after collecting specimens or playing in a stream and found Julia gone, she'd run to her cot breathlessly and throw the mattress off. Each time, the coin had been there. She still remembered it so clearly. One side depicted a sunrise falling upon a leopard with a child riding on its back. A flowing American flag filled the center of the opposite side. A Greek letter *a* floated above it, and the words *Duty, Honor, Country* were inscribed around the outside. She had assumed the coin was a Park Service souvenir like others sold at the gift shop. One day, in what Tallie remembered as her seventeenth year, she had asked Julia about the origin of the coin. She'd never seen Julia turn so pale. The next day, she'd decreed that since Tallie was almost an adult in age, and most certainly one in ability and wisdom, there was no further need to leave the coin as a crutch, and Tallie never saw it again.

She hadn't thought about it in years. She hadn't seen it when she emptied the cabin, nor was it included in the few items Louis had rescued from Julia's broken body when he found her after her fall. Tallie would have loved to have had it, to hold on to a tangible reminder that Julia had, in fact, cared for her.

That need to connect with someone who cared for her ate at Tallie. She immediately thought of Jackson. Aside from her conversation with him the previous day, she had ignored his calls and texts in the attempt to set him free to pursue a life with someone more suited to him, but he kept calling her, and now she needed him.

She sent him a quick text to assure him she was fine. Barely a second passed before her phone rang, and she picked up.

"I was going crazy with worry, wondering why you weren't answering," he said.

"I couldn't call from the plane, and we ran into some problems when we got here."

"Like what?"

"For starters, the man I thought was the missing girl's father showed up here."

"What?"

She could imagine him jumping from his seat and rushed to assure him. "He's also a trusted colleague of Major Norris's. Evidently, he's been following me since we arrived in Idaho. He said General Kaswell had assigned him to protective duty over me because of some picture a photographer snapped of me guarding the plane. I hear Bodie offered some quote that makes me sound like a clairvoyant."

"I've heard about that photo too," Jackson said, breathing out a long sigh. "I called Bodie about his quote, and he fell all over himself, telling me how sorry he was and that his PR person used a comment out of context because she thought tying him to you right now would broaden his appeal and sell more books."

"Poor Bodie. He's a victim of his own imagination. He had half of Cutler convinced I was an alien the night of the crash." She laughed as she pictured her innkeeper friend and his wild assortment of outfits.

"I told him not to say another word or I'd do some PR of my own and share a few pics of him in his inspiration costumes."

"You're awful."

"I'm just protecting the woman I—"

Tallie's breath caught as she anticipated what might be coming next.

Jackson's voice sounded forced as he finished. "The . . . woman . . . I admire most in the world."

She was both relieved and disappointed by his closing. But she didn't need another distraction at the moment, and she silently thanked Jackson for realizing that in time. "Any word on whatever I caught in my snare? Sorry to dump that on you."

"I called the sheriff's office and left a message. No one has reported back yet. I'll let you know as soon as I hear something."

"Thanks."

"And never think you're bothering me. If I can do anything to help from this end, I'm here. I've had only two work-related calls so far today. The conversations are short and sweet when your answer to 'When is General Kaswell planning on making his decision on the UN job?' is 'I'm sure you can understand that he's still grieving privately and will be making a public statement when he's come to a decision.'"

"I'm proud of you. How do you like the new assignment?"

"It's not what I expected since your father isn't yet the UN ambassador, but the facility is pretty intriguing, and I like my bunkmates."

"You live there?"

"For now. Most of these guys are married to the job. They're in intel."

"As in CIA and NSA?"

"As in every three-letter government agency you can think of."

"Good to know I have a friend on the inside."

"More than a friend, Tallie." The hurt in his voice stung her. "But yes. I'm here for you, whatever you need. I'm worried about you."

She twisted a strand of yellow hair around her finger and savored the warm feelings Jackson stirred in her. "I'm okay. Except Julia's in my head a lot."

"You've been through so much, and you're trying to find your missing father. Your mind is probably on overload. Maybe, when you're second-guessing your own instincts, your brain defaults to Julia's. Trust her and follow your instincts. She trained you well."

"Thanks, Jackson. I'll be in touch."

She ended the call and immediately missed the comfort she felt when he was near. She did trust him and his counsel. *Trust that voice, Tallie.*

"Okay, Jackson. I will."

Are you listening, Tallie?

"Yes, Julia. What am I missing?" The old instinct returned to her. After walking around the room for several minutes, looking for evidence, her eyes always drifted back to the mattress.

Are you listening, Tallie?

She heard Julia's question rattle around and around in her mind until she couldn't resist the urge any longer. As foolish as it sounded, she lifted the end of the mattress to look. Nothing. She lifted one of the sides and found, as she'd expected, nothing again. She berated herself for her folly, but still, she could not resist lifting the other side of the mattress's end. She fell back in shock, repelled by the mattress, as if it had been a snake. The coin was there. Julia's coin, or an exact replica. Her flesh prickled as a sheen of sweat rose on her skin, as if Julia might appear from the dead. When her heart rate slowed, she told herself she'd merely seen what she wanted to see. Surely there was no coin. Certainly not Julia's coin. After a minute, she inched back to the mattress and lifted it again. There it was! A coin exactly like Julia's!

She studied it closely, needing desperately to make sense of the find. She saw a military influence there, and the crazy situation began to make new sense. Julia and Cai and Major Norris had all served in the same unit in Mogadishu. Was leaving a coin some sort of military signal they shared? If so, had Cai left it as a message for Major Norris? And what was its significance?

She used her phone to search the internet for symbols related to Mogadishu and found the primary emblems on the coin in the shield of Somalia. This coin was somehow related to the team's UN mission to Mogadishu.

A knock on the door pulled her from her thoughts. She peeked through the viewing aperture and saw Marlene standing outside the door, so she opened it.

"What's going on? I can tell by your face that you found something."

Tallie opened her hand, revealing the coin.

Marlene's head tilted to the side. "That's the Mogadishu challenge coin."

"Challenge coin?"

"Yeah. Branches of service, even units and divisions, design coins to commemorate service and specific campaigns. This one was cast to represent our fathers' company when they served in the UN peacekeeping mission in 1993." Her mouth shifted to the left. "The leopard represents Somalia. The child riding it was supposed to represent the tame and peaceful Somalia the soldiers hoped to restore once the rebels were defeated."

"But it didn't turn out that way."

"No, as we both know all too well. Where did you get this?"

"Let's find your father. I'll tell you both at the same time."

Tallie followed Marlene to a table in the lobby café, where she waited while her friend made an excuse to pull her father away from Burke so the three could talk privately. She handed the coin to Major Norris, who remained silent as he turned it over in his fingers. "I found it under the mattress," Tallie explained.

He nodded as if not at all surprised it was there. “We traveled to Somalia with the platoon, but after the failed raid on Mogadishu, Cai and Julia and I were singled out to run the retaliatory strike on the rebel stronghold. Our commander needed a secret way to communicate the day of the strike with us, so he used these coins, placed under our mattresses, to signal that the day had come.”

A waitress came to take their order. When they asked for more time, she smiled and left.

“Each soldier deployed to Mogadishu was given a few of these coins. The leaders in communities where we deploy love to collect American military tokens, so soldiers spread them around to build goodwill. We did the same in Mogadishu. Julia and I decided to keep one of ours so we'd never forget. Cai came home with at least one of his coins as well. He tucked one into his pocket the day of the raid, thinking it might bring him good luck.” Major Norris winced. “We used them as our own secret calling cards. If he came to my office and I wasn't there, he'd leave his coin on my desk. I'd do the same when our paths didn't align.”

Tallie was lost in thought.

“I know it probably sounds foolish that grown men, especially military leaders, would leave secret messages with coins, but the tradition is an honored one that goes way back.”

“You taught me that once,” Marlene said. “A penny left on a veteran's headstone means the veteran has been visited. A nickel means the visitor who came attended boot camp with the fallen veteran. A dime means the visitor served with them, and a quarter means the visitor was with the veteran when they died.”

Major Norris placed the coin on the table with a deliberate snap. “That's right. It might seem silly to some, but it's a simple, silent way to honor fallen warriors.” He looked up at Tallie. “It's proof that the tall white-haired man the maid spoke to Burke about had to have been Cai. He must have left this for me to find, to mark his trail.”

Tallie picked up the coin, closed her eyes, and tightened her fingers around it, hoping to feel a connection to her father.

Norris rested his hand on her shoulder. “This is good news, Tallie. Cai was here.”

“But we still don't know where he went from here or how he is. And we don't know what happened to the sick or missing US Citizens.”

“What other clues did Burke's colleagues miss?” Marlene asked.

Tallie glanced left and right, as if searching for the answer. “Talk to me, Dad. What am I missing?”

CHAPTER SIX

JACKSON VISITED THE LOBBY SNACK machine and stared at the heavy electronically locked door leading down to *the* floor, the sublevel floor more guarded than the upstairs security floor. It was the place where the really important work was happening, where Mak and Rich and the other spy guys were evidently listening in to the chatter.

Chatter meant intel, and intel fired up every one of Jackson's journalistic instincts. More personally for him, any chatter about Tallie could provide information on what threats were coming at her and how best to protect her. He longed to be part of the team dealing with that.

One member of the team was always on the main floor, guarding the entrance and screening incoming personnel. Jackson marveled at how these guys didn't even trust one another to come through without having their persons and belongings checked. No wonder they hadn't given him a golden key to the place. Still, he attempted to climb down the stairs once, making it only as far as the door's keypad before he was castigated with a warning and a look that deterred future attempts. The elevator was also a no-go. His Rich-issued keycard got him *into* the elevator, but the only floor buttons that responded to his touch were levels one and two. He was stuck in the ugliest, loneliest building in the civilized world with excitement and purpose happening a few meters beneath him. It was maddening. It almost made his old *Kensington Courier* job seem enticing.

He took his soda and pack of nuts back to "the fridge," his new code name for his sterile office, determining that he had his own intriguing work. After all, he was the go-to PR guy on Cai Kaswell, and he was Tallie's trusted partner. He checked his phone. No calls. He checked his department-provided inbox. No emails. He decided to follow up with the sheriff's office about Tallie's wild-animal catch. At least that was something.

He recognized the voice that answered as that of Deputy Kwiatkowski, the officer he and Tallie had met the previous morning. Jackson introduced himself and offered a cheery greeting, hoping to find the hard-nosed officer in a better mood than he'd been the previous day.

"Jackson James, eh? The guy with the pretty lady tracker?"

"Yep, that would be me."

"What was the lady's name again? It was something unusual."

"Tallie . . . Tallie Brown. I'm actually calling to check up on something for her. She rigged some traps or snares yesterday and heard at least one of them release. She'd like someone to make sure no animals were caught or hurt."

"Oh, she caught something," the deputy said with worry in his tone, "but it wasn't any animal."

Jackson straightened in his chair. "What? Are you saying a person stepped into her trap?" His first thought was that Burke was Tallie's catch.

"I'm not saying anything else. Sheriff's orders."

The notion that someone was on Tallie's trail sent shivers down Jackson's spine. His hands shook so badly he nearly dropped his phone. "Please listen to me. Tallie put finding Emily ahead of her own safety yesterday, and now she might be in danger. I need to know what or who you found on that mountain."

There was a long pause before the deputy spoke again. "I could get fired."

"Tallie could get hurt . . . or worse. You wouldn't want that to happen, would you?"

"Of course not."

Jackson heard the deputy's breathing deepen and knew the situation was causing him distress. Trying to ease the officer's worry, he said, "You saw the military chopper land and that officer who came for her. She's important to national security. I am too. We work for General Cai Kaswell. You'd be helping us save Tallie and, in turn, helping your country."

"But if you work for the government, how do you not know all this already? And why would someone else in the government want to make it seem as if all the bizarre stuff that went down yesterday never happened?"

Prickles formed on Jackson's arms, and he fought to keep his voice confident and steady. "Let's just break it down together, okay? We'll figure it all out."

"All right. I hope I'm doing the right thing."

"Trust me. You are." Jackson opened his laptop and prepared to take notes. "You were saying Tallie's snare caught something."

"That's right. The sheriff and I hiked up to the cliff after dawn to make sure no other trespassers were camped up there. We didn't see any animals, but we found this guy who looked like he'd been hit by a truck. We thought he was dead at first. He barely spoke English, but we got him down the mountain and called 911. An ambulance came and took him to the hospital."

Jackson typed some notes. Then he scooted forward in his seat, set the phone to speaker so he could use both hands, and asked, "What hospital, Deputy?"

"Mercy Hospital, but it doesn't matter. You won't find anything on him. He's no longer in the system"—the deputy continued in a whisper—"as if he were never there. And that rescue? We were ordered to delete the report, as in 'make it appear it never happened.'"

Jackson fell back against his seat as the import of what he was hearing bore down on him. A man had followed Tallie on that mountain, a foreign national connected to someone high enough in the government to make public records vanish.

"Are you still there?" the deputy asked.

"Yeah. I'm just . . . I'm just . . . typing some notes."

"Sure, I get it. I'm just glad you're taking this seriously, 'cause honestly, this whole situation is creeping me out."

How does all this tie to Tallie? It was all Jackson could focus on. "Who ordered the report to be thrown out?" he said at last.

"The word came to us from the county commissioners' office, but when the secretary called us, she seemed as confused as we were. It must have come from higher up."

"Who would the county commissioners answer to? The governor's office?"

"Or higher. Everything about the whole situation is so odd, starting with those trespassers."

"Trespassers?"

"Yeah. That land wasn't a campground. It was some farmer's unused acreage. Those people shouldn't have been there in the first place, but when the father called us to report that his daughter was missing, we headed right over and found the girl's mother sitting in a camp chair. As soon as she saw us, she jumped up and started crying about her little girl. We didn't see her husband, so we assumed he was out looking for Emily. Once we got the mother's story down, we put the Amber Alert out. Then, almost immediately, Tallie showed up out of nowhere. We were suspicious of her because we couldn't figure out how she got there so fast. It was literally minutes after the alert went out."

Jackson typed more notes and checked the time of the alert on his own phone. "What time did your alert go out?"

"Four fifty-four a.m."

It matched the time of the alert on Jackson's phone, but Tallie was long gone by then. Worries flew through his mind as he typed questions the deputy's comments raised. This had been no simple rescue of a lost child. So what was it? "How long was it before you were able to interview the father?"

The deputy blew out a rush of air and finally said, "We didn't see him until Tallie arrived, and then he was gone again. He helped us control the crowd but we never got a chance to talk to him. After Emily was rescued, he and his family just disappeared. See? I'm telling you, nothing about this adds up."

Jackson drilled back down on the man caught by Tallie's trap. "So the father wasn't the man in the snare?"

"No. I saw him earlier, and the hurt man wasn't him. A friend of mine who served in the Peace Corps treated him in the ER. He thinks he was from Africa. Maybe Somalia."

Jackson sucked in a breath. *Somalia.* The rebels attempting to tie Tallie to Cai Kaswell were Somalian. Maybe Burke really was there to protect Tallie.

"That means something to you, doesn't it?" the deputy asked.

Jackson avoided the question. "I'm writing everything down."

"Finding that guy changed everything for the sheriff and me as well. Once we found him, we knew this wasn't a game."

"You thought it was a game before that?"

"Well . . . yeah. I mean, think about it. It all felt staged, including the arrival of your friend Tallie. How likely was it that a trained tracker would just happen by that remote location minutes after we sent out the alert? At first, we thought the whole child-rescue call was some sort of twisted stunt, like a crazy game of hide-and-seek that got out of hand so its organizers fell back on plan B and called it a rescue."

"And now?"

"Man . . . I don't know anymore. By the end, when reporters and dozens of bystanders showed up, I was half-expecting a camera to pop out and tell us we were on TV or something . . . like a blooper show or hidden-camera thing."

"Because?"

"Nothing adds up. That little girl didn't act like most kids who've been rescued. They're usually traumatized, but not this child. She was tearing up a little because of the lights and crowds, but she was pretty chipper for a child who had supposedly fallen from a cliff and spent hours alone in the dark. And then during all the hubbub after the rescue, that man, woman, and the girl just disappeared. And then there's the major from the chopper. I served six years in the army, and I know the look of duty on that man's face was real. He was there for a serious purpose, but I just can't figure out how all the pieces fit together. I can't explain how someone like Tallie Brown or an army major got duped into some charade."

The prickles on Jackson's arms made him feel itchy and unsettled. He stood and paced across the fridge's floor. "And now there's no record of any of this."

"Not on any computer, but they can't erase what people saw. But you never heard any of the rest of this from me, right?"

"Not a word."

Jackson's mind went on overload. He wasn't even sure if he'd muttered some sort of thank-you before ending the call and trying Tallie's phone four times in manic succession, to no avail. Had Burke subdued the Somali rebel? But why hadn't he told Tallie this detail? And was he the one who had erased the report? And if so, why? Jackson didn't trust him and had just fired off a text to her with the details of the call when the door to his office flew open. Mak and Rich filled the doorway, and neither of them looked as if they'd come to invite him to baseball night on the second floor.

Mak took Jackson's arm, and Rich picked up his cell phone and then his laptop, ripping the cords and connectors from it.

"What the heck," Jackson argued. "That's my personal phone."

"You'll get it back," Rich said flatly, as if they had every right to do what they pleased. "Take him down to the Crib."

Jackson mounted a second argument, but Mak's hand clamped down on his arm.

"Come on," he said without the usually affable voice Jackson trusted.

"What the heck is going on?" Jackson attempted to wriggle loose from his friend, but his efforts proved futile.

Mak's reply was curt. "We're moving you downstairs."

"No way! Why?"

Mak raised a warning eyebrow Jackson's way. "Consider it a promotion."

"It doesn't feel like a promotion."

Rich gritted his teeth and growled at Jackson. "Then, consider it a matter of security."

There was no clarification as to whether that "matter of security" was about an outside threat or if it was something they'd enforce if Jackson didn't comply. Rich rushed Jackson's computer upstairs while Mak rushed him down the hall to the elevator and used his own keycard to select floor S1—sublevel 1. Before Mak shoved him into the elevator, Jackson saw two men wearing body armor lope down the stairs from upper floors and settle into the lobby. They didn't convey Mak's and Rich's sense of urgency, but they were armed and dressed to face anything.

Now he felt like Deputy Kwiatkowski, unsure and off guard, and he didn't immediately ask questions. The door closed and then opened on the lower level. He wasn't instantly impressed by what he saw—a dozen or so acrylic-walled cubicles, some filled, some empty, where men and women sat poring over computer screens. It appeared that everything they saw was being transmitted to a large wall-sized screen divided into numbered stations that matched the numbers on the cubicles, so everyone saw everything. Another testament that these people clearly didn't even trust one another.

Jackson placed his hand on the elevator door slot and held the door open as he took it all in. The room itself wasn't very impressive, but the mood was electric, with people typing at light speed and calling out to one another, which led others dashing from station to station as if the fate of the world depended on every keyboard stroke and appearance on those screens.

"What is this place?" Jackson asked.

"It's where we comb through the chatter. We catch a word here, a call there, a name, a place, and we try to make sense of it, like trying to make whole fruit from a smoothie."

Jackson was busy processing that visual as Mak directed him to a more private acrylic-walled cubicle with a docked tablet connected to a hanging remote screen. He lifted the tablet from its dock and said, "You'll get your laptop back after Rich runs some diagnostic tests on it. In the meantime, log in here."

"Not until you tell me what all this has to do with me and my call."

Mak sat on the edge of Jackson's desk."We have a list of keywords that trigger alerts to our team. That conversation you had with the Idaho deputy just triggered a bunch of them."

"Such as?"

"*Tallie Brown*, *Somalia*, *danger*, *government*, to name a few. Some of them would have slipped by without alerting us, but all of them together in one conversation? Let's just say that if you were in any other location, a carful of guys like those upstairs would be pulling up out front and hauling you off to an installation for questioning."

Mak's words were stern, but his tone was friendly, so Jackson felt he could still trust him. "I'm worried about Tallie."

"And, it seems, for good reason. What time did she get her Amber Alert?"

Jackson's hands flew up. "Wait, wait. Are you telling me you were listening in on my call?"

"Not every word."

"Just the metadata," Jackson tossed back sarcastically.

"Exactly. Intel like the time the call was placed, its duration, and the caller's and recipient's phone numbers."

"I know there's more. You can also collect other information alongside the call metadata. Like topics—excuse me—*keywords*."

"Maybe. The point really should be that your call verified some chatter we've been following, and it's not good for your girlfriend."

It was the first time anyone had truly linked Jackson and Tallie together as a couple, and it strengthened his urgency to warn and protect her. "There are a lot of strange incidents and people surrounding her right now. I tried reaching her before you broke into my office, but she didn't answer."

Mak pulled a chair over and sat down beside Jackson. "So let's begin with what *you* know."

Jackson told the story about the missing child and Tallie's rush to rescue her, but Mak drilled down beyond the facts to the reasons Tallie had left the house without notifying Jackson, as if he were now on trial.

"She felt overwhelmed. She's been through a lot lately."

"Like her mother's accident/murder/suicide?"

"Accident," Jackson replied emphatically.

"We're still checking that out. Okay . . . so she's fragile, brilliant, lonely, unstable—"

"She's not unstable!"

"Excuse me . . . prone to erratic decisions."

Jackson hated how Mak was portraying Tallie, yet he didn't dare defend her with the truth. These guys knew a lot, but he was beginning to wonder whose interest they served and whether he could trust *them*.

"Let's get back to the details."

Jackson took a breath and organized his thoughts, wondering how much information he should share. Every instinct told him the missing-child scenario had been orchestrated to draw Tallie out into the open. What he didn't know was why or what he could do to help her. But these guys, if he could trust them, were his best hope at answering those questions. He pulled himself together and cooperated with Mak.

"Someone must've sent her a separate Amber Alert before the public alert went out, because she was on the road before my phone received it."

Mak tapped on the tablet and scowled. "What time did you get your alert?"

"The deputy said their alert went out at four fifty-four a.m."

"I pulled up Tallie's phone records. She got the alert at four ten."

"If Tallie's been on your radar, how did you not catch that discrepancy before now?"

"It's like I said, a lot of things are happening right now. We do our best, and with our best efforts and a little luck, we can stop bad things and catch bad guys, but some things slip through, and then we scramble to play catch-up."

"Clearly." Jackson didn't try to hide his irritation. "The rescue *was* a setup."

"It appears so." Mak rubbed a hand over his face. "Do you think the deputy and sheriff are on the up and up?"

"They must be. They tried to turn away Tallie's offer of help. They even called her old Park Service boss to verify her credentials before they let her past them."

"Okay. Let's say we trust them. Let's talk about the missing child's family."

"I guess you already know your buddy Burke was there, acting as if he were the father. And the deputy said the entire report was deleted. Who'd want that or have the power to do it?"

"First things first . . . hold on." Mak tapped on his screen. "The guys upstairs pulled the names of the mother and child. They really are mother and daughter, but they're actors. One of our guys called the mother. She claims their agent called with an offer to audition for a commercial for some child safety device . . . a GPS tracker."

"You believe that?"

"As far-fetched as it sounds, the story checks out. They both have SAG cards proving they're registered with the Screen Actors Guild. The mother thought the sheriff and his deputy were also auditioning. She said the commercial director was there to get her daughter into position. He was very complimentary about her performance, but as he was leading them out of there, she heard people in the crowd mention that they'd showed up because an Amber Alert was issued."

"Like she didn't know what she was doing. I don't believe any of this. Who hired them, and who is this director? Someone should interrogate him."

"They're all registered with a non-union agent who says the German company that makes the tracking device hired them. They offered compensation that was above scale and wired it in advance, so the agent thought the offer was legit. Our boys reached out to the company. They're real, but they didn't book this commercial. We're tracking the money transfer now."

"And the public Amber Alert?"

"Officially, it was labeled an accidental release. Someone in the state pulled some pretty powerful strings and had the entire incident erased from the system." Mak sat on the edge of the desk. "Right now, government employees up and down either know nothing or are assigning responsibility to another department."

Jackson began pacing. "Someone staged a rescue emergency convincing enough to get a sheriff to buy it, lured Tallie out with a private alert early enough to get her into those woods alone, had a guy in place to grab her, *and* has the power to cancel an Amber Alert?"

Mak shook his head. "It's a lot. Just be grateful she's with Major Norris and Agent Burke now."

"Tallie told me things aren't adding up. She isn't sure she trusts him."

"Burke?" He scoffed. "She doesn't trust anyone right now—including you, it seems. She did leave without telling you where she was going."

"That's a cheap shot. It was personal."

"It might have gotten her hurt or abducted or worse. Be glad Burke was close enough to keep an eye on the situation. He'd have handled things if Tallie's snare hadn't taken the attacker out."

Mak walked away, and Jackson was glad to see him go. "But we'll never know, will we?" he thought out loud. Jackson shoved his keyboard in frustration over what Mak said, but as he reflected on their conversation, he knew most of Mak's observations were painfully true. Tallie was fragile right now. Bringing her to Idaho and the Jackson family enclave had been good for Jackson but had made Tallie feel even more isolated and alone.

"Please tell me I can still trust you."

The fact that she'd felt she needed to ask was proof of his failures. But not anymore. Mak, Major Norris, and their teams' priorities were American security and finding Cai Kaswell. Jackson had only one priority, and it was crystal clear—protecting Tallie—and he'd move heaven and earth to succeed.

CHAPTER SEVEN

When Tallie arrived at the office of the resort's head of security with Marlene and Major Norris, Cooper Burke was heading down the hall. "The file is loaded and ready for viewing," he said as he opened the door, allowing the three to enter.

"This is Sergeant Pasqual, head of security and a former Miami detective." Burke pointed to a man sitting in front of a dozen monitors.

He stood, extended his hand, and bowed in a show of drama. "I'm here to help with anything the American government needs. Anything at all. I want to get to the bottom of this as much as you do. As a spokesman for the resort, I can tell you that these incidents are bad for business, but as an American citizen working down here, my first concern is to find my compatriots."

Norris spoke in a flat, clipped tone, making it clear that he had no time for gratuitous testimonials. "Let's get to the videos, shall we? And let's start with a glimpse of the check-in of the last guest, the man with the white hair, assigned to room 612."

They all pulled up chairs, and the feed from the security camera nearest room 612 began to play. Tallie felt her heart thunder in her chest as her tall, distinguished father appeared on the film. She blinked to clear her burning eyes, telling herself to hold it together. Major Norris glanced her way, loss etched into his expression, and then he abruptly ordered Sergeant Pasqual to cut the feed.

"Very well, Major. So you have identified this man?"

"Yes, Sergeant." He glanced Tallie's way again. "Now let's see the camera outside Agent Gonzales's room."

Pasqual hurried to load the video recording of Agent Gonzales's arrival at her room. From time to time, someone in their group would ask Pasqual to stop and back up the feed or speed it up to skip footage that had nothing to do with the missing agent's stay, but Tallie was struggling to focus on anything but the thought of her missing father.

When they'd watched the film twice, Norris turned to Tallie. "Did anything catch your attention?"

She hated to admit defeat, but she answered, "No."

Marlene's answer was the same, as was Burke's.

"All right. It's five thirty. Let's take a break and grab some dinner."

"Sounds good to me, Daddy," Marlene said. "These little green eyes are fried." She stood and waited for Tallie to rise, and when she didn't, Marlene said, "Come on, sugar. We'll be clearer-eyed if we step away for a few minutes. And we still have all the footage of General Kaswell's visit to go through."

Tallie couldn't put a finger on it, but something in the video feed bothered her. "Could you bring me back something? I want to run through the skipped footage."

"We skipped it because there was nothing relevant to our search," the major replied.

"Maybe not, but I need to know that for myself."

His rough face softened. "I understand." He looked at Pasqual. "Do you mind running it again for Miss Brown?"

The man looked at his watch and paused before saying, "I'd be happy to, but did you say you also plan to view the video of another guest's arrival tonight? I'm off the clock at six."

Tallie rolled her eyes at the patriot's waning interest in solving the crime when it bled into his dinner hour.

"I'll do it," Burke said, "if you'll also grab me something to eat."

"Gladly," Norris said, but Tallie noticed a hint of disappointment on Marlene's face as she and her father exited. Tallie figured her friend was mourning the loss of Burke's company at dinner.

He looked at Pasqual. "Would that be agreeable to you, Sergeant? I began my career with the NSA working security after I left the Rangers. I'm familiar with several systems. I think I'd be a quick study if you'd honor me by brushing me up on your specific system."

The gushing sergeant spent two minutes explaining things before Burke went rogue and began operating the system like a pro.

"You're an excellent teacher, Sergeant. Thank you."

The security specialist stood proudly and nodded. "It was my pleasure, sir. Anything for a fellow vet."

The man turned sharply on his heel, military-style, grabbed his coat, and made his way to the door. As it closed behind him, Burke glanced at Tallie, who pulled her blonde hair forward to conceal her grin.

"What's so funny?"

She fought her smile but lost the battle. "That was a bit over-the-top, don't you think?"

"Nah, I made his day. You have a pretty smile."

Tallie blushed and resumed her previous professional demeanor. "Will you pick up the video right before Gonzales entered her room, please?"

"Yes, ma'am." Burke seemed pleased he was able to crack her stoic veneer, if only for a moment. He refocused and started the footage exactly where she'd asked.

Tallie scanned every movement of guests and staff, allowing Burke to skip only footage showing when the hall was completely empty. She asked him to stop and back up a few times, but the footage rolled by for half an hour without any leads.

He glanced at the door. "I'm starving. I thought they'd be back with the grub by now."

Tallie's stomach rumbled, and her eyes grew wide. "Oh my. Excuse me."

"You're starving too. Do you have any mints or candy in your purse?"

"I don't carry a *purse*, but I do have some protein bars in my *pack*."

A subtle smile teased his lips as he quietly studied her.

"Why are you looking at me?" she asked, growing uneasy under his stare.

"You're a unique woman, Miss Brown. I . . ." His eyes bored into her for several more moments, and Tallie couldn't read the expression on his face.

"What?"

"Just an observation. Let's get back to work."

"I'm trying to trust you, but you're making me more uneasy all the time."

He turned sideways in his chair toward her and winced, bending forward over his left side, the side she'd seen him protecting earlier that morning.

"You're hurt."

He waved her off and swiveled forward with another wince and a groan.

"Lift your shirt."

"It's just my ribs," he said, dismissing her.

When he didn't move to lift his shirt, she knelt in front of him, grabbed the fabric, and did it herself. What she found set her back on her heels for a moment. Swelling had set in over a distinct purple line surrounded by a field of purple and red.

"When did this happen?"

"You might find the details entertaining." Burke laughed, and pain flashed across his face.

Tallie reached toward him, and he recoiled from her attempted exam. "Can you breathe comfortably?"

"Shallow breaths are okay, but I'm not up for any cardio right now."

"I don't think a lung is punctured, but you could have internal bleeding. I'm a trained medic. Let me look more closely at this." She gently touched the affected area. "A rib appears to be broken. You need an X-ray and something for the pain, and you should have been icing that area. I'll get s—"

"Wait." Burke took her hand as she stood to leave. "The pain isn't that bad. And we need to talk."

Apprehension shuddered through Tallie. She sat back in her seat. "All right."

He took a careful breath, tucked his shirt back in, and began. "I followed you in my car when you walked down that road yesterday morning. When that bread truck pulled over to give you a ride, I panicked, trying to decide whether to blow my cover and pull you out or trust that your famed skill set could keep you safe with whoever was driving. Once I read that Amber Alert, I knew where you were headed. I decided the best course of action was to follow the truck and trust you."

He shifted in his seat and rolled his shoulder as if trying to find a more comfortable position. "While the sheriff and deputy detained you at the site, I got ahead and noticed that the girl's mother was alone. I told her to say I was with her and let me be the buffer between her and the press. That's how you found me there beside her. When you headed into the tree line, I followed."

"I heard you when I found Emily. I thought you were an animal."

He winked and smiled at her. "Our government would be sorely disappointed if, after all the money they invested in me, I were foiled by a civilian. But it wasn't me you heard. You're a very good tracker, Tallie Brown—I saw that for myself yesterday—but the truth is I'm even better."

There was confidence but no arrogance in the man's words this time, and it was Tallie who now smiled at meeting a person who not only appreciated her talents and knowledge but could actually best her. "Prove it."

"Okay. I watched you rig a snare with a sapling and a rope to take care of whatever you heard rustling in the trees behind you." He pointed to his ribs, and Tallie's hand moved to her mouth in surprise.

"You? You were hurt by my snare?"

His eyebrows wriggled in reply. "That wasn't a forest creature moving through the brush. It was a man with a gun who'd followed you and was waiting at the top of the cliff for you after you went down to rescue the little girl. We fought; I stumbled back, forgetting where that snare was rigged, and . . ." He spread his arms wide.

Tallie was absorbed by the revelation that someone had targeted her. "Who was the other man?"

"He was a foreign national . . . a trained warrior, judging by the beating he gave me and, from his dialect, probably Somalian." The look on Burke's face told Tallie he knew more than he was admitting.

The mention of a Somalian man tracking her increased Tallie's heart rate and put her on high alert. She'd only recently learned that Somalian rebels were the shadows Julia had run from for twenty-one years. Surely it was no concidence such a man was on that mountain yesterday. He had come for her. The question was how much of this did Burke know and could she trust him?

He shouldn't know anything about her father's role in Mogadishu or her connection to the general, so she decided to put Burke to the test. "Why would a Somalian come for me?"

"Cai is more hated than loved because he has stopped coups, captured and killed leaders, and made peace in places rebels didn't want it. In short, he's halted people's power and their cash flow. That's why they hate him. And you're a pawn in their game because you're now someone Cai cares about."

"General Kaswell is a good man. I'd imagine the list of people he cares about would be quite extensive."

"Yes, but you showed his loved ones a particular kindness, and he recognizes what that action has cost you—your privacy. And because of that newspaper photo, the world sees a personal tie between you. All that puts you in a separate tier."

She needed to know what else Burke knew, and she repeated her question. "But why would a Somalian man, in particular, come after us?"

"Obviously, Miss Brown, you've innocently become caught up in something not of your doing."

Burke wasn't willing to divulge more, but he obviously knew something about Cai Kaswell's tie to Somalia. Was it simply what he'd said before, about her father's success in stopping rebel plots, or was it more? A new question loomed over Tallie. Was Burke helping her find the general to protect him or to expose him? She tapped into every skill she had in reading people as she asked him, "What's your purpose in coming down here?"

"To protect you."

"And what about Cai Kaswell?"

"As I told you when you arrived, I'm protecting you because he asked me personally."

She studied him for several seconds, searching for any sign of a lie—increased blinking, fidgeting, stressed breathing, or facial twitches. She saw none, but then, he would have been trained to avoid such easily readable signs.

"Keep your head down. Trust no one."

Not even this man, Julia?

A siren in the distance pulled Tallie's eyes away, breaking the bond growing between them. She was beginning to like Burke, and that made her wary again. She silently thanked the siren and Julia for raising her guard. "Shall we get back to the video?"

Burke's eyes widened and he drew his head back, as if surprised by Tallie's abrupt end to the conversation. He straightened, cleared his throat, and shifted in his seat, hiding his discomfort beneath a tightened jaw. She believed she had, perhaps, even wounded him. *Good,* she thought. *Better to keep him off guard.* Secretly, it saddened her to be so untrusting and cold, but she had a job to do, and time mattered.

The video feed began again, showing a bellman guiding a guest and pushing a luggage cart to a room. Tallie recognized the bellman as the same one who'd checked Gonzales and several other guests in that same day, but there was something about his routine that caught her eye.

"Can you do a facial recognition on that bellman and show every clip of him settling guests in their rooms?"

"Do you see something?"

"Maybe," she said as she leaned closer to the camera.

Burke glanced at her, and she caught pleasure in his expression. He clearly loved his work, especially when success was in sight, and this potential lead had energized him again. "What are we looking for?"

"Every detail of his routine." Tallie narrated the bellman's process. "He points the way at every turn, follows the guest to the door, bows, and if my lip reading is correct, he appears to ask them to allow him to do the honors of opening the door. Then he's holding the keycard. He inserts it, opens the door, and holds it for the guest. They enter, and the door closes." Tallie checked her watch. "Let's also see how long he stays in the room."

Burke glanced at his own watch. "Tell me when he leaves."

Several minutes passed before Tallie said, "Now."

"Three and a half minutes."

"Okay," Tallie said, "Let's see if that exact routine is repeated with the other guests."

Burke pulled up five clips that preceded Gonzales's arrival. Together, he and Tallie noted the exact same routine. Another siren sounded. Tallie turned her head to the sound. "There must have been an emergency at the resort." She stood, debating whether to respond to the siren. "Maybe we should head out there and see if they need help."

"Not now, Brown. The resort has plenty of security people. This is our priority, and you're onto something. Let's stick with it. Besides, whatever it was, it's over now. Maybe that's what's been holding up the major and the food."

"Maybe." She sat down again. "Let's run Gonzales's footage and see if she received the same service as the bellman's other guests."

Tallie and Burke leaned closer to the monitor, narrating each step.

When the bellman and Gonzales neared the door, Tallie shot her hand forward toward the monitor. "He's handing *her* the keycard!" She shot around to face Burke. "And he's wearing gloves! He never did that with the others."

"You have an eagle eye!" Determination showed on Burke's face as he addressed the bellman on the screen. "All right, bellman. Let's see how long you stay in the room. Miss Brown, do the honors."

Tallie kept an eye on the clock as three minutes ticked by, then four, then five, and the door still remained closed. Her phone buzzed, but a quick glance at it showed an unfamiliar number she assumed was spam, so she ignored the call and kept counting the time passing by in the video. Ten more minutes passed before the door in the video opened. The bellman in the footage exited and then turned back to face the closed door. There was a slight motion in his arm, and then he stuffed something into his jacket pocket before walking away.

"Did you see that?" Tallie asked. "Can you get a tighter shot of whatever was in his hand?"

Burke rewound the feed and zoomed in. "It's a cloth. He's wiping evidence from the door handle."

"I'm pulling up the general's footage. Let's see if his arrival was handled like Gonzales's." His phone buzzed, but he quickly silenced it.

"Do you need to take that?" Tallie asked. "It could be the major."

"I will. First the footage, then the phone." He typed a few more characters, looked at the screen, and announced, "Got it."

The two leaned close, Tallie nearly breathless, hoping the footage would confirm their theory that the bellman was the culprit or at least one of the people involved in the disappearances.

She watched her stately father walk down the corridor—tall and handsome, gentle yet strong. She barely knew him, yet she already loved him. She wanted to jump into the monitor and save him from what she felt sure was about to happen. She placed her elbows on the table and moved her fisted hands up to her mouth to stifle the warning cry she wanted to shout out to him.

Burke laid a gentle hand on her shoulder, and she knew in that moment that she had revealed too much, maybe enough for Burke to detect the truth behind her tie to Cai. Tears welled in her eyes, and she blinked them back, diverting Burke's attention back to the screen. "The bellman's wearing gloves again."

"And he's handing the keycard to the general."

"Now we count down to see how long he lingers in the room."

Burke and Tallie were silent for the interminable eleven minutes when the door remained shut. Tallie could only imagine what was happening in that room. A struggle? Was the bellman trying to manage the giant man's limp and drugged body?

Burke's voice was nearly a reverent whisper when the door opened. "Eleven minutes and seventeen seconds." He looked at Tallie. "And he's wiping the knob."

"There's something significant about making Gonzales and Cai touch that keycard."

"I hate to say it, but the fact that the bellman is wearing gloves when he hands them the keycard suggests there's something skin-absorbable on it."

That was Tallie's thought as well. "A toxin? A paralytic?"

"That'd be my guess. And once the victim is disoriented, the bellman must have some way to keep them under."

"The rooms had to have been preselected to have the exact card rigged with a paralytic agent," Tallie said. "That implies a conspiracy with someone else in the hotel, maybe including the front desk clerk. But how do they get the victims out, and where are they now?"

"The security cameras in a place like this could be hacked by a twelve-year-old," Burke said. "It would be so easy to loop back to seemingly innocent footage and hide an army marching down that hall."

Tallie's heart sank at the thought that her brave father, who'd come to rescue his countrymen, had himself been tricked and drugged. No matter how many times she'd told Major Norris she could handle this assignment, it was deeply personal to her.

And then she heard Julia again. "*Whining doesn't help. Work the problem.*"

She blinked again to clear her moist eyes.

Burke touched her shoulder again. "I know you're worried about the general, but at least you've given us a lead."

Tallie nodded. "Agents investigating similar crimes in other cities could look for these same routines with the bellmen who served the other missing persons. Who knows where all this might lead?"

Burke's voice was thoughtful and contemplative when he said, "Yes. Who knows?"

"You almost sound despondent. This is good news."

"Yes . . . yes, of course it is. It's a bit embarrassing that America's best didn't see clues you caught right away, even after we viewed these feeds dozens of times. If we had, we wouldn't be looking for Cai right now."

Tallie touched his arm. "We'll find him and all the others."

"Of course we will." Agent Burke flashed her a confident smile. "Why don't you take a break while I shoot these clips up the line so they can be distributed to the units working the other locations where disappearances occurred."

Tallie nodded and stepped into the hall to look at her phone. There were many missed calls from Jackson earlier in the day. She decided to check in with the major before calling Jackson back, but his voice was uncharacteristically frantic when he answered.

"Tallie! Why didn't you return my calls?"

Chills shot through her. "Besides Jackson's, the only missed calls I have were from a spam number."

Norris moaned. "I was afraid to touch my own phone until I could sanitize it, so I called from the restaurant's line. I was scared to death something happened to you too."

"What do you mean me *too*? What's happened?"

"It's Marlene. She's in a coma or something. We're in an ambulance headed for the local hospital. Are you with Burke?"

"Yes," Tallie answered, shaking.

"Put him on."

Tallie opened the door, and the worry on her face was soon reflected on Burke's. He rose to his feet slowly and eyed her with a sideways glance. "What's going on?"

She put the call on speaker and said, "He's here, Major."

"Burke, get Tallie out of there, now. Do you hear me? Someone targeted Marlene. She's sick, Burke. Very sick. Tallie's in danger."

Burke stepped to Tallie. His left arm slid around her and pulled her behind him. Ignoring the pain she knew he was feeling, he placed himself between her and the door while, almost seamlessly, he used his right hand to pull his sidearm from its holster and aim it toward the doorway. "What happened, Major, so I know what to watch for?"

"We waited for our food by the pool. I left for a minute, and when I came back, she was . . . she was . . . it was as if she was dead." His voice broke.

"Major, did she touch anything while she was waiting?" Tallie asked urgently.

The major cleared his throat. "We ordered drinks. They arrived right before I left the table."

"And Marlene?"

She was drinking hers when I walked away. Now that I think about it, neither glass was at our table when I returned and found her."

"We found something in the footage, Major. We think a skin-absorbable neurotoxin or paralytic was applied to Gonzales's and Cai's keycards. Someone might have used the same thing on your beverage glasses."

"I'll pass that along to the doctors at the hospital." He mumbled some threats to the culprits under his breath, things Tallie knew he could make good on. His voice shifted into an authoritative tone. "The culprits know we're here. I'm flying Marlene back to D.C. as soon as she's stable. I advise you two to do the same. It's too risky for you to stay down here."

She looked at Burke, whose arm tightened around her.

"You make the call," he said. "We'll play it your way, but I've got you. I promise."

A few hours earlier, she wasn't sure about this man at all; she'd even accused him of being a threat, but she now believed he did have her. So much had changed in a few hours. She had no real proof. Just instincts. She hoped her radar was spot-on.

"I'm staying, Major. Burke and I need to check out this bellman."

"Burke, consider her as you would my own daughter, do you hear me?"

Warmth and hope swelled through Tallie over the major's reference to her. She bit her lip and found Burke studying her.

"Roger that, Major," he said.

"Whoever is doing this is always a step ahead of us," Norris said. "I don't want you two going off half-cocked and walking into another of their traps. Do you hear me?"

"We hear you," Tallie said.

"Good. Call it a night and start fresh in the morning. Under the circumstances, I'd rather you two share a suite with a pullout so we don't have one of you mysteriously disappearing, but, Burke, mind what I said about treating

Tallie like my own daughter. I plan on avenging the injury done to Marlene. I'm just as willing to kill two birds if you get out of line. Get my drift?"

Burke smiled at the loving threat. "Loud and clear, Major."

"Good. And, Tallie, no venturing off on your own. Do you read me?"

"Loud and clear." The call had barely ended when Tallie pushed back on Norris's orders, stepping away from Burke. "We need to see the resort manager right away."

"He's probably gone for the day. It's after eight."

"His office should be somewhere in this administration corridor." She started into the hallway, but Burke stepped in front of her.

"You heard what the major said. We've had some great success. Let's shut down for the night, grab some dinner, and find a suite. We'll be more effective when we're rested."

"But our suspect could be leaving the area as we speak."

"Not if he's also interested in targeting us. In either case, we've got his picture. There's no hole deep enough for this guy to hide from facial-recognition technology."

Tallie again stepped away from Burke and challenged him. "But we could be interrogating him sooner rather than later."

"Or stepping blindly into a setup. I know you don't want to hear this, but I side with the major on this one."

Tallie kept her pleading eyes on Burke, and he eventually buckled.

"Okay, but first things first. Grab your things. We'll swing down to the front desk and see about getting us a suite."

Tallie grabbed her rucksack, and they headed toward the lobby and the front desk.

"No touching buttons or knobs or any surfaces with bare skin, understand?" Burke said.

"I've got gloves in my pack," Tallie said.

"Unless we're the cleaning crew, wearing gloves at an ocean resort will be odd, and we're trying to stay under the radar here. Just don't touch anything. I'll use my elbow."

"Got it."

"And we're not taking the first or second room they offer us either. Our suspect is not the only operator in this resort. We don't want to walk into a trap someone's prearranged for us. Just follow my lead."

They reached the elegant lobby with its blend of Caribbean and Spanish decor. Burke slid one arm around Tallie again and whispered, "Play it cool" as they approached the reservation desk.

"May I help you?" the attendant asked.

"A suite, please, with two bedrooms, if possible."

The woman eyed them and asked, "*Two* bedrooms?"

"In case I snore," Burke answered.

Tallie understood the game.

"Ocean view or poolside?" the woman asked.

Burke turned to Tallie and flashed her a smile. "What do you think, babe?"

She sputtered, taken aback by his use of the word *babe*, then finally said, "An ocean view would be nice."

"Ocean view it is," the woman said as she typed. "Let me check our availability."

"On second thought," Burke said, "I saw the pool. The glow of the tiki lamps is very romantic."

Tallie picked up on the game quickly—move the room a few times so the culprits wouldn't have time to lay a trap. "The pool *would* be nice," she said with a slight wink to Burke.

"So poolside, then?" The woman typed the change into the computer. "Pool level or higher? I have a two-bedroom vacancy on ten."

"How about pool level?" Burke said. "We'd be able to enjoy the glow of the of firepits and lamps through the atrium doors."

"True. Final answer?" the attendant said with a laugh that seemed more annoyed than humorous. When Tallie nodded, the woman said, "Very good, then. Moving you to room 1113. One of our bellmen will assist you with your bags."

As if he'd heard his cue, the bellman arrived.

Burke slid his credit card forward and completed the registration. "No need for a bellman. We're traveling light."

The bellman had reached for the keycard on the counter but pulled his hand back when his services were dismissed. Instead of heading back to the main door, Tallie noticed he headed down the hall toward the first-level rooms. Fear struck her, and she wondered if he was attempting to reach their suite before them. She didn't know if her panic was justified or pure paranoia, but she turned back to the woman and said, "On second thought, I'd prefer a suite with an ocean view on a higher floor after all."

Without questioning her, Burke agreed to this erratic change. The front desk clerk's eyes widened, but her taut smile remained pasted on as she scrolled through the offerings on her screen. "I'd love to accommodate all your preferences, but I have only one available suite on the third floor. It's ocean view but only a one-bedroom with a pullout."

"Perfect," Burke said. "We'll take it."

The woman handed them two key cards. Tallie noticed the woman's dimmed smile, and as they walked away from the desk, she remarked, "I think she hates us."

"Let her. We're getting a room we chose, not one she and her colleagues rigged."

"And she handled the keycard with her bare hands." Tallie took comfort in that, at least.

"I noticed that too. That gave me the courage to take it from her."

Once they reached the room, Burke opened the door for Tallie. "Let's sweep it for bugs and cameras." When they were confident all was secure, he headed for the door. "I'm going to follow up on your suggestion and see if the manager's still here. I feel safe leaving you in here until I get back."

"I want to go with you."

Burke shook his head. "No way. Every doorknob, elevator button, and surface in this place could be rigged with toxins. I'm not taking that chance. We've gone over this room. You're safe in here, and I want to keep it that way."

"Safe? Any employee can make a keycard to this room."

Her point left Burke visibly flustered. "Under the circumstances, it's the best compromise I can offer. You've got a gun. Shoot them if they try."

Tallie's jaw dropped at the complete ridiculousness of his response.

"Return the calls you missed, and I'll swing by the administration office to see if the manager happens to still be in. I won't be gone long. I promise."

Frustration seared through her as he exited the suite. Surely, she was just as safe with him as she was in the room, so why not take her? Tallie would have fought Jackson if he acted this arbitrarily, but she hesitated to push Burke too far. *Why?*

CHAPTER EIGHT

Each unanswered call to Tallie's phone caused Jackson to lose another piece of his quickly dwindling mind. He knew each message he left sounded increasingly crazy, and he dreaded the realization that he was becoming *that* guy—the overprotective, neurotic psycho girls ran from. Mak had insisted Jackson could relax with Agent Cooper Burke protecting Tallie, but that had done nothing to ease his concern. He had good reason to worry, he told himself, and information he needed to get to Tallie before something bad really did happen to her.

Mak had given him all the info they were able to dig up on the Somalian man who'd been stalking Tallie and tasked Jackson with organizing the info into meaningful reports—family ties, criminal records, known associates. Jackson's spine never stopped tingling as he read about the terrorist.

He stretched his back and rubbed his eyes. Both were worn out from sitting for hours, staring at one distressing report after another about the rebel's past on a computer screen in a sublevel room where the only light was from overhead bulbs. But nothing he'd read gave him any ideas about who might come for Tallie next, and his frustration and fear doubled.

Mak popped by, dressed in shorts and a half shirt. "How's it going?" he asked, which Jackson interpreted as "How much progress have you made?"

Between his worry over the terror suspect, Tallie's safety, and his failure to connect with her, Jackson was a ticking time bomb, and Mak's added pressure was the catalyst that caused him to snap. "Do you mean have I found the intel your team of brainiacs missed?"

Mak stepped back and his hands flew forward. "Whoa. Where's that coming from?"

Jackson dropped his head onto the keyboard. When he lifted it, he leaned back in his chair and covered his face with his hands. "I'm sorry."

"It's harder to do this work when it's personal. Tallie hasn't returned your calls yet?"

"No. I'm worried about her, Mak."

"Well, I don't know if this will ease your worry or not . . ."

Jackson sat up. "What? Have you heard something?"

"She and Burke have cracked a big lead, not just in General Kaswell's disappearance but perhaps in dozens of international missing persons' cases."

Professionally, the news was great. Personally, it felt like a stab in Jackson's heart. Work was keeping Tallie too busy to answer his calls, and Burke, a man Jackson didn't trust, was now her ally.

"I know what you need," Mak said. "Come with me." He led Jackson down the dimly lit hall to a small gym with big equipment. "You'll find clean workout gear in those cupboards. Take your frustrations out on the weights."

Jackson's runner's body was not completely foreign to weightlifting, but it humiliated him when Mak did arm lifts with heavier weights than Jackson could bench press. He headed for the treadmill instead and started running his frustration off. Soon his phone rang, and in his enthusiasm, he tried exiting the machine without stopping it and nearly face-planted.

"Tallie?" he said with embarrassing breathlessness. "Sorry. I was just working out." It was true, though most of his breathing issues were caused by his relief and excitement over her call.

"I can't talk long. We've had a big break in the case."

"I heard. That's great." He tried to maintain enthusiasm over her success, as much to impress Mak, who was in earshot, as for Tallie. He stepped into the hall so he could lessen the need to disguise how he really felt about Agent Burke.

"A resort employee was involved," Tallie said. "Agent Burke and I saw him on the security camera feed, and we know how the perp disabled the victims."

Her use of the word *we* sickened Jackson. Burke was part of that *we*. Tallie trusted him. Jackson needed her to trust him as well. "I think your report is headed to my desk."

"To PR?"

"No," he said with pride. "I've been reassigned downstairs. I'm working intelligence on your case."

"That's great. We really are working together again."

"Not as closely as you and Burke."

"Jackson . . ." She was bordering on being annoyed with him, but he pressed on.

"If you see us as partners on this case, maybe you'll take what I'm about to say seriously."

"Is this another of your astute observations about Agent Burke?"

"Don't forget you've had your own reservations about the guy."

"That was before I gave him a chance. Agent Burke is a . . . a skilled agent. He's helping me find my father."

The Cai Kaswell card trumped all others with Tallie, and Burke held it firmly in his hand. Jackson felt like a jealous jerk, and he knew he should apologize for losing sight of Tallie's primary mission, but he couldn't because he wasn't sorry at all. He'd risk angering Tallie if it made her keep her guard up. "It's just that from here, it sounds like you aren't too happy with your new partner right now."

"I'm just frustrated. Burke is heading down to see if the resort manager's still here, and if he is, he's going to interview him. I wanted to be there when he questioned him about his criminal employee."

"Why aren't you?"

"Because I'm talking to you instead," Tallie snapped.

"Then, hang up and go. Do it. And I'm not being sarcastic. I want you to hear every word that guy hears or says."

Her tone returned to normal. "It's all right, Jackson. I guess it doesn't matter who gets the suspect's information."

"Maybe, maybe not. I have news, and I need you to hear me out. Yesterday was all a setup. Everything about that rescue was really about getting to you."

"Burke told me about the armed Somalian guy tracking me. Burke's the one who took the rebel out. He may have saved my life."

Jackson stepped farther into the hall and lowered his voice so Mak wouldn't hear his next few comments. "And you believe him? Yesterday, you thought *he* was a threat."

"Things have changed. He was badly injured protecting me in the woods. My father obviously trusted him enough to assign him to protect me. Norris trusts him enough to leave me to his care."

Jackson's instincts rose to a new threat level. "What? Norris *left* you?"

"Marlene's been poisoned, Jackson. I just got off the phone with Major Norris, and she's doing better, but she was in a bad way a few hours ago."

"Tallie, that could have been you! You're the one they want, and we both know why. You need to get home."

"No. I need to work this lead."

"With *Burke*?" Jackson spoke the man's name as if it were a curse word. He didn't care.

"Yes. I trust him, and more importantly, I need his skills right now."

That comment stung worse than Jackson cared to admit. "Then, answer this. If he was so good at protecting you, why did he let you get into that bread truck? He didn't know who was driving that thing. It could have been a kidnapper."

"Don't do this, Jackson."

"I just don't trust him, Tallie."

"Because I prejudiced you toward him. If you don't trust him, at least trust me."

"I do. You know I do. But maybe you could trust my instincts a little too."

The seconds of silence that followed caused a new layer of sweat to break out over Jackson's body. *Don't hang up. Please don't hang up.*

"All right. How about we come to a truce? I'll take everything you said under advisement and watch Burke's every move, but Jackson, I need *you* to do what *you* do *there*, but I also need *Burke* and what *he* can do *here*. Okay?"

Jackson was gritting his teeth so tightly he thought his jaw might crack. "Okay." It was spoken in surrender, not in any level of agreement.

"I've got to go."

"Please be careful."

"I will. I'll call or text you tomorrow."

"Tallie, I'm sorry. It's just that I—"

"I know. You worry about me. Thanks, Jackson."

The call ended with Jackson's deepening feelings for Tallie left unsaid. She had placed him in the friend-zone, on the back burner, and Burke, a man he didn't trust, was her new number one. His temper rose again over the futility of the situation, and he slammed his fist against the wall, forgetting that it still held his phone. The corner of the screen cracked, and a new panic hit him as he worried whether he'd severed his lifeline to Tallie. Luckily, it still worked, but it now served as a visual reminder of his increasing distance from the woman whose love and trust he was struggling to earn.

He'd barely crossed the threshold back into the gym when Mak set his weights down and said, "I take it the call didn't go well?"

Jackson grunted and gathered his things to leave.

"Wait. I get it. You want to be there for her. That's noble, but she's in the best of hands. You can trust Burke."

"No, I can't. Because I don't."

"As an agent . . . or as a man?"

"Neither."

"There's no need to worry about him hitting on your girl." Mak grabbed a towel and wiped his face. "Burke has already punched his ticket on the love train."

"What's that supposed to mean?"

"He's engaged to Penelope Drummond, a rich babe whose daddy owns Drummond Engineering. In fact, Bartrum Drummond handpicked Burke for his little girl, so Burke's future is set. Even if he were a lousy operator, which he's not, there's no way he's going to mess up that bright future for a girl he met on an assignment."

The news gave Jackson little comfort. "Okay, let's say he's not trying to swoop in and steal my girl, but what if he's not the courageous soldier everyone believes he is?"

Mak balled the towel and tossed it into the dirty-laundry basket. "I've worked with him. Trust me. He's the total package."

His unequivocal praise of Agent Burke weakened Jackson's argument but not his unease. "All right, new topic. You compare the security in this place to that of the NSA, but you guys don't actually work for them, do you?"

Mak eyed Jackson curiously and answered, "They contract with us privately, but if you're asking if our names are on their pension rolls anymore, then the answer is no."

"So you admit that you guys work black ops, on the dark side of the line."

Mak straddled a weight bench near Jackson, sat, and leaned in to look Jackson in the eye. "Let's define *black ops*, Pulitzer. We don't go rogue or defy the law or shred the Constitution. Yes, we straddle legalities when lives are on the line because we go into places and investigate situations where the government might need deniability. We're warrior ghosts, and now so are you."

"Is that your group's name—the Warrior Ghosts?"

Mak laughed. "Heck no. Nothing lame like that. We keep it cool and simple—Blue 12."

"Is there a Blue 1 or a Blue 50?"

"Are you asking if we're the twelfth best team?"

"Well . . . are you?"

"We're color coded by specialty. Blue means intelligence gathering. The number is the location of the base."

"So you're D.C. intelligence."

"Right." Mak dragged the word out until it sounded incredibly cool. "But we're number one at what we do. And now you're Blue 12 too."

There was no denying that being lumped in with the likes of Mak and Rich swelled Jackson's ego, but he was fighting for Tallie, and he'd risk being kicked out of the band of brothers for that. "Are you telling me not one of your teammates has ever lost their footing while straddling that line?"

Anger flared in Mak's eyes. "I'm going to forget you asked that question because you're new and you've lost your mind over a girl."

Jackson decided to bear down on that nerve of Mak's he'd just irritated. "So it's happened."

Mak pressed his knuckles into the padded bench. When the emotions released, his shoulders sagged. "It's rare, but it happens. Temptation and greed have pulled a few good operators off that line."

"Is money the only reason they falter?"

Mak stood and pointed a finger Jackson's way. "I know where you're trying to go with this, Pulitzer, and I'm not jumping on board."

"Does ego and the need for power also pull them off the line, Mak?"

Frustration, anger, and pain all flashed across Mak's face. "You've got to have an ego to do this work, but in the military we learn to follow orders no matter what. We still adhere to that code, but . . ."

Jackson held his breath and waited for Mak to find the words he wanted.

"But after getting fifteen or twenty years of experience, some operators burn out, and they start having opinions and questioning decisions."

"What's the fallout?"

Mak filled his mighty lungs with air and blew it out in a long steady exhale. "One termite and some eggs can destroy a building."

"Put that in soldier terms."

"If a soldier or an operator questions his leaders long and loud enough, he'll eventually convince others to follow him."

"And things break down."

"It's only happened a few times, but when life or death depends on trusting the guys to your left and right, a guy like that is operational suicide."

"And you don't think there's even a tiny chance that could ever happen to Burke?"

"No way." He shook his head. "Burke's the last guy I could see that happening to. He's a soldier's soldier. The guy you want standing beside you on the line. I know because Rich and I have deployed with him more times than I can count. I think he's Rich's best friend. Trust me, he bleeds red, white, and blue. Now, grab your stuff and get over your preoccupation with Burke. We've got our own work to do."

"Yes, we do," Jackson said under his breath. And job number one was to find out whether Burke could possibly be a termite.

CHAPTER NINE

Tallie shoved her phone into her pocket, but ending the call didn't prevent Jackson's doubts about Agent Burke from creeping into her thoughts. After two minutes of debating the consequences of disobeying the agent, she hid her gun beneath the back of her shirt, gloved up, left the room, and took the stairs down to the main level. Tallie recalled passing administrative-looking offices through the corridor to the left when they'd accessed the security room to view the footage. Still, she had no idea which door led to the manager's office. She hoped she'd find a door conspicuously marked as such, but just in case she didn't, she decided to call the front desk to at least get the manager's name and office location.

The voice of the desk clerk who answered the call was unfamiliar, and Tallie was glad she was equally unknown to the clerk when she asked for the boss's name.

Curiosity tinged with a note of worry colored the clerk's voice over the request. "Has there been a problem? We'd be happy to do anything in our power to make your stay as perfect as possible."

"No problem. In fact, I'd like to know the manager's name so I can note it when I leave my recommendation on a travel site."

"Oh, wonderful!" the clerk gushed. "I'm sure if senor de la Fuente were in town, he would have been happy to thank you in person for your kindness."

If senor de la Fuente were in town. She and Burke hadn't considered this hitch. "When will he return?" Tallie asked.

"Not for another week, I'm afraid. He and his wife are in Brazil on vacation."

"I see. Perhaps we could give a copy of our note to senor de la Fuente's assistant manager."

"That would be senor Serrano."

"And is he here this evening?"

"I'm afraid not, but he's the dashing young man at the mic during breakfast who welcomes our newest guests. You've probably already seen him going from table to table."

"That's very helpful. Thank you."

She ended the call before the clerk asked for her name or room number. She had names now, at least, so she headed down the hall, hoping to match one to a door. Instead, she heard a muffled voice she felt certain was Burke's coming from behind an unmarked door.

Tallie homed in on Burke's intense but hushed conversation with someone, unable to catch any particular words. Jackson's doubts about Burke began replaying loudly in her head. She wondered who Burke was speaking to and why he was speaking so low, as if attempting to conceal his conversation.

Not trusting someone she should was as dangerous as trusting someone she shouldn't, and since skulking about and spying only added to her feelings of doubt and worry, she decided to be forthright. She knocked on the door.

"Come in." The greeting was offered in a mature woman's voice layered with European intonations.

When Tallie entered, Burke's expression made his displeasure apparent. He offered an abrupt thank-you to the woman and exited, giving Tallie a dark scowl as he passed by. She offered the reddish-haired woman a sheepish smile. "I'm sorry to have interrupted your meeting."

"No apology needed. Agent Brown, is it?"

Agent? Tallie decided not to quibble over titles. The woman remained seated and studied Tallie as if she were a precious objet d'art on a limited museum tour. Needing to hide from the attention, Tallie dropped her eyes to the desk, where a leather portfolio lay. Tallie caught the artistic outline of an eight lying on its side, the mathematical symbol for infinity, with three embossed letters—*IBT*—arched above it. Initially, Tallie assumed the letters were the woman's initials, but something about the combination of letters seemed familiar. Her study of the insignia ended when the woman covered the portfolio with a stapled set of papers, as if she were tidying her desk.

Her smile persisted as she said, "No wonder Agent Burke has more than business on his mind."

Tallie's face flushed hot at the innuendo. "He doesn't . . . I mean . . . we are not . . ." Her adamance on the matter got diluted by her embarrassment. She hated thinking that the unknown woman's unnerving interest in her was because she was making assumptions about some presumed relationship with Burke. "We're just working. It's just work."

"Maybe for you."

"Again, my apologies for interrupting," Tallie blurted. She hastily left and closed the door, nearly running to catch up to Burke. "What did you tell that woman about us? About me?"

Burke spun and pulled her into the obscurity of a stairwell, and his lip curled. "Nothing. More importantly, what did I tell *you*?"

"I know I didn't listen to your instructions. It's just that I really wanted—I needed—to sit in on that meeting."

"There was no *meeting*," he grumbled as he climbed the stairs two at a time.

Tallie raced behind. "What do you call your conversation with that woman?"

"Useless. She's the head of housekeeping. She doesn't handle personnel issues, and the manager already left for the day." There was a snarl in his voice. "We'll have to wait until morning, as I suspected in the first place." He thundered down the hall.

Tallie half ran after him, afraid he might get to their door first and lock her out. "Please, Burke. Wait up," she called out.

Burke spun around and pointed an angry finger as he stepped in her direction. The elevator door opened between hers and Burke's positions, and the two were creating a scene as a white-shirted waiter exited the elevator, pushing a room-service cart. The young man saw Burke storming his way toward Tallie and blocked the hall with his cart, saying something about protecting the beautiful young lady.

"Mind your own business," Burke growled back.

"I cannot," the young man argued back in Spanish. "I am a gentleman."

The implication that Burke was not a gentleman apparently hit a nerve, and whether in shame or fury, Burke balled his fist and stepped toward the young man like an angry bull. The waiter responded like a frightened matador, with only his cart to protect him. With one well-timed thrust, he pushed it toward Burke, causing him to turn suddenly. The cart slammed into his already-battered ribs, doubled him over in a yowl of pain and a flurry of expletives.

"Stop!" Tallie yelled before round two began. Two room doors opened over the ruckus and several vacationers emerged. They watched as Tallie dropped her rucksack, grabbed the young waiter, who was again brandishing his cart, and pinned him to the wall. "I appreciate your kindness, but you're mistaken," she said in perfect Spanish. She pointed to Burke, who struggled to straighten. "This man is my friend. He would never hurt me."

It took a few seconds for the waiter to relax and accept that it was safe to leave Tallie in Burke's care. Tallie pulled a few bills from her pocket and set them on the cart with a gracias and a smile. The waiter hurried away, watching over his shoulder as he delivered food to one of the gawking guests.

Burke made it to their suite and opened the door, holding it ajar until Tallie was inside. Once he was inside and the door closed and locked, Tallie reached to check his injured side, but his hand shot forward and he recoiled from her, rejecting any help she offered.

Tallie fell back against the wall. "You're making this personal."

"Trust matters in this work. I can't trust you."

It was the look he gave her, more than the words, that hurt most, but even his words couldn't have hurt her more if they'd been delivered on the tip of a knife.

"What do you want to do about food?" Burke asked as if Tallie were a prisoner in his protection.

"I'm fine. I've got a protein bar in my pack."

"Fine. You take the bedroom. Lock both doors."

"You're leaving again?"

"That stunt you just pulled proves you don't feel a need for my protection."

"And leaving me behind for that meeting implies you don't respect my abilities."

"So I was right. You wanted to tag along because you either don't believe I'm competent enough to conduct an interview or you don't trust that I'll share my findings with you."

Jackson would list an even uglier third worry, the question of who held Burke's loyalties. Julia's warning to trust no one kept playing in Tallie's head, but Burke's expression, a mix of betrayal and hurt, was jamming her instincts, making her unsure about whether or not she should trust him. Trust was hard for her, but so was rejection. Julia had left her strong in some ways but weak in others; she was easily disarmed by mind games. She went back to the things she knew. Her father respected Burke enough to have assigned him to protect her. Norris trusted him enough to have left her in his care. However arrogant and controlling the military may have made him, Burke had the endorsement of military men who cared about her. She'd take another chance on him as well.

"I'm not good at trusting," she finally said.

Burke pressed his hands into the front of his thighs and stared at the floor, apparently dismissing her words.

"I'll try to be a better partner," she added.

His head lifted and his hand came forward as if to stop her. "*Client.* You are my *client*, Miss Brown. Good night."

Tallie's heart sank as she watched the door click shut, but she had to admit she was relieved to have time alone and space to think. The broad pendulum swing between Burke's concern for her safety and his bitter disappointment left her feeling whiplashed. She hadn't felt that way since . . . since . . .

She knew exactly when. Burke's reaction to her disobedience could have been pulled from Julia's book on discipline, where it was not enough to simply identify and correct the alleged misdeed. Instead, Julia had used every violation of her rules as an opportunity to break Tallie's will and torture her by withholding approval and companionship.

Was that what Burke was doing, and if so, why? Or was he truly as wounded by her perceived mistrust as he'd appeared?

She paced as a wrestle ensued within her. So many oddities made the way forward unsettling. Burke had said the manager had already left for the day, but the manager wasn't even in town. He'd also said they'd have to wait until the morning before he could conduct an interview, so perhaps he meant he'd be speaking to the assistant manager. That made sense. The assistant manager could still give him the info they needed on the employee captured in the video, but would that evidence be enough? They had no video of the suspect actually drugging any of the guests. Would the time stamps of his entrances and exits and the discrepancies in his handling of the keycards be enough to convince management to give them the bellman's name and address? Would it be enough to call in the authorities?

She missed having Major Norris and Marlene to lean on. If the doctors at the hospital were able to stabilize Marlene, the two were probably back in the States by now. Hopefully the major would call soon and give her an update, but meanwhile, the only person left in the country she thought she could count on was barely speaking to her.

She prepared for bed and plugged in her phone and smartwatch, both of which reminded her of Jackson. Part of her wanted to call him, to hear from someone who believed in her, who built her up. Burke had left her confused, and Jackson was her safe zone. Her North Star.

She sat on the edge of the bed and weighed her easy options. If she gave Jackson a replay of the last hour's confrontation, he'd be on the next plane to

Mexico to save her, but his first concern would be to rescue her, not to save her father. And while heading back to the States would keep her safe for a while, there were no guarantees another Somali rebel wouldn't come for her eventually, plus, she'd likely lose any hope of saving her father.

Yes, one call to Jackson and she'd be whisked away to a temporary sense of safety, but she knew that wasn't what she or her father needed right now. Her life had been squandered by people who claimed to be protecting her. She made a decision. From this point forward, wise or unwise, she'd prefer to make her own decisions about what was best for her. Either she was wise enough and strong enough to handle the work Major Norris entrusted to her, or she wasn't. Julia had believed she was strong, but Tallie needed to know that for herself.

Two hours passed before a text appeared on her phone. *Heads up. I'm coming in. I didn't want to frighten you.* The door opened, and Burke entered sheepishly.

"Did you enjoy a quiet supper?" Tallie asked with noticeable snark.

Burke smiled. "Now you're upset with *me*. I deserve it." He found the bedding for the pullout in the closet, tossed it on the sofa, and sat down. "Truthfully? I never left the floor. I was sitting in the armchair at the end of the hall, watching the door the entire time."

Tallie leaned against the doorjamb to her room and folded her arms in front of her.

"You challenge me, throw me off my game," Burke said. "I'm not used to that."

Tallie offered no response other than her silent patience.

"During active duty I was an army captain—special forces, no less—where everyone followed me unconditionally. In private paramilitary, it's the same deal. I make decisions and people follow. People hire me to do dangerous things or to get others out of dangerous situations and keep them alive. In return, I expect their unquestioning obedience. But you're different. You don't blindly follow anyone."

"That's not completely true." Tallie thought of Julia. "I did once, and I found that my loyalty was misplaced. I won't make that mistake again."

She saw the slight raise of one of Burke's eyebrows, as if her confession shocked him.

"Then, we have a great deal in common." He ran his knuckle across his lips as he thought and then aimed his finger her way as he delivered his next point. "Would you agree that there may be multiple paths to achieving the same objective?"

His timing of such a question puzzled her, but she considered it and said, "Yes."

"And that some paths might depend upon challenging existing paradigms? Upon thinking outside the box?"

"I suppose so. Is that what you're doing?"

"I do what needs to be done to achieve mission goals," he said.

"So where does that leave us?"

"It leaves me eating some humble pie. I should have had more faith in your abilities. You do know how to take care of yourself. I'll remember that, but trust goes both ways, so I'll begin by telling you everything I learned in that meeting with the director of housekeeping."

Tallie kept her guard up.

"She's sending the manager an email with the details of why we need to meet with him, so he'll make time for us when he arrives tomorrow."

Tallie knotted up over the news. The manager was out of town. Did the housekeeper mean she was emailing the *assistant* manager, or was she lying altogether? Or was Burke? Tallie's throat grew tight. Time would tell. "Thanks for letting me know."

"There was something else."

Tallie tensed again as a smile lifted the corner of Burke's mouth.

"She told me one of the resort's nicest hot tubs is on the balcony of this floor, and a gym is at the end of the hall. Could I interest you in either of those?"

"Only if our suspect is hot-tubbing or giving a treadmill a go."

"Not likely."

Tallie didn't find his Cary Grant–style deflection helpful or calming. Delays were jeopardizing their success and perhaps her father's life. "What time is the manager expected tomorrow?"

"He generally arrives at about nine."

The arrival matched the schedule of the assistant manager, who according to the front desk clerk, made an appearance in the dining room for breakfast. Still, the reference to the *manager*'s arrival raised Tallie's guard again, and without realizing it, her doubt must have shown on her face. Burke read her mood instantly.

"You're still upset about something."

She played that card instead of denying the point. "I'm worried about the risks of waiting so long to follow our lead."

Burke's frustration was evident, but he took a few deep breaths and replied in a controlled voice. "This is when you have to trust me and *my* abilities. Remember our deal?"

Tallie pressed into the jamb, weighing every word.

"Don't bail on me now, Brown." Burke untied his shoes and tossed them aside. When he finished, he stayed bent over and sighed. "I'm sorry about my temper earlier. What you said to the waiter . . . that I was your friend and that I'd never hurt you . . . it meant a lot to me." He lifted his head and faced Tallie, rubbing his hands nervously as he spoke. "I can get so focused on my mission goal that I become callous to the people who'll be affected. You made me think about that today, Brown. I can't get it out of my mind."

He seemed like a broken man in that moment, and Tallie wondered if she were responsible for the change. Part of her wanted to comfort him, but a voice inside her still warned her to keep her distance. She missed Jackson and his way of centering her.

"Good night, then," she said as she turned and closed the door.

She prepared for bed and laid down with three items on her prayer or hope list—that by morning she'd hear from Major Norris that Marlene was improving, that she and Burke would get back on track as partners, and that they'd be refocused on the only thing that mattered—finding her father.

* * *

By seven thirty the next morning, Tallie emerged from her room, dressed and packed and ready for the day. Burke was lying on the pullout sofa, where he'd spent the night. Upon hearing her enter, he opened his eyes, stretched, and smiled approvingly, his mood and confidence fully restored. "No woman rocks khaki shorts and T-shirts like you, Brown."

Tallie blushed. Two minutes in and she was already playing defense. "I thought we should get an early start."

"We've got ninety minutes before the meeting. Relax while you can. The rest of the day could get crazy."

"Why not be ready in case he comes in early?"

He laid his arm across his eyes and chuckled. "You are relentless, Brown. All right. At least give me a chance to take a quick shower. I considered using the one in the pool area, but I didn't want to leave you alone."

Burke's quick shower stretched into twenty minutes. Afterward, he packed his toiletries and answered two apparently urgent emails before they finally loaded up to leave the suite. A knock sounded on the door. Burke pulled his gun from his holster and held it by his side. He looked back at Tallie, gesturing for her to move into the bedroom and away from the doorway as he cracked the door open as far as the security bar allowed.

"Good morning, officers," he said loudly enough for Tallie to hear. "How can I help you?"

"Please open the door, sir. We're conducting an investigation."

"What sort of investigation?"

"The door—open it, please," another man said.

Burke holstered his gun and opened the door, allowing two security guards to enter. Their attention was riveted to Burke's holstered gun and then to Tallie as she joined them from the bedroom.

"One of our resort employees called in sick today because of an injury he said he received from an American guest on this floor. He should have reported it right away, but he said he was embarrassed because the attacker was a woman. We're going room to room to identify the assailant and take statements from everyone involved. Perhaps this is all a simple misunderstanding caused by a lazy employee. I hope we can clear this up together without involving the local authorities." He turned to Burke. "I see you are armed, senor. Do you have a permit to carry that weapon in Mexico?"

"Of course. Would you like to see it?"

"Yes, please." They turned to Tallie. "You too, miss. Do you also have a gun?"

Tallie's neck prickled. "My gun is in my pack."

"Do you also have a permit to carry it in Mexico?"

Burke presented his permit to the guard and then looked at Tallie. "Where's yours? Go ahead and show it to them."

A sheen of sweat broke out over her body. "The major made all the travel arrangements. If he got a permit for me, he must have taken it with him when he left."

Burke's face tightened. He turned to the guards and smiled with his hands spread wide as he explained further. "We are all colleagues in law enforcement. Miss Brown and I were sent here by our government to conduct an investigation of our own. I came ahead, but Miss Brown arrived with two other American agents who unfortunately had a medical emergency and were forced to return home early. They must have left with her permit."

"Aha, I see. I'm sure we can sort this all out. Please gather all your belongings, Miss Brown, and come with us while we verify these details."

Tallie fiddled nervously with her hair until she'd twisted her blonde strands into a rope. "What if we call the man with my permit? He could fax it over or read you the number."

"That would be helpful. You can make that call from our office, but we will still need to inspect your weapon, file paperwork about this violation, and of course, there is still the matter of yesterday's altercation. Other guests witnessed it. They said the woman was young and blonde. Do you have anything to report about the incident?"

Tallie shot Burke a panicked glance and caught his effort to suggest she deny any involvement, but she shook that suggestion off. "There was a misunderstanding between the waiter and Mr. Burke. I intervened, but I didn't hurt him."

The two officers shared a knowing glance, and one reached for her arm. "Please come along so we can discuss this *intervention*."

Burke groaned "Fine. Let's get on with it. But I'm coming along."

"As you wish, senor."

The resort's security officers led the way down the corridor that held the administrative offices and past the room where Tallie and the others had watched the video feeds. Her hopes lifted as she thought about the very accommodating sergeant who'd helped them the previous day.

"Wait!" She halted and smiled at the officers. "Sergeant Pasqual helped us yesterday. Isn't he the head of security?"

"Yes," one officer replied, "but today is his day off."

"Surely you can contact him," Burke said. "He met our entire team. He can vouch for Miss Brown and her credentials."

The officers smiled politely. "No, we would not bother the head of security over something we can clear up ourselves. Come along." They continued leading the way.

Burke checked his watch and scanned each door they passed as the security guards led them to the last door on the right and had them take a seat while they conducted a search of Tallie's satchel in another room.

Burke pulled out his phone. "I'm calling the major."

"We left the States in such a hurry. What if he didn't file a permit for me? What if *he* and his authority were my permit?"

"We'll know soon enough." Burke made a call but received no answer. Tallie watched his frustration increase by the second. "I'll text him, but he should be up by now. And the time of day is irrelevant. You always take a call when you have men in field."

Tallie's eyes misted, and Burke took her hand. "Don't worry. I'll stay with you until we get this sorted out."

"I'm not afraid for me. I'm worried about Marlene."

Burke turned fully toward her. The haunted expression he'd worn the night before returned as his eyes shifted around the room, finally resting back on Tallie's. "Are you serious?"

"Think about it. She must have taken a turn for the worse. It's the only explanation for why Major Norris isn't monitoring his phone right now."

He glanced everywhere, finally setting his eyes on the floor as if trying to avoid making eye contact with Tallie again. "I don't get you, Brown. You're a real piece of work," he whispered tenderly. He bit his lower lip and turned to stare blankly ahead. "You're detained in Mexico and sitting in the hotel security guards' office, possibly about to be charged with assault and for carrying an illegal weapon, and you're worried about someone else."

She squeezed his hand back. "Look who's talking. You stayed in Mexico to protect me and help me find Cai." She looked at his hand holding hers. "Thanks for your help."

He sniffed and rubbed a hand under his nose before looking at his watch again. Tallie remembered their nine o'clock meeting with the hotel manager. Burke's dedication to her over the last few hours diluted her doubts about his loyalties. If there had been a miscue about the manager or assistant manager, she accepted that it had been on the part of the director of housekeeping. They needed the suspect's information, and the only way they'd get it was for Burke to attend that meeting; the only way he'd do that was for her to assure him she'd be all right.

"You need to go to that meeting, Burke."

"You're job one right now. We've given the team a huge lead. Someone else can pick up our suspect another time." His feet bounced on the floor, and the fidgeting of his hands increased. "I've got a bad feeling about this situation, Brown."

Burke's concerns caused cold fear to sweep over Tallie.

"Listen to me," he said in a whisper. "I can get us off this resort and across the border by nightfall. What do you say we call this op a wash? How about you put your safety first for a change?"

She was about to consider the new plan when her father's face flashed across her mind. What would a delay cost him? And if he was the world's best hope for peace, the risk could be immeasurable. She wasn't trying to be a martyr. She didn't want to have her freedom curtailed when she had barely tasted what it meant to really be free, but neither could she put her fears ahead of all the people who'd been kidnapped. She trusted Norris and Burke to sort her situation out later, and she was about to tell Burke as much when the guards entered the room carrying a stack of papers.

"We have good news. The police have located your permit in the database. They will create a new document for you to carry so you don't have this difficulty again, yes?"

The relief the news brought left Tallie giddy. "Thank you, thank you! Do I need to pick it up somewhere?"

"They will fax the temporary document here, but still, these things take time. Please use that time to fill out this accident report about yesterday's altercation. Every violation must be documented. I'm sure you understand."

What Tallie understood was that she wasn't leaving their office anytime soon. "Burke, you should keep that appointment," she reiterated.

His head slipped into his shoulders. "Even with my offer to get you out, you're still set to proceed with the plan?"

"It's like you said earlier. We're a lot alike. We do what needs to be done to achieve mission goals, so go. I'll be here, just filling out forms."

He stared at her for several long seconds. "All right," he said in surrender. "All right, then."

"I'll hurry through these documents and join you as soon as I can."

"Sure, sure."

Two more hours passed before the guards were satisfied that she and her gun were properly verified, permitted, and documented. Tallie was finally ready to leave when Burke arrived at the security office.

"I'm sorry that took so long. Are we all done here?" he asked the officers, who nodded and gestured that Tallie could leave.

She hefted her pack as Burke led her away from the guards to the lobby. "Long meeting," she said.

"Yeah, I'm sorry. He wouldn't release the name of the employee until we ran through all the footage. Even the video wasn't enough to convince him."

"What did?"

"A threat to charge him and the resort for negligence and impeding our investigation."

Burke's failure to mention that the man he spoke with wasn't the actual manager unnerved her, so she asked him straight out. "So did senor de la Fuente give you the bellman's name and address?"

He answered without addressing her question directly. "Our suspect's name is Gerardo Ibarra. He was a recent hire who came onto the payroll with a few others who were recruited because they spoke nearly perfect English. He quit yesterday, but the manager did give me his address."

"Great! Let's get him."

Burke led Tallie to a table at the lobby's small café. "We've got a few minutes. Take a seat. Can I get you something?"

Her hands flew to her hips, and she glared at him in disbelief. "We need to get this guy now. General Kaswell's life could be in danger."

"Shhh," Burke warned. "Keep your voice down and don't draw anymore attention to us than we already have. Gerardo might not be here today, but we don't know if he has a buddy or two still inside this place."

Tallie lowered her voice. "We don't have time—"

He gestured for her to lower her voice even further.

"We don't have time to sit and sip," she hissed.

Burke shot her an overexaggerated smile as he moved behind her and pulled out a chair, gesturing for her to sit. "First of all, we haven't eaten any real food since yesterday's lunch. I can't do my best work when I'm starving."

Irritated, Tallie reluctantly lowered into the chair and scooted forward as he moved her closer to the table. While doing so, he leaned next to her ear, as if to whisper sweetly, and said, "Second, we can't get there in my rented sedan."

"Why?"

Burke took his seat across from her, coaching her as he spoke. "Your scowl will draw negative attention. We've already raised quite a stir here. Just smile and act like we're a happy American couple."

It's a game, she repeated in her mind. Part of their undercover assignment. She smiled awkwardly, having no skill in the art of subterfuge.

Burke continued to smile pleasantly and speak in whispered tones meant for only her ears. "Gerardo's address is in a small inland community called Lugar de Sueños, the place of dreams."

"Such a sweet town harbors kidnappers and possible murderers?"

"The name is aspirational only. A lot of workers for fancy resorts live there because the rent is cheap and their wages go farther. On the other hand, because it's cheap, it doesn't have great infrastructure, like paved roads. We need an SUV."

Tallie beamed back a disingenuous thousand-kilowatt smile. "Why aren't we getting one *now*?"

"The management wants to make nice. They've arranged for a four-wheel-drive vehicle to be delivered in the hour."

Tallie picked up her napkin and placed it in her lap. "I didn't know."

"I get it. You want to save Cai. For reasons you'll probably need to sort out with a therapist someday, you feel committed to saving the man whose family you couldn't save."

He had no idea how right he was or how deeply his tongue-in-cheek comment pained her. She bit her lip to still its trembling and redirected the conversation back to the mission. "If we have to wait, let's formulate a plan while we eat. I'll have a burger and a diet Coke with lemon."

"Good call. I'll be right back."

She wanted to trust Burke, but something about the continual shifts in his demeanor felt off, and she hedged her bets with a quick text to Jackson. *The suspect lives in Lugar de Sueños. We're heading there soon.*

A sense of security swept over her when Jackson's reply came almost instantaneously. *Got it. Please be safe. I'll be here. And thanks, Tallie, for inviting me to lean in on this.*

She smiled. Jackson's new military friends were teaching him their lingo. To *lean in* was a military term that implied readiness and the willingness to assume responsibility. He must have known she'd understand what those few words implied for her. That he would be there, at the ready, if she needed him. She pocketed her phone as Burke returned with their drinks.

"Is that Jackson checking in?"

"Yes."

"How are things on the home front?"

"Good. Complicated." She took a sip and hoped Burke would drop the line of questioning. But he didn't.

"Relationships are always hard for people like us."

The statement rolled off his tongue with a startling matter-of-factness that left Tallie dumbstruck for a moment. She sat back in her chair. "We are not the same. I'm neither ex-military nor a federal agent."

"Those are just the vehicles through which we devote our abilities."

"And what specific similarities do you see between us, aside from our committment to do what needs to be done to achieve mission goals?"

"Devotion to mission is no small thing." He batted the saltshaker around between his fingers, as if the topic were uncomfortable. "It's admirable, but it gets in the way of more personal pursuits."

Tallie weighed his assessment. It was certainly true of Julia, but was it equally true of her? Julia was a loner. Would it always be so for Tallie? She hoped not. She returned to her drink and drew in a long, slow sip before saying, "But you're engaged. I saw the announcement on General Kaswell's refrigerator."

"Was." He looked at his watch with its screenful of information and opened the calendar app. "The cancelation notes should be going out in a day or two."

"I'm sorry. What happened?"

"I started questioning my long-term career path a while back, and we went around and around for a year, debating what to do. She wanted me to take a job as head of security for her father's company, one of the US military's biggest suppliers. It was a win-win for all of us, or so she told me. She'd get the man she loved *and* the lifestyle she wanted. Her father would have bragging rights that his head of security was a trusted son-in-law with a deep background in military and federal intelligence, all of which would go over big with his patriotic board and investors. And me? Well . . . I'd have a six-figure salary, nice perks, status, and a more impressive résumé that I could parlay into a board position or even into a political career down the road."

"Did you love her?"

"I thought I did." He poked at his lemon for several seconds. "Things changed between us when she set so many conditions on our relationship. I realized I didn't love her enough to reinvent myself to her liking, and she didn't love the man I had become, so we called off the wedding."

Tallie remembered Jackson saying something similar about his relationship to Dawn. *"She loved the man I was, and the man I was loved her, but I'm not that same man anymore."*

Tallie and Burke sat in silence, sipping sodas and looking out the window for the promised vehicle. Burke finally asked Tallie, "Do you love *him*?"

She wasn't surprised by the question. Burke seemed to love asking uncomfortable questions. "Jackson and I have only known each other for a short time."

"How does he make you feel?"

She stirred her drink while deciding how or whether to answer. "It's complicated."

Burke scrutinized her face as if she were a fingerprint at a crime scene. She felt herself folding forward, hiding her face from his gaze. She wanted the questions to stop and a return to their more professional relationship, but when she glanced up, she saw admiration in his eyes.

"I really wish you wouldn't stare at me like that."

"Maybe I can provide some important insight for you."

"Such as?"

"I see it in your eyes whenever you speak about Jackson. You doubt whether you're good enough for him, don't you?"

She stirred her drink again with her straw. "I wouldn't put it that way," she replied with more than a little defensiveness. "Like you and your ex, we're very different. I'm not sure we'd make each other happy long-term."

For a moment, the man was speechless. He leaned into the back of his chair and tipped his head to the side, holding her in his gaze as a look of wonder lit his face. "Hear me when I tell you that you never need to question your worth. You deserve someone who knows that. Someone who appreciates you. You're very special, Miss Brown."

She was ready to defend Jackson's opinion of her when what Burke said next slammed her thoughts together like two colliding freight trains.

"Everything they said about you is true. How did they put it? Oh yes . . . 'a woman with an incomparable dichotomy of talents.'"

Her breathing hitched and her skin prickled. "*They* who? Who said that about me?"

There was a break in Burke's confidence. His smile froze, becoming a placeholder to sustain the moment while the tiny shifts in his eyes and brows told Tallie he was scrambling to come up with an answer.

"Major Norris and General Kaswell."

Plausible candidates. Tallie would have accepted that answer and been honored by the compliment if it weren't for the mild panic in Burke's eyes. Either he had revealed something he wasn't supposed to, or he was lying.

Tallie couldn't imagine the words *dichotomy of talents* coming out of the major's mouth, but Cai Kaswell's? Perhaps. But it was high praise from a man who knew her only as the woman who had stood guard over his family's remains . . . unless . . . unless he knew more about Tallie than she realized. But how much more? Did he know she was his daughter? Did Burke?

Burke's words were a blur as she focused on the possibility that her father had figured out who she really was. And then she heard Burke say, "You have no idea how special you are. You truly don't know." His brow furrowed, narrowing his eyes. "You're strong and resilient. I've witnessed firsthand how that million-dollar mind of yours sees bright goodness in the world despite its ugly realities, goodness for which you're willing to sacrifice your personal wants. And somehow, you've managed to remain completely unimpressed by all this."

Tallie shivered at the thought of having her worth assessed by him. "What is *a million-dollar mind*?"

There was another second's pause. Burke's eyes missed a blink and his mouth froze, and then he said, "Just a figure of speech."

Their food order arrived, and Tallie picked at her plate in silence.

"Not talking to me anymore?" Burke asked after a few minutes. "I'm sorry if I made you uncomfortable. Can I give you some more advice?"

"Would it matter if I said no?" Tallie answered.

Burke set his burger down and wiped his mouth with his napkin. "Not in this instance, because it's that important." He leaned forward and slowly reached across the table, peeling her fingers away from her glass until they rested in his hand. "Please listen to what I'm about to tell you. Go home and get out of this business, Brown. You've got the abilities and the desire, but you're too kind. Too innocent. Maybe things will work out with this Jackson, but if they don't, find another way to save the world, one that won't harden your heart or get you killed."

Tallie pulled her hand back. "Are you asking me to give up on finding General Kaswell?"

"Yes. Yes, I am. You have no idea what this could cost you."

"And no matter what you think your amateur analysis revealed, you don't know anything about me or my 'incomparable dichotomy of talents.'"

Burke's expression darkened, and he leaned back in his chair. "I'm trying to protect you."

Part of her believed he was telling her the truth, or at least a partial truth to conceal something he didn't want to share. She said, "When Major Norris told me to leave Mexico and go home, you said it was my choice and you'd help me complete my mission to find Cai Kaswell. Why the sudden change?"

"I didn't know you then," he said and looked away.

A chill snaked up her spine, and a pregnant silence ensued while Tallie wrestled with the myriad possibilities of what Burke's intentions could be. Maybe he really didn't think she was capable enough or smart enough or tough enough. All she knew was that this man stood between her and finding her father, and he was not going to deter her from interrogating Gerardo Ibarra.

She was about to tell him that when his attention was drawn to something outside. She saw the subject of his interest—a black SUV pulling up to the front doors. Burke rose before the driver, a young woman, entered. Neither acknowledged the other at first, and yet Tallie saw a spark of recognition pass between them as soon as they made eye contact. Once she saw Burke, the young brunette smiled and moved his way, extending her hand with a key.

"You are Mr. Burke?" she said.

Tallie noted the unique nuances in the woman's voice, the hints of both German and Spanish accents. And she noticed something on the leather fob from which the key dangled. The woman's fingers concealed most of the artwork, but Tallie felt sure she could make out a familiar infinity symbol and pieces of what could be the letters *IBT* embossed into the leather, the same insignia embossed into the director of housekeeping's portfolio.

"And you must be Maria," Burke replied. "Thank you for bringing the vehicle."

"You're welcome. It is yours to use as needed. When your investigation is complete, just park it in the lot and bring the key to the front desk clerk."

"Will do. We're in your debt."

She said goodbye and walked away toward the valet station, where another car was waiting for her. Burke drained his glass and bored his eyes into Tallie. "We have a vehicle. It's time to fish or cut bait. Do you take my advice and let me escort you across the border, or do we go after Ibarra?"

"I want to get Ibarra, but first, I want to know what the plan is."

Before Tallie had time to stand, Burke leaned over the table toward her, his eyes narrow and cold. "Do you think we're just going to walk in there and *get Gerardo Ibarra*? Are you really that naive? You're brilliant, but you're in over your head, Ms. Brown. Someone could die today, or worse. Do you understand that?"

Her racing mind could barely process all the random inconsistencies popping up like warning signs around her. She looked at Burke, trying to figure out what he'd said, but something wild and desperate lurked in his eyes, and she knew she dared not press him.

"Aren't you smart enough to know when to call it quits?" he growled before lowering his voice and dropping back into his chair in a huff. "This is why I never allow myself to get personally involved." He turned away from her, as if not seeing her actually made her disappear. When he turned back, his face had morphed from hard and obstinate to fear-filled and pleading. "If you aren't smart enough to protect yourself, at least let me protect you. Say the word and we're out of here, mission aborted, on our way home to the States and safety."

Tallie wondered what horrors he'd seen in the field that left him so divided inside himself—both dedicated and terrified of duty. Julia was like that, dedicated to combat readiness while being crushed by fear.

She and Burke were close to getting answers about her father, and she wouldn't walk away now. It wasn't grand bravery. She didn't know if she was safer saying yes or no to Burke's half-crazed offer to abort the mission. What if this was Cai Kaswell's hour of need? She knew she could never have peace knowing she forfeited a chance to save him. And besides, was she really safe anywhere now that someone had succeeded in taking her father?

She kept her voice calm and measured as she reasoned with Burke. "Let's make a plan and get Ibarra."

"With what intel? All I have is a location."

"We know what he looks like."

"On grainy security-cam footage while he was dressed in a uniform and hat. Face it. We're going in blind, Brown, like kicking down doors in Afghanistan. If you want to do this, we make the plan as we go." Burke stared at her as if hoping to break her will. When she still didn't bend, he stood and pointed a finger her way, saying, "All right. You want to get to Cai Kaswell so badly that you're willing to throw all caution to the wind? Then, so be it. This is on you now. When it's over, however it ends, remember you offered yourself as the price to save the world. Load up."

Tallie picked up her rucksack. It and its materiel grounded her and made her feel back in control. She followed Burke to the vehicle and loaded her things. He had only his sidearm, so they drove to the rented sedan, where his own canvas satchel of equipment was locked in the trunk. After loading that into the SUV, Burke pulled out of the resort and onto the main road.

Tallie spent the first few minutes trying to make sense of the appearance of the letters *IBT* on both the portfolio and the key fob. She concluded that the letters could designate the management company that owned the resort. It made sense. Burke said the management was providing the vehicle. The same management company could have provided the portfolio to their valued director of housekeeping. She moved on to a new concern. "Don't you need a map or GPS coordinates to find this place?"

"The GPS is useless over there. I was told directions would be easier to follow."

"Where are they? I'll navigate for you."

Burke tapped his temple. "They're right up here."

His arrogance was unparalleled. "How much time until we get to Lugar de Sueños?"

"An hour."

Her stress ramped up. "During your meeting, did you get any intel on Gerardo's household? Does he live alone? Does he have a family we need to deal with?"

Burke ran his hand through his hair a few times before answering. "Don't worry. He'll be alone."

Burke's assuredness was either reckless or based on intel he hadn't shared with Tallie, intel he refused to share now. She turned in her seat, needing to read Burke and not merely hear his replies. "What if Cai isn't there? What's the next step?"

"We get information." Burke lifted his left hand from the wheel and massaged his brow. "Just stop with the questions! I need to think."

Burke's vagueness reaffirmed Tallie's earlier worries. Either he really was winging it as he'd said, or he had an agenda he wasn't sharing. Instead of cowing Tallie, he'd merely succeeded in emboldening her. "I want to hear everything you know about this guy, right now."

He slammed his hands on the steering wheel and moved his focus from the road to the view from the side window and back to the road, avoiding eye contact with Tallie.

"Answer me, Burke."

"I tried to do the honorable thing and give you an out! Whatever happens now is your fault."

"Are you trying to frighten me? Why are you so angry? Why are you shutting me out?"

"I am reacting to a rapidly changing situation. No one expected you to identify that suspect and send us on a manhunt, and when you did, I tried to persuade you to pass the information on and head home, but no! So I'll make the plan based on the conditions on site. Me. *I* make the plan. I'm running this op because you have zero authority down here. You will simply stay in this vehicle and do what I say. Got it?"

There was something manic about him now, as if he were being squeezed or torn by two onerous options. The last phone conversation with the major replayed through her mind, the one in which Major Norris had all but threatened Burke if he didn't protect her. What if Norris had told Cai she was his last living child? Burke may have been told that protecting her was the first priority. If so, his offer to get her out of Mexico would make perfect sense, but Tallie had made that option a nonstarter, leaving Burke only one choice, a choice that put her in danger on his watch.

"I know you're in a position you didn't want to be in," she said. "And I know why."

Haunted eyes met Tallie's when Burke swung his head around to face her. He inadvertently stomped on the brake, throwing them both forward but soon regained his composure and drove on. "You do?"

"Yes. You're caught in a vise of conflicting orders and loyalties."

This time, Burke purposely pulled the vehicle to the curb and stopped it. "Explain."

Tallie laid her hand on his shoulder. "Major Norris warned you to protect me, and you're trying your best to do that, but you also know that would mean abandoning Cai Kaswell until a new team could arrive, and we both know that could be too late. So your only options are to evacuate me to protect me, or take me with you to save Cai, and I'm making that more difficult because instead of agreeing to stay back and stay safe, I've been fighting you to let me help."

Relief washed over him. "So we're killing the op and heading back to the States?"

"I know you're not trying to patronize me. You see me as a colleague, but you also see me as a client you've vowed to protect. You're trying to ground me from this rescue to protect me *and* you're trying to save Cai, and you can't do both, so I relieve you of your responsibility to me." She pulled out her phone. "I'll text that to Major Norris right now if it'll make you feel better."

His reaction wasn't what she'd expected. Beads of sweat dotted his brow. He looked more tortured, not less, after her statement, lying his head on the steering wheel and bouncing it slightly. When he raised his head, he said, "Don't" and restarted the ignition. When he skidded out onto the road, he kept silent, with his eyes focused forward.

The phone still sat in Tallie's right hand, and while she didn't want to start another confrontation by having him catch her disobeying his orders again, she couldn't do nothing. She decided to start by verifying whether IBT was a management company.

She turned her body away from Burke, doing as good a job of avoiding further conversation with him as he was doing with her. She surreptitiously typed the letters into the search bar. More than a dozen results came up, but none seemed to fit a management company. She drafted a quick text to Jackson. *Busy here. Please search* IBT. *Is it a management company or anything interesting?*

She shoved the phone back into her pocket but felt it vibrate immediately, signaling Jackson's reply. Comfort settled over her like a blanket at the knowledge that Jackson was always there for her, at the ready. She feared escalating Burke's wrath if he caught her texting Jackson back, and as she suspected, her silence set Jackson off in a worried panic, launching a series of texts and phone vibrations. She knew her silence worried him, but keeping him on alert was enough, and hopefully he'd discover what IBT meant and provide some backup from his end.

CHAPTER TEN

Jackson's order from Mak's latest fast-food run sat before him, encased in white Styrofoam. "Double patties?"

"Have I bungled an order yet? You, however, still owe me a fish sandwich from yesterday."

"You said the chicken salad was good."

"Yes," Mak said with a raised brow, "but it was no fish sandwich."

"Point taken. I'll square things when I grab dinner."

"Good man." Mak pistol-shot Jackson with his fingers, shoved an onion ring into his mouth, and took a seat at his station.

Jackson leaned back and pulled his already-loosened tie over his head. *I might not bother wearing one tomorrow*, he thought as he opened the burger box. He looked forward to adopting the casual dress standards that belied the importance of Blue 12's work. He felt welcome around Mak and was anxious to be welcomed by the rest of Blue 12's pack. That would take time—perhaps a lot of it—but the other guys assigned to the Crib seemed to be warming up to him; they shared jokes with him or made others up about him on an almost hourly basis. These were strange rites, but Jackson found them positive ones.

Halfway through his burger, a text came through from Tallie. As soon as he saw her number flash on the screen, he dropped his burger and picked up the phone, smearing mayo and ketchup on the case.

Mak saw the spectacle and handed him a napkin. "Tallie?"

"Yeah. Hey, listen to this. She's asking about IBT. Do they run a management company?"

Mak shrugged. "No idea. You're the guy they tried to hire."

"I thought they were just a philanthropic think tank, but if they supplied you guys, they're clearly more than that."

"Burke probably knows more about them than I do. Tell her to ask him."

Jackson knew chugging a quart of Cholula hot sauce would pain him less than sending Tallie back to Burke. He quickly texted, *Infinity Brain Trust. The company that tried to hire me. Why are you asking?*

While he awaited a reply, he began a search of the three letters and found nothing related to any sort of management enterprise. He texted Tallie again. *No results about a management company, but they outfitted this site, the station for one of Norris's op teams, called Blue 12.*

There was still no reply from Tallie, but Jackson's mind became stuck on the idea of a think tank supplying military gear. He wondered why they'd have access to such goods unless they had some involvement with the military community. He dug deeper, using some of the government resources Mak had opened to him, and found a few articles printed in inter-governmental journals about IBT. One mentioned their partnership with a company called Drummond Engineering, which was owned by Bartrum Drummond—the future father-in-law of Agent Burke.

Before his imagination ran off at a Kentucky Derby pace, Jackson told himself that Burke may have told Tallie about his fiancée and that could have led to a mention of Drummond and IBT. It was possible, but it didn't feel right. Tallie wouldn't have asked him to check something unless it had raised an alert in her.

The other two heavily redacted articles listed IBT with four other three-letter entities: IMT, ICT, IFT, and IPT. It also mentioned a group called the Conservancy. Jackson tried plugging those letter combos in using *Infinity* for *I* and *Trust* for *T*. His first choice for the *M* in IMT was *mind*, but he discarded that, assuming IBT covered *brain* and similar topics. He instead plugged in *military* for the *M*. Seven more heavily redacted articles popped up, and Mak appeared, hovering over his desk.

"What are you digging for, Jackson? You're setting off all kinds of alarms."

"Like security alerts?"

"Big time."

"What words are pinging the system?"

"*Infinity, conservancy, military, IMT, IBT.*"

"Pretty much everything I've typed," he muttered. "Did you know there are ties between IBT and Burke's sugar daddy, Drummond?"

Mak's eyebrows wriggled. "I didn't, but that's not surprising, I suppose. Drummond probably has his fingers in lots of philanthropic groups."

"But why would a think tank like IBT set off security alerts unless they're doing more than delivering humanitarian goods?" Another thought came to him. "You said you guys arranged secure transport for IBT clients. Do you remember who you moved, when, or to where?"

Mak's mouth went slack. "What are you getting at?"

"Tallie found out how the kidnappers disarmed their victims. She and Burke are supposedly on their way to get the suspect right now, and she's texting me about IBT. There's got to be a connection. Humor me and check it out . . . please." He hoped his information was enough to earn him a spot at Mak's computer station.

Mak stood at his station and typed for several minutes. His curse got the attention of everyone in the room as he stared at his screen, both hands pressed to his head. "J. R.," he called out to a man in another cubicle. "Get Rich on the line. Tell him I need him ASAP."

As if he'd heard Mak, Rich passed through the floor's security checkpoint at a run. He glanced curiously at Jackson and then at Jackson's screen and asked, "What did you stir up this time, newbie?"

But before Jackson could answer, Mak asked, "Why is IBT pinging alerts today?"

"I hope it's because they had the misfortune of putting the word *infinity* in their name. There's a lot of chatter over that word today."

Mak put a hand on Rich's shoulder. "Did you ever meet the clients we moved for IBT?"

"Which time? We've transported a lot of people for them."

"Watch the big screen."

All the eyes in the room looked up to the big screen in the center, where two spreadsheets were displayed. One listed the jobs Blue 12's members had performed for IBT and was titled IBT Billables. The other listed every American and international missing leader of government and business with their home country, the country from which they were abducted, and the dates the abductions had taken place. This sheet was titled Missing and Presumed Alive. The last name on the list was Cai Kaswell's.

Mak began deleting unnecessary columns until only two remained on each sheet—date and location of abduction. Next, he filtered the Missing and Presumed Alive sheet by places where members of Blue 12 had deployed to move IBT clients, and when the results flashed across the screen, a somber gasp could be heard across the room. The locations of nine international abductions matched the places and dates where Blue 12 had been deployed.

Mak raised his arms and used them to cover his head. "Rich, who ordered these jobs?"

"Major Norris." Rich rubbed his fingers deep into his eyes. "Notify the major that we have a situation here. Ask him to get over here, pronto." He pointed and swept his arm across the entire room. "Listen up, people. I want everyone on IBT, IMT, and—forget that—stick every stinking letter of the alphabet between *I* and *T* and scour every site for whatever you can find. A three-day weekend to the first one who can nail down what this Conservancy is. Go!"

CHAPTER ELEVEN

TALLIE WATCHED OUT HER WINDOW for more than a half hour as the city's luxurious shopping and entertainment district shifted into bustling suburban neighborhoods, which eventually faded into blocks of rundown residences and shops running toward the edge of more rural terrain. Some of the buildings were no more than lean-tos constructed from plywood or cardboard owned by tired, bedraggled people. Buildings became more sparse and paved roads ended as agriculture consumed the land, watched over by armed guards in trucks posted along the acreage. The SUV trundled along the rutted road, beyond tended fields of produce laid in quilt-like rows and on to wild acres of trees and viny growth, broken only by an occasional shack or cluster of run-down, inhospitable hovels. Tallie suspected that the presence of armed guards meant that behind the innocuous fields of vegetables and corn lay plots of marijuana, nightshade, and possibly coca, the plant behind cocaine.

She'd spent most of her childhood in obscure shanty towns and squatter settlements, places where she and Julia could become part of the invisible poor while Julia served the indigent locals as a teacher or nurse or research scientist. Poverty didn't frighten Tallie, but the desperation it sometimes bred did, and she saw that hopelessness in the eyes of some of the villagers she and Burke passed.

The hairs on her arms rose as she noticed that same desperation in the eyes of the armed man guarding the road Burke turned onto. More a trail than a road, it was rutted so badly that the trip felt like a carnival ride of deep forward dips and shifts left and right. They passed a decrepit bus parked in a junglelike clearing by the side of the dirt trail. It was guarded by another armed man, illustrating its worth to the community. Tallie assumed it was the area's one form of transportation to move shifts of workers to the resorts and hotels in the city.

She smiled at the sight of children kicking a soccer ball in a field and women gathered by a cooking fire, some with small children bundled on their backs. There were no house numbers or street names in the village, so she found it a cause for wonder when Burke accurately snaked through the patchwork paths and parked the car amid some overgrowth a hundred yards from one of the finer buildings in the community—a block-and-wood structure. He had the vehicle's door open and one leg out before he said, "Wait here." His tone was unequivocal and underscored by the shutting of his door without further explanation.

Tallie rebelliously exited through her door and met him at the back of the SUV. He glared at her as he opened the door and silently unzipped his satchel to grab an extra magazine and a silencer, which he slid into his hip pocket.

"I should go along. I'll stay out of harm's way, but I'll be there if you need backup."

"No."

"Stop and think, Burke. You have no idea what you could be walking into."

His soft close of the door was punctuated by a stern glower. "Be quiet and get back in the vehicle."

She grabbed his forearm and dug in to make him hear her. Respect, more than anger, reflected on his face, so she carried on. "I don't know why you're being so GI Joe with me, but you're letting it cloud your judgment." The tension in his body eased for a moment, and Tallie softened her hold. "Please, Burke. You said it yourself back at the resort. I possess some unique skills. Let me help you."

His head tipped toward her and his lips parted, as if he were preparing an important reply, which he fought and finally refused to voice.

Tallie ended the silence, jumping back in with, "This is my fight too. Let's bring Cai Kaswell home together."

His brows pinched and he pulled back from her grasp, as if her touch caused him pain. "You're obsessed." In three steps he was at her door, holding it open.

She walked up to him to make another attempt to persuade him. Instead, he drew near her face. "Get out of my head, lady. I don't need anything from you, and I can't wait to hand you off. Get in." She reluctantly complied, his words leaving her puzzled and dazed. He issued her a final smirk, shut her door, and wagged a warning finger her way, as if daring her to cross him once more. With that, he was gone.

"I can't wait to hand you off."

What did Burke mean?

Tallie replayed his words again and again. *"I can't wait to hand you off."*

To whom? To Cai Kaswell?

More-sinister options presented themselves, like the Somalis. But he had protected her from them. Or so he'd said.

Tallie had tried not to label Burke a threat, but the oddities in his behavior and comments weren't adding up. She'd told him he didn't know what he was walking into, but what if he actually did? She worried she was becoming as neurotic as Julia, seeing threats and dangers at every turn. *I am not Julia*, she told herself. "I'm reasonable, logical," she assured herself. To prove it, she began reassessing the data before she tagged Burke an enemy.

She filtered her previous theory about his actions through a less flattering lens. He had said he was assigned by Cai Kaswell to protect Tallie, but that was unverified. The only comment Major Norris had made on the matter was, *"I can see Cai doing that."* Norris trusted Burke. He'd left Tallie in the agent's care when he'd left with Marlene. That was a powerful endorsement, wasn't it?

The hours Burke had spent scouring the video feed with Tallie, his protective posture when Norris had assigned her safety to his care, and his excitement when she'd broken the case open were points in the agent's favor.

Still, Tallie could no longer shake off how Burke had ordered her to remain in the suite while he attempted to meet with the resort manager alone and how the unplanned security check of her gun permit had conveniently locked her out of the morning's critical meeting. She found that curious, and she felt uneasy over Burke's claim that he'd met with the resort manager when she knew the man was in Brazil. There was also the matter of how he had so accurately navigated his way to this place, a place he'd supposedly never been before, to interrogate a man he had supposedly never met before. And now he was conveniently excluding her from that interrogation as well . . . for her own safety? She didn't feel safe leaving the vehicle, but neither did she feel safe staying inside. She had dismissed Julia's primary directive—trust no one—when she had decided to trust Burke. But in her attempt not to be like Julia, had she blinded herself to evidence and warning signs that he was not to be trusted?

Tallie hadn't felt this vulnerable and blind since she was nine, when they'd lived in a remote village in the cork forests of northern Tunisia. Julia was tending a fevered child, and instead of taking Tallie along as her assistant, as she usually did, she left her in their one-room stone apartment with tasks to keep her occupied, and she instructed Tallie not to leave the room alone. Hours into the work, Tallie heard children squealing and ran out to find them chasing a fennec fox through the dirt streets. Long after the playful fennec had eluded the other children, Tallie was still following its tracks, until she'd roamed far from home and into the path of boar hunters whose guides were funneling the beasts their way.

One of the boars chased Tallie up a tree, where she sat for hours, hoping the animal would tire of the wait and leave. Instead, bats came to roost in the treetops and the boar remained. Terrified to climb down, and now terrified to stay in the trees, she cried and called out for Julia to find her, but more hours passed without rescue.

Tallie heard an engine once and held her breath, waiting for Julia to burst through the brush and save her, but no one came. And then the mist that often fell in the forest turned to snow. Between the icy tree limbs and Tallie's shivering, she found it harder and harder to maintain her perch in the tree. Fatigue added to her misery, and she slipped and caught herself several times before help finally arrived. She saw headlights bursting through the darkness, followed by gunfire, which frightened the boar and the bats away. Julia had come!

In Tallie's elated relief, she'd ignored the fact that no engine sounds had immediately preceded Julia's arrival. Instead, the truck lights had suddenly cut through the darkness and then the truck had rolled up. It was then that Tallie knew the first engine sounds, hours earlier, had signaled Julia's arrival, followed by hours of agonizing delay before Julia had actually helped her. Her tears of gratitude had turned bitter.

"You arrived hours ago, didn't you?"

"Yes."

"Why didn't you get me? I was freezing and frightened. I thought I was going to die."

"Don't you know I'd never let that happen? Hopefully, my delay will help you learn a lesson that will keep you safe in the future."

They'd returned to their apartment and sat before a warm fire, sipping broth, when the lesson resumed. *"How did this happen, Tallie?"*

Tallie remembered the shame she'd felt as she listed her mistakes, from her disobedience of Julia's original instruction to remain in the apartment to her ignominious hours spent treed by a boar.

"And?" Julia had demanded.

"I didn't notice the boar tracks."

"Why?"

"Because I was chasing the fennec."

"Chasing a prize narrowed your focus. You saw only what you wanted to see, and you nearly got yourself killed."

Tallie wondered if she had repeated that mistake with Burke, seeing only what she'd wanted to see because she was too busy chasing another prize—her father. Jackson had tried to warn her about Burke, but she had summarily dismissed his concerns, despite knowing she could trust Jackson. What if he was right?

Children and curious adults soon filtered her way in awe of the fancy vehicle and the newcomers in the village. She studied them as they studied her and the vehicle, pointing her way as they chattered among themselves. Tallie didn't sense a threat from them, but she knew how quickly a presumably friendly climate could change. She would not allow herself to become stuck in this SUV like she'd allowed herself to be stuck in a tree. She needed to know whether Burke was a friend or an enemy, and she needed to know now. She rifled through her rucksack for her gun and its silencer and grabbed the keys Burke had left dangling from the ignition. She'd at least make it more difficult for anyone to steal her one means of escape. A thought flashed through her mind about Gerardo Ibarra's skill at dispensing paralytic powders. She quickly dug in her med bag, pulled out a pair of latex gloves, and put them on.

Slipping out of the vehicle, she headed for the block house. The gun bulged under her shirt, causing the mothers to gather their children and scurry away. The young men, however, excitedly followed along behind her.

In Spanish, Tallie asked one of her admirers, "Who lives in the block house?"

"No one," a young man replied. He explained that it wasn't a home. It was the community building—part school, part church, part government center. Prickles rose on Tallie's arms.

"Does a man named senor Ibarra live in your village?"

The boys looked at one another and shook their heads.

Only a few logical possibilities gave Tallie any hope for Burke. The resort manager could have lied about the suspect's name, or Gerardo Ibarra could be living and working under different names. Tallie knew accepting those possibilities forced her to ignore facts unfavorable to Burke like she'd ignoring the boar's tracks while chasing the fennec.

How could Burke have known he'd find Gerardo, or whomever their suspect was, here, at the community's building, at this precise time? He couldn't have unless the two had talked, which meant Burke knew the suspect, a man whose name was probably not Gerardo Ibarra. It looked more and more like

Burke hadn't planned to raid a suspect's house. He'd arranged a *meeting*, and that implied complicity between Burke and Ibarra.

"Did you see a man go into that building before my friend and I arrived?"

The boys again looked at one another, then at the ground. One boy spoke up. "Yes. A stranger, but he's been here before."

"Do you know his name?"

"No, senorita."

Tallie thanked the boy, but she needed to send her little posse away for their own safety, and for hers, before they drew additional attention her way.

"Are you the boys I saw playing soccer over there?" She pointed to the field where she'd spotted the children playing.

Six animated voices replied that they were, and they also pointed to the weedy field across the way. Tallie nodded appreciatively and pulled six fifty-peso notes from her pocket. She waved the small fortune at the boys and said to her new friends, "I'll give each player a fifty-peso note if you play a game right now."

The boys snatched the wad and ran off joyfully toward the weedy field. Soon, happy chatter and the chaos of a pickup game replaced the grim silence of this working community. Finally alone, Tallie surveilled the building's perimeter. Each wall had two glassless windows with curtains that moved in the breeze. The two on the front flanked the door, the lone exit. She stood close to the open window and listened for voices, identifying Burke's and one other's who must be Gerardo. Both were softly speaking Spanish. Burke was appealing to Gerardo, whose only response was a clearly spoken no and muffled phrases that, from their negative tones, appeared to support that position.

Carefully moving around the building to avoid detection, Tallie managed to catch glimpses of the situation in the room. The space was empty except for four chairs in the front of the room and eight benches that sat in two rows of four. She assumed the chairs were for the village leaders who sat in front and that the benches were there to accommodate the people lucky enough to get a seat at all.

She watched Burke move erratically in a small perimeter behind the rows of benches. His gun hung idly in his hand as he spoke to Ibarra, who sat in one of the wooden chairs in the front of the room, holding something Tallie couldn't see well enough to identify. Ibarra appeared to be in control of the meeting. The situation confirmed her greatest fears. Burke hadn't come to arrest Ibarra. He'd come to cut a deal with him, and he was failing.

A phone rang, and Tallie panicked, fearing it was her phone giving away her position. She fumbled to silence it and was relieved to find it wasn't hers after all. She checked it for a signal in case she needed to get a message to Jackson. As she suspected, there was no reliable signal to be had in this little outpost, but a satellite phone would work under these conditions. She'd never seen Burke with one, and she hadn't seen one in his bag of materiel, so she assumed it was Ibarra's. But if Ibarra had such a device, it was further evidence that he had important information someone wanted immediate access to, and she needed to prevent that information from being conveyed.

Trusting her logic, she moved to the door, grabbed the handle, and burst through the entrance with her gun pointed at Ibarra, who held a phone. Instinctively, Burke swung in the direction of the new action and pointed his gun at her, but Tallie remained focused on Ibarra, whose hand slowly lowered in capitulation, moving the satellite phone away from his mouth. Aware that someone was on the other end of the call, Tallie gestured for him to be silent and set the phone down. He nodded, indicating his willingness to comply as his arm and the phone lowered, but then he smiled and threw the phone at her. Tallie reacted instantly and squeezed off one rapid-fire shot, obliterating the device. Burke fired also, directly into Ibarra's chest.

Tallie rushed over to Ibarra and checked for a pulse, knowing there'd be none. "He's dead." Her anger toward Burke spewed out in muted fury. "Why kill him? He's not armed. He posed no threat!" She began a frantic search of Ibarra's pockets. "Now we can't get any answers from him about Kaswell or the others."

"Brown."

Tallie ignored him. Finding nothing in the shirt pockets, she moved on to check the trouser pockets.

"Brown!" Burke repeated more sharply. "What is this pathological obsession you have over rescuing Cai Kaswell?"

She looked at him, hoping to sear him with her disappointment. "You couldn't possibly understand."

Burke's eyes narrowed and his face flushed red as he growled, "You idiot. He's the reason they want you."

Painful confusion weaved through her mind like wisps of toxic gas, poisoning her confidence. She no longer knew when he was lying, when he was telling the truth, or when he was simply toying with her. He wasn't pointing his gun at her anymore, so she focused on what she could control and continued searching the dead man.

There was nothing in Ibarra's left pocket, but his wallet was in his right, and when she pulled it out and opened it, she sank to the floor. Tucked into a clear flap where a driver's license would go was another Mogadishu challenge coin.

"This man took Cai Kaswell." She held up the coin and muttered to herself. "This was his. I found one in his room, but he must have brought several to leave a trail for the major."

"What's on that coin?"

The sound of Burke's voice was like an alarm to Tallie, pulling her back to full alert. She quickly tucked the coin away in her own pocket. She had her proof about Cai's abductor and, sadly, about Burke. She stood and spun on him. "You don't get to ask me anything. I have questions and you're going to answer them." She pointed her gun his way. "You never needed to question Ibarra, did you? You were in on everything from the start. It was a lie. All of it!" she cried out, as much over her profound disappointment in herself as in Burke.

Burke bent slowly and laid his gun on the dirt floor. "You've got to trust me, Brown. More now than ever."

"I can't trust you," she said as she slumped against the wall. "You're a liar and a traitor."

"Lying is a part of this job, Brown. We play the part needed to get the job done. But I'm no traitor. Everything I've ever done is out of love for our country."

"Stop! Just stop!"

"Hear me out, and at the end, you can shoot me or have me arrested, whatever you want. We've only got minutes—two groups of vehicles are heading this way to pick you up. Ibarra sold us both out to the Somali rebels. They made that call, and he told them you're here. My employers were waiting for Ibarra's information. When they realize they can't reach him, they're going to come for us both. Pray they get here first because my people want you as an asset. The Somalis want you as a hostage."

"You set me up."

"You insisted on finding Cai Kaswell. This was how you could find him."

"No! I insisted we find *Ibarra* and question him. I expected my *protector*"—Tallie delivered the word with a sneer—"to contact Major Norris to report our findings and arrange for Cai's rescue. I never signed on to be your prize. What's the going rate for me? A million dollars for my 'brilliant mind'?"

Burke's brow shifted as Tallie tossed one of his many slipups back at him. "I tried to save you. Remember all the times I tried to persuade you to go home? I even bargained with Ibarra for your freedom, but he refused. I'm your only hope right now. Please, trust me, Brown."

The entire surreal situation made her sick. Keeping her gun pointed at Burke, she moved to a corner in case she wretched. "Start at the beginning. You've got three minutes, and then I'm getting into that SUV, whether I let you come or not."

Burke spoke quickly. "I work for a group of international leaders from every sector of life. They call themselves the Conservancy because they're dedicated to saving the planet and its people from catastrophe. I'd been fighting America's battles for fifteen years, and I'd seen the same insanity repeat and repeat and repeat. One president would send us off to fight for a noble cause, and four years later, after blood and treasure were lost protecting an arbitrary line on a map, the next president would enter and pull back, abandoning all we'd suffered to gain."

"You weren't just fighting for a president," Tallie replied angrily. "You were fighting to uphold the Constitution and protect the millions of citizens it represents."

Burke dropped into a chair and gazed up at Tallie. "I laid my life on the line for my country so many times, and I'd gladly do it again if that would keep North America and the world safer and stronger, but I finally realized that the real battle is more insidious. It's ignorance and complacency at home. Aside from the ones who stand on that line, and their families, how many citizens consider the sacrifice that's gone into creating and protecting this country or what's actually written in the Bill of Rights, or in the Constitution that soldiers vow to protect and defend with their lives?"

Tallie was moved by the passion of his argument. "People are imperfect."

He jumped from the chair and looked at her as if she were daft. "It's more than that! Social media has changed the world, Brown. We're like sheep, following the loudest voices." His pacing increased and his rambling grew manic. "If we're going to follow like sheep, then it makes more sense for the wisest minds to chart the future rather than allow a few politicos to draft policies that enrich themselves while the rest of us scratch and fight for crumbs. I thought the Conservancy's ideas sounded mad at first, but I decided to listen one day, and now I think they have a better plan."

Tallie watched the unraveling of this man with alarm. He had appeared so together and confident only hours earlier. "And how does putting power in the hands of fewer people make the US better or the world more free?"

"They harvest the brightest minds and pay them a hefty stipend so they have no motivation other than to do good."

"And to wield power. This Conservancy would end up with more power than a president or Congress, and they wouldn't be elected by the voice of the people."

"Presidents and the Congress become leaders with their own agendas, including to simply get reelected."

"So the people would have no voice? That's akin to slavery," Tallie argued.

"How can it be slavery if everyone is guaranteed a home, healthcare, a job, and an education?"

"And who makes this come true? How do they do it?"

He stopped and glared at her as if she'd picked a raw nerve.

"And what about the individuals who don't comply? Would the Conservancy jail them? Kill them? Give them a paralytic to force them into submission?"

His mouth hung agape until all his features went slack, like melting wax.

"I understand the flaws in our beautiful, wonderful system of government and how someone who's fought to make life better for his countrymen would ache over those flaws, but you also fought for freedom, Burke, and it's not freedom if someone else controls the basics of life. The system you're describing reduces people to being well-kept children. There is no Utopia when individuals have no voice . . . no self-empowerment."

"But some rise and others tank, and the mighty take what they want. Some will always see war as a way to get their share."

Tallie stepped toward him. "You were bargaining with Ibarra for my freedom. Why didn't you want me to be inducted into this system?"

His eyes softened, and a smile pulled at the corner of his mouth. "You still see the US and Cai Kaswell as those bright beacons of hope. You reminded me of how I once felt. I wanted to believe in all that again."

"Believe in it. Maybe we need to work for better candidates and to better educate our citizenry, but don't help overthrow something inspired and aspirational to people across the globe because you've become disillusioned."

Burke crumpled over and whined, "I want to believe again, but I don't know, Brown. I don't know anymore." He straightened and pled with her as he moved toward her. "I wish we could just load up in that SUV and drive away from here, but the Conservancy supplied it and it's being tracked. Letting them take us is our only chance now."

The childlike loss in his voice so disarmed Tallie that by the time he reached her, her guard was down. While his eyes were on hers, he shot his hand forward and snatched the gun from her hands. She fought back, thrusting her right palm into his nose while she punched her left into the tender center of his chest. The blows sent Burke back a step, but his longer arms allowed him to get off a direct blow to her nose just before he stumbled. Stunned, Tallie knew he had the upper hand and could shoot her if he desired, but the shot never came, so she reacted before he regained his balance. With a leap and a turn, she brought her right foot against the side of his head.

Burke fell to the ground and scrambled to his knees. Still in control of the gun, he wiped blood from his nose, leaving a crimson smear, and nodded approvingly at Tallie's bloody nose and the swollen red bulge on her cheek. "That should do it," he said.

Tallie maintained her battle stance, her feet spread apart for balance and her hands poised to fight off another offensive blow if needed.

"I'd heard you were good," he said as he used his sleeve to dab at his gushing nose. "You didn't disappoint."

"Is this all a game to you?"

"I'm trying to give us a tiny chance of surviving this situation," Burke muttered as he paced and pieced his plan together. "The Conservancy will believe Ibarra went rogue, but they already question my loyalty. I hope our battered appearance will support the claim that you fought hard to escape before I subdued you."

Tallie grabbed her aching, bleeding nose and tried to make her head stop spinning. "Do you even hear yourself? Is this your better world?"

"I'm a survivor, and I'm trying to make you one too. I could have shot you, but I didn't. I'm trying to save your life."

She coughed. "And what if I tried to escape right now?"

He raised the pistol and pointed it her way. "I'd shoot you enough to save you."

Tallie believed him. She took a deep breath and choked on blood.

"I think we broke each other's noses," Burke said. "There's a clean handkerchief in my pocket, but my hands are covered in blood. Pull it out, please?"

Tallie grabbed the cloth and held it out for Burke.

He smiled at her and pointed to her face. "You need it more than I do. Suck in a good breath and blow hard to clear the blood out, but don't wipe it away. The worse we both look, the better."

The fabric held a faint aroma Tallie didn't detect until she brought it close.

Burke nodded and looked away. "That's better."

She held it out to him.

He shook his head. "It's best if they see what you did to me. Just drop the handkerchief on the ground."

"Now what?"

"We wait for them to come and hope like crazy that they buy our little drama. I may not survive this, but you will, and I will have kept my word to you. You'll be reunited with Cai Kaswell."

"Twisted words," she spat back at him. "You never tried to call Norris this morning, did you?"

Burke showed no pleasure in admitting with a shake of his head that he had not.

"And the security check?"

"All prearranged the night before, when I sat outside the room alone, deciding whether to follow through with the plan or rescue you."

Tallie's stomach felt as if it would flip, and her head ached so badly she could barely follow Burke's ramblings. "I don't feel well."

"Come. Sit," he said as he led her to a chair. "You'll feel better soon." Once she was settled, he checked his watch and looked outside. "I hear children playing."

"I paid them to play soccer so they wouldn't get caught up in all of this." The mention of children reminded her of Emily. "What about that Amber Alert and that missing child?"

"All arranged by the Conservancy so I could assess your compassion, ingenuity, and abilities."

"So Emily was never lost."

Burke shook his head slowly, shifting his eyes away from her, as if he were ashamed. "She and her mom thought I was directing them in a commercial."

"A commercial?" Her tongue felt thick in her mouth. "That's why you were there beside the mother."

"Yes, and when I left her side, she simply thought I was directing Emily in her rescue scene."

"You lied to them too."

"If it's any comfort to you, Emily was never in any danger. Our people walked beside her and her dog on a parallel trail. We hoped you'd be so focused on following Emily and the dog's trail that you'd ignore the second trail three meters to the side."

Tallie thought about the fennec and the boar. Once again, she'd missed a threat because she was too absorbed in chasing a prize—Emily. "That's why the dog left the trail so often. He was chasing your team."

"I suppose so. They had Emily scuff her feet at the edge to finish the trail, and then they lowered her and her dog down the embankment in a harness rigged over a branch of the tree growing there."

"I should have seen all that."

Burke cleared his throat and rubbed a knuckle into his eye. "Your only concern was Emily, not yourself."

Tallie spoke slowly. "And the Somalian?"

"We knew he was following you, and we allowed him to inject himself into the game to see how you'd respond. The team was impressed by how you handled yourself."

"And yet you said I messed up the plan. What was the plan?" she mumbled.

"You were expected to suffer Cai Kaswell's fate when you checked into your room down here. You'd fall asleep, we'd get you out, and you'd wake up at Conservancy headquarters, where you'd see and hear about their goals. But you picked up on how Ibarra disarmed the victims, and I became conflicted as I worked with you. Your loyalty to country, joy for life, and compassion for me . . . You made me doubt my loyalties. Elena saw my confusion."

"Elena?"

"The redheaded woman you thought was the director of housekeeping. She sensed I was having second thoughts about delivering you. She knew the truth before I did."

"I can't feel my fingers or feet. What did you do to me?"

"Shh . . . you'll feel better in a while. I promise. We need to prepare before they get here. They're going to destroy our phones when they arrive."

Tallie vaguely sensed his touch on her wrist.

"I'm removing your smartwatch and sticking it into your boot. Let's hope they don't search you that closely. Major Norris and the team just might be able to find you if they home in on that watch's signal."

Burke suddenly tipped his head, as if to better hear something. "Vehicle engines. Two, maybe three. Someone's here." He looked out the window. "It's the Conservancy's team, but don't be afraid. They won't hurt you. You're very important to them, and I'll do everything in my power to set you free again. It might be my last noble act on this earth, but if need be, I'll give my life to freeing you, because Elena was right. You've become personal to me, Brown."

Tallie didn't hear his final words. The paralytic powder in the handkerchief had done its work.

CHAPTER TWELVE

Jackson watched the staff move like hummingbirds, flitting from their stations to Mak or Rich, who gathered their printed reports like cards in their hands. They eventually scanned each piece of new info and assigned it to one of three outcomes:

- send back to the intelligence unit for further review
- viable and ready to be posted to the large monitors
- scrap as insignificant

Very little was getting scrapped.

A whispered nervousness passed through the Crib, like a quiet tsunami, sending researchers back to their desks in a musical chairs–like scramble. All eyes were on the door, and Jackson soon understood why when an all-too-familiar voice bellowed out a string of expletives that served no informational purpose other than to put everyone on alert that he had arrived.

"Rich! Mak! Before you tell me why you asked me down here, I want you to tell me why Burke hasn't checked in with me in twenty-four hours!"

The two operators looked at one another, knowing full well that Major Norris was not going to like the answer.

"He's not answering our calls anymore either, Major," Mak said.

Rich rubbed his shaved head as if delaying the coming upsetting news. "That's one of the reasons we called you down here. We think Burke may have gone rogue."

Norris halted instantly. After a lengthy pause, he bellowed across the room again. "Can anyone in this room come up with any other plausible reason Burke hasn't checked in?"

All eyes darted away from Norris and to the floor, and Norris turned back to Rich and Mak.

"Sure. He could have lost his phone or his charger, or he could be on a drinking binge, or maybe he fell off a cliff," Rich said.

"Thank you, wise guy. Let's hold off on calling a brother a traitor until we've ruled out accidents or blatant stupidity."

"Ordinarily, I'd be the last one to call my best friend a traitor," Rich said, "but there's more."

Norris drilled down on Rich. "Opinions or proof?"

"At the very least, some pretty incriminating circumstantial evidence."

The major's tall frame bent forward until one hand pressed against the desktop. Leaning heavily into it, he groaned in a low rumble. "Is Tallie Brown still with him?"

"Oh, I'm sure she is, wherever that is," Jackson answered, scowling.

Norris shot a look Jackson's way. "You've got something to say? I'm listening."

"Tallie texted me that they were headed to a village called Lugar de Sueños to pick up the suspect, a guy named Gerardo Ibarra. She didn't trust Burke when she met him, but then he won her over. I think her doubts were returning when she sent me that text. She wanted to make sure I knew where he was taking her."

Norris drilled into Rich and Mak. "What do we know about this suspect?"

Mak took the lead. "He's a lackey, not the mastermind. Prior to this he was just a small-time dealer for one of the cartels. This gig at the resort was his first legit job in years."

"So someone hired him because he's dispensable," Norris said.

"That's how I read it," Rich said.

Norris pressed his palm to his forehead. "Have you assigned someone to get a read on Burke's and Tallie's phones to verify their location?"

"They're still at Lugar de Sueños," Mak said.

"Good."

But from Jackson's view, Norris didn't appear to think it was good at all.

"You." Norris looked at Jackson, then moved his gaze to Rich and Mak. "And you two. In a conference room with me, right now."

The four men gathered in a small room. Jackson noticed relief on the faces of the other researchers and assumed it was either because Norris brought a new level of confidence with him to the sagging effort or because they were grateful not to have been summoned into the meeting. More interesting was the effect Norris's disappointment and worry had on the leaders of the group. Rich and Mak were quiet and delicate in presenting their reports, and

Jackson wondered if their respect for Norris made the bad news more painful or if they, too, feared the man.

"Don't read me a book about everything you *think* you know. Give me bullet points on what you *do* know. Now."

Mak deferred to Rich, who slapped reports on the table each time he made a point. "We know Burke was in on that Amber Alert Miss Brown answered."

Norris grunted. "We talked when we met in Mexico. Burke explained his presence there. He said General Kaswell asked him to pull personal protective duty on Tallie because of the news interest she was generating."

"Did he also tell you the whole event was a trick to lure Miss Brown out?" Rich said.

Norris's jaw ground left and right. "Continue."

"Tallie received a preprogrammed alert on her phone before the missing child was reported to the sheriff. Burke received that alert too. His phone's metadata proves that. They arrived at the scene in the middle of nowhere mere minutes after the sheriff issued an alert. Burke's phone data also shows a text about the Somalis' plan to grab her, and it didn't come from us. He let their guy get close enough to Tallie for an intervention to be required."

Norris rubbed his face so hard over this news that the right side turned as red as the scarred left. "Tallie fought him off?"

"Burke intervened while Tallie was down the embankment with the child."

Jackson knew most of these details—he'd even discovered some of them—but hearing them laid out this way made him feel small and inadequate to support her. Things were way beyond his control.

"And it gets messier," Mak added. "We now know the actresses who played the mother and daughter were hired by a small German holding company with ties to Bartrum Drummond."

"Burke's future father-in-law," Norris said.

"Not anymore, Major," Mak said. "At least, according to Penelope Drummond's Instagram page."

"So Drummond isn't going to have a personal soldier for a son-in-law."

Rich changed his stance, as if getting settled before delivering the next bit of news. "His claws are deep into Burke, wedding or not, Major. And he's snagged us as well, it seems."

"What are you talking about?"

"Here's where it gets personal." Rich spread some more papers out on the table. "Drummond is tied to IBT, who contracted with you to have us transport anonymous VIPs around the globe. Check out the dates and locations on this spreadsheet. We led caravans of vehicles, but we only made a point to meet the drivers. We never met the passengers. We may have been ignorant coconspirators in delivering kidnapped business and government leaders from their hotels into their captors' hands."

Norris's face turned gray as he stared at the sheets. "Drummond claimed they were humanitarian missions." He grabbed the back of a chair and squeezed it until his knuckles turned white. "Are we still getting signals from Burke's and Tallie's cell phones?"

Mak checked the computer screen. "We have five signals—a satellite phone, two cell phones, and two others . . . watches maybe."

"Tallie has a smartwatch!" Jackson chimed. "I have the number." As he scrolled through his phone, he felt his throat tighten at the wonder of how happy and simple the day had been when he'd convinced Tallie to buy the watch.

He knew his rapid blinking was setting off a hundred signals to these body-language readers that he was falling apart over all the news about Tallie.

Mak gave his shoulder a pat. "That's good, Jackson. Real helpful. Thanks."

It probably wasn't helpful at all. They probably already had all that information, including the color of her watchband, from hacking into the phone store's records. But what could he do? Tallie wasn't answering calls or texts to her phone or her watch. He was useless to her, and that realization was crushing him.

It appeared to be crushing Norris as well; he hung his head as he leaned over the table littered with condemning paperwork. "I want everything you have on Drummond, and as for any other intel you have, just give it to me straight. What's the long and short?"

"It gets worse, I'm afraid," Rich said. "IBT is just one think tank owned by a large-umbrella corporation called the Conservancy. IBT focuses on education and intellectual pursuits, but the other trusts cover financial interests, journalism, social media, scientific and medical research, and military intelligence. The names associated with each of these trusts are among the best and brightest minds in the world, and they claim their purpose is to develop policies and forecast future trends in their respective areas."

"And the missing leaders all fall into one of those categories," Mak added.

Norris wiped his hand over his face. "What are you implying? If someone they want doesn't accept their invitation to join, they just kidnap them?"

"Tallie texted me asking about IBT," Jackson said. "She's onto them. What if they know that? Or what if Burke's whole plan was to kidnap Tallie for them? They've got General Kaswell. What if she's leverage to make him cooperate?"

"Leverage against the general? For what?" Rich shook his head. "He's grateful to her for respecting his family at that crash, but even if they do have Miss Brown, how could they possibly think she's important enough to him for the general to be manipulated? That's a bridge too far for me, logically."

Jackson and the major exchanged a knowing glance. Jackson wasn't about to have Tallie's life risked because Mak and Rich didn't know the truth of her relationship to Kaswell. He huffed and was about to spill what he knew when Mak piped in.

"Don't worry, Jackson. We're not saying she isn't important."

Norris laid a hand on Jackson's shoulder and gave him a look that stopped him from sharing what he knew about Cai and Tallie. "She matters to all of us." He spoke softly and with a tenderness far different from the tone he used with his team. "We're going to get her back no matter who might have her, and I want Burke too. This is personal . . . to all of us."

"Drummond *is* pretty persuasive," Mak said.

"And he's set us up so we look dirty too," Rich added.

"Are you two yahoos trying to excuse Burke's betrayal?" Norris said.

"Not at all," Rich said. "We're just pointing out that we look just as bad as he does. We're implicated in those kidnappings. We've got IBT's initials on our gear. We're easy scapegoats. If the Pentagon or Capitol Hill gets wind of this, we're going down."

Norris tried to calm the panic rising in the room. "Let's verify something instead of speculating. What assets can we scramble to get some real-time intel down there?"

Mak stepped out of room. "Dante! What drones are near Lugar de Sueños?"

The thirty-something researcher typed something and brought up a list on the giant monitors. The listed items were identified only by acronyms and numbers. Coordinates were listed beside them. "El Chapo's Sinaloa Cartel has two birds monitoring a camp near there."

"Can you hack into them?"

"Yes . . ." Dante's eyes grew wide. "But we could be bringing the cartel down on Burke's position."

Mak looked back at Norris. "It's your call, Major."

Norris straightened and stared at the fact sheets on the table. "Mak, grab that drone. We just need eyes on that village for a few minutes. Then get me everything you have on this Conservancy. Rich, put a call into Drummond, pronto."

Mak and Rich headed out to attend to their respective assignments. Jackson started to follow them when Norris asked him to stay and close the door. "I'm sorry, Jackson. I never should have involved Tallie in this."

Though he wanted to pile on and indict the man for anything and everything that had happened to Tallie as a result of that decision, Jackson refrained. Norris was taking it all very personally, and causing him to unravel wouldn't benefit anyone.

Norris walked to the glass wall and stared out over the bustling room of people trying to rescue Tallie. "In the beginning, soon after Julia took Tallie, I went along with her demands to keep her stable and to protect Tallie. I fooled myself into believing I'd find a way to get her away from Julia and back to Cai and Deidre, but I failed them. The Kaswells were picking up their lives and moving on, and I told myself that keeping the secret of what had really happened to their baby protected them from further pain. That was partially true, but I was also lying to myself. I kept that secret because I didn't want to be hated by the man I respected most in the world. Regardless of the medals I've won, that decision makes me the worst kind of coward." He sat on the edge of the desk and dropped his eyes to the floor. "Tallie hates me because I made the choices that cemented their fates. I told her about Cai and invited her to make her own choice this time because I didn't want her to accuse me of repeating that mistake. But I shouldn't have. I should have protected her." His voice broke, and he coughed to clear the emotion. "I got it wrong both times."

Jackson never would have believed he could feel sympathy for the military rock, but it came in an overwhelming flood. He didn't know what to do—whether to offer him some touch of physical support or to speak words of absolution. He sat beside the man who'd shaped and tortured him for years, the man who'd given him the chance to exchange his lofty dreams of personal glory for a life of service. "You did the right thing," he said. "She never would have forgiven you if you'd bypassed her, and there was no way she would have stayed behind once she knew."

Norris smiled through trembling lips.

"How's Marlene doing?" Jackson asked.

"Better. Almost back to full speed." He bit his upper lip. "Thanks for asking."

"They're two amazing women."

"They are. Tallie gave me the information about the neurotoxin the doctors needed to save Marlene. Now we're going to save Tallie." Norris set his hand on Jackson's shoulder. "It's time to go on offense."

"There has to be something I can do to help."

"Right now, just keep us out of the weeds and focused on Tallie. Doing that is more important than you know." Norris stood with his old swagger and opened the door to the Crib. "Rich! Mak! What's the word?"

"Dante has a bird tracking three vehicles pulling up to a block structure in the village," Mak said.

Norris's jaw tensed and bulged. "Get that bird's pictures on the big screen now. I want to see who comes out of that building and what their condition is. Do we still have a beat on those phones?"

"I'll check. You should know we've got photos of an SUV that was already parked nearby. We assume that was the vehicle Burke and Tallie used to get there. We've got a shot of the tags. We're running them now for registration info."

"Wait, look!" Dante pointed.

Fear ripped through Jackson like a cold knife, and all chatter in the Crib silenced as everyone watched the events playing out on the screen. Three armed men and a red-haired woman exited the three vehicles that had just arrived. Two other men followed them into the building, pushing a gurney. Minutes later, a collective gasp was heard as everyone witnessed two of the men carrying a still, blanket-wrapped body by its arms and feet. When they reached the first vehicle, the body was unceremoniously tossed into the back.

Jackson didn't realize how badly he was shaking until Mak wrapped an arm across his shoulders to hold him up.

"That's probably Ibarra," Mak said.

The stark reality of the situation slammed Jackson. "He's dead. What's that mean for Tallie?"

"That's actually a hopeful sign," Mak said. "It might mean Burke fought back. If he did, then we haven't completely lost him."

That news was some relief, and then Burke appeared under an armed escort, arguing as he kept looking back over his shoulder. The reason for his concern was soon evident when Tallie appeared, limp, lifeless, and battered on the gurney.

Jackson's hands flew to his head and then to his mouth as he cried out, "She's hurt! They hurt her!" He couldn't watch, and yet he couldn't bear to look away.

The redheaded woman fussed over her all the way to the second vehicle, where Tallie was carefully transferred to a bed in the back.

"She'll be okay," Mak said. "You saw how they're caring for her. Right now, it's Burke I'm worried about."

The men guarding Burke threw him face first against the vehicle, leaving him stunned and bloodied before they shoved him into the last SUV. When all the doors were closed, the vehicles began pulling back out with Tallie in the middle vehicle and Burke riding in the one pulling up the rear.

"Oh, oh, oh, oh!" Dante yammered. "We've got trouble!" He pulled the drone back, widening the view to show two heavily armed trucks spewing a cloud of dust as they sped down the dirt roads in pursuit of their hijacked drone.

"Tallie!" Jackson yelped.

"I read two RPGs and two M240s on those trucks," Rich said. "If they find that caravan, they'll destroy those SUVs."

"Unless they're armored," Norris corrected. "Let's hope they are. Head the drone away from that caravan," he barked, "and let's hope those trucks follow it."

The Conservancy's first two vehicles broke right at the first turn, speeding away from the cartel's position, but the third vehicle was cut off by the arriving cartel trucks.

"Oh my," Mak muttered. "Burke bought himself a mess of trouble this time."

"We're losing sight of Tallie!" Jackson hollered.

Norris pointed at the screen. "Dante, don't lose those first two vehices."

Dante pounded his keyboard in utter futility. "The cartel changed the frequency. I'm not controlling the drone anymore. They are."

One man exited the SUV containing Burke and took aim at the hovering drone above. In three shots, the screen went dead.

"Dante!" Norris yelled. "Get us another asset in the air. Don't lose that caravan."

A female voice across the Crib called out, "The phones and one watch went dead before they left the building, but we're still getting a read on one watch. We're tracking it."

"Don't lose that signal! Dante, what's the word on a new drone?"

"I can't raise any, Major. It's like the cartel took them all off-line."

Jackson turned on Norris. "Now what? Do something!"

Norris swung around to Rich. "What's the word from Drummond?"

"The official word is that he's unavailable. Would you like me to take a team over there and shake that tree?"

"No," Norris said with a diabolic glint. "I've got a better idea. See if you can scare me up a flight to Drummond Engineering Corp."

"You want me to procure a chopper for a ten-minute flight to Fairfax?"

"That's right. Drummond Engineering has a helipad on its roof. I want you and three others in full gear. We're going to remind these traitors exactly who they're toying with. And, Mak, I think it's time to do a little housekeeping around here."

"Sir?"

"Grab some men and some trucks and load up every piece of garbage that has the IBT logo on it. Meet us over at Drummond's place, and bring a pack of matches."

"Yes, sir!"

Jackson grabbed Norris's arm without worrying about the man's reaction. "Give me something to do, or I'll lose my mind with worry."

"Help Mak load those trucks. It's time to turn the tables on them."

CHAPTER THIRTEEN

Stephen Norris loved the precision of his team. Even Jackson caught hold of Blue 12's rhythm as he worked beside Mak to load the IBT material into a truck. Mak's convoy of trucks left first, but Stephen was in the air in thirty minutes, accompanied by Rich, three other wall-sized men, and a woman with a gun the size of her body. He never wanted to take these soldiers' loyalty for granted. He understood how precarious the line was between a leader's patriotism and their egotism. His team had followed him into the political equivalent of hell and back, and he knew they'd do it again and again, if need be, but that kind of loyalty was a heady drug that could turn well-intentioned leaders into dictators. He'd come far too close to that line in his career, and he was afraid Drummond had completely crossed over. He'd know soon enough. Three minutes out from their destination, he shot Rich an approving wink. "Good work on the chopper."

"Your name still carries a lot of clout, Major."

"That's good to hear. If things go sideways at Drummond's place, we're going to need whatever I've got left to get Cai and Tallie back."

"Whatever you need, we're on board, sir."

"I appreciate that. We're playing hardball when we land."

Rich smiled. "Understood." He touched his headpiece. "Mak says he and his team are in place, but the guard at Drummond's front gate won't let them in." He pressed his bald head against the glass and scanned the bustling North Virginian corridor below. "We're approaching Drummond's place, and yep . . . there's Mak and the boys."

Stephen stretched his neck to see where Rich was pointing. A satisfied smile pulled at his normally stern mouth at the sight of the group's two trucks at the company's front gate, loaded with desks and beds and anything else Drummond had secured from IBT.

"Who's driving that second truck?"

Rich smiled. "Jackson James. He's a good man."

"Do you think he's licensed to drive a big truck like ours?"

Rich laughed. "Major, I think that's the least of our worries today."

"Copy that." Stephen laughed. "Rich, patch me in to Mak."

"Roger that. Go ahead, Major."

"Mak, tell the guards you can either deliver the goods to their loading dock or dump them on the sidewalk."

"Roger that," Mak said.

A call came through the pilot's radio, denying them the right to land. He relayed the info to Stephen, who unbuckled his seat belt and walked to the cabin, his lips pressed tightly. "Hand me that radio."

When the mic was in his hand, he said, "Tell Drummond that Major Stephen Norris is calling. He can let me land nicely, or I can tell my men down in that truck by your gate to target that prized thousand-gallon saltwater tank in your boss's office with their M82."

Several moments of silence passed, and then the voice came back on. "You are cleared to land."

"We appreciate your cooperation," Stephen said sarcastically. The soldiers cheered at the news, and he couldn't help but laugh at that first victory. He returned to the mic. "One more thing. Ask my good friend Bart how much he'd enjoy having the press run down here to cover the fire at your complex."

"What fire?"

"The one we're going to set in your street unless someone orders the guards at the gate to let our trucks through."

As the helicopter slowly landed, Stephen saw the gates roll open and Mak and the team drive through. Up on the roof, three armed security guards appeared, tasked to meet the craft and its occupants. Stephen exited first. He looked at the men and said, "Seriously?" as heavily armed Rich and his associates exited the chopper. Stephen actually grew nervous thinking that one of Drummond's yahoos might be foolish enough to start a war on the company roof.

The door to the roof opened again, and a tall older man rushed out yelling, "Stand down! Stand down, you imbeciles. I didn't authorize him to land so you could have an armed spitting contest." Drummond's security staff immediately obeyed their boss and lowered their weapons. "Take his men to the executive lounge and order them anything they want. Major Norris and I will be in my office. Don't disturb us until we call for you."

Stephen nodded to Rich, okaying the plan, and his team filed away after Drummond's security team. "Good to see you, Bart. Impressive run you just did. I see you've been putting that fancy Peloton to good use."

"How did you know I—" He stopped, likely because he already knew the answer.

"So nice of you to come down and meet me in person," Stephen added.

"I only did that to prevent you and your morons from kicking down my building's doors."

"You know me too well. And, by the way, does your invitation for my men to visit the executive lounge extend to my team on the ground? I'd advise you to say yes since the alternative is for them to follow through on their initial mission."

"Which is?"

Stephen leaned in and narrowed his eyes. "To pile up every stick of furniture and every piece of technology you gave us bearing the IBT insignia and set it ablaze right here on your corporate grounds."

Drummond's previous confidence and pomp fled, evidenced by the conspicuous sag in his shoulders, a silent admission of guilt. "Then, you've figured it out too. I'm sorry, Stephen. I hope you'll believe me when I say that I'm as worried about this IBT situation as you are. Come with me, please. I have so much to tell you."

Drummond led the way to his office, an elegant sprawling suite that accommodated him and three personal assistants. The walls were lined with photos of Drummond Engineering's military hardware being used in various military theaters across the globe. There were more than a dozen framed photos of Drummond himself, standing beside camo-clad generals, admirals, and lesser officers of every military branch. Stephen stopped by a picture of himself standing with Drummond and Cai at a D.C. event. His expression must have revealed his worries over his friend, because Drummond also stopped as he shook his head almost imperceptibly.

"How is General Kaswell doing?"

Stephen swung on him. "You tell me."

Drummond sputtered for several seconds. "Why . . . how would I . . . ? Are you saying . . . ?"

Stephen pinned him against the hanging photo using his forearm as a restraint against Drummond's neck. "When I leave here, I want to have a doctoral-level understanding of IBT and the Conservancy—the who, the where, the why, the how, and the what your part is in this is. Are we clear?"

His captive made no effort to break free, but the man's flushed and then paling coloring prompted Stephen to back off.

Drummond's knees nearly buckled as he gasped for breath. "My reputation is being ruined by the Conservancy, and IBT is but a small part. You could have done me a favor by simply killing me."

"Don't leave me regretting that decision. Start talking."

Drummond stretched his neck and coughed softly as he made his way to the sofa. "I had nothing to do with this. You've got to know that." He dropped into the cushion and bent forward, staring at the floor. "The director's name is Joseph Howard, the former owner of Mercury Intel and about a dozen other international companies."

"Joseph Howard?" The name was a familiar one to Stephen, and he prayed this Joseph Howard was not the man he once knew.

"Joseph went by J. J. then, for Joseph Junior. We both landed at Mercury after college, where I met him. He was a good guy back in Mercury's early days. A true red, white, and blue patriot who loved the United States. I left the company and veered into military hardware, but J. J. stayed. His computerized simulation software made Mercury billions and made him a rock star to the Pentagon brass, but Mercury took his skills for granted and didn't compensate him to the level he deserved. He decided to take a job with a competitor, and then he ran Mercury into the ground and bought her back two years later for pennies on the dollar."

Regret hollowed Drummond's face. "We were both enjoying great success, and we lost contact over the years. I reached out to him when I heard that his wife had passed away from an apparent suicide. Their only child, a daughter, was quite young when her mother passed. J. J. vowed to devote more of his time to his little girl going forward, so he turned Mercury over to his board and bought an international development company that specialized in government contracts—building military bases, embassies, consulates, and the like. Then he hired people to run that business as well so he could stay closer to his daughter."

Stephen's hands trembled as pieces of the puzzle began to fill in.

"He didn't stick with his plan. When the opportunity to develop the military's next generation of software came to him, he jumped at the chance, but when the final program was ready for testing, some of the military's IT pros had reservations about the programs."

"I remember there were security issues with Mercury's software. Like a backdoor the company built into the program."

"Yes. J.J. did that, but he has a golden tongue. The louder the IT people protested the sale, the more bases and expos he visited, giving speeches and building his following into a patriotic cult. The highest-ranking decision-makers felt he was a trusted patriot, and they set aside their concerns to buy his cutting-edge package. He became Mr. America, and the sale closed despite the experts' reservations. But then he lost his way."

Drummond paused to collect his thoughts, but Stephen pressed him on. "I'm listening."

"J.J. was invited to speak at one of the party's conventions on the topic of national security. He had the crowd on their feet, and afterward, he was installed as the head of one of the most powerful political-action committees in American politics. Surely you've attended some conference and heard him speak."

"Can't say that I have. Unlike you, I haven't spent my career trying to be one of the popular kids on the playground. I wasn't into procurement. I was more of an end-user kind of soldier."

Drummond's eyebrows narrowed. "I don't know what I was thinking, believing I could have a civil conversation with a social moron like you."

Stephen ignored the jab. "Let me guess. J.J. parlayed his popularity into even more powerful connections with politicians, the military, and the companies that support our military."

"Yes, but his reach is much broader than that," Drummond said. "He hosted elite charity dinners for worthy causes that drew celebrity athletes, Hollywood's A-listers, and media moguls. They love him too, and they repeat whatever line he throws at them."

"Is that why you broke ties with him?"

"I started pulling back from him some time ago when I realized the nice guy I once knew had built a propaganda machine of blindly loyal influencers willing to pick up their proverbial swords to support and spread any idea, person, or action he put forward, no matter how radical."

"Expanding his circle of influence exponentially. And now he's dropped off the face of the earth and decided he knows what's best for everyone."

Drummond nodded soberly. "That was his reaction to a personal tragedy."

"Did he lose someone else he loved?"

Drummond's eyes closed and his head bowed for a few silent seconds. "His daughter."

Pained silence hung in the space between the two men. Stephen had almost lost his only child twice in just a few weeks. He had fortunately been able to save her, but as much as he hated to admit it, in those hours when her life hung in the balance, he'd became familiar with a father's hunger for retribution. He knew all too well the lengths a father would go to save a child . . . or might go to avenge the loss of one.

"The death of his child made him hate the free world? Who did he blame?"

"Himself, mostly. She committed suicide, like her mother, after she returned home from deployment."

Stephen winced. "She was a soldier."

Drummond nodded and crossed one leg over the other as he leaned back into the sofa. "Against his wishes. The sad thing is J. J. discovered the military actually gave her confidence and strengthened her. He started bragging about his soldier daughter in his speeches, especially after she'd been promoted and was doing well. And then she went to Somalia on a peacekeeping mission. Everything went wrong on that mission, and a few months after returning home, she took her own life."

The word *Somalia* hit Norris like a lightning strike. He clasped his hands to still their shaking. *Howard . . . daughter . . . suicide . . . soldier . . . Somalia . . .* There was no denying this was the same man. "You said his name is Joseph Howard?"

"Yes, but once he took over Mercury, he began using a more formal iteration: J. Rutherford Howard."

It was a name with which Stephen was devastatingly familiar. Mr. Howard had not been his reportedly charismatic self when Stephen met him at the man's lavish estate to deliver his part in Julia's ploy to fake her death—the news of his daughter, Diana's, passing.

Drummond leaned forward, his expression turning curious. "If I didn't know better, I'd swear you'd seen a ghost. You can't know how much it pleases me to think something I've told you put a fright in you for a change."

Drummond's glee reset Stephen's determination. He pulled out the revolver tucked into the back of his trousers and aimed it at Drummond's prized aquarium. "It brings me pleasure to put a fright in you as well."

The businessman leaped to his feet, sputtering apologies.

"Shall we return to the topic at hand?" Stephen asked.

Drummond slowly lowered back onto the sofa. "You're insane. What more do you need from me?"

"How did this grieving father, J.J. Howard, set his sights on world domination?"

"He placed part of the blame for his daughter's death on the United States' international policies. He tried to effect change in those policies by using his charm and intelligence to gather like-minded people in government, media, and education, but he saw corruption everywhere and became disillusioned with government in general. That's when I began suspecting he was working outside the normal channels. I don't know how or by whom he's amassed his fortune, but it's the size of a small nation's gross national product. And he went dark with the rise of social media, funneling his decidedly anti-government propaganda through his vast army of celebrity puppets. That's why I finally parted company with him."

"Is that why you also parted company with Burke?" Stephen asked.

"Cooper?"

Stephen counted almost six seconds before the man took another breath.

"Oh no." Drummond's face twisted into worry. "Of course. It all makes sense now." He scooted to the edge of the sofa and leaned toward Stephen. "You have to believe me when I tell you I loved Burke like a son, but he took a new job without telling Penny it would require them to relocate to some remote island. He almost had her convinced to go, saying it would be a paradise, but he let it slip that returning home would be difficult and that she should plan not to see us for a few years. That was the deal breaker for her. She tried to convince him to work for me instead, but he wouldn't hear of it, and she called off the engagement."

"Tell me more about this island. Is this Howard's own personal Eden?"

Drummond sighed and flopped back like an expiring balloon. "Perhaps. I don't know."

"You said Burke described it as a paradise. What else did he tell Penny?"

"I don't know anything more."

Stephen needed this info, and he wasn't above scaring this man to get it. "Perhaps you'd prefer I find Penny and interrogate her instead."

"No!" Drummond jumped up again. "You wouldn't!"

"Then, talk to me."

"What do you want me to tell you? It must be tropical, or at least warm, and beautiful all year round. I'm just deducing that. Do you want me to simply make up other details to satisfy your need to intimidate me? How would that help Cai or anyone else?"

"It wouldn't, but if I find out you've lied about anything or withheld intel, I'll be back, and you'll like that visit even less."

"Oh, I have no doubt you'd love nothing better than to smash a few doors and knock me around in the name of patriotism, but not everyone is an enemy, Stephen."

"Why didn't you notify me or someone else as soon as you suspected Joseph Howard had gone rogue?"

Drummond hung his head and groaned. "I don't know. I wish I had, but it felt gestapoish to turn someone in to the government on nothing more than a hunch." He raked his fingers through his thinning hair. "We can't destroy the Constitution's freedoms because we disagree politically with someone. Heaven help us if the day comes when a difference of opinions is ground for labeling someone a traitor."

"It's so much more than that with Howard. He's trying to overthrow governments, Bart."

"I know, I know. And worse, I fear. If he hacks into our defenses . . ." He shuddered.

Stephen's hand moved to his mouth, and he mumbled, "He could hijack our tanks and ships and silos."

"I believe he could, and worse. I have some very worrisome invoices for parts he's ordered over the years. He may have armed that island."

"Are you talking nuclear silos?"

"Not yet. Our satellites would have picked up something like that, but if you're capable of disarming the world and you've loaded your island with the best materials, scientists, and engineers and convinced them your actions are necessary to ensure world peace . . ."

"He could easily build what he needs to become a superpower." Stephen stood a few shaky moments longer before finally slipping down into a chair across from Drummond.

"But honest to goodness, Stephen, sometimes you scare me more than Joseph Howard. You make everything so personal."

The observation stung Stephen. Was he on the right side of the line? His methods might get extreme occasionally, but he reasoned that necessity warranted extreme measures. This was such a time, and if Bart Drummond's fear of him helped move the effort along, so be it.

"You have no idea how dangerously personal this situation is, Bart, to everyone. A member of my team was set up by a group who drew her out with a fake Amber Alert. They specifically used European-born actresses your company hired a few years back for an ad promoting some device you guys made. Want to explain that coincidence to me?"

Drummond's face twisted, and Stephen knew the man was honestly trying to recall the event. Moments ticked by and then Drummond shot forward, success beaming on his face. "He had access to their names and hiring info because that ad was for one of Joseph's goodwill projects. We applied military technology to build prosthetics for children hurt by landmines."

Even Stephen couldn't offer a snide comment to that.

Drummond pled with him. "Can't you see how cunning he is? He's like the mafia of goodness, requesting favors from those he's helped and implicating anyone who crosses him."

"Let's say I believe you. Do you have enough pull with Howard to get someone recruited into his inner circle?"

"Like who?"

"I'll be in touch with a name or two this afternoon."

Stephen exited the office and radioed his men. Mak's team had off-loaded all the IBT material, so he ordered them back to base. He ordered Rich's team back to the chopper. As soon as the bird was in the air, Stephen turned to Rich. "Are we still able to get a beat on Tallie Brown's watch?"

"No, sir. It went dead about an hour ago."

Stephen bit down until his jaw bulged. "So they found and disabled it. What was the last position?"

"About fifty miles southeast of the pickup point, near the coast."

"It sounds as if Drummond was telling the truth about the Conservancy's location. Get Jackson James and anyone you can spare to scour the southern waters for communication traffic, unusual air and sea transport, and anything else that could indicate a city in the middle of an ocean."

"That's a third of the earth. Can you narrow that down a bit?"

"No. And that's why I need you to start yesterday."

CHAPTER FOURTEEN

GAUZE.

Everything Tallie felt and heard and saw and tried to say seemed wrapped in gauze. Two voices flitted through her mind. Both were female. Both were soothing and calm. Her lips couldn't give voice to the random thoughts darting in and out of her consciousness, so she tried to raise a hand and reach the beings attached to the voices, but her hand barely lifted from the white linen upon which she laid, if it moved at all.

"Lei, she's coming around," one voice said.

Soon gentle hands were on Tallie, smoothing her hair back and adjusting tubes that pulled on her skin.

An IV. Tallie tried to pull on the tube, but the second voice drew near, talking softly as hands held hers, machines beeping and humming in the background. Tallie blinked several times, forcing her mind and eyes to work in tandem to identify what was happening around her.

A brown face hovering over her placed a straw near her lips and said, "Hello, sweetie. My name's Livvie. Just rest and sip this. It'll help you awaken from the veil drugs."

"Drugs?" Tallie mumbled.

"Yes, Tallie," the woman said sympathetically. "Some people awake rested and clear, but the veil drugs leave others muddled and nauseous. I'm afraid you fall into that second category, poor thing. But don't you worry," Livvie chirped cheerfully. "We're going to take special care of you. You're our honored guest. The director himself wants to share supper with you when you're ready."

Tallie felt as if she were swimming through sand, powerless and unable to ascertain her surroundings or what had happened to bring her here. One name came to her, and she uttered it. "Burke."

"There you go," one of the women said. She must be the one Livvie had called Lei. "This is very good. You're coming out of the fog now. So you've met our dashing Captain Burke." She turned to Livvie. "Was Captain Burke Miss Brown's escort?"

"I don't think so. Captain Burke is not listed on her escort form."

Tallie's mind was like a kaleidoscope that offered little more than jagged glimpses of her memories. She was slowly putting pieces together, but nothing made sense.

"Burke?" she muttered.

"I'm sorry, sweetie. He's not here," Lei said.

Tallie could now see the women were both dressed in nurses' attire. Everything in the room indicated that this was a medical facility with top-rung equipment.

"See him. I need to see him," Tallie repeated with all the emphasis she could manage.

"Livvie?" Lei asked. "Can we locate him?"

"We can ask around, but he's probably escorting other guests."

Lei brushed Tallie's hair back from her face. "Was Captain Burke your contact, Tallie? All guests get one."

"I'm not a guest."

"Of course you are," Livvie replied. "A very important guest."

"No. A prisoner. Kidnapped."

"Oh no, Lei. She's really deluded. Did the doctor leave orders for meds for her?"

"No. Just an authorization for sensory deprivation therapy."

"Really? In her state of mind?"

The words would have increased Tallie's anxiety, but the women and their voices, so soft and caring, were her only defense, so she placed her trust in them.

She was already undressed down to her underwear beneath a hospital gown. The women spoke soothingly to her as the gown was removed.

"Have you ever heard of a sensory deprivation tank, Tallie?" Lei asked. "It's restful and quiet, and it helps calm the mind and body."

They covered Tallie's body with a sheet and wheeled her down the hall to a room. Inside, there was with a podlike tank with its cover raised.

Livvie held Tallie's hand and smiled. "I'm placing this monitor on your wrist. We'll get constant feedback on your heart rate and respiration."

"And we'll be right here, monitoring you every minute," Lei added. "If you feel uncomfortable, or if you need anything, just call out and we'll hear."

Sleep still pulled at Tallie, but her eyes pled with them, and in return, she saw compassion in their faces.

A sling transferred Tallie into the tank, which was filled with several inches of body-temperature water in which Tallie floated with no effort.

"Are you comfortable?" Livvie asked.

Powerless, Tallie closed her eyes.

"We're going to close the lid now, Tallie. You won't be able to see or hear anything. That's expected. Just relax and breathe. Let your mind wander where it wants. And remember, you're not alone. We're right here all the time."

The pod lid closed, and the weightless darkness surrounded her until Tallie couldn't hear or see or feel anything. Panic hit her for a moment, but then two memories came to her. One was of a woman taking her to a black pool of water in the darkened forest. The woman was small, almost as small as she was. The woman was Julia, her mother and yet not her mother. Tallie panicked again at the confusing thoughts until the darkness took her back to that moment in the forest when Tallie was a child. Julia laid a finger to Tallie's lips and told her not to make a sound, and then the two of them laid down together in the dark silence of the inky pool, seeing nothing above them but stars. Feeling safe and at home in that darkness, with only the calls of birds and the whisper of trees around her, Tallie became so much a part of the terrain that small animals had no fear of drinking from the water that cradled her.

Her second memory was more recent, of repeating that experience in another body of water, a swimming pool. She'd been floating so still and serenely in the water that a man had thought she was dead. She recalled the terror on his face when he'd found her and then his anger when she'd fled the water and challenged his arrival at her quiet place. That misunderstanding had turned into friendship and then something more. Jackson. His name was Jackson James. The simple thought of his name flooded her with warmth and comfort. She knew he was her safe place. The true north that centered her. She needed him now, and she missed him with a loneliness that was almost physical, but there was pain there too. A fear of disappointment or rejection.

She tried to get back to the center place where Jackson meant happiness and peace, but with no sense of space or time other than what her thoughts conjured, her mind whiplashed her here and there, to the streets of Jakarta, the shores of Matamata, the wetlands of Mongolia, and on and on. She couldn't get back to Jackson. Only to Julia. No matter where she saw herself, Julia was always there, running her on to a new place, teaching her, correcting her, protecting her. Always before . . . before Jackson . . . there had been Julia.

Deprived of her other senses, her emotions poured forth in tears of joy over happy times and tears of loneliness and sorrow. She missed Julia and was angry at her. She missed the mountain home in the Gifford Pinchot National Forest they shared, and she missed another place, a house with photos of happy faces, of a mother and a soldier father and two baby girls.

More tears poured from her, but she couldn't separate her emotions anymore. Every emotion and want and hope and dream poured into the same ocean, draining her and drowning her in the same moment.

Tallie had no idea how much time had passed when the lid opened to a darkened room that seemed bright in comparison to the tank. Livvie's and Lei's worried faces peered down on her.

"Hey, Tallie. How're you doing?" Lei whispered.

Tallie cried unabashedly when she was able to reach for their hands. Weak, trembling, she managed to climb from the shallow tank with their strong support and move over to a shower, where fresh water rinsed her still-shaky body. When she stepped out, the women wrapped her in soft warmed towels and compassion-filled hugs.

"Feel better now?" Livvie asked.

Whatever the doctor's intention had been in ordering the sensory deprivation therapy for her, it had done its job, helping her swim through the drug-induced confusion and reconnect with the feelings and memories that placed her back in control. Now Tallie remembered how she'd gotten to this place. She remembered everything. And whether or not these gentle women believed her, Tallie knew the truth. She was not a special guest. She was a captive, and Burke had done this to her, but where was he now?

She had more questions than answers. Burke had said bringing her here was the only way to protect her. He had also said he'd find a way to get her home. Could he be trusted? Who was the director and why was he so anxious to meet her? And was her father, Cai Kaswell, here? How would she get them both away from this place?

She still felt weak, she and allowed the women to report her condition to the director.

"It just so happens that the director has a scheduling conflict anyway, so he'd like to reschedule your supper invitation for tomorrow morning instead," Livvie reported. "He just wants you to rest and recuperate today, but he wants us to take you to the garden to get acquainted with your new home."

Tallie counted it a gift to finally be clear-headed again and have some time to think and observe this place. As the women helped her dress and wheeled her out to the garden, she posed questions, and her companions proved to be fountains of information. "What is the veil drug?"

"That's just what Livvie and I call it because of the cocktail of benzodiazepine drugs used to veil your arrival from your memory. Remember that clause in the agreement we each sign when accepting the invitation to come here? The one that says we accept the colony's transportation terms used to protect its location? That's how they do it."

"It's just the price we pay to protect our little paradise," Livvie added.

Tallie knew it would be pointless to explain that she had never agreed to come here.

They exited the medical building, and Livvie waved her hand across the horizon. "We really do live in paradise, with great schools, beautiful surroundings, gorgeous weather, abundant organic food, and a small group of like-minded people who are all working for the same noble goal."

Tallie scanned her surroundings, noticing a wide diversity of nations represented in the people she observed and in the languages they spoke as they greeted her and interacted with one another. Her first observations were that the people seemed content and busy discussing projects and goals. Perhaps she was the exception. What if things really were as Livvie and Lei said? That the people here truly were happy to have been brought here?

"But . . . what if someone decides not to stay?" The words slipped out, and the two nurses looked at one another as if the question were ridiculous.

"They administer it again before you leave," Livvie said, "but hardly anyone ever chooses to go. Look around you. Why would they?"

Lei stopped pushing the chair. "How are you really feeling, Tallie? The fact that you, the director's special guest, with all your talents and abilities, asked that question worries me." She looked at Livvie. "Maybe we should call the doctor."

The thought of further intervention prompted Tallie to change course. "What I meant was what if I can't find my own special niche? I'm alone. What is community life like? What are your responsibilities here?"

Relief showed on Livvie's face. "Ohhh! Well, everyone here contributes to the whole. We function as a model for the global society we're helping build. Lei and I work in the women's triage team. You've seen our primary job, to make sure new arrivals transition as comfortably as possible."

"We also give each new arrival a basic physical," Lei said. "We take some blood and check vitals. On a small isolated colony like ours, even the flu could wreak havoc."

As they exited the building's long hall onto a perfectly manicured garden path teeming with vibrant color and delightful scents, Tallie sucked in an admiring breath.

The women evidently noticed her pleasure, because they stopped talking and slowed their pace, allowing her to soak up the beauty around them. Tallie smelled the sea beyond the stretching palms ahead. All around her bumblebees, butterflies, and tiny hummingbirds flitted about, adding the thrum of their wings to the scene. Crayon-colored exotic birds called from the trees, and drops of cool water misted her as it fell from fountains from which the birds drank. The place truly felt like a paradise.

They pushed her over to a bench and transferred her there. The spot had a view of the ocean beyond. Tallie looked left and right to assess the size of the island. Judging from the glimpses of water she could see, she knew that either she was situated at the point of the island or the island was very small, perhaps only a mile or two in diameter. Her silence during her thoughtful calculations caught the women's attention.

"It's beautiful, isn't it?" Lei said.

"The most beautiful place I've ever seen," Tallie said, and she meant it. "Tell me more about what life here is like for you."

Lei sat on the bench next to Tallie while Livvie stayed standing, leaning on the chair's handles.

"Two hundred years ago, my husband's ancestors were slaves who dreamed of a better world, so it was a source of great pride to his parents when their only son became a professor of philosophy at Princeton. They died a few years ago. John wanted to keep building on their dream, and now he's here, as the head of a think tank, designing models for a better society."

"So he's among the elite here."

"No," she said emphatically. "There is no class structure here. No matter what work we do, we all live the same and contribute to the whole. Even the children. They grow up understanding that we all work for the good of the whole. Our three children attend marvelous schools taught by some of the brightest minds in the world, and a few hours a week, they each take shifts in the childcare unit or pick up trash or serve wherever they're needed."

"That's admirable. But where do you live?"

"In a private family home provided by the Trust, like everyone else."

It all sounded noble and moral, but Tallie noticed a new quietness fall upon Lei. "What's your story, Lei?"

"It's a . . . little different," Lei began. "Neither my husband, Jack, nor I were professionals or influential in any sense of the word. We met in South Korea, where I was born. He was in the army and I worked in a little shop near the base. Our son followed in his father's footsteps and joined the military. Jack sang in a community choir with Livvie when we received the news that our only son was killed in Iraq." Her eyes fell to her hands as she continued. "We were devastated. We dropped out of everything, and we wanted to die too."

Livvie reached to take Lei's hand, and the personal bond between the two women became evident.

Lei smiled and carried on. "Livvie's husband, Brian, had already been offered a position here, and Livvie knew we needed something . . . a change of scenery . . . a new reason to trudge on in life. Brian inquired to see if there could be a place for us here in this paradise, and our story of loss touched the director. He sent us the same package he sent Livvie's family—plane tickets and hotel reservations, along with a letter for us to sign, indicating that by using the travel vouchers, we were both accepting the offered positions and agreeing to relocate under the Conservancy's terms. That was just fine with us. When he brought us here, we were just a grieving grocery store checker and a factory worker. He gave us new lives and purpose and training. Now I'm an RN and Jack manages food distribution on the island. We're not changing the world, but we support the people who are."

Tallie was moved by Lei's story. Maybe this director wasn't the power-hungry tyrant she'd believed him to be. Maybe he was a good man who'd lost his way. Everything Burke had told her about the director and his plans sounded so egotistical and crazed, but perhaps there was more to understand here.

"We're going to let you have some quiet time." Livvie set a walkie-talkie down beside Tallie. "I'd feel better if you didn't try to walk alone just yet. When you're ready to move about, just push the button and call for us, and we'll come help you take a little stroll."

Their honey-sweet smiles beamed her way, and then they were gone, leaving the chair behind. Tallie couldn't reconcile what she was experiencing with the fear she'd seen in Burke back in Lugar de Sueños. He'd killed a man because of those fears. What was happening here that these women didn't know or understand?

"Work the problem, Tallie."

Julia was right. Tallie organized her thoughts, sorting out what she knew from what the women had made her feel. The two columns didn't add up. She leaned her head back and let the sun warm her face. It would be so easy to buy into this paradisiacal plan. She had almost no one to leave behind. She thought of Jackson and their last few conversations. He would miss her, but he would be all right. Love would come to him from someone else. Someone who was more than she could be. She was spiraling again, but then she heard that voice of wisdom once more. *"Work the problem, Tallie."*

"Yes, Julia." She smiled at the thought of someone catching her speaking to a dead person. *I need more information. More than I can gather sitting on this bench.*

She flexed her feet and felt them react to her will. She might not be ready to walk, but she was ready to transfer to that wheelchair and follow the paths to see more of this place. The chair was slightly out of reach. She scooted along the bench to get closer and stretched again. It was still too far away. Tallie anchored herself to the bench with her right hand and stretched until her left fingers could touch the chair's metal frame. *One more inch*, she told herself, and with a determined final reach, her body bent farther, past its center. She felt herself tipping and tightened her hold on the bench rail, but it was too little too late and she dropped forward onto the packed-sand trail.

The shock of the short fall stunned her momentarily, and then she scrambled to get her weakened limbs under her and steadied in order to lift herself up. She felt strong hands slide under her arms and carefully support her efforts, and she closed her eyes in embarrassment, knowing either Lei or Livvie or both would soon be giving her a gentle scolding. She turned her head to receive the loving rebuke for not calling them, but the face she saw and the voice that spoke to her turned her limbs back into jelly.

"M—" He halted on that first letter as his expressions jumbled into an indecipherable palette of emotions.

Tallie had referred to him as her father so many times in her own mind and in conversations with Jackson and Marlene that she almost let the word slip from her lips, but she too held her tongue, instead answering, "General Kaswell."

"Are you all right?" he asked with fatherly tenderness as his eyes scanned her scraped hands and he brushed sand from her cheek. His strong but gentle face, with its silver hair and handsome features, came within inches of hers.

"Let me help you up, M—"

Tallie almost dared believe he was about to say her name, her real name, the one he and her birth mother gave her, but instead, he stuttered and said, "Miss Brown."

Her limbs went limp from sorrow and shame. Sorrow because he either still didn't know or wasn't willing to admit that she was his daughter and shame because she was too timid to express her greatest desire, to claim him and be claimed by him. Instead, she said, "You're here. I hoped to find you."

"I can't tell you how sorry I am that you did," he whispered as he placed her on the bench and sat beside her, grabbing her hand. "Your being here is my worst nightmare. Is it true you were picked up while trying to rescue me?"

His gaze melted her with a warmth that radiated through her. She felt his hand squeeze hers. Never in her life had she felt more safe and loved. "Yes, but how did you know that?"

"I overheard two security guards talking when your flight arrived. They mentioned Burke's part in all this. When I find him . . ." Kaswell's eyes shut, and he cursed under his breath. "I caused this. I chose him to protect you from paparazzi, and he turned out to be your biggest threat."

"It's not your fault. No one knew his loyalties had changed. And besides, Major Norris ordered me home after we figured out how the kidnappers were disarming their victims, but I refused." She paused, daring herself to say more. "I had to find you."

"Why, Tallie? I've brought you nothing but heartache."

He had teed up the perfect moment for her to tell him everything about their connection, about how she was his daughter Molly and had survived the car crash twenty-one years ago. That Julia had kidnapped her, stolen her . . .

Tallie froze, and her tongue locked in her mouth as guilt rushed in. Hadn't Julia also cared for her . . . protected her . . . loved her, in her own way? Tallie didn't know what to do with those feelings, so she dipped her head and changed the subject. "Have you found a way off this island?"

Kaswell studied her as he released her hand and slumped. "Not exactly, but I promise I'll at least find a way to get you home."

Tallie missed his protective touch immediately. She boldly retook his hand, and her courage was rewarded when he placed his other one on top of hers, cradling it. "What about you?" she said. "I can't leave if you're forced to remain here."

His eyes crinkled in the corners as they began to glisten. "I'm profoundly touched by your willingness to sacrifice yourself for me, but you won't need to. I can leave . . . under certain terms."

"What terms? Who's keeping us here and why?"

"The less you know, the better right now." He patted her hand and redirected the conversation. "We've never had a chance to just talk about you. You're a marvel to me. I want you to tell me all about you and your life. Where did you grow up? You told me your mother was a soldier. Tell me about the woman who raised you."

His kindness emboldened her to try again to tell her story, but there was something about his penetrating gaze that held her back, as if he already knew the answers to the questions he was asking. Tallie hung her head, unsure how to answer, where to begin, or what she'd do if he didn't believe her. While she prepared her response, Julia's voice arrived in her head, ready to weigh in as well.

"I didn't bring you out here to pout. You can do that somewhere else. People are counting on us. What's the problem?"

Tallie fidgeted as she tried to identified the problem. Plain and simple—she was afraid.

"Fight through it, fix the problem, or get away from it. Don't let it control you."

"Okay," she answered, as much to Julia as to her father. "I had a rather unconventional childhood. We traveled all over the world for the first fifteen years of my life."

She felt his hand tighten over hers. "Were you happy, Tallie?"

"It was my normal. I never knew anything else."

His face pinched as if her answer pained him. "Too much change is hard for children. I saw it in my own family. My daughter Meghan never recovered from losing her sister."

Tallie wondered if he was baiting her, drawing her out on the topic of their shared family. His eyes burned into her as silent seconds ticked by. A lump filled her throat, leaving her unable to respond. She felt as if a cord were tied between them and that he was reeling her in, away from Julia, away from aloneness and sorrow, to a safe place he was offering her.

Her lips trembled, and his eyes began to glisten. "Was Diana good to you?" he asked.

A shock zipped through Tallie. "Did you say . . . ? You called her Diana. You . . . know?"

The muscles of his taut face went limp, as if her words confirmed what he'd already suspected, and harrowing pain and guilt aged him before Tallie's very eyes. He inched forward and then retreated, as if he were as unsure about what to do in that moment as she was.

"Not until a few days ago, I'm ashamed to say," he finally said. He leaned closer. "I felt a connection to you that day I met you at the inn, but I kept excusing it away. It seemed too incredible to even consider, but it's so clear now." His eyes were love-filled and sad as he released her hand to cup her cheek in his palm. "You're our Molly. You're my little girl."

Tallie fell into his arms, and he tightened them around her. Words seemed insufficient as both laughed and cried and held on to one another. Her father's hand ran over and over her hair, as if she were a little girl.

"What convinced you?" she asked into his shoulder.

He pulled back and rubbed a knuckle over his moist eyes. "I couldn't make peace with that earring of yours. I knew it was one I'd had made for my girls, and no matter how hard he tried, Stephen couldn't provide an explanation that satisfied me for why you had one. But it was your face that haunted me. You're a cross between Deidre and Meghan. My heart knew it before I had proof." His eyes misted again. "They loved you and missed you every day. We all did."

"I wish I could have met them. I saw the family photos in your house."

His mouth quivered. "Then, you know we never forgot you or gave up the hope of finding you."

"I saw that, but it was also hard to see what my life could have been like if . . ."

"So much waste." He sighed.

"I think Julia was trying to set things right in the end," Tallie said. "She included Deidre on a text she sent out the day she died, directing her to Cutler's Ridge to find me. I'm the reason she and Meghan were on that plane. When I saw that Cessna go down, I still thought I was Julia's natural child. By the time I found out who I really was, my mother and sister were already gone, and I thought I could never reveal who I was to you."

"Why?"

"To protect you and your reputation."

He closed his eyes and shook his head. "Yet you still tried to save me."

"I've long admired you as a public figure, but when I heard that you were my father . . . I can't explain it, but I just knew it was true. And even though I didn't really know you, I already loved you."

He pulled her to him and cried into her hair. "I've loved you every second of every lonely, painful day these twenty-one years, Molly. Nothing in this world, not my career or my reputation, could keep me from claiming you."

He kissed her forehead. "We've got some hard things to sort through. I know Norris got caught up in this somehow, but now is not the time to worry about the past. I just want to look at you and learn about you and find a way to get you off this island."

Tallie heard Lei's and Livvie's voices and knew they were coming their way. "We have company."

Her father stood and bent forward, whispering, "Don't tell anyone who we are to one another right now, Tallie, all right?"

Tallie nodded. "All right. But you can call me Molly when we're together, if you'd like."

"I've caused enough hardship in your life. I won't upset it further by asking you to change your name from what you've always known. I love you. You're my daughter Molly, but you're also Tallie Brown."

His broad hand pulled her cheek close so he could place a soft kiss there. Then he winked at her, gave her hand a final squeeze, and stepped away, standing there as if he were just making her acquaintance.

"General Kaswell," Livvie called out when she came into view. "I see our two special guests have already met."

He stole a glance at Tallie and replied, "Yes, we have. Miss Brown and I have just enjoyed a lovely conversation."

"We're glad we found you, General," Lei said with a sweet rebuke.

"I didn't realize I was confined to quarters."

"Oh, you're not." Livvie pulled a two-way radio from her pocket. "Brian has been searching for you. He and his committee expected you to attend the afternoon session of the Brain Trust meeting. I'll tell him you're on your way."

Tallie noticed a slight scowl in her father's face over the mention of the words *Brain Trust*. She'd heard a similar reference before, but the memory was fuzzy.

"Point me in the right direction, ladies, and I'll hurry along. And if Miss Brown has no plans for this evening, I'd appreciate the chance to join her for dinner."

"That's just perfect," Lei said. "Miss Brown was calendared to have dinner with the director this evening, but something unforeseen came up and he's left us for the mainland."

"Which mainland?" he asked.

"Oh, General," Livvie replied with a curious smile. "Now, hurry on. You're the guest speaker at today's meeting."

Tallie's father shot her a reassuring glance, and she soaked up every detail of his face before they parted. "Until this evening, Miss Brown?"

"I'll look forward to it, General."

CHAPTER FIFTEEN

Jackson came through the meeting room door, and Major Norris stood to greet him. "Did he buy it?" the major asked.

"It appears so." Jackson displayed an email on his tablet. "The personnel director is ecstatic that I reconsidered the job offer, and I already signed and returned my relocation agreement. I fly to Mexico City tomorrow, and a car will be waiting at the airport to take me to the Casa de Maya Hotel for my final interview."

"Where they'll drug and kidnap you."

"And take me to where I'll hopefully find Tallie."

Norris took a deep breath and tried to hide his discomfort over this plan. "Are you sure they're not suspicious about this sudden change in their fortunes?"

"Pretty sure. IBT knew almost everything about me when they offered me the job the first time. They sought me out because of my newspaper work, and since I didn't know who the Conservancy was, I basically told them everything else going on in my life. They knew I had accepted a job working with General Kaswell and that I was in a relationship with Tallie and I didn't want to leave the area at that time."

"So how did you explain your change of mind? Did you tell them your career and your love life both blew up?"

"Wow." Jackson sighed and rolled his eyes. "Thanks for that delicate summation of my life."

"So that's a yes?"

"I played ignorant and used a tad more tact. I told Howard's personnel guy that my job didn't work out because I was told the general had not yet accepted the position, and I didn't want my future to remain in limbo. They asked about Tallie, and I told them we basically broke things off amicably back in Idaho and I'm anxious for a change."

Norris pressed his thumbs into his temples. "They know you're going to run into Tallie and Cai, both of whom you know and neither of whom are there of their own will. That leaves only two scenarios: either they think they have some way to pull your loyalty away from Cai and Tallie and to their cause or they plan to add you to their collection of hostages."

"There's the original scenario, that they know I'm trying to rescue the others and they're planning to—"

"Don't even say it. I'll kill you myself if you get yourself hurt. Understand?"

"Loud and clear."

The two men shared a knowing glance. "Are you sure about this, Pulitzer? Really sure?"

The once-detested nickname no longer offended Jackson. He knew Norris had come to respect him, even care for him, and that the current use of the former slander was simply a reflection of Norris's concern.

"This is all on me, Major. You couldn't keep me from going now that I know there's a chance I can reach Tallie."

Norris smiled, but there was no humor in it. "That's what Marlene said too." He fell back into his chair. "Like you, there was no way she was going to stay back and miss a chance to bring down the people who almost killed her and then kidnapped Tallie. Once she heard you'd managed to get on the island on your own terms, she asked for that second IT slot Bartrum Drummond arranged."

"She's our third member?"

"I ordered new IDs and backstories for her and another female operator, just in case I can't find the courage to pull the trigger and let Marlene go. I'm worried about the Conservancy's willingness to move up the timing of your arrival. No matter how deeply we build Mak and Marlene's covers, the Conservancy's personnel guy has to wonder why three candidates popped up in a week."

"I think the timing did raise a red flag with him, because he told me he couldn't bring me in for a month. I panicked and figured I'd have to join your assault team to get on that island, but I played it cool with the recruiter. When I agreed amicably to his terms, he doubled back and asked me again if I'd be willing to delay my arrival for a month. I told him sure but asked if I could get paid for the waiting period. I guess my financial motives sounded sincere and cooled his concerns, because he laughed and said he'd try to get me in on the next flight, and then the itinerary and tickets arrived."

Mak rushed through the Crib to Norris's door, opening it without a knock, and Norris stood. "What the—"

"We've got a situation," Mak said. "Guess who's showing up on our security camera."

Norris leaned over his desk. "Spit it out."

"Burke's on the property. He wants to come in. He knows the risk and consequences, but he says he's the only chance Tallie and Cai have."

The blood drained from Norris's face while Jackson could feel his own heating like it was about to explode. "You can't trust him! He's the reason Tallie and Cai are in danger!"

"We all know that, Jackson, and he must know we're aware of his part in all this," Norris said. "But he has knowledge we need. Mak? I want you and Rich to screen him and bring him in, and not as a brother in arms. Let him know he's no longer trusted around here. Am I making myself clear?"

"Copy that, Major."

Jackson saw the grimness of Norris's expression. Burke was someone he'd trained and led into battle. Someone he cared about, probably even loved. Burke had lost that trust, and that loss made Norris's pain excruciatingly personal.

"You deserve to be in on this interrogation, Jackson, if you want to," the major said.

Jackson held back his earnest desire to make a snide comment about Burke and his fall from grace. That knife would stab Norris more than Burke, so he simply nodded and followed the major on the elevator ride to the first floor.

"We put him in Jackson's old office," Rich said. He wore the same look of hurt and betrayal Norris did.

Without further word, Norris, Jackson, and Rich made their way to the office door, where Mak stood guard over his former friend, who sat in a chair against the wall.

Burke was a sight. His hands were secured behind his back with a zip tie, and he was dressed in filthy pants and an oversize hoodie that covered most of his face. He looked up, revealing a bruised and bloodied face. "I'm so sorry, Major. I'll take whatever punishment is coming, but you have to hear me out first."

His mouth was split and swollen, but not as badly as one of his eyelids, which left him little more than a purple slit through which to see. His left cheek had a gash surrounded by raw cuts, as if the entire side of his face had been worked over with coarse sandpaper. Jackson looked more closely and realized that much of the dirt on Burke's clothes was actually dried blood. The man had been through a war of his own.

Norris sat on the edge of Jackson's former desk and studied Burke while Rich moved to flank Burke, with Mak on the other side. Jackson wasn't sure if the three of them were going to beat the man further or continue shooting guilt-stares his way until he broke, but neither situation was one Jackson wanted to be involved in, so he leaned against the wall behind the desk, as far from what was about to happen as possible.

"I hear you have intel that might help us rescue the people whose lives you endangered," Norris began. "But don't think for one second that makes you some special kinda hero."

Burke dropped his head again. "I'm not asking you to forgive me or even to understand. I lost my way. I see that now."

"Why didn't you come to one of us?" Mak asked.

"We shed blood together." Rich moved close to Burke's face. "We'd have helped you."

Burke's eyes glistened. "I know. I know," he said as his head bobbed almost imperceptibly. "But we shed too much blood and treasure, both us and the locals we enlisted to help us, and look how it turned out. Look at Afghanistan. We pull out and break our promises, and everything our men and women sacrificed becomes meaningless. I wanted to believe there could be a better way, and now I've done the same thing to Tallie."

The mention of her name by this man flipped a switch in Jackson, and he turned on Burke with his finger jabbing out every word. "Don't say her name. Don't you dare!"

Mak laid a hand on Jackson's arm. "Breathe, brother."

But Jackson wasn't finished. "A man who befriends a woman to deceive her is a dog. What did you do to her? She was unconscious when they carried her out of that building!"

"Would you believe me if I told you she helped me see how off-base I'd gotten? I tried to convince her to go back home, but she was determined to find Cai Kaswell. I killed the man who was planning to sell her to the Somalis. Drugging her was my last hope of getting her into the Conservancy's care. I knew they'd keep her safe, and I hoped she'd be able to be rescued from there."

As much as Jackson hated to admit it, everything Burke said about Tallie's decisions seemed like choices she would have made. "You created this mess, traitor. Don't think I forgive you because you finally tried to clean it up."

Burke flinched, and Jackson hated the words as soon as they left his mouth. Who was he to deny anyone forgiveness after everything he'd done? After Cai Kaswell and Norris had given him a chance to redeem himself?

"I deserve that. You must be Jackson James."

Jackson kicked the tile floor. "I'm sorry. I have no right—"

"You have every right. You love her. And you're spot on about everything. I aided and abetted an enemy, who I now see was not promoting better policies. I think he's trying to bring down governments, including ours."

Norris sat back and released a groan. "This director has the codes to disarm any military hardware run by a computer. Start talking, Burke, and begin with some actionable details."

"I've been to the island a few times, working security. I wasn't conscious for the flights, but I have something in my pocket that should help."

Rich looked at Norris, who nodded, and then produced a knife from his own pocket and cut the restraint on Burke's hands. Burke pulled a slip of paper from his pocket and handed it to Norris. "These are the coordinates for the Conservancy's island. While we were en route to the island, the Conservancy's caravan got hit by some local group tracking us from a drone. Probably cartel members."

Jackson noticed that none of the men in the room admitted they were the ones who'd brought the cartel down on that caravan, nor did they reveal that they knew anything about the attack.

Burke continued. "The cartel cut the vehicle I was in off from the caravan. One of my escorts shot the drone, and the driver got the cartel's men, but not before they got him. I managed to talk him into releasing my restraints so I could check his wounds. Before he died, he said, 'I didn't sign up for this,' and he gave me those coordinates for the Conservancy so a rescue could be set for the people being held against their will. He told me security on the island monitors a one-mile air perimeter around the coast."

While Rich refreshed Jackson's old computer and pulled up a map of the coordinates, the rest of them, including Burke, gathered around the screen to find the island.

"There's a small island or atoll slightly due east of those coordinates," Mak said, "and nothing else for over a hundred miles in any direction."

"A good place if you want to get lost and stay that way," Rich said.

"Could a submersible get in there undetected?" Norris asked. "A DPV?"

Burke frowned. "I don't know how sensitive their equipment is or whether it could detect a DPV's motor."

Jackson couldn't stand being in the dark, so he asked Mak, "What's a DPV?"

"Diver propulsion vehicle: a handheld motorized swim aid that pulls a diver through the water over long distances."

Burke stepped back into the conversation. "I think you'd be safer dropping SEALs off outside that perimeter and having them swim in with their gear."

After an hour of questioning, Burke's information had been gathered and his usefulness appeared as exhausted as he did. Norris thanked him for bringing the intel to the team, but he also nodded to Mak, who pulled another zip tie from his pocket. Burke cooperated and put his hands behind his back. When he was secured, Mak tried to stand him up, but Burke stumbled and fell back into the chair.

Norris stepped toward him and asked, "How long has it been since you've eaten?"

"What day is it? I've been driving the Conservancy's SUV for thirty-six hours straight."

"You must have had no wallet or credit card on you. How did you pay for fuel?"

"I picked the pockets of the dead. It's probably best if you don't know anything else."

"Copy that." Norris nodded to Rich. "Take him to the holding cell. Get him cleaned up and tend his wounds while Mak rustles him up some grub. Let's meet downstairs in an hour to finalize our plan."

Jackson watched the sorrowful scene as Mak and Rich exited with a very humble and broken Burke. He didn't know exactly where the holding cell was or what being "held" entailed, but he felt oddly numbed by the decision. He still didn't like Burke, but he understood how circumstances could lead people to make choices contrary to their norm. Burke had fallen, hard, but he had been certified a hero many times, and he had provided verifiable info that would hopefully save Tallie, Cai, and others. Jackson was just glad he wasn't the one who would have to weigh Burke's actions and render a decision on his future.

"Sit a minute, Jackson," Norris said as he fell heavily into the desk chair. He pressed his fingers deep into his eyes and blew out a long rush of air.

"Are you thinking about Burke or Marlene?"

"Everyone. Tallie, Cai, you, my impetuous daughter, and a young man whose life is ruined. The sad thing is I understand what he's saying. I don't fault him for his frustration. I lost a lot of good men in those places, so I feel it too. I fault him for not coming to his brothers and for not trusting the chain of command or our system of government. He was willing to scrap the Constitution for some idealogue's philosophies."

"What will happen to him?"

Norris's head tipped to the side, and his eyes closed. "I wish I knew."

"And what have you decided about Marlene?"

"I guess I'll give that third slot to her." He sat up and looked Jackson straight in the eye. "Watch out for her, will you, Pulitzer?"

"You know I will."

"Mak will be able to fight off trouble she can't handle on her own, but she listens to you. You might be able to keep her out of trouble in the first place."

Jackson rolled his eyes. Tallie and Marlene were two women with minds of their own. If anything, he'd be chasing after them and grateful if he could keep up.

Norris checked his watch. "Marlene's and Mak's new identities should be ready soon. When does your flight leave?"

"Six a.m. tomorrow."

"Mak and Marlene are scheduled for a red-eye flight tonight. Hopefully all three of you will be 'processed' and end up on the same flight to the island. Now we've just got to figure out how to smuggle a small army out there so they don't see us coming."

"Copy that, Major." Jackson stood and held his hand out to Norris, who stood and took it and held it as he studied Jackson.

"I chose you years ago because I believed in your goodness, that no matter what life threw at you, you'd be a man of integrity."

Jackson thought about his fall from journalistic grace. "Sorry I lost my way for a while."

"No apology needed, Pulitzer. You're every bit the man I believed you'd be and more. Now, let's go set things right—together."

CHAPTER SIXTEEN

Livvie and Lei had moved Tallie out of the observation suite and into a private room with a glorious view of a lush green lawn dotted with colorful flowers. That view stretched to a steep cliff that dropped off to the ocean beyond. She could, perhaps, understand why entrance to the island was by "invitation" only, but why could people not come under their own power, awake and alert? And, more curious, why could they not come and go at will?

She added these questions to the growing list of topics she wanted to discuss with her father tonight.

Her father.

Just acknowledging him brought prickles to her arms. She had found her father, and he loved her. Their meeting at the bench had taken her by such surprise that she hadn't had time for the wonder of this new relationship to wash over her, but it had during the ensuing hours, leaving her giddy and warm and nervous over their planned supper. How would they greet each other this time? Would they hug like normal fathers and daughters did, or would the awkwardness settle back in before they felt comfortable together?

Each thought increased her anxiety until she began to feel sick. She needed something to do. A project or an assignment to keep her normally occupied mind and hands busy. The spartanly furnished room left her few options, so she headed to the closet that had been stocked with two pairs of shoes in her size and three new outfits—slacks and a top, cargo shorts and a T-shirt, and a light sweater and skirt. All the items were things she might have chosen for herself, and all fit her perfectly, but the idea that someone she'd never met knew her so well that they could predict not only her size but also her taste in clothes unnerved her.

She settled for the shorts outfit, which almost perfectly matched the set she was wearing the day she was drugged and kidnapped. She combed her long blonde hair and pulled it back in a tie. While fiddling with the resulting ponytail, braiding it, and twisting it into a bun, a knock sounded on the door.

The wrestle over how to handle the greeting was quickly resolved when she opened the door and her father extended the one arm not busy holding a bag. He drew her close and planted a kiss on her head. "You look beautiful," he said with a proud smile.

He barely had to bend his neck to reach his tall daughter's head, and Tallie realized she'd gotten her height from her handsome father. She held him in the circle of her arms for several seconds, enjoying the feel of his strong hug, as if she were filling a space held in reserve just for her.

"Thank youuuu . . ." Her voice faded out, revealing her unsurety over what to call him.

"To make us both more comfortable with each other, please know I won't be offended by whatever you decide to call me—Cai or Kas. I answer to either. Or . . . you're welcome to call me Dad . . . if and when you'd like to."

Prickles rose on her arms again. "I'd like that very much."

Her father beamed at her. "Me too, but we'd have to reserve that for when we're alone."

"I understand." She allowed silence to fill the space where words seemed inadequate.

"I'm afraid I didn't do very well on the menu," her dad said. "The only dining option open to newbies like us is cafeteria food, unless we're invited to dine with the director."

Tallie heard the scorn in his voice as he mentioned their captor.

He walked to the tiny table and set the bag down. "I figured with all the traveling you've done, you're probably familiar with most cuisine."

A veiled sadness shrouded the question. She answered with a simple nod as she joined him near the table.

He studied her, rolling his lips as his gaze fell back on the bag. "Knowing Diana, I also imagine you've primarily lived in remote places these twenty-one years . . . eating simple foods. She wasn't one to cook when I knew her."

"I did most of the cooking."

His eyes glistened again, and Tallie's throat tightened. She sensed he had spent the hours away from her regretting the stolen years and imagining how and where'd she'd been all that time.

"I remembered what you said this morning, about how seeing the family photos made you realize everything you've missed because of—I mean, while you were away from us. It gave me an idea for tonight's dinner. I asked the cafeteria workers to dish up a sampling of Kaswell family favorites so you could know your family traditions a little better."

Her skin prickled at her first invitation to enjoy Kaswell family traditions. She noticed how the former sharpshooter's nimble hands, trained to squeeze a trigger with a butterfly's touch, shook as he pulled various containers from the bag and set them on the table. He fumbled with the lids and then waved his hand over the feast with an awkward flourish.

"Our first offering is chicken pot pie." He glanced her way and said, "Your mom made an amazing chicken pot pie with vegetables from her garden. If I needed to find her, I'd just head outside, and chances were she'd be pulling weeds or digging in the dirt . . ." His voice trailed off, as if he were lost in the memory. He started, then blushed. "I bet you'd have been right in there beside her, pulling weeds and talking about school and life and boys. She'd have loved that." He shot Tallie a quick smile that trembled despite his efforts to remain cheery.

He lifted the second container and breathed in the steamy aroma. "Sliced turkey and stuffing with gravy, a Thanksgiving staple." He looked at Tallie and asked, "Did you celebrate Thanksgiving wherever you were?"

Tallie replied in tiny shakes of her head, noting that each movement seemed to cause him greater dismay.

"Christmas? Easter?" He became more distressed with each question.

Again, Tallie shook her head.

"How about your birthday? Did she at least acknowledge that?"

"I don't think she knew what it was." Tallie stepped forward, and he opened his arms to her, pulling her to him and laying his head on hers.

"My poor girl." He spoke quietly. "We had balloons and a cake for Meghan's birthday every year on May twenty-first, but we never forgot it was your birthday too. We'd buy a giant bouquet of balloons and flowers and take them to the cemetery." His voice broke, and he pressed his lips to Tallie's head, labored pauses in his breathing. Moments passed before he spoke again. "We never accepted that our Molly was dead, but our pastor pushed us to memorialize you somehow, so we bought a plot and set an angel statue there. We had a marker made with your name and birthdate but no death date. Just the word *Lost* and the date of the accident."

Tears burned Tallie's eyes at the reference to her birth name. "It's okay. It's okay."

He coughed, stepped back, and wiped his eyes before tipping her face up. "The word *lost* didn't just apply to you. We were all lost after you disappeared."

He kissed her forehead and tucked her back against him. "Meghan never recovered. That little girl cried for you every day, which ripped your mother apart. Deidre never forgave herself for the accident, and our marriage suffered because I knew that, ultimately, I was the one who'd failed all of you. And you?" His embrace tightened. "I can't imagine how confused and frightened you must have been."

Tallie didn't know what to say. Each point he made added to her profound sense of loss. Yes, she had her father back, but his return came with an awakening to everything Julia had taken from her. But even knowing that, she couldn't and didn't want to wish away her own past and the only life she'd had, the life that had made her who she was.

She stepped back and held her father's hands, hoping she could bring him and her some peace. "Thank you for telling me all this. Knowing you all thought of me is both wonderful and painful. I can't remember anything solid before Julia. Perhaps that's because I was sick for so long after the accident. When I was with her, I was timid and fearful of disappointing her, but in other ways, I was fearless, climbing hills and mountains and able to adapt to new cultures and languages."

Tallie felt her father's struggle as he tried to camouflage the complex mix of anger, sorrow, and wonder swirling across his visage. "I . . . I would have loved to have seen you then," he muttered. "It's hard to imagine how different all our lives could have been had we each not lost so much."

"But we lived the lives we were left as well as we could, and we are who we are because of what we've suffered and triumphed over. My friend Jackson would say that someday, somehow, in the grand scheme of life, God will compensate us for all we've lost. I hope so—I dearly do—but at least you and I have each other now, and a chance to grieve together and make new memories." She squeezed his hands in hers. "We'll eat pot pie and birthday cake while you tell me stories about my mother and Meghan, and we'll eat turkey at Thanksgiving and sing carols together every Christmas from now on. We'll hold tight to those we've lost and to one another, and we'll never be alone again."

Her father squeezed her hands back and smiled. "And let's begin celebrating with this good food. Sit down. I'll serve. And I want you to tell me where you've been and a favorite memory of each place."

There was something in his laser focus on making the most of the day's opportunities and his deflection away from her discussion of future memory-making together that left Tallie guarded. Still, she began telling stories as they ate, studying him all the while, and hoping to allay her worries. By the end of the meal, the two had returned to a comfortable place where the dialogue was less about past losses and more about the present.

"I wish I had my phone so I could take a picture of us and preserve this moment," Tallie said. "It must have been left behind in Mexico."

"Or confiscated," her father whispered. "No cell phones or cameras are allowed on this island. I've inquired."

She gave that some thought. "Lei and Livvie had a two-way radio. Why no phones?"

"The director wants to control all information coming in or out of the island."

"And the people agree to that?" she whispered back.

"You'd be amazed what compromises people are willing to make to have a comfortable life in paradise. But I have the feeling they're beginning to wake up. Not everyone is as blindly happy here as they want you to believe. Are you up for a walk?"

Tallie noted his eyebrow raise, indicating that he had multiple reasons for suggesting they head outside. She pushed her chair back and agreed immediately.

"I've discovered a path that leads to a tidal pool," he said.

"Sounds lovely. Lead the way."

The path was steep, providing a satisfying challenge Tallie adored. Her father reached a hand to her several times, and she took it, but he soon realized she didn't need his help at all.

The views from the path were exquisite, providing glimpses of coral reefs, brilliant florals, and brightly colored fish swimming in a small lagoon. While her father skipped a few stones, Tallie scouted out the residents of the pool, naming them off one by one.

"You can climb like a goat and rattle off the names of sea life like a scientist. Your education didn't suffer."

She hesitated in answering. "Every day was spent learning. I have two master's degrees, one in biology and one in environmental studies."

"You're a scientist. What else don't I know about you?"

"I speak seven languages. More if partial proficiency counts."

"Did Diana teach you all that?"

She knew the answer would hurt him, so she shrugged and tried to change the subject, but he encouraged her to continue. "It's okay. I want to know all about you, even if it was Diana who helped you reach your potential."

"We treated each new place and experience as a learning opportunity. My life was like bootcamp—rigid, strict, demanding. Never boring or ordinary.

Whether she was teaching me to shoot or fight or navigate by the stars, excellence was required, and we repeated the exercise a hundred times if that's what it took to master the skill."

"That was your childhood?"

"It was all I knew. I longed for what I saw between other children and their mothers, but I accepted that all Julia had to give me besides education was her approval, and I lived for that."

Her father paced as he wrestled with the information. "I don't know what to say, other than that I'm sorry."

"I didn't understand why she trained me like a soldier, but I do now. She was preparing me to face a situation exactly like this. She wanted me to have the tools I'd need to survive the people who might come for me. I know it hurts you to hear that, but—"

"It's not that. Yes, it hurts me, but not for the reasons you think."

Tallie's conflict of loyalties hurt her more than she would have suspected. As excited as she was to be reunited with her father, guilt pricked at her with every mention of Julia and the twenty-one years they'd shared together. Her choices were to erase her life and begin anew or evade the topic of her past the best she could. She quickly changed the subject. "Let's just enjoy this beautiful place. It is a paradise, but why would a man build such a beautiful place and then feel the need to drug people to bring them here?"

"For power."

"Burke said the director was trying to make the world better."

"Perhaps it began that way, but something went wrong, because this is not how a good, benevolent person does things."

"Have you met him?"

"No. Neither this place nor this director was on my radar. He should have been. He's been influencing political and military decisions for years, but I was focused on diplomacy and left procurement to others. I flew to Mexico to figure out why American execs and officials were disappearing, and I woke up here. That was three days ago. No one has made any attempt to explain my purpose in being brought here, and the director, whose 'special guest' the nurses purport me to be, hasn't requested to meet with me. I've asked to see him, but all I've had were delays."

"What happened at that IBT meeting this morning?"

He huffed. "A few so-called experts in foreign affairs presented their theories on current geopolitical hot spots and then asked for my opinion."

"I take it you disagreed."

He huffed again. "Their assessments were inaccurate and their proposals insane."

"How'd that go over?" She chuckled, and Cai studied her as if she were a miracle.

"I want to replay that sound forever." He laughed as well, and Tallie thought his laughter was equally magical.

"As you obviously guessed, my opinions were not well-received." He laughed again and stared at her as if forever preserving a glimpse of her in this happy, peaceful moment. But then his smile faded back into that look of sorrow and worry. He reached down, grabbed another stone, and threw it rather than skipped it into the water. "They thanked me for my time and invited me to leave."

"At least they let you leave. Maybe that's hopeful. The director supposedly wants to meet with me tomorrow."

Her father picked up another, larger, stone, took four giant steps, leaned back, and hurled it into the sea with a prolonged, agonized groan. The effort ended with him bent over, sucking in deep gulps of air. He spoke to Tallie from his bent position. "I've been a failure as a father, so I know I have no right to give you fatherly advice—"

"That's not true. And I'd welcome advice from my father."

"It *is* true, Tallie. I've done some terrible things in my life, and everyone I love has paid for it."

"You're talking about Mogadishu, aren't you?"

He dropped to sit in the sand and drew his knees close. "You know about Mogadishu?"

Tallie sat a few feet from him. "I know you didn't know those civilians were in the building when you fired that shot."

"That part of the story is true. It's what I did after the shot and the fire that I'm ashamed of."

"You nearly died rescuing people from that inferno."

"The inferno I caused with the shot I never admitted to firing."

Tallie was at a loss for words to console him.

He laid his head on his knees. "I built a career on a lie."

"From what I've been told, you were asked not to confess because everyone thought you could do more good as a hero than as a martyr."

He turned his head and looked at Tallie. "Not everyone. Not the people injured or the families of those killed in that fire. And surely Diana didn't think that when I came home to a hero's welcome and she was stationed near a dying coal town."

"She was unstable."

"And I made her worse. I knew Diana had been part of the search party looking for you after the accident, and I saw the newspaper article about how she found Sophie Bodeil, who'd wandered off, chasing the search party's lights. I heard the strange rumors being whispered through Cutler's Ridge about the child the Bodeils adopted and then gave up in the same year the town debt was forgiven and expensive renovations were made. I didn't want to put the pieces together, but then I saw you and your earring, and I knew the truth. Diana took you to punish me, and her father bought everyone off."

Tallie took his hand. "She made that choice. Not you."

"As you said, she was unstable, so those choices *are* on me, just as I'm ultimately responsible for the deaths of Doc Henley and Petty Bodeil, who unknowingly got caught up in Diana's kidnapping plot. The list of people who would still be here or whose lives would be better if I had just confessed to pulling the trigger that caused that fire goes on and on."

He seemed unwilling to be comforted, so Tallie sat in silence beside him, waiting for the right moment to diffuse his pain with reason. She scooted near until her head could rest on his shoulder. He answered her brave offering by laying his head on hers. She felt her spine turn to butter in the sweetness of his response.

"What about the hundreds, maybe thousands of lives freed because you gave them the courage to push the rebels out of their villages? And what of the lives saved because you brokered peace deals in places that had known only war for generations?"

"It still doesn't make what I did right. And look at what I've done to you. After all the loss and hardship you've known, you were finally beginning to enjoy a normal life, but because of me you were drugged and kidnapped and brought here."

He straightened and stared out at the sea. She longed for a return to the closeness they'd shared a moment earlier, but pain lines etched into his face, and she gave him the space he desired.

"I caused this to happen to you," he whispered.

"That's not true."

His eyes dipped and came back up to meet hers. "I love how you see me—as good and brave and noble." He took her hand and rubbed his other hand over it as if it were a magic lamp. "Poor Meghan grew up with a guilt-ridden mother and an absentee father who left her to travel the world, making amends for his wrongs. It broke something in her and left her looking for love and acceptance in empty places. I think she grew to hate me. You and I, Tallie, already have a better relationship than she and I ever had. That's why I can be completely honest with you. I hurt Meghan, and I'm the one who's hurt you. You were a blank slate, completely off the grid, until you were photographed watching over the crash that took Deidre's and Meghan's lives. Sending Burke to protect you was another of my mistakes. My concern for you drew this director person to you."

"What do you think he wants from me?"

He looked away from her and threw another stone. "You're exactly the kind of person he recruits, from what I've observed: brilliant and multitalented with strong opinions."

Tallie heard the reservation in his voice and noted that he turned away from her to offer his assessment. "But you don't really believe that's why he brought me here, do you?"

"No." He turned back toward her. "I could be wrong. At least, I hope I am."

"Do you think he knows what we are to each other?"

"If not, it's a pretty strange coincidence that he wanted both of us."

"For what purpose?"

"To coerce me into doing what he wants."

"Which is?"

He cupped her jaw in his large hand. "It doesn't matter if it gets you released and sent back home."

"I'll gladly stay here if it means we can be a family."

He squeezed her hand. "First, we get you home." He brought her hand to his lips, kissed it, and held on to it, keeping her close. "If you're still willing to listen to that fatherly advice I spoke of, don't trust anything the director says. He may try to convince you that he has our best interests at heart, but don't believe him. If I have any fatherly capital with you, Tallie, trust me on this and don't trust that man. Please."

CHAPTER SEVENTEEN

Jackson exited the taxi and entered the hotel quietly while all the bellmen were busy helping other guests. As promised, Mak, who had arrived previously but had not yet checked in, left a jacket in a lobby chair, reserving the space for Jackson. It was near enough to the front desk to hear the conversations there and was within eyesight of the front entrance and the restaurant. Jackson set his single bag beside the chair and moved the jacket off the seat. After picking up a copy of an American newspaper, he sat down and checked in with Mak through the communication devices given him back at the Crib.

"I'm in position," he said.

"The major's daughter should arrive shortly," Mak said. Jackson spotted him near a tall potted plant, appearing to check his phone.

Dread and excitement coursed through Jackson at the prospect of what was about to occur. The Conservancy had booked Marlene and Mak into the Casa de Maya Hotel, where Jackson had already been booked for the same night. Red flags went off for the major, who feared the Conservancy had detected a plot afoot. To lessen that possibility and to protect the team in the event the op went south, he'd had them all fly into Mexico on separate airlines with communication devices, security protocols, and a no-contact order between them. As an added precaution, each was given a prophylactic dose of anti-paralytic medicine, and Mak carried extra doses in case they'd be needed.

Marlene arrived as inconspicuously as a fully feathered peacock in a barnyard of banty hens, dressed in a tight-fitting red skirt, red heels, and a white knit tee with her mop of flaming red hair piled loosely on her head. She seemed to enjoy women's jealous scrutiny as much as she enjoyed men's favorable attention, nodding and smiling at every female stare and male hat tip or approving glance. It was a wise strategy that made it possible for her to make eye contact with Jackson without drawing notice. He lowered the paper and hid his smile. The woman certainly knew how to make an entrance.

"Please tell me that's Marlene," Mak whispered.

"Bingo," Jackson said.

"Do you believe in love at first sight?"

"Evidently, the major does. That's why he sent you to the airport before she arrived at the Crib for her briefing."

"If any of these creeps touch her, I'm going to take them out."

"I think he's counting on that."

Her Southern accent was on full display as she strode to the front desk with a senior-aged bellman following behind, pushing her luggage on a rolling cart. She flirted shamelessly with the young clerk and checked in using her ex-husband's surname—Bodine. As planned, she repeated her room assignment—1420—loud enough for Jackson to hear.

"Did you catch that, Mak?"

"Roger that and sending."

Mak's fingers flew over his phone as he texted the room number to the other members of the team already on site.

Jackson focused his attention on the swap of desk clerks as the younger clerk was asked to help someone else while a new clerk, a woman, stepped in to complete Marlene's check-in. She dismissed the older bellman and called for a younger employee to guide Marlene to her room. If things went down as Tallie and Burke had suspected, the woman and the younger bellman were Conservancy plants inserted into the staff to see that certain expected "guests" were drugged and prepped for transport to the island. Jackson hoped only one bellman was involved. He watched carefully to see who would be called to assist Mak when he attempted to check in.

Burke had schooled Jackson and his colleagues on the items used to disarm the Conservancy's guests—keycards, glasses, and who knows what else dusted with the paralytic agent. Knowing what was about to happen to Marlene, Mak, and himself didn't stop Jackson's stomach from knotting.

Marlene followed the next step of the plan, delaying her arrival at her assigned room, which would afford Rich and his team the necessary time to set their security protocols in her room. She feigned a panic attack over a missing piece of luggage, sending the bellman out to the curb to search there, where she said she may have left it. The search went on until Rich texted her to say things were in place, and then she tipped the bellman and asked him to take her luggage upstairs while she grabbed a bite to eat. The bellman balked when her request upset the Conservancy's planned protocol of guiding the chosen guest directly to their room and administering the drug before he left them. Marlene remained unflappably charming and immovable despite the bellman's persistent offers of room service and his other efforts to get her to her room. In the end, she headed for the lobby restaurant anyway, and the bellman headed to her room to deliver the luggage.

Thirty minutes later, Mak moved to the front desk and the process repeated, except he had only one rolling bag that required no bellman. After repeating his room number—1425—which Jackson overheard and relayed to Rich's team, Mak used a tour of the exercise room and pool to give team members time to secure his room. Jackson checked his watch as Marlene exited the restaurant. She pulled a pin loose, releasing her long red hair, flipping a strand as she passed him—the signal. Her timing was perfect, and he knew the team should be ready for his check-in. He too was assigned to the fourth floor, in room 1418.

The older bellman was assigned to lead him to his room, handling the keycard and opening the door for Jackson. Curious about the change in protocol, Jackson looked down the hall and saw the younger bellman previously assigned to assist Marlene exit the elevator. He was carrying a tray with three drinks and three envelopes. Jackson watched the younger man open the door to room 1420—Marlene's room—and enter. After quickly tipping his own bellman, Jackson rushed him out so he could glance back down the hall and watch Marlene's door. As expected, the Conservancy plant exited with only two drinks and envelopes on his tray and headed for Mak's room, 1425.

Rich's voice came through the coms. "The cameras are planted, and we've got eyes on you three blind mice. Our hosts probably have their own eyes on you, so keep your voices low and face the floor when you speak so they can't read your lips. Copy that?"

Marlene and Mak said, "Copy," and Jackson followed suit.

"The protocol seems to have changed," Jackson relayed. "The bellman assigned to Marlene has drinks and envelopes on a tray."

"Copy that," Rich said through the coms. "Did everyone hear that? Bachelor number two is leaving courtesy cocktails on your nightstands with a card from the hotel manager. Delivery of the powder could be either via the glass or the envelope."

"Copy that," Mak said.

"Got it," Marlene said with an understandable tremble in her voice.

"No worries, Miss M. We've got you," Mak said.

Jackson heard a knock at his door.

"A special delivery is waiting for you, Jackson," Rich said.

Jackson opened the door and recognized the gloved bellman. He wanted to punch the guy straight out, but he managed a smile and said, "I didn't order any room service."

The bellman's smile widened. "Complimentary." He pushed through the door and set the glass on the nightstand, setting the envelope beside it. In a thick Spanish accent he added, "Gift certificate."

Jackson couldn't stand pretending he didn't know what game this guy was playing, so off the cuff he said, "I'm interviewing for a job with a company called IBT. Did they send you here with this?"

The bellman's eyebrows narrowed nervously, and his lips parted as if he wanted to reply to Jackson's comment. Instead, he answered, *"No hablo inglés"* and fled from the room.

The joy of rattling the Conservancy's crony was short-lived. Rich came over the coms. "What in the—Jackson! You want to tell me what that was about?"

His head dropped in shame as the enormity of his gaff sank in, but as he raised it to say, "I'm sorry," Rich's voice came over the coms.

"Keep your head down before you blow this entire op!"

Jackson moved to the bed and sat on the edge with his face toward the carpet. "I-I-I'm sorry. I couldn't handle having that weasel grin at me as if we don't know what he's up to."

"I hope it was worth possibly losing our best chance of rescuing Tallie and the general. You may have put the three of you in danger too. What if that weasel tells the Conservancy we're onto him and they decide to eliminate the problem? Was your little spitting match worth that?"

Jackson sank down onto the bed and cursed his foolishness. "Of course not. I-I-I wasn't thinking."

"No, you weren't, and that's why we don't let *amateurs* in on these ops. You're too big a risk. I'm pulling you."

Rich's words bit like a viper, but the thought of letting Tallie down made Jackson panic. He jumped from the bed and paced by its side, keeping his face downward. "No, you're not. I'm still in. No matter what. I'm still in!" Without waiting for further argument, he picked up the glass and rubbed his hands over it.

"Calm down or you'll blow what's left of your cover, Jackson. They can see what I see, and . . . wait!" Rich said. "What are you doing?"

"I'm sorry I was so foolish. Pull Marlene and Mak, but I'm going through with the plan. I'd rather get stuck on that island with Tallie than wonder what happened to her."

"All right, all right." The anger in Rich's voice turned to worry. "What do you think, Mak?" he asked.

"I agree that we pull Marlene, but I'm still in. I trust you, brother, if things go south."

Marlene piped in. "You have about as much chance of pulling me out as you've got of catching a greased pig in a lard factory."

"What?" Mak laughed and the mood changed.

"I believe you get my drift, buster," Marlene replied.

"The name's Makai, ma'am, but you can call me Mak."

"Shut it down, you two," Rich ordered. "Jackson, tell me everything you're feeling as it happens."

The effect was so soothing at first that Jackson didn't realize the drug's impact. Before he was unable to speak, he slurred out. "Relaxing. So tired."

"That sounds about right," Marlene assured him, having been through this days earlier. "And, Jackson, I get what you're feeling. I feel it too. Let's just stick to the script and bring this network down."

Jackson thanked her in his heart.

Rich's voice came back through the coms. "I see the bellman lurking in the hall. He must have eyes on you, Jackson, and he's waiting for you to drop."

And *drop* was the last thing Jackson heard.

* * *

A smiling Arabic man in a golf cart arrived to pick Tallie up the next morning. "Good morning, Miss Brown. I am Malik," he chirped. "I hear you're meeting with the director today. I'm your driver."

His cheeriness could not ease the flight response encouraging her to run. She'd struggled over what to wear for an hour. She had only three outfits, but slacks and a tee gave her the best chance of speed and movement if she needed to flee or fight, so she'd chosen them.

"Thank you," she said as she stepped into the cart and took her seat beside Malik. "What happens at these meetings?"

"I can't say that I know. I've never received an invitation myself. After intake, my family and I moved into our condo, met our supervisor, and became part of the community."

"You've never met the director?"

The man flinched. "Well . . . not . . . personally. I've seen him in the auditorium and on screen, of course, but he's a very busy man, flying here and there, trying to fix the world's problems."

Tallie had noticed that all the residents' answers about the director were glowing but vague, as if they were repeating lines from a brochure with no personal knowledge.

"What problems is he trying to fix now?" she asked.

The man sputtered and stammered for a few seconds before saying, "That's above my clearance, Miss Brown."

Clearance? She took a different approach. "I keep wondering what assignments I'll get. What's your job here on the island?"

"I'm a handyman, I guess you'd say. I fix what needs fixing. Now, my wife, she's a teacher over at the school. We both love our work."

"And your children? Are they happy here?"

His face lit up with pride. "They are the reason we came. To give them the best prospects for a successful life. My wife and I poured everything we had into them. They're special. Very bright. Their early test scores caught the attention of the Brain Trust. Our daughter, Jana, is eighteen now. She wanted to head back to the mainland and study law, but the Conservancy's international law committee offered to allow her to study under them, with a guaranteed position when she passes the bar. She won't have to wait seven years to make a difference in this world. She'll be contributing while she learns."

Tallie thought she heard a tinge of regret in the man's voice.

"Our son, Zain, is very talented with computers," he continued. "At fifteen, he's already learning how to write code for the island's defense system."

He was another child whose future rested solely on the island. "That's remarkable," she said, but her mind was spinning over Malik's other, less charming, comment. "This island has its own defense system?"

His eyes widened as if he'd revealed something he shouldn't have. "I don't really know much of what that entails. I probably misunderstood Zain. Don't pay me any mind. Not any mind at all."

Malik immediately became guarded, and Tallie knew she needed to work fast to restore the man's comfort. She wriggled up in her seat as if enthusiasm were about to explode from within her. "It truly is thrilling. I can't wait to hear how I'll contribute."

The trick worked; the man's face visibly relaxed again. "If the director wants to meet with you personally, I'm sure he has many exciting projects waiting for you."

"I hope so," she added with an extra measure of eagerness. "Could you give me a little tour of the island while we drive and tell me how things run here?"

"Of course," he said proudly. "It's all very streamlined. At last count, there are only about two hundred and six of us. But three more are expected to arrive tonight."

Her heart hitched at the thought of three more people being torn from their homes and lives. "Where are they from?"

"I'm afraid you're asking the wrong person. I don't have that information."

Suspicion and tension tightened his face, and Tallie returned to the topic he was most comfortable with. "So where does everyone live and shop and work?"

His smile returned again, and his left arm began pointing. "Private homes are situated on the left side of the island, nearest the water. The condo buildings are two streets back, but they're tall, so every place has a beautiful ocean view. The dock and market are south, the director's house and auditorium are on the north point, and most everything else for public use—schools, the infirmary, each trust's enclave, utility buildings, and security—is spread out in the center."

Tallie noted the use of the words *for public use*, implying there were facilities that were closed to the residents. "Security . . . is that the building where your son works?"

"After school only," he corrected.

"Of course." She pointed to a random building. "All the buildings are white, and they look so similar. It'll take me weeks to figure out what's where."

"The architecture here is based on the Conservancy's themes of equality, economy, and function. Sameness in design is more economical, but it also assures us that no group or occupation appears more important than another. As for finding your way around, just memorize the numbers on the buildings."

Malik identified each building they passed as Tallie constructed a map in her head. She formulated less-invasive questions and was able to get him to reveal a little more information about what each space was used for. The security building was in a cluster of buildings, near the infirmary. When she and her father were ready to leave, that building would play prominently in their plans.

Malik checked his watch. "We should head straight to the director's house now. You wouldn't want to be late for your appointment."

A sheen of sweat broke out over Tallie's skin as she recalled her father's advice not to trust anything the director said. She steeled herself to remain aloof and detached as the little cart approached the sprawling white-stucco home perched on the north peak of the island.

It wasn't the majestic palace or armed compound she expected a man trying to run the world would choose. It was larger than the other private homes but not grand by mainland standards. Most of the outer walls were formed by atrium doors that were open and inviting, allowing ocean breezes to ripple the gauzy curtains and leaving no clear definition between the inside and outside.

The view was breathtaking, and the gardens that surrounded the home were equally spectacular in their natural array and beauty, but no other efforts had been made to aggrandize the home, making it seem as though the man lived by the standards he espoused for everyone else—equality, economy, and function.

The cart's motor stopped, and as Tallie stepped off, a short older man emerged from the house, impeccably dressed in a white linen shirt and slacks. His smile beamed with so much love that Tallie turned to see if it was intended for someone else coming up behind them, but there was no one else. The hand that was waved in greeting was meant solely for her.

"That's the director, Miss Brown," Malik said. "I'll return for you when he calls me."

The cart's exit felt like the cutting of an umbilical cord, leaving Tallie alone and vulnerable.

As if noticing her discomfort, the director hurried down the pebble path to her. "Welcome, Tallie, welcome," he said almost breathlessly as he rushed to her. "How are you, my dear girl? You're even more beautiful than your photo suggested."

There was something about him that weakened her defenses, leaving her without the will to rail on him for the abuse she'd endured in Mexico at his associates' hands. His welcoming smile quivered as the moments ticked by and his hand remained outstretched and empty as the two continued to study one another.

"Have we met before?" Tallie asked.

"Do I seem familiar to you?"

Tallie scanned his face. "Slightly. But I don't know why or who you are."

"I'm someone who cares very deeply about you. In a way, you inspired this place. Do you like it?"

His ridiculous assertion that she, someone with no knowledge of this man or place, had somehow inspired it all pulled Tallie out of the veil of intrigue he'd created. "Yes, it's beautiful. That's why I find it especially ironic that you decided kidnapping was the best way to get me to come see the place you say I inspired."

He dropped his hand to his side. "I am sorry about the emergency arrangements, but my associates did what was needful to protect you from the rebels."

"And hiring an American agent to betray my trust and drug me . . . was that also to protect me?"

He reacted to her indictment, but not with a cagey reply or returned insolence. He smiled at her as if her anger was endearing. "You have your mother's fire and temper."

"You knew Deidre Kaswell?" The words flew from her mouth with a hunger she thought had been satisfied by being reunited with her father. She wished she could recall the admission as soon as the words left her lips. No one was supposed to know about her ties to the Kaswells, and she waited to see how the man would react to her admission. But he appeared more disappointed than surprised.

"Not Deidre. Julia, your true mother. The woman who raised you."

Tallie found no less thrill in connecting with someone who knew Julia.

"I knew her very well, in fact," the director added.

The sadness in his tone gave Tallie chills. "Who are you and how did you know her?"

"Come inside with me and you'll understand." He bent his arm, inviting her to take it.

She hesitated, and then, figuring he'd had more than ample opportunities to harm her if that was his wish, she took his arm and allowed him to lead her inside.

The interior of the home was white and airy. The entryway led to an open living area that was modestly furnished—two wood-framed chairs with tufted teal cushions, a striped sofa to match, a sofa table, a few end tables and lamps made from driftwood. The space spread into the dining area with a wood dining table and ten chairs. The entire space tied into the large kitchen with high-end appliances, a luxury he'd obviously allowed himself, but judging from the table size and number of chairs, he evidently entertained here.

Aside from the restaurant-quality kitchen, everything appeared simple, functional, and even handmade, down to the amateur island-themed artwork. Childlike sculptures, possibly products of an elementary art class, provided enough sea creatures and birds to fill the sofa table, and Tallie recognized some of the subjects of the oil and pastel paintings, like the tidal pool and a few of the gardens she'd passed today. This man clearly valued his small community, and his pride over its few children was evident.

Warmth and welcome filled the space, and as Tallie scanned it, her eyes fell on a simple corner shelf unit that held framed photographs. She looked at her host and saw hesitancy as he waved his hand forward, inviting her to view them. She had barely moved when she recognized the young woman whose shoulders were wrapped in a black stole for her senior portrait. Every inch of skin on Tallie's body prickled and her eyes stung at the sight. It was Julia when she was Diana, young and beautiful and smiling. Tallie inched to the photo, wanting desperately to see who Julia once was and dreading the idea of seeing who her serious, somber mother might have been. She knew how insane the thought was. If Diana had been well, she never would have taken Tallie. Whatever happened between that happy photo and the day Diana had decided to keep Tallie had changed everything in so many lives. When Tallie turned back to look at the director, she knew Mogadishu was not the only event that had changed the course of Diana's life. This man was also the cause.

"My name is Joseph Howard," he said.

"How—" Her knees quivered, and she immediately straightened her posture, as if Joseph were Julia, equally insistent on perfection and excellence. When he smiled at her, she relaxed and cocked her head to the side, comparing the man before her to the woman she'd called Mother. "Diana's father?"

"Yes."

Tallie fixed her gaze on the family photo of her host as a young man. He was well-dressed in a suit and tie, seated beside a lovely dark-haired wife with an infant in her arms. Another photo pictured the mother and toddler at the beach. The last photo was of a sullen adolescent with long hair in a plaid jumper and white boots, sitting alone on a swing.

"She never spoke of family," Tallie said, "of her father. All those years . . . we were alone, poor, hunted, afraid. Why didn't you help us?"

"I thought she was dead, Tallie. She wanted me to think that."

"But why?" The words came out as a moan more than a question.

"Because I failed her . . . in every way a father can fail a child." Joseph reached for Tallie's hand and led her to the sofa. Long grief-filled breaths escaped him as he sat beside her and gathered his thoughts. "I created encrypted software for military applications. I thought I was making the world safer, but while I was busy building an empire and being important to other people, I ignored the signs of mental illness in Diana's mother until it was too late. She took her own life, Tallie, when Diana was only a child." His eyes shone at the memory, and his voice broke as he began again. "Diana witnessed it, and it shattered her. I promised myself and Diana that I'd change my priorities and put her first in my life, and I did, for a time. I turned the day-to-day operations of my software company over to my board, canceled all speaking and philanthropic engagements, and moved into the international construction field, which I could supervise from home."

"You raised Diana alone?"

He closed his eyes and shook his head. "I wasn't strong enough to trust my board for very long, and I came to realize two ugly truths about myself. I fed on being needed by powerful decision-makers, and I loved the adoration I received when I spoke. Soon I was as busy and absent as before, and Diana needed medication to remain stable." He stood and walked over to the photos, returning with the senior-year portrait. "What do you see when you study her expression? What does that smile tell you?"

Tallie studied the image more closely and saw so many emotions—yearning, insecurity, hopelessness.

"When I look at this photo, I see her taunting me with a secret." He set the photo on the coffee table and sat back down. "As soon as she left her portrait appointment, she headed into town to the enlistment office."

"Without your approval?"

"I'd never have given it. She was all I had, and she wasn't well. That's what kills me. I knew she was struggling, but I wasn't home enough to help her." He dropped his head into his hands and massaged his temples. "She was eighteen, but she waited weeks to tell me what she'd done. She said she enlisted because I loved the military so much."

"She wanted to make you proud?"

"No. She was mocking me. She said she thought she'd have a better chance of seeing me on a parade field or at a military base than she would at home." He stood and replaced the portrait on the shelf, as if needing to walk more than he needed to tidy the room. "I tried to cancel her enlistment. I called in every favor to get her declared unfit for service. It only alienated her further from me, so I surrendered."

Tallie wondered what her life and Julia's would have been like if Julia could have called on her father for help.

"She left for basic training and didn't contact me again until after she returned from Mogadishu. I didn't even know she'd been deployed to Somalia on that *peacekeeping* mission."

His sarcasm was bitter, and Tallie wondered if that assignment had broken him as deeply as it had his daughter.

"And then, out of the blue, she called me when she returned home. She'd been stationed on some base in West Virginia, and she'd done something terrible there that she feared would hurt me. When she called, she said she was in trouble, expensive trouble. She didn't tell me the whole truth at the time. Only that she had a child and that the truth about the baby's father would ruin not only her but me as well if I didn't pay off a blackmailer named Petty Bodeil.

The man somehow knew Diana's father was very wealthy, and the price he requested for his silence was that I satisfy the debts of his hometown, Cutler's Ridge, and fix the flood damage that had destroyed much of the downtown area. When Diana came to me, she didn't mean for her request to come across as a threat, but that's how I read it."

His face twisted as if he might cry, and then he began tapping on his head. Tallie wasn't sure if the tapping was intended as punishment, but after a minute or two, he stopped and stared blankly at an unknown spot in the air and continued.

"She was looking out for me, trying to protect me and my good name, but I refused to see that at the time. I can't remember much of our conversation that day, but I imagine I let her know I wasn't pleased that our one and only contact in six years was because she'd shamed our family and needed my money. *My* money." He spat the last words out like snake venom. "The words sicken me now. I sacrificed my family to make that accursed money."

He bit his trembling lip and leaned forward, folding into a weeping lump. Tallie laid her hand on his shoulder, but she too was bleeding out on the inside, leaving her no words of comfort to offer him. His pain had caused her pain, as she realized how his mistakes had cost her the life she was meant to live. Day after day, week after week, each time she'd thought she'd rounded the last corner, uncovered the last lie and secret, there was another and another, and she wondered if there could ever be an end to the hurt.

Joseph sat up and straightened. "Whatever our conversation, in that instant, I knew I owed it to her to help her no matter the reason, so I sent teams of contractors to Cutler's Ridge to do whatever Petty Bodeil asked. I did it for Diana and for her child, but I'm sure she felt I did it to protect myself and my precious reputation. I began to see her child as a new chance for all of us, but I never got to meet my granddaughter because the next word I received about Diana came months later, when Major Norris visited me to tell me she had taken her own life. In that moment, I thought she preferred death to being my child. Can you imagine how deep that pain went?"

"Yes, I actually can."

"Yes . . . yes, I suppose you do, child. You lived with the aftermath of my failure as her father, her sense of loss and betrayal. But hopefully you see how my daughter loved you and molded you. Major Norris told me she was heroic in Mogadishu." His voice broke again. "I never got the chance to tell her I was proud of her." Joseph coughed to clear his voice and wiped his fingers across his moist eyes. "I blamed myself for her death, and I lost all hope of ever meeting her child, who seemed to disappear into thin air. At first, I assumed the father had her and that I had lost another person from my life. I made myself two promises. The first was to atone for my part in Diana's agony." He raised his arm and pointed to the island view visible through the open doors. "So I started the Conservancy in hopes that fewer mothers and fathers would have to send their children to war. I gathered the smartest people and kept our work under the wire for years, holding summits in foreign countries, where we discussed public policy changes to make sure all people have access to the basic needs of food, water, land, healthcare, education, and a healthy planet. I took my suggestions to governments, but they had already become drunk on the same power trip that had sucked me in."

His voice rose in volume and passion. "Look at who we choose to run our governments. When I saw a brutal world leader's poll numbers rise among his own abused countrymen because he was photographed with a movie star, I knew it was pointless to hope for governments to solve our problems. That's when I bought this island and began bringing the best minds here, where we could not only discuss policy changes but enact them too."

"By kidnapping people?"

His disappointment was not only evident but nearly palpable. His hands flew to his head, and he crouched and moaned. "After all I've told you, is that all you care about? I do that for security. The work we're doing is too important to risk premature exposure to the world." As if illustrating his next words, he drew his shoulders inward and bent low, drawing his arms close to his body and wriggling his fingers until he looked like a mouse before he said, "We need to remain obscure, hidden, off the grid."

Joseph's own instability sent chills through Tallie, and she wondered if Julia's paranoia had its roots in his genetics. It frightened her to think of this man's power and the plans he was implementing. His dreams may have had a noble beginning, but somewhere, he'd lost his way and his mind.

He straightened his posture and then his clothes. "Do you understand?" he asked.

She had been too preoccupied with his antics to immediately remember the topic, but she quickly recalled that it was about his reason for bringing people here drugged and, in some cases, against their will. "I hear what you're saying."

"Good." His right hand chopped into his left as he made each new point. "No one has to stay. They get three days to decide. Three days to walk along the island, smell the first pure air they've breathed in years, sit in on the most stimulating discussions in their specialty, and get a personal testimony of our mission."

"And then?"

"If they choose to leave, we administer our proprietary, untraceable cocktail that affects their short-term memory, and we send them back to where we picked them up."

"Unharmed?"

"Completely unharmed, except for a nasty headache and the loss of a few days."

Tallie had heard the reports about the victims who were sent home sick and confused with terrifying gaps in their memory. It wasn't the innocent practice Joseph tried to paint it to be. "Why do you say I inspired all this if the island and the plan were built years ago?"

"I always knew Diana's child was out there somewhere." Joseph took her hand. "I tried for years to find you, and when I failed, I wondered why I bothered to care if the world destroyed itself. Understanding the suffering that caused my daughter to kill herself became my next mission. I scoured the internet and pieced together every minute of Cai Kaswell's life, especially the mention of his *heroic* service in Mogadishu. I sent men to pay Somali rebels for their side of the story and the villagers who saved Kaswell for theirs. I discovered what really happened that morning in Mogadishu. I also figured out what really happened with that car accident where everyone assumed you were dead. I paid those rebels to hound the doctor in Cutler's Ridge to get me proof of your identity, but once again, I failed."

He released her hand and wiped at his eyes. "Then, after suffering over Diana's death for twenty years, I received a strange text several weeks ago. I didn't recognize the number, but the message upset me so much that I put my IT specialists on it to find the source. The message began, *If you're reading this, I'm probably dead* and ended with a reference about a daughter.'"

He leaned back, relishing this part of his story. "My IT staff was able to track down the name of every other person who received that text. Some were from that small mining town—Cutler's Ridge—and one went to Deidre Kaswell. Then you appeared in the papers. The girl with no history, who kept a vigil at the crash site where Deidre and Meghan Kaswell died."

He stood and stared out the window for a few moments as a serene pleasure softened his face. "Though I couldn't prove it, I knew you were Cai and Deidre Kaswell's daughter Molly. Diana got you from the Bodeil family after their daughter rescued you in the woods and then faked her own death because she hated me and had no one else to trust." He turned back to Tallie and sat beside her again. "You became her reason for living after Mogadishu, and now that she's gone, you've become my legacy."

Sweat poured over Tallie's body as her defenses rose. She inched away from Joseph, and in response, he reached his hand to her, smiling and saying, "I know I've overwhelmed you. What I should have said is that I want you to see me as your grandfather."

Tallie cocked her head to the side and replayed the words over and over, decoding every intonation, every eye movement, and the spread of his smile. She believed what he said. He wanted her to love him as a grandfather. Could she? Should she?

He patted her hand. "You don't have to answer me this instant. I know you've connected with your father and that you already feel a love for him. I ask you to consider, as a woman of science, that his investment of but a moment's worth of DNA is far less than what Diana gave you. She was your mother. She made you who you are today . . . this brilliant, sensitive, strong woman I've learned so much about and who I now see before me."

Tallie started to speak, but the words and her thoughts became so tangled that she stopped with only a mutter. "I love my father."

"Understandable, but why not love us both?"

Could that be possible?

"Tallie, I'm not excusing what Diana did. It was wrong, but what she did *for* you is remarkable, perhaps giving you a priceless gift. Think about it. Your mind is enlivened while remaining relatively untouched by the world and its problems and prejudices. Socially, you're a blank slate, capable of unlimited hope and awe and love for everyone because your broad view of the world's cultures and people has opened your eyes to the potential in all mankind. We see the world the same way, Tallie. You're the perfect person to continue my work when I'm gone."

Tallie processed Joseph's beautiful, flattering words. It was true that her purloined life had been spent living in countless countries and many cultures, most of them among the poorest of the world. She did feel love, empathy, and compassion for them, and she also knew they were capable of great things if given access to the things most first-world people took for granted, things like nourishing food, clean water, and education. The issue plaguing her, she knew, was that she struggled to extend that same grace and love to herself, to see her own potential to rise and fit in. To believe she was equal to and deserving of a first-world life instead of discounting herself as odd and lacking. And Joseph and his failure with Diana was at the crux of that.

As if sensing her inner struggle, he squeezed her hand and smiled at her with so much love that her blame faded and her heart began to swell. Her father had also failed, hadn't he? And she had forgiven him. And Jackson had struggled because of his own failures, and he'd found redemption. The same could be said for Norris and even Julia. So why not for this man? Overriding her defenses, she allowed his offer of more family to distill upon her mind. If losing a daughter had destroyed him, could finding a granddaughter save him?

Then she remembered her father's warning, that she shouldn't believe anything this man said, but it was hard not to share his hope for a better world. She lowered the barrier between Joseph's plan for the world and her view of it. Were they so very different? Could it be possible to tweak his methods and salvage his vision?

One unanswered point picked at her, leaving a gaping hole she needed him to fill. "You said you made yourself two promises. One was to atone for your part in Diana's pain by making the world a better, safer place. What was the second?"

He crossed one leg over the other and set his hands on his knees, as if posing for a portrait. "To make everyone who contributed to Diana's distress and death pay."

A chill zipped up her spine. "You mean my father."

"Yes, and Major Norris, among others. They each had the obligation to tell the truth about what happened that night. That truth would have freed Diana. She'd have had no reason to fear her government or the Somali rebels."

"Her fears about the government were the result of her paranoia, and you're the one who stoked the Somalis' interest in hounding us. You nearly drove her insane."

"I've owned up to my sins," he replied defensively. "Now Cai Kaswell and Stephen Norris must own up to theirs."

"Haven't they already paid for their mistakes in years of guilt and in service to their country? Can't you forgive them? Julia wanted to be forgiven before she died. It brought me to you, to this moment. Can't we take advantage of this gift and look forward instead of being chained to the past?"

Joseph stood abruptly. "No! Surely you must also want everyone responsibile to pay for what they did to Julia."

"But what do you want from them? A confession? Imprisonment?"

"Confession is nonnegotiable, but where and how and to whom is negotiable. We all have choices, Tallie. They will have choices also."

"Which you feel you have the right to decide. You want to be their judge, jury, and sentencer. What gives you that right?"

"They know. Ask them."

CHAPTER EIGHTEEN

THE SWIM WAS MORE THAN Stephen's aging body was able to handle, but Rich and Burke saw his struggle and came to his rescue a few hundred yards from shore before his burning muscles and lungs gave completely out. Rich quickly added Burke's pack to his own back while Burke pulled Stephen onto dry ground.

"Thanks for the lift, Burke," Stephen said as he lay gasping for breath and fully spent on the beach behind a large rock. "How are you managing with those battered ribs?"

"Okay, sir. Rich wrapped me tight. Thanks for bringing me along and giving me a chance to redeem myself."

Rich slapped Burke on the back of the head. "Don't make us regret it, knucklehead."

"Don't worry. My knucklehead days are over." Burke laughed and grew thoughtful. "I'll take whatever legal action is coming my way. I'm just grateful I can face that storm from this side of the line."

"If we get off this rock, we'll stand beside you." Stephen rose up on one elbow and then stood slowly. "Now, give us the lay of the land."

Burke used his hand to shield his eyes from the sun as he pointed above. "See those giant wind turbines? Behind them is a solar farm. Between the ocean breezes and the sun, the residents have a never-ending supply of power and massive underground batteries to store the excess they produce. More than enough to power anything the director has a mind to install, if you get my drift."

The ominous report left Rich and Stephen silent for several moments.

"Where does the director keep his choppers?" Rich asked.

Burke pointed to a position right of the wind farm. "From what the dying driver told me, the landing pad and the helos are in that area."

"Mak and I worked out the flight plan before he left for Mexico," Rich said. "We just need to get everyone to that pad and hope the directors' two Apaches are fueled and ready to fly."

"Apaches." Stephen rolled his eyes at the extravagance of the owner. "I'd like to know what he promised some general to get that purchase authorized. But they'll give us plenty of flight miles per tank and just enough seats to get our people to the Ecuadorian mainland."

Rich smiled. "Then it's just a flight home from there." After scanning the shoreline and the steep ascent ahead, he stripped off his wetsuit and dug in his pack for dry clothes. "What's the best route, Burke?"

"The only security gap I ever found was straight up that cliff. That is, unless they've addressed that weakness since I escaped from their people in Mexico."

"That's going to be a haul."

"Like Normandy, and the stakes are just as high," Stephen muttered.

"Copy that, Major. I'll ready the gear," Rich said.

"Thanks, Rich. Give me an hour or so to peel this wetsuit off and put on some dry clothes and I'll be good to go."

Rich laughed. "Sure, and I'll draw you a hot bath."

"Okay, smart guy. Give me five, and Burke, check the weapons and distribute the coms."

"Roger that, Major."

Stephen turned his head to study the island prison.

"Thinking about your daughter and Tallie?" Burke asked.

"And how much I regret letting either of them out of my sight. How long is recovery during intake?"

"It's different for everyone. Weight, general health, and the dose of paralytic they received determines their recovery period. Some people pop out of bed, hungry and ready to walk in an hour. Others need a day or two to feel like themselves."

"What about our guys?" Stephen said.

Rich piped in. "Mak just touched the glass lightly; that and his size should help him recover quickly. I'm not even sure he was fully out when they grabbed him. Jackson might be a mess for a while. He rubbed every inch of that glass."

"And my girl, Burke? What do you think is happening to her right now?" Stephen said.

"The women in intake are angels. They're giving her a day at the spa."

"Thanks for saying that, whether it's true or not." Stephen tied his boots and took several deep breaths. "I think I'm ready to tackle that wall."

"You're sixty years going on forty. I'd say you're battle fit," Rich said with a wink. "Still, how about letting me head up first and anchor things?"

"Roger that."

Burke pulled the climbing gear from a pack. "I'll take the rear and cover you two in case security comes calling."

"Sounds like a plan," Stephen said. "Don't get yourself captured, Burke. We need you to identify the targets up top."

Burke laughed. "Thanks for making me feel needed, Major. But, just in case, head for the white buildings. They're your primary targets."

"You said all the buildings on the campus were white." Rich's head cocked back.

"Did I?" Burke teased. "Then, I guess I'd better not get myself captured or killed."

The three men laughed and began the arduous climb up the ragged cliff face. Rich arrived on top and pulled Stephen over the edge a few minutes later. Burke crested the top and signaled for his friends to take cover behind a clump of shrubbery. Once they'd caught their breath, Rich pulled out a satellite image of the island taken using the coordinates Burke had provided before they'd set out.

"Orient us from this location," Stephen whispered.

Burke silently pointed left and raised two fingers to indicate a distance of approximately two kilometers to the airfield. "Security is straight ahead a half klick."

"Roger that," Stephen said. "When we break from here, Rich'll head to the airfield to see if those Apaches are there and fueled up while Burke and I head to the security building and get control of communications. Then we'll start searching this rock for our people."

"Roger that, Major," Rich said.

The men had barely made it ten yards when Burke pointed to an approaching guard and groaned. "Grab cover! Grab cover!"

The men ducked behind leafy scrub growth, but not before the security guard noticed movement and headed their way. "Stay down," Burke said. "Maybe I can convince him I'm supposed to be here." He stood up and brushed himself off nonchalantly, waving the young armed guard over. "It's just me, Agent Burke. I climbed the ridge to check this weak spot in the security perimeter. It needs some reinforcing. I suggest you report that to your superior."

"What are you even doing here?" the guard said in a heavy French accent. "We were told your team was lost to us in Mexico."

"I was, for three days. A cartel gave chase and caught us. I hid in the jungle until they gave up looking for me and just made it back on this morning's flight."

The guard assumed an aggressive stance, raising his gun at Burke. "No. We were told you were lost, as in you turned sides."

Burke raised his hands and stepped back. "Why on earth would I come back here if I changed sides?"

"Explain it to the director. Now, walk."

The man nudged Burke forward with the barrel of his gun. Burke complied and began heading inland. He glanced back, supposedly at his captor, also making eye contact with Stephen and Rich. The younger man signaled that he was ready to come to Burke's aid, but Burke shook his head.

The exaggerated motion caught the interest of Burke's captor, who turned him around and headed back to check the area for any missed comrades. Burke tried distracting the guard with small talk, but the man would not be deflected. As he and his captor neared the brush, Burke's mouth spread into a wry smile aimed in his friends' direction, and then he dropped to the ground and kicked the captor in the kneecap. The man fell backward with a yowl. Rich broke from the bushes to secure him, but the guard squeezed off one round straight into Burke's chest.

Rich reached the shooter and twisted the man's neck until he went limp. As soon as Rich determined that the assailant was dead, he rushed to Burke to check on his condition.

Stephen was right behind, pulling the guard's body. "Let's get these guys back in the brush in case someone heard that shot."

Rich pulled Burke behind cover to assess him and stuck his finger directly into the bullet wound. Burke barely acknowledged the pain the action should have caused, and Stephen knew he wasn't going to make it.

"Rich'll fix you right up," Stephen lied, blinking back tears.

Burke managed a weak smile. "It's okay. Just tell me I went out as a good guy."

Stephen bit the side of his mouth and knelt down beside Burke, laying a hand on his arm. "You're not just one of the good guys. You're one of the best guys, do you hear me?"

As the color drained from Burke's face, he managed to say, "The campus is small. The security building is the largest on the island. Next to the infirmary marked with a red-and-white flag. Everything . . . you want is in that security building—the computer hub, communica . . . communica—"

"Don't talk, Burke," Stephen said. "We'll find it."

His breathing turned shallow, and he struggled to get enough breath to continue. "Tell Cai I'm sorry, and when you find Brown . . ." He swallowed and gasped as his spittle turned red. "Tell her I died trying to keep my promise." His head fell limply to the side with a final exhale.

Rich blinked rapidly and tightened his arms around his friend. "He was bleeding out too quickly. I couldn't . . . there was nothing we could do for him."

"You did what he wanted most—proved to him that you saw him as your brother again." Stephen transferred his hand to Rich's shoulder. "We need to move now, in case someone heard the shot."

Rich laid Burke down carefully on the ground. "Copy that."

* * *

Marlene woke up to the last thing she wanted to see—two smiling women hovering over her. It took only a few minutes for her to get her bearings. Her last experience with the paralyzing powder had made her wise enough to touch the glass very lightly, just enough to put her under, and as Burke had predicted, her previous experience with both the paralytic and the antidote administered at the hospital had left her less susceptible the second time. She asked for a drink of water, and then her professional and personal missions took over. "Well, this is quite a reception. You'd think I was your only new arrival." When the women didn't take the bait, she continued. "I'm not you're only new arrival, am I?"

"No," a woman whose nametag read *Livvie* said. "But don't worry yourself about the others. You're our personal guest, and we're here to make sure you're comfortable and happy."

The second woman approached her with a pill in a cup, and Marlene was having none of it. "Back up and listen, Florence Nightingale. I arrived with two men. Where are they and what have you done with them?"

The women sputtered, and the second woman headed for a red button on the wall. Before she reached it, Marlene jumped onto her feet, caught the woman in two strides, twisted her arm behind her back, and wrapped her own free arm around the woman's neck. Her captive fought to get away, her opposite hand coming up to tug futily at Marlene's arm. Marlene put more pressure on the woman's shoulder and wrist, holding them securely behind the woman's back. "I don't want to hurt you nice ladies, but put a cork in your programmed spiel and speak some truth. Where are my friends?" To accentuate the urgency of an answer, she pulled the woman's arm a little higher until the woman moaned in pain and her wriggling stopped.

"All right, all right!" Livvie squeaked. "The larger man was moved to a private room over an hour ago. The other man is struggling to come out from under the cocktail."

"Let's all three visit him."

"Let Lei go, please," Livvie said. "All we've done is try to help you."

"Listen, lady, this isn't my first trip on the director's crazy train. One of his little kidnappers almost killed me last week. I'm lucky to be alive, so don't try to convince yourself or me that all you're doing is making people feel comfortable and happy. You're aiding and abetting a mass kidnapping operation, and unless you want to leave paradise for a one-way ticket to a federal pen, you'd better do as I say and take me to my friend."

The woman's wild-eyed expression sobered.

"You don't have to threaten us," Lei said. "We'll help you. And to prove we mean what we say, I'll warn you that the entire building is under video surveillance. Security is probably on its way here now."

Marlene released her and smiled. "If my big friend was moved to a private room an hour ago, as you said, those cameras are already disabled. Now, take me to the little guy."

The women complied, leading Marlene to a suite down the hall, where one male med tech was monitoring Jackson from a chair while reading a book. Livvie entered the room first and inquired about his patient while Marlene and Lei stood just outside the door.

"He's going to be out for a while. Whoever administered the cocktail to him nearly killed this guy."

"What are you doing for him?" she demanded.

Marlene heard honest concern in the woman's voice and trusted the pair of nurses enough to whisper to Lei, "Get me a bedsheet."

While Lei ran her errand, Livvie dismissed the tech and took over. She pulled a bag of liquid from a cupboard and hung it on a pole, preparing to administer the fluid through an IV already installed in Jackson's arm. The tech stood by and argued about his dismissal, ignoring Marlene, who entered behind Lei, armed with a bedsheet twisted into a rope. With one quick movement, she lassoed the man's neck and crossed the fabric in back, tightening it until he passed out. After he was down, she tied him up quickly like a rodeo calf. Her attentions turned to Jackson just as another man hurried into the room and directly to Jackson's side, where he grasped Livvie's arm in his left hand, stopping her work.

"I assume you're Mak," Marlene said.

"Yes, ma'am. I'm a medic." He touched Jackson's forehead and took his pulse. "I'll take over here."

"Mak, I'm Marlene, the major's daughter."

"Nice to meet you," he said, never taking his eyes off Jackson. "I recognized you from your entrance at the hotel."

"Livvie isn't a threat, Mak. At least not anymore. We've reached an understanding, haven't we, Livvie?"

"Yes," Livvie replied with pleading in her eyes. "I really just want to help. This man needs an IV."

Mak clearly wasn't ready to trust the woman with Jackson's life just yet. He removed the IV bag from the hook and asked to know where the supply of Ringer's solution was. Livvie pointed to the cupboard. Mak released her arm and walked her there, under guard, pulled a new bag from the cupboard and read its label. When he was satisfied it was safe to use, he walked Livvie back to Jackson and watched carefully as she set the new bag and adjusted the flow. When Mak was satisfied that Livvie was actually helping Jackson, he offered her a nod of approval.

"Always a SEAL?" Marlene asked.

"Yes, ma'am."

"He should get better now," Livvie said.

Mak pulled a syringe from his pocket. "This is an anti-paralytic. Now he'll get better."

Livvie set her hand on Mak's arm. "That IV bag already contains the antidote to the paralytic. I promise. Now he just needs time and rest."

Marlene checked her watch. "Neither of which we can afford."

Mak glanced out a window. "The rest of the team should be on site by now. I found the computers that monitor the cameras and set them in a loop so the security team will see footage, but it'll repeat every minute. Once they notice that, they're going to storm the security building next door. We need to get out of here and get Jackson to a safe place until the whole team can assemble."

Marlene turned to the women. "Does Tallie Brown have her own place here?"

"No," Lei said. "She's just in a private room here in the infirmary."

"Does Cai Kaswell?" Mak asked Livvie.

"Yes. It's not far from here."

Mak picked Jackson up, Lei maneuvered the IV pole, and Livvie led the way through some garden paths to hide their exit. Marlene covered the rear, watching and hoping she'd see her father appear. She worried about him. He still saw himself as a door kicker, but she knew the years and the strain of secrets had taken a toll on him.

They reached Cai's door, and Mak knocked. When no one answered, he had Marlene fish a small tool from his pocket.

"Allow me," she said as she worked the tool to unlock Cai's door.

"Is it proper for a man you barely know to say, 'I love the way you pick a lock'?"

"Save it for when we get off this island, sailor." She looked up from her work and asked him point-blank, "We are going to get off this island, aren't we?"

Mak gave her a quick wink and a half smile brim with confidence. "Yes, ma'am. You can count on it."

She got the door open, and the group hurried inside and closed it behind them. Mak laid Jackson on the sofa, and while the nurses settled their patient in, Marlene did a quick surveil of the room to get some indication of how Cai was and where he might be. She headed into the bedroom to lift the mattress, hoping Tallie had shared the story of finding his challenge coin under the hotel mattress with him. Sure enough, inspiration paid off when Marlene pulled out a note from Cai to Tallie.

It felt wrong to read it, but she was convinced the information contained would be critical to the group's success in saving their friends . . . and perhaps the free world. Knowing she had it was enough for now, so she set the letter back where she'd found it and headed back into the living room.

"How's he doing?" She nodded to Jackson.

"A little better, but not great," Livvie said. "We'll keep pushing fluids to flush the toxin out."

Marlene crossed her arms and towered over the sitting nurses. "So what's your story? I can't believe everyone on this island prison thinks life here is worth giving up everything else."

Lei dropped her gaze to the floor. "Once you make a decision, you live with it."

"You don't have to," Marlene argued. "We're allowed to make mistakes and change our minds. That's freedom. This—whatever this is—is not. People back home are worried you were murdered."

Livvie sighed long and low. "People? Most of us don't have people to notice that we went missing. Or do you mean government people and lawyers? Because we walked away from everything and defaulted on all our responsibilities, as if we'd died."

Lei pulled her shoulders back and said, "The director is so generous and welcoming. I'd feel like an ingrate for wanting to go back." She took Livvie's hand. "So we make the best of it, and we've tried to help others make the best of it too."

Mak shook his head as if the entire conversation were insane. "Making the best of *this*? This little project is not about happy island life or making the world better. Your benefactor bought you, plain and simple. You might have a nice place to live, but you're his now, and so is everything you do and create. Why do you think he's asking you to improve a world you're not allowed to return to and experience?"

"He's afraid the island will get overrun with people who want to come here once they hear about it," Lei said.

Mak jutted his finger forward. "Don't buy it! This place is about power. *His* power. Every article you write, every program you code, every scientific breakthrough you discover becomes his and makes him stronger. You give him the material he needs to stay relevant on the airwaves and sway people's opinions. Your citizens are increasing his influence."

"What are you saying?" Livvie asked.

Marlene leaned close and looked the woman in the eye. "He's saying that your generous director has less-benevolent motives for his work. He wrote the programs used by the US military, and experts think he can manipulate the air and naval fleets across the world using his software. He could neutralize our defense system."

Lei's hackles rose. "Well, maybe that's a good thing. Would it be so bad if he stopped all the ships and tanks and planes and *war*?"

Mak laughed sarcastically. "Not all. Ours. Do you really believe a world without the US military would be safer?"

"What if it is?" Livvie asked.

"What if the last armed nations aren't friendly ones?" Marlene said. "I don't think this director or any one individual should get to decide what leader gets to command the last superpower on Earth, do you?" Livvie didn't reply, so Marlene dug back in. "Let's say he does manage to disarm everyone else. Will he disarm this island, or does he get to keep his toys?"

Mak pulled the window curtain farther aside and said, "Marlene, look. The major and Rich are on the move across the garden. I'm going out to lead them here." He handed her a gun. "No one leaves."

"Absolutely not."

Jackson stirred on the sofa and tried to sit up, then groaned from the effort and sent his hands to his head, as if he were trying to keep it from splitting open.

"Whoa, buddy. Take it slow and easy," Marlene said.

"Marlene? Where's Tallie?"

"I haven't seen her yet. We're in Cai's place. These two ladies are the island's nurses." Marlene looked at the women and smirked. "They're currently our *guests*."

Jackson looked at the gun. "I take it our rescue mission is only beginning."

"Mak is gathering the rest of the crew. I think Daddy, Rich, and Burke were surveilling the island. We're waiting for directions."

"Got it."

The door opened then, and Marlene's father and Rich entered. Her father made his way directly to Marlene and caught her in a quick hug.

"Where's Burke?" Jackson asked. He must've caught the telling glance that passed between Mak and Rich too. "No! He didn't betray—"

"No." Marlene's father was clear and direct. "He died protecting us. He used his last breath to direct us to our targets."

"It's messed up," Mak said. "Especially after everything he's been through."

"He's dead? I can't believe it. He died saving us?" Marlene's voice broke as she searched her father for injuries. "Are you all right, Daddy?"

"I'm fine," her father said, wrapping his arm around her.

She buried her face in his shoulder as another knock, rapid and panicked, battered the door. Rich ordered the women back near Jackson while he and Mak and Marlene's father positioned themselves near the door, at the ready in case of a fight. The knocks repeated, followed by Tallie's voice calling out for Cai.

Jackson rose shakily and rushed forward, dragging his IV pole along. He was nearly breathless as he opened the door. "Tallie, are you okay?"

Tallie stepped back in shock, trying to process his presence there. Once she recovered from the surprise, she hugged Jackson and scanned his face and then the others'. "What are you . . . ? How . . . ?"

"There's no time for explanations now," Marlene's father said. "So you don't know where Cai is either?"

"He's not here? We have to find him." She turned to Marlene's father. "The director is Joseph Howard, Diana's father. He's not stable. He holds you and my father responsible for everything that happened to Diana, and he's set on making you pay."

CHAPTER NINETEEN

It wasn't until Tallie saw the shocked expression on everyone's faces that she realized what she had revealed about her relationship to Cai. Jackson and Marlene sucked in worried gasps, while Livvie and Lei assumed the same open-mouthed look of shock Rich and Mak wore.

"Did I just hear you right?" Rich asked as he turned to the major for confirmation.

Norris placed a hand on Tallie's shoulder and stepped in to refocus the group. "All you need to know for now is that it's true. Tallie is Cai's daughter. Now, let's zero in on what we know of his circumstances, formulate a plan, and find him, shall we?"

"He left a letter for Tallie," Marlene said as she hurried to retrieve it. Tallie's hands trembled as she read the first letter she'd ever received from her father. The longer she read, the more she feared this first letter would be the last.

> *Tallie,*
> *I'm growing accustomed to your name. I actually like it. Short for Talitha, the girl raised from the dead. You're a miracle to me—my miracle—and I can't take that for granted.*
>
> *Before I deployed to Somalia, your mother and I took you girls to Nashville. Your grandma came along to watch you in the evenings so your mom and I could have some alone time. We spent those hours dreaming about the future, about our girls' future, where we'd live and what our life would look like. We made contingency plans in case I didn't make it back home. Never in a million light-years could we have imagined it would be you who would leave us and never make it home.*

But you're back now, and I'm dreaming those dreams your mom and I started for you long ago. I'm imagining what you'll look like in ten years and twenty. I'm picturing you married to some lucky guy who deserves you, and I see you as a mother, sharing the strength you got from Diana and the gentleness of your birth mother. I'm picturing all this, and now I'm going to make sure those dreams come true . . . for me and for you.

Joseph Howard sent for me, and I'm going to make a deal with him to let you go home if I promise to stay. It won't be forever. I'll find a way home, but I need you to go now, Tallie. I need the joy of imagining you doing all the things your mother and I dreamed for you. Live free for all of us. Warn the world about how fragile freedom is and how hard it is to win back once lost. Do it for me and Meghan and Mom. When Joseph gives you the choice, take it.

Please.

Love you always and forever,
Dad

Tallie wiped at the tears trailing down her cheeks. "He's gone to see Joseph. We've got to get to him."

"We will," Norris promised, "but our first priority is to shut down Joseph's capability to seize control of our fleets and arsenals. Rich and Mak, dismantle all the servers stored in the security building. Getting home will mean nothing if we leave Joseph the tools he needs to intimidate the world."

"Roger that, Major," Mak replied.

"Rally back here?" Rich asked.

Major Norris nodded. "Copy that."

"Leave us each a gun," Marlene added, glancing at the two captive nurses. "No offense, ladies, but I'm tired of fighting with bedsheets and bare hands."

Rich and Mak grabbed their packs and pulled three firearms out, handing one each to Jackson, Tallie, and Marlene, and then they left.

The major turned to Tallie. "Do you know where Cai would be meeting with Joseph?"

"Most likely at his house. I went there today in a golf cart. It's probably a half mile from here, maybe a little more, but the path is level. We can make it on foot pretty quickly."

"We?" Norris looked at the remaining crew. "You girls are staying here to defend our rally point."

Tallie squeezed the gun in her hand and felt her heart rate slow and her mind focus. Once she had the gun stowed in the back waistband of her pants, she stepped to the door and looked back at Norris. "With all due respect, Major, I just found my father, and I'm not letting him sacrifice himself so I can leave here without him. There's no way I'm *not* going."

Norris looked at Marlene. "You too?"

"We won't go OK Corral on you, Daddy, but we're not staying behind."

"Neither am I." Jackson said from where he leaned against the wall. He brandished his gun and attempted to follow Norris, but his legs failed him and he fell against Livvie and Lei. Norris tapped his shoulder and shook his head. "You can barely stand, son. The best help you can offer right now is to stay here and keep these women from alerting the island's cavalry."

"We won't do anything to stop your escape," Lei said.

Norris eyed the pair. "Forgive me for not taking your word on that."

"I feel fine. I want to help," Jackson pled.

"I know you do, but you didn't recover from the toxin as fast as the others. I'm afraid you'll just slow us down."

He looked at Tallie. "I'm failing you again."

"No, you're not. I know what you went through to come here, and I know you did it for me. That means more than you can possibly know."

"But I'm worthless to you now."

"No, you're not," she repeated. "If there's a hole in the plan, you'll see it. That's what you do, and you'll do whatever it takes to fill it. Like the major said, right now what we need most is for you to stay here and protect the rally point so we have a safe place to come back to."

His head dipped in futility, as if he were feeling utterly useless, and then he seemed to understand that Tallie didn't have time to massage his ego. He quickly pulled himself up and smiled at her. "I'll hold down the fort. You go get your dad, but please be safe, Tallie. Please."

"I will. I know I can always count on you to have my back." She placed a light parting kiss on his cheek and left with Norris and Marlene.

* * *

Jackson lingered at the window after Tallie's group entered a line of heavy growth and disappeared.

"You're in love with her," one of the women said.

"Is it that obvious?" He gave a somber chuckle as he turned toward the nurses. "We've only known each other a few weeks, but I already know she's the most extraordinary woman I'll ever meet. I only wish she were as clear about my feelings for her as you are."

"She doesn't know you love her?" the other woman said. Her name was Lei, according to the nametag she wore.

"She thinks I'm temporarily smitten and that I'll wake up and realize we're wrong for each other." He dropped his head into his empty hand, the other still limply holding his gun.

"You're not a very good guard," Lei said.

When he looked back up, he found both women smiling at him.

"I trust you." He smiled back. "Besides, I wouldn't shoot you ladies even if you made a run for it."

Lei tilted her head to the side, as if she were sizing him up. "You're not like the rest of them."

"I think we've already established that fact, along with the notion that I'm a worthless hero."

"Quite the contrary," Lei said. "I think you're a very special kind of hero. You didn't come here to destroy Joseph's island. You leaped blindly into danger to save the woman you love."

Jackson revisited his failed heroic effort. "I could never rest knowing she was stuck in this tiny world. She deserves more. You all do." He studied the women's faces and saw their resistance to his statement. "I don't disagree with Joseph's wishes. Don't all sane people want an end to conflict and plenty for all? Of course we do, but I disagree completely with his plans for achieving those goals."

"What would you do instead?" Lei's friend—Livvie, according to her nametag—challenged.

"Well, for starters, I'd fire Joseph Howard because he's too desperate for power. My father taught me that if you want a good leader, you should find the smartest man for the job who *doesn't* want it."

"A man like George Washington," Livvie answered numbly. "He walked away from the presidency when he could have been a king."

Lei looked at Livvie. "That's right. I'd almost forgotten that. The children on the island aren't taught American history, and it's been so long since I was in school."

"Joseph says the founding fathers were oppressors who don't deserve to be commemorated," Livvie explained to Jackson.

"I don't know how he can dismiss all the good they've done." Jackson spread a hand toward the couch, inviting the women to sit down while he turned a chair to face them and sat down as well. "They were flawed men, but they were also brilliant and inspired."

Lei leaned forward and rested her elbows on her knees. "Joseph says the Constitution is an antiquated document."

"That's not true. The founders never intended their work to be the end of the struggle for liberty. They knew it was just a rocky, fragile beginning. It's a miracle we have the Constitution at all. The men at the convention had to cobble votes together around the weaknesses and prejudices of the people in their day. They knew it was flawed, but they put forward the best document they could pass, expecting each generation that followed to strengthen and improve it. It was a beginning, not an end."

"Isn't that what Joseph is trying to do?" Lei asked. "Improve the system?"

"No. He's bypassing our Constitution and other countries' as well. He believes we, the people, are too lazy or stupid to manage our own governments, especially when, in his view, governments were founded by flawed individuals. And they were flawed, if you judge the leaders of the past by the standards of our day. Who could survive being judged by the sensibilities of people two hundred and fifty years in the future? But judge them within the context of their own time and they're visionaries."

The women were listening but silent.

"Put yourselves in their places," Jackson continued. "Someday your children and grandchildren will look back on this moment, and what do you want them to see? People who were content to surrender their rights and freedoms in exchange for a waterfront view? Or people who argued and debated issues and tripped and fell sometimes, trying to strengthen their government for their children?"

Livvie folded and unfolded her hands. "You're not teaching us anything new, but people wear out. The news is so terrible. When you don't know how to fix things, it's easier to pretend you don't see it. We don't have to pretend here. At least, we haven't had to so far." An unhappy look crossed her face. "But the young people aren't content at all. Even the ones who were little when they arrived are growing bored and antsy."

Lei began to speak and stopped herself before apparently deciding to voice her thought. "Livvie's right. Go next door to the computer-hub building, for example. You'll find a young technician named Zain, who'll tell you he's ready to leave this island." Lei winked at Jackson and removed his IV, replacing it quickly with a bandage. "He might be able to help you with a few other things as well."

Jackson nodded slowly as her meaning sank in. "Can I trust you ladies to stay here and watch the fort?"

"You can," Lei said, placing a gentle touch on his arm. "But take that gun with you."

Jackson secured the gun in the back of his belt and stumbled to the largest building he could see, the one the women called the computer-hub building. The damaged door took him aback. It bore signs that Rich and Mak had entered by force. The large outer lock had been cut, and the door lock was blackened, as if it had been chemically burned through. Jackson entered slowly, announcing his arrival in soft calls.

Mak met him with his gun raised but lowered it when he saw who it was. "Sorry, brother. We can't take chances. Who's guarding the ladies?"

"They're guarding each other, on the honor system."

"Whoaaaa, bro. You'd better hope that works out." Mak walked him through the building that hummed with water pumps and turbines. This was not just the communications center. It housed the essential machines that delivered water and power to the people.

Rich was kneeling in front of a stacked column Jackson assumed was the island's mainframe. He was in the company of a dark-haired teen who was bound and gagged. He looked to be about fifteen.

"Zain?" Jackson asked.

Rich looked up from the mainframe he was working on. "You know each other?"

"Livvie and Lei told me he's a computer genius."

"So he says," Rich grumbled. "All the more reason not to trust him." He pulled out a panel, typed on his keyboard, and grumbled some more.

"You look like you're having problems," Jackson said.

"All the life-sustaining systems—water, power, heat, sanitation—run through this mainframe. If we use explosives to blow it, the island won't have any life-sustaining services, and we'll need to evacuate everyone." He sat on his haunches and shook his head. "I could rework things if I had time, but I don't. A security guard could come by any minute."

"Zain wants off this island as much as we do, according to the ladies," Jackson said. "He could help you if you let him."

Zain nodded excitedly, and Jackson removed his gag so he could speak. "You can get me off this island? I have grandparents in Jordan. If you can get me to them, I'll help you crash the server. I know every piece of this hardware. I run the equipment for the director's weekly video bulletin."

The thought of video capability intrigued Jackson. "Where is the director when he films the bulletin?"

"At home, but I control the feed from here using a high-def camera installed in the clock on his desk."

"So you can communicate with him from here?"

"Easily."

"Did you hear that, guys? Think we can undo his restraints now?"

Mak looked to Rich, who nodded. "Are you planning a little show of your own, Jackson?" Mak asked as he pulled out a knife and cut the zip ties restraining Zain.

Jackson arched his eyebrows. "If you destroy Joseph's mainframe, he'll be up and running again in weeks or months. But what if we can destroy his influence?"

Rich's eyebrows rose in approval. "You mean pull his web pages down?"

"I have something more permanent in mind." Jackson smirked.

"A broadcast?" Mak asked.

"The mother of all audio broadcasts."

Zain frowned and shook his head. "The director limits our signal strength so we remain hidden to the outside world. He flies to the mainland to do his interviews for the networks because we can't transmit that far."

"Our military sat-phone could." Mak wriggled his eyebrows and smiled.

"And I just happen to know the phone number of a small-town reporter who could use an AP-worthy story," Jackson said.

Rich handed him the satellite phone, and he punched in the number of his protégé at the *Kensington Courier*. "Jenna? It's Jackson James. I'm about to pay you back for stealing your story a few weeks ago. Put your phone on speaker. Good. Now, invite the AP to a video conference and prepare to broadcast through your phone. And how fast do you type, because I'm patching you in live to the story of your career."

CHAPTER TWENTY

Tallie heard shouting as she, Major Norris, and Marlene neared Joseph Howard's home. "That's Joseph. He's arguing with my father," she said. "I've got to get in there and calm them."

The major stopped her from bolting toward the house. "Arguing is much better than shooting. Let's keep it that way. Let's surveil the perimeter and see if any armed security guards were invited to this party."

Tallie followed along but not without worry, keeping her eyes and ears peeled to the angry sounds coming through the open atrium doors and windows. The noise from inside drew the attention of a male security guard doing rounds in his golf cart. The little rescue band hid behind trees and watched him rush into the house and exit nearly as quickly, as if he had been dismissed, yet he remained nearby, as if he were uneasy about what was happening in the house.

"That complicates things." Norris touched his ear and held a hand up, signaling to the women to wait. He reported to Mak and Rich on the coms and turned back to Tallie and Marlene. "Our guys are ready to crash the mainframe, but doing it will also affect the essential services and leave these people in dire straits. Jackson's with them now, and he has another idea. I think it's worth a try, but I need some help with the details."

The news heartened Tallie. Jackson was evidently better, and he'd come up with a plan to stop Joseph without harming the island paradise or its people. "I trust him," she said. "What details do you need help with?"

Norris relayed the go-ahead for the plan back to Mak, Rich, and Jackson, and then he signaled for the women to sit. "Tallie, you said Joseph wants me as well as Cai, so the plan is to get me inside that house and get Joseph to sit at his desk in front of a camera set up there."

"You can't just show up at his house," Tallie argued. "This is his island fortress. How will you explain your arrival without him fearing he's under attack? He'll panic and kill my father."

"That's the detail I need help with. What story will Joseph buy?"

"How *did* you get here?"

Norris's shoulders sagged as he thought of Burke again. "Burke died leading us in."

"Wait, what? Burke was here? And he's dead?" The world stopped for a moment as Tallie replayed her last conscious moments with the man. Her voice broke as she muttered, "He said he'd give his life to free me from here."

Norris placed his hand on her back and said, "He kept his word. He wanted you to know that."

"He was so lost and disillusioned about his military sacrifice and the world in general. Please tell me he made peace with his doubts."

"Yes, he did." Norris looked into the women's faces. "He found his way back to his brothers and to his country. Let's not waste his final sacrifice."

Tallie sniffed and wiped her eyes. "I think we can use it to defeat Joseph."

"What are you thinking?" Norris asked.

"Burke felt sure the Conservancy doubted his loyalty. Joseph would believe he turned on him, but you've got to convince Joseph that Burke helped you come in the way I did, or he'll worry that Burke led an army here." She turned to Marlene. "Who else arrived with you today?"

"Mak and Jackson. Mak and I were recruited as IT specialists."

"That had to have been arranged very recently."

"Three days ago," Norris said.

Tallie nodded as an idea formulated. "The intake nurses made it sound as if Joseph knows who comes and goes from here each day. Jackson was recruited by someone in the Conservancy. Joseph probably knows too much about him, but he may not have had time to receive details about Mak. Use him as your cover. Tell him that Burke arranged for you to come in undercover this morning as an IT guy named Mak."

Marlene shook her head. "You still need a reason for *why* you came here. If he thinks you came as his enemy, he'll kill you and Cai."

"Then, I'll have to convince him I came here as an enemy to Cai," Norris said.

Tallie's mouth felt dry, and her hands felt sweaty. "It's still risky."

Norris shrugged. "It's the best plan we've got. Now on to the next hurdle. I've got to get past that guard. I need a distraction."

"Is that all?" Marlene quipped. "I've got that covered. You just say when and get ready to run." She hugged her father. "Please be careful, Daddy."

"I will." He looked at Tallie. "I'm proud of both you girls. It'll be all right. I trust my team. Tallie, you cover us. Make sure Marlene gets back here safely. Then I want you two to keep your eyes on that armed yahoo. Don't let him enter that house or signal for reinforcements."

"Got it." Tallie nodded.

"Good girl. Now, Marlene, just keep him occupied for thirty seconds."

She winked at her father, saying, "Piece of cake," and wandered into the open area, turning around in circles as if she were trying to get her bearings.

The guard raised his weapon without convincing authority and sidled over her way. "I don't recognize you. Are you new here?" he asked.

"Yes. Marlene Bodine," she said in a breathy voice barely loud enough for Tallie to hear. "This morning. I just . . . I guess I'm not . . ." And then she pulled off a five-star partial-faint timed to make sure the man arrived in time to catch her. While the guard supported her weight and fussed over her health, the major sneaked along the perimeter and entered the house undetected.

Marlene had performed her role well . . . too well, perhaps, because the guard seemed unwilling to allow her to leave his care. He was trying to get Marlene into his golf cart as he muttered something about needing to drive her back to the infirmary. Tallie knew he had to be stopped or he'd soon find the nurses missing and likely call out more guards. When she and Marlene locked eyes, Tallie drew her hand across her throat, signaling that Marlene needed to stop the driver. Marlene signaled her understanding with a nod. She pretended to awaken in a fright, thrashing her arms at the man until she managed to get behind him and wrap her arm around his neck, catching his throat in the crook of her left elbow and tightening her hold. The man gave one gag before slipping to the seat of the cart in a lump. Once he was subdued, Marlene raised a thumb to signal that things were under control before she drove her sleeping victim into the tree line, where Tallie trusted that her friend could keep him under control when he came to.

With Marlene safe but occupied babysitting the guard, Tallie's attentions were torn between only two worries—what was going on in the house and wondering if more of Joseph's loyal followers would show. She made another pass around the house, listening to every word that slipped through the open windows and doors. Seeing no one, she pressed close to one of the open glass doors, where she could both watch the road leading to the house and hear well enough to know if and when she'd need to enter the conversation going on inside.

* * *

Stephen heard elevated voices echoing ahead. One was Cai's, while the other—Joseph's, he assumed—was reciting a litany of Cai's sins and the reasons he deserved to suffer. Stephen heard his own named mentioned and knew what line to play against Joseph.

His hands shook. It wasn't about his fear of Joseph or the threat posed. His team would see to that. It was more about his worry over his first meeting with Cai since he and Tallie been reunited on the island. There had been no time to ask her what Cai knew about his own part in her abduction. It was all so exhausting. He was worn down from the twenty-one years he'd spent keeping Tallie safe and leveling Julia's mania when she went off the rails. He was ready for the lies and secrets to be over—so ready that Joseph posed the lesser threat to his future. Losing Cai's friendship, and likely facing his wrath, worried him more, but even that didn't matter anymore. He'd gladly offer himself to Joseph or Cai for whatever retribution they felt they were owed so long as Marlene and the others got safely home.

It had already been a hard day of loss and sorrow and worry. He was getting older, and the weight of responsibility was harder to bear these days. Maybe he was getting soft in his old age, or maybe it was just that his heart had softened too much for this work. All he knew was that he needed every ounce of grit and will he could muster to outfox Joseph Howard, and willing to die for a good cause, he steeled his nerves, dug deep into his reservoir of strength, and announced his arrival in full voice before approaching the living room. "Joseph Howard? I hear you're looking for me."

"Yes. Wait . . . what? *Who* are you? I'm not ready for anyone yet. You weren't invited, not yet. Not yet! How did you get here?"

Tallie had been right about Joseph's mania. The panic in his voice made Stephen's skin crawl. The situation was more fluid and unpredictable than he'd imagined, and he quickly adjusted his game plan. "It's me. Major Stephen Norris. We have a mutual friend, Cooper Burke."

"Burke brought you here?"

"He sure did."

"So . . . the turncoat turned again, did he?"

"Not exactly. His life and career are ruined. All you left him with was a little information, which he offered to sell me for the right price."

"And what information is that, Major?"

"Who's on your current guest list and how to pose as an IT guy in order to be here when the great Cai Kaswell is brought to his knees."

"I see . . . I see," Joseph said. "Well . . . do come in, but if you have a weapon, please hold it over your head as you enter."

Stephen entered the room slowly and found his host sitting in a chair with his back to an open atrium door, alight with sun, nearly blinding Stephen. Joseph had a gun pointed at Cai, who was seated on the far-right side of a sofa.

"Thank you for coming, Major. Please, join us, but first, lay your gun down on the floor, very carefully, please."

The manic pleasure in the man's voice zipped chills up Stephen's spine as he did as Joseph instructed.

Cai turned and said, "Hello, Stephen."

Stephen nodded, hoping Cai would see through his ruse. "Cai."

"So glad you could make it, Major," Joseph said. "Before we begin, please lift your shirt and turn for me so I can check you for weapons."

Stephen complied, lifting his shirt and turning slowly to prove he had no gun tucked into his waistband.

"Now lift your pant legs, please, one at a time. I'm aware that socks make very convenient holsters too."

Glad he hadn't tried to sneak any additional weapons in, Stephen complied, and when his host was assured that his latest guest was clean, the man said, "Take a seat next to your friend, please. I assume he's why you're here, that you came to save an old friend. Or are you still friends?" He tapped the barrel of his pistol against his chin as Stephen settled onto the sofa farthest from Cai.

"I hope threatening General Kaswell's life with this gun will keep you in line too, Major, but now I'm not sure. Maybe neither of you'd care if the other died."

"We're not the barbarians you believe us to be," Cai replied.

"We'll see. How much do you actually know about the connection we all share, General? I've already told you I'm Diana Howard's father. I believe Major Norris was in command on the mission you all shared in Mogadishu."

"That's right," Stephen confirmed.

"Major, you know the details of this story more intimately than the general. Please, humor me while I catch him up. I assume you know by now, General, that Diana came home afraid of her own government and the Somalis, thanks to you two."

Cai didn't answer, but Stephen squinted and bobbed his head around until Joseph's annoyance at the distraction came to a head. He swung his gun toward Stephen and barked, "What exactly is wrong with you, Major?"

"The sun. It's directly behind you and blinding me. If this interrogation is going to last very long, would you mind moving somewhere else?"

Joseph huffed and ignored him, carrying on with his explanation to Cai. "I know you and Tallie Brown have spent time together. How long have you known that she's actually your daughter Molly?"

"Known? Just a few days. My heart recognized her the minute we first met, but my mind couldn't accept it. Accepting that truth was probably as painful for me as it was for you when you found out Diana was alive all those years. We both failed our girls."

Stephen applauded Cai's reply, especially when he saw how it unnerved Joseph, whose lower lip twisted and trembled before he pushed back. "I've atoned for that sin already, Major. But I wasn't the one my daughter was hiding from. It was you."

Feeling a little more pressure was in order, Stephen doubled down. "You can't face it, can you?"

"Face what?" Joseph spat back.

"She and Tallie were poor, afraid, and desperate for twenty-one years, but who did she reach out to? Not you. Me. How does it feel to know that she trusted the man you think betrayed her more than she trusted you? Who did she think was her biggest betrayer?"

Joseph turned his gun on Stephen. "You . . . you!" He growled the words more than spoke them. He stood and walked to where the major sat, pressing the gun barrel to his head.

Stephen tried not to flinch. He glanced Cai's way, hoping for a last show of caring from the fellow warrior he loved like a brother, but Cai appeared completely unaffected by the possibility of witnessing Stephen's execution. Either he was a spectacular actor, or Stephen's worries were true—his friend was no longer his friend because he now knew of Stephen's complicity in Tallie's hijacked life.

His thoughts turned to Marlene, the one person who would mourn his loss if this moment proved to be his last. He'd made her nearly as much a hermit as Julia had made Tallie, situating his brilliant, exceptional daughter in a library in backwoods Cutler's Ridge. He'd told her it was for her protection from the slimebag ex-husband who'd beaten her, but it was also because he'd needed her there; he'd needed someone who would wrap her arms around Tallie Brown if and when she ever made it out of Julia's hand. The women had become friends, good friends. They'd at least have each other if their fathers perished here, and he took some comfort in that.

"You did this, Major," Joseph finally sputtered. "Do you know your friend's part in all this, General?"

Stephen saw a new opening, and remembering Jackson's instructions to get Joseph behind the camera, he made his move to put Cai on alert and upset Joseph's script. He hoped Jackson was monitoring every word. "Your first mistake is in assuming that Kaswell and I were ever friends. He was a showboat when I led him, and he's been an opportunist ever since."

From the corner of his eye, he saw Cai's body flinch. Stephen had his attention. Now he needed to throw out a lie or two that would clue Cai into the ruse and bring him into the game. "You want to talk bitter? See this scar on my face? I got that doing what he did that night, but he became an international hero, and I got shipped off on a rinky-dink assignment to a base in a coal-mining town." He stood as if angry. "You want my story? My real story? Not the one the brass ordered me to say to protect their Silver Angel? Then, sit down at your desk and I'll tell you what I know. Write it down—all of it—and I'll sign it."

Joseph's face brightened with joy. "Like a military tribunal! Yes, yes!" The man was losing his grip on reality. He hurried to his desk, and as he moved, Stephen shot Cai a wink. Relief washed over him when Cai returned a guarded nod. They were on the same page.

Joseph set his gun beside his computer, within quick reach, and pulled a tablet of paper from his desk. He grabbed a pen from the drawer and chuckled as he made scribbles on a blank page to test the pen. "We could do this electronically," he said with glee, "but I want your confession and your undeniable signature in ink, on paper, so no one will ever question its authenticity. And in case either of you has a notion about charging me to get this gun, please know that I've made very good friends among our elite army rangers. They were quite anxious to repay me for my support of the military, and I accepted their offer to train me on the firing range. I'm sure I'm not as good a marksman as either of you, but I'm quite fast and deadly accurate, so feel free to test me. I'd enjoy that immensely." He chuckled. "Now, please begin, Major."

Stephen sat back down. "Diana was an outstanding soldier. Did you know she helped develop the gun Cai fired that night?"

As hoped, the mention of Diana's name, married to a compliment, distracted Joseph. He leaned forward and said, "I didn't. Thank you for telling me that."

"That's why she was there with us. She was the munitions expert who trained Cai on the weapon. We cared about her very much. So did our informant from the local village." Stephen held his breath as he waited to see how Joseph would react to the bread crumb.

Joseph grew thoughtful. "I traveled to that village in 1994, after attending my daughter's supposed funeral. No locals recognized her photo when I showed it to them." His tone turned bitter. "But they sang praises of Cai Kaswell, the man who'd walked through fire to save them." He smiled and looked at Stephen. "You have a right to feel cheated, Major. They knew it was Cai Kaswell's gunshot that set off the fire, but they forgave him because he tried to make it right." His tone was mocking as he sneered.

Cai bolted forward. "They knew I fired that shot?"

"You didn't know that?" Joseph's eyes glazed as if the concept were completely incredulous. He laughed. "You've carried the guilt of that night all these years, not knowing you were forgiven?" Another cackle escaped his lips. "Oh . . . it pleases me so much to think you've been living with that guilt all these years. It's what you deserve." He picked the gun back up and pointed it at Cai. "Yes, they knew. They said that during those weeks when your burns left you swinging between life and death, you screamed out and cried, 'I'm sorry,' pleading over and over for forgiveness. They forgave your mistake and focused on all their people you rescued as they nursed their hero back to life. And what was happening to my daughter during those weeks? When she found out your team executed that raid after a cease-fire had been called, she was terrified. You two moved on with your careers, but it affected her deeply. She was *afraid*, gentlemen. My sin is that I never gave her the chance to tell me about those fears, but Tallie knew them. Suffered under them. Have you ever been afraid? Oh, I want you to feel it now. I want you to know how bone-deep fear feels."

Cai moved to the front of his seat and asked in a voice filled with calm, "Is that why you built this island, Joseph?"

Emotions swirled across Joseph's face like paint in moving water. Stephen inched closer to Joseph's position while the man's mind wandered. He hoped to make a grab for the gun before the man lost all reason, but Joseph caught the change in position, which appeared to clear his focus.

"You missed your calling, General. You should have been a counselor. You're quite good at probing other people's thoughts."

"Let's see how good I really am," Cai said. "I think you've convinced the world and all those people you lured here that your purpose is to advance peace, but that's not true, is it? You built this place, and then you used your power and influence to gather more people with power and influence, and I think you did all that not for peace but for the exact opposite . . . to strike fear into those you hold responsible for Diana's death."

"You're not wholly right. My initial plan was to try to make a world where other fathers and mothers wouldn't have to bury their children because of war. But I dug into the facts of what happened that night in Mogadishu, and I banged on the doors of Congress for help, and you know what it got me? Empty promises of future hearings. That's when I decided they'd abdicated their right to be part of the process. I'd have to do it myself."

"What about those mothers and fathers whose children you were trying to save?"

"I couldn't trust something this important to them. Look at the percentages of those who even show up at the polls. They're followers. They want to be led, so I'm giving them leadership that requires nothing from them."

Stephen pretended to be fascinated by the concept, and asked, "What exactly is your plan?"

A new light entered Joseph's eyes. "Since you're not going to live to see the full finale, I'm happy to share it with you. It's brilliant. You've heard of banks that were too large to fail? Well, I've made myself an influence too powerful to doubt. No one can bring me down because the people who make the decisions love and trust me. I capitalized on that trust to build this paradise and handpicked intellectuals I knew I could influence. After all, who's going to contradict the man who holds their ticket to Utopia? I quote Doctor This and Professor That's research, and whatever I say is truth, whether in an interview with a news agency or on social media. I can sow division among the populace, deflect attention to causes I control, elevate the leaders or parties of my choice, and craft the agenda I want because power comes down to two things, friends: money and messaging. I have the money, and I own the ears of the people who influence everyone else, so if I say it or tweet it, a thousand other people will carry my message to a million more."

"But you didn't just want to control the messaging, did you?" Stephen asked.

Joseph leaned back as a bizarre peace, a mix of serenity and insanity, spread across his face. In theatrical style, he spread his hands wide and closed his eyes, saying, "But once you control the messaging, you can do anything else you want."

Cai huffed. "Like ground the US fleet?"

Joseph fell forward, smacking his hands on the desk. "Oh, General. Think bigger. Think redeploying that fleet or selling it piece by piece to the highest bidders. I will cause excruciating pain to this government and all the people who hurt my daughter."

Cai buried his face in his hands. When he lifted his head, he pled with Joseph. "I, of all people, understand the pain of losing a child. I thought I'd lost my entire family until I found Tallie, but I never wanted to punish innocent people because of my pain. Keep me. Kill me, if you like. I'm the one you want to hurt most."

"You're but a start, General, and I *will* hurt you. But first, I'll enjoy your suffering as you watch American might crumble, knowing you were the cause. But that will be but the beginning of your pain."

Stephen heard Jackson's voice in his ears. "We've got what we need, Major, and we streamed it all to the AP."

Stephen chuckled and said, "Copy that. Well done."

"What?" Joseph asked. "What did you say?"

"Look into the camera and say hello to your former audience, Joseph Howard. You're finished. Your halo is gone."

Joseph flailed his gun wildly from Cai to Stephen and back. "What are you saying? What do mean?"

"Check the light on your video camera," Stephen said with undeniable pleasure. "You've just broadcasted your maniacal, egotistical war plan to the entire world. Those big-name influencers you've been counting on are bailing on you and distancing themselves from you as fast as they can."

Joseph began frantically typing on his keyboard, growing more manic with every stroke.

"It won't do you any good," Stephen said with a grin. "Our team disabled your entire network . . . with the help of a few of your not-as-loyal-as-you-thought citizens."

* * *

Tallie entered the house when the major told Joseph to look in the camera, and she rushed into the room as Joseph stood and aimed his gun at her father. "Don't! Please don't!" She ran up to Joseph, startling him as she stood in front of the gun. Her father and Stephen moved quickly to intercept Joseph, but their actions only made the man more frantic, putting Tallie in further danger.

"Back up," she said to the men. "He won't hurt me if you just back up, please."

"No, Tallie," her father argued, and Joseph swung his gun toward him.

"Please put it down, Grandfather. I could never love the man who murdered my father."

"Tallie," Joseph muttered pitifully. "Of course. I'm so distraught that I don't know what I'm doing. You're all I have. I need you. You alone can help me." He reached a trembling hand to her, and she took it.

"It'll be all right. It'll be all right now," she said.

"Oh, Tallie, my sweet girl. You know I love you. You'll help your grandfather, won't you?"

"It's going to be okay. I'm here. I'm here now. Just give me the gun." She continued to speak soothingly to him as she gingerly took the pistol and slid it toward her father.

Joseph crumpled over the desk, leaning on it for support. "Tell your father about our plans, Tallie. Tell him you love me. Tell him you'll stay with me."

She placed a hand on his back and looked back at her father as she said, "I'll help you get better, Grandfather, but I won't help you with your plans."

"Foolish girl," he groaned with a dark rumble. "Wrong answer." He bolted back up, moving behind her with an object in his hand—a knifelike letter opener he'd picked up from the desk—and grabbed her as he pressed it to her neck. She cried out as the tip of the blade broke her skin.

"No, stop!" her father shouted, but Joseph continued to speak as though he hadn't heard him.

"Stupid, stupid, stupid girl," he snarled. "For all your brilliance, you forgot the first rule of warfare. Surely Diana taught you that—self-preservation."

Her father flinched and jerked, his eyes darting around as if looking for an opening to disarm Joseph. He glanced at Norris, who was equally wary, his hands spread forward to try to calm Joseph. The manic man responded by pressing the point deeper into Tallie's neck. Tallie gasped when a trickle of blood flowed from the wound, and panic drained the blood from her father's face as he said, "Okay, okay!" before retreating.

Both her father and the major looked on helplessly as they backed up. Tallie understood. One wrong move would give Joseph the satisfaction of taking her life and leaving her father blaming himself for his final failure—his last family member's death.

She heard a whisperlike cacophony of sound come from somewhere. When she saw the major cringe and touch his ear, she knew it was likely the frantic, worried cries of Jackson. Her eyes burned as she considered what he was feeling as he listened to every word through the coms.

But Joseph heard the sounds also. "You've all got coms!" he said, his voice wild. "Well-played, Major. How convenient for me. Tell your men to ready my chopper. I leave safely with Tallie, or she dies."

The nightmare wasn't ending, and once again Tallie questioned whether it ever would. Whether she'd ever know a day's peace. She wondered what Julia would say or do right now. None of Julia's words of wisdom came to mind, but her actions did. Tallie recalled Julia chastising her for wandering off or for venturing too far into a river. Her concern was always about keeping Tallie safe, even when her words or actions pained Tallie as a child. She remembered the letter Julia left her, warning her to run, and she wondered now if Julia's father was on the list of people she was trying to protect Tallie from.

As the letter opener pressed deeper into the skin covering the artery of her neck, Tallie thought of Julia, but she spoke to Joseph. "You didn't deserve Diana. She was better than you."

"Neither did you. She was ill, but you're a fool. You could have inherited an empire, had the power to mold the world in whatever way you chose, but you threw it all away, and now you're going to comply or die."

The hours spent sparring with Julia returned to her with clarity, perhaps for just such a moment as this. Along with those memories came the skills ingrained—the ability to calm her breathing and remain as still as a bird on a wire when all she really wanted to do was crumple and cry out. She recalled, even under pressure, the body's most vulnerable points, the angles and thrust needed to inflict injury, and the will to use all those tools when needed.

"Not today." Tallie moved as deftly as a hummingbird as she grabbed Joseph's knife-wielding hand with both of hers and yanked it down, away from her neck. She sank her bodyweight into the motion, then ducked backward underneath his arm and shoved the knife into his side with a quick jab that she knew would wound him but not fatally. Dropping his hold on the letter opener, he gasped, stumbled, and sank to the floor. Tallie let it fall, kicking it away from him. She knelt on the stone floor next to him and lifted his small frame into her arms as he sputtered and gasped again, looking up at her like a fearful animal. Their eyes met, and while she showed him mercy and compassion, she was no longer chasing fennecs. She saw clearly the danger the man and his ideas posed.

"You won. Rightly so, child. I'm so sorry. So very sorry. I didn't mean what I said. I'm not a well man. Get me to my chair, will you? I can't . . . I can't breathe. I need my medicine."

Tallie looked to her father, who came to her side. Together they helped Joseph into his desk chair. The older man reached to open his desk drawer, and her father slammed his hand down, denying Joseph access to the drawer. Joseph shrank back and whined. "Surely you wouldn't deny a wounded man his medicine."

Carefully, cautiously, they allowed him to open the drawer, from which he removed an inhaler, placed it to his mouth, and pressed the button, releasing the contents in a soft puff.

Angry voices flared up outside.

Norris touched his ear again, and his face grew stern. "The locals heard the entire broadcast. They know they were duped, and they're coming for Joseph."

"We can't let them have him," Tallie replied. "He's unbalanced. He needs help."

She turned to assure Joseph that she'd protect him, but she found the man devoid of fear. Instead, a peaceful smile graced his lips.

"Are you all right?" she asked him.

"Quite all right, my child."

"What's happening? Your coloring is off." She reached for his pulse and found it slow and thready. "Something's wrong. What did he take?" she asked as she reached for the inhaler to check the name.

Her father shoved himself between her and the desk. "No, Tallie. Don't touch it!"

Norris pulled Joseph's head back and checked his pulse for himself. "Thready."

Joseph's head slumped to the side and Tallie reached for him, crying out, "Grandfather!"

Her father wrapped his arms around her. "He had this end all planned out. An inhaler filled with toxin."

"Find the antidote!" Tallie reached for the drawer, ready to rifle through it, but her father prevented her again.

"No, Tallie, no! You could be poisoned too," he said. "The toxin could be all over the drawer."

Tallie pulled back and wrapped her arms around Joseph. "Please, Grandfather, tell me where it is," Tallie begged. "Let me help you!"

"Don't cry, child," Joseph said faintly. "I'm going home . . . to Diana. Be happy for me."

After a few moments, his head slumped to the side, and Norris removed his hand from Joseph's neck. "He's gone."

Tallie looked away and walked to a window, where she could see angry people, some with fists raised, some with guns, surrounding the house.

"I'll tell them," Norris said. With a look back at Tallie and her father, he headed out the door to face the angry mob.

"No," Tallie said. "I'll tell them. He said I inspired him to create this island. It's my responsibility."

Her father walked with her outside to the porch, where dozens of shouting people—some angry, some fearful—were already gathered. Others were making their way up the path. Among them were Jackson, Mak, and Rich, who were coming at a dead run.

Marlene moved up to the porch too and spoke in an undertone so as not to be overheard by the mob. "This could get ugly and violent. The guard I took down mentioned Joseph's cache of guns."

Tallie moved forward, flanked by her father and Major Norris, and faced the crowd. "I know most of you heard everything your director said, and I know you're confused and angry. He brought you here under the pretense of making the world better, and I think that was his intention, at least in the beginning. But he lost his way, and in that process, he led you astray as well."

A man called out from the angry audience. "Where is he? We want to hear from him."

Tallie took a deep breath and said, "I'm sorry to tell you that Joseph Howard committed suicide a few minutes ago. He had preloaded his inhaler with a deadly dose of the veil drugs and used it after he learned his plans had been broadcast."

The crowd was instantly subdued, and then their voices turned to a churning swell of diverse emotions. Some of the people dabbed at their eyes while others muttered in confusion and still others grew angrier.

"Who are you to tell us about the director?" another man shouted.

Tallie took her father's hand. "I'm Tallie Brown. The woman who raised me was Joseph's daughter, Diana. I know how you feel—confused and angry and lost. He brought me here against my will, just as he brought many of you, and like you, he wanted me to believe in the world he said he'd build. But it was all a charade. A lie." She turned to her father and Major Norris. "But this man is General Cai Kaswell, my father. He and Major Norris are going to help us figure out what to do going forward."

A low hum spread through the crowd of disaffected citizens.

"He's just part of the problem," a young woman hollered. "One of the current talking heads we wanted to get rid of."

"We don't want you here!" came another shout. "Get off our island!"

A guard brandished a gun and yelled, "We can make you leave."

Tallie's father and Major Norris pulled their daughters behind them, and Rich and Mak moved in front of them all, fully armed. Jackson ran to the porch and shouted, "Are you ready to fight the entire world? You can't hide here anymore. You're not the only ones who heard that broadcast. The whole world did. Anyone with a signal tracer can find you and this place now."

Another voice yelled, "You ruined everything . . . everything we've spent years building."

A woman cried out, "What will happen to us now? This is our home. We walked away from everything out there. We have nowhere else to go."

Their anger turned on Tallie with shouts of "You did this! You and your friends!" As the murmuring ramped up again, Livvie and Lei stepped forward and faced their peers.

"Just hold on, everybody," Livvie said. "It's our own fault. We did this as much as the director did. We tried to convince ourselves that we were working *around* the system, but we knew the truth." She seared her gaze into one man in particular, and Tallie assumed it was her husband, the chair of the Brain Trust. "Shame on all of us," she said. "Most of you are supposed to be the brightest lights in your fields. Deep down, you had to know what Joseph had you doing. Shame on us for inflicting this on our own children, but that's not even the worst part of it. We weren't content to hide here in our own little Utopia. We wanted to decide how everyone else should live too."

Lei moved forward and dabbed at her eyes. "We had a little civics lesson today, and I remembered things I'd forgotten or, rather, things I wanted to ignore, like the Constitution and the price others, like my own son, paid for the freedom we've abused. We're not leaders or heroes or founders. We're tyrants, and maybe traitors too. I don't know anymore. I can't see my way forward from here. I only know one thing. My boy also wanted to change the world, but this isn't how he would have done it."

"Go to your homes now," Cai said. "When there's something new to report, we'll announce it to everyone."

Their anger diffused somewhat, and the group began to disperse, mumbling as they filtered away.

Rich stepped up next to Norris. "I don't know how this is going to end, but we've definitely succeeded in setting the world on fire. Half the Pentagon called our sat-phone. They're ordering us back to D.C. ASAP, and they're sending us armed transportation."

"They don't trust us to come home on our own?" Norris asked.

"They don't know who or what to trust right now," Rich said.

"Can't say I blame them." Cai winced.

Tallie returned with him to the house and stared at the chair where Joseph's body remained. His tentative arm slipped loosely over her shoulder, as if he were unsure of what she needed in that moment. They stood together in silence for several long seconds before she turned toward him, burying her face in his shoulder.

"I wish I knew what to say to you right now," her father whispered, placing a kiss on her head.

"I'm just glad you're here. I don't even know what I'm feeling. I can't explain it, but finding Joseph helped me make peace with Julia. I've been so angry at her for taking me away, but I also love her more than ever. Can you forgive me for that?"

"There's absolutely nothing to forgive. She was the only mother you knew, and you're just beginning to understand that she loved as well and as much as she was capable of doing."

"Joseph too. They were both so broken. Me too, I guess."

Her tears poured hot as her father held her in his arms, whispering, "It's going to be okay," over and over.

People entered softly and retreated, giving the pair their privacy. When the tears stopped, Tallie lifted her head. "Don't ever leave me. Promise me that you and I will always have each other."

Before he could answer, Mak and Rich entered. "Would you like us to move Joseph's body?"

Tallie's father deferred to her. "Yes, please," she said and watched the men handle Joseph's body with respect as they moved him to his bedroom.

When they returned, Rich said, "Major Norris told us to spread the word that military transport is coming. Not everyone is taking the news well."

"We're arranging guards for the house to make sure no one unwanted comes in," Mak added.

Her father thanked them, and then he and Tallie moved to a window to observe the people as they responded to the news. The island became a hive of motion as the residents fearfully prepared for the military's arrival. Rich and Mak headed out to find some of Joseph's most disgruntled citizens to train them to guard key buildings and records from Conservancy loyalists who might attempt an insurrection or attempt to destroy proof of Joseph's reach and goals.

Tallie was grateful for the aloneness the guards provided, giving her time to sort out her losses and gains, the guilt and the hope. Somehow, she ended up on the sofa with her father's arm still around her.

"How are you holding up?" he asked.

She shook her head. She had no words to express the chaos in her mind. They sat a while longer, and then she finally said, "I was never really sure until today, but I am now. She loved me, in her own way."

"Diana?"

"She'll always be Julia to me. Am I a terrible person because I remember how she protected me more than I'm angry because she abducted me?"

"Not at all," her father whispered and kissed her head again. "I understand, and I can even appreciate all the good she poured into you. Everything your birth mother and I gave you and everything Julia gave you combined to make you the amazing woman sitting here with me today, my daughter, a survivor who's triumphed over things that would have dropped battle-hardened men." He framed her face in his hands. "Do you have any idea how proud I am of you and how very much I love you?"

"I love you too, but everything is such a mess. I can't get the image of Joseph out of my head, and even though he's gone, the world still has to deal with the division and damage he and his philosophies have caused. The entire world's in chaos. Life feels scary."

"Today was a win. People saw him for what he was, and hopefully, they've learned not to follow anyone so blindly again. Hopefully, they'll read more, think more, ask more questions around the dinner table."

"The dinner table . . . that sounds nice." She laid her head down on his shoulder. "Tell me we're going to be happy."

He paused before answering. "You're going to be so very happy. And you've got a young man waiting outside who wants to help you find that happiness."

Tallie noticed the obvious absence of his own place in that future. She lifted her head and studied his face as a sickening understanding passed between them. "No," she said softly. "Tell me we're *both* going to be happy."

"We are." He combed a single finger through her pony-tailed hair. "I'm going to be happy because every day will be filled with memories of Deidre and Meghan and dreams about my beautiful daughter Tallie and her amazing life."

"Tell me we're going to be happy *together*. Please." Her voice was but a whimper as she slumped against him. "I just found you. I can't lose you again."

He pulled her close. "You'll never lose me or my love. Remember that, Tallie. But my secret's out. In a way, I'm glad not to carry that lie around, but there will be repercussions. I don't know what they'll be, but it doesn't matter." He brushed a tear off her cheek. "All that matters is that you're free and safe. But we have a little time. Tell me your dreams. What do you want to do with the rest of your life?"

She hugged him close. "Right now I just want you to hold me." She drew a breath that caused her shoulders to shudder.

Norris entered quietly, head down, his hands folded in front of him.

"What is it, Stephen?" Tallie's father asked.

Norris shook his head. "It can wait a little longer."

"No. Let's face it head-on. Give it to me straight."

"Our transport is two hours out. A company of men from Fort Bragg are being assigned here to inventory the weapons, and then specialists will be called in to disarm this place."

"And Joseph's people?" Tallie asked.

"They're all being transported stateside for debriefing. Some may face charges."

"And us?" her father asked.

Norris shrugged. "The brass has gone silent. I don't know if that's good or bad." He turned and left.

Tallie put her head back on her father's shoulder. "Can we forget what might happen when we get back? Could we just dream for a little while longer?"

"I'd like that." Her father brushed stray hairs back from her face and pulled her close again.

"Where shall we go?" she asked.

"My choice?"

Tallie nodded into his shoulder.

"Then, close your eyes, sweet girl. We're packing our gear and hiking up a mountain in the Smokies to a sweet little estuary off the Little Pigeon River that's filled with brook trout."

They dreamed on for an hour about peaceful places where Kaswell family memories had been made, until Jackson walked in timidly, paused, and turned to leave again.

Tallie's father called out to him. "Don't leave, Jackson. Will you stay with Tallie until the transport comes? The major and I need to get a few things ready in case I'm hauled off to the brig."

Tallie cried out, "Don't leave, Dad!" as Norris walked in behind Jackson.

"I don't think that's going to be a problem, Tallie. Cai, I just heard from a friend at the Pentagon. The world heard everything, including your admission of guilt and your offer to sacrifice your freedom and even your life to stop Joseph. Add that to Joseph's own admission that the Mogadishu shot was an accident and the news that the villagers knew everything and forgave you long ago. You're trending on all the social media platforms. There's no official word yet, but it seems people are willing to forgive a man who takes responsibility for his mistakes. I'm happy for you."

He started to exit the room, but Tallie's father caught his arm and stopped him. "I suppose I can learn from everyone else and forgive a man who took responsibility for his mistakes by spending most of his life protecting the victim of his error."

Norris blinked and nodded. "Thanks, Cai."

"Thank you, Stephen, for keeping my girl safe. Now, let's give these two some time together while we round up as much evidence on this Conservancy as we can. Joseph had moles all over the globe. Let's start digging and see what we can find."

Norris and Tallie's father left the room, leaving her and Jackson in awkward silence.

"Are you okay?" Jackson asked after a moment.

"I will be."

"Good. That's good."

"You saved the day, just like I knew you would."

"No," Jackson said with a humble tilt of his head. "Maybe just a tiny piece of the world." He smiled and pinched his fingers close.

Tallie laughed and walked to him, finding his arms open and waiting for her. "I've learned a lot this week."

"I'm sure you have."

"No . . . I mean about myself and about love."

Jackson's head tipped again and Tallie continued. "Joseph brought me here and wanted me in his life because he wanted me to carry on his legacy. His love was about what I could do for him. My father offered himself in order to free me. His love was about what he could give. I recognized it because that's how you love, but it's also how Julia loved. She wasn't soft and she didn't sing lullabies, but everything she did was about taking care of me . . . about keeping me safe."

"Sounds like you've made peace with everything."

"I'm getting there. I've also come to realize that the voice I hear in my head isn't Julia's. It's mine. It's what she taught me and who she helped me become. This is where Julia was leading me all along—not to follow her but to find myself, and I think I have."

"And now you have your father."

"And you, if you're still interested in teaching a fast learner about bedtime stories and lullabies."

Jackson slipped his arms around her waist. "I think that could definitely be arranged."

EPILOGUE

The buzz in the courtroom of the United States Court of Appeals for the Armed Forces increased as the gavel fell. Reporters from every quarter of the globe rushed forward to interview General Kaswell, forcing his chief of security to pull him from the room while his communications specialist fielded questions.

Tallie waited in the wings for his arrival. "Have I told you how handsome you look in your uniform, Dad?"

He smiled as his cheeks reddened. "Only about seventeen times. But keep it up. You're good for my sagging ego."

"Sagging?" Jackson said. "You just hit a homerun in there. 'Censure without prosecution.'"

Tallie used her sleeve to polish the bars on her father's dress uniform. "And, according to the major, the president is ready to reoffer you the post as United States Ambassador to the United Nations."

"That's why he put your staff in place," Norris added.

"Oh, Stephen." Tallie's father sighed. He shook his head and wrapped an arm around her. "My reputation is tarnished. I don't deserve the post."

"That's why the people love you, Dad. You're someone Jackson's father would approve of."

"A battle-scarred has-been?"

"'The best man for the job he doesn't want,'" Tallie said.

"Exactly," Jackson agreed.

Tallie's father brushed the praise away. "All right, all right. It's almost time to go. I need to change. You should too."

"I will on the plane," Tallie said. "I've got my rucksack ready to go."

"Julia trained you well," he said.

"Now it's your turn." She grinned.

"Happy to pick up where she left off."

Norris pulled her father aside as Jackson sidled over to where Tallie stood. He wiped a hand across his sweaty brow and leaned on her shoulder. "For the record, those reporters are relentless. Everyone wants an exclusive with your father."

Tallie took him by the shoulders, stood him up, and straightened his ruffled hair. "Payback is rough, isn't it, Pulitzer?"

"Touché!"

"No worries." She placed her hands back on his shoulders. "I'm confident these shoulders can handle the job, Mr. Future Director of Communications. Will you miss being a black-ops specialist?"

"Hmm . . . maybe a little."

"I hear Mak and Rich have extended an open invitation for you to share baseball night with Blue 12 whenever you're here in D.C."

"It's not the same. I'm only welcome on the second floor. They canceled my keycard."

"I know that's disappointing, but if all goes as expected, you'll soon have a new keycard—to the UN. How great is that?"

He bobbed his head in humble agreement. "Pretty stinking awesome, I'd say. And my parents are flying out so I can show them the bright lights of New York City."

"They're proud of you, as am I."

"Then, I've got everything I've ever wanted." He kissed her softly.

Her father's chief of security replied to a message on her coms. "Your driver just checked in. Your car is here, General."

"Thanks, Marlene. I just need a moment."

"Roger that, General. You've got to leave in five to make your flight."

Tallie chuckled. "You've got to stick to the schedule, Dad. Marlene needs us to make that flight because she's scheduled to go off duty at eight. The word on the street is that she and Mak are having their first big date tonight."

"Okay, okay. I'll change and be back in five."

As Tallie's father left, Jackson shot Marlene a look. "Poor Bodie."

Marlene rolled her eyes. "He's booked at Comic Con in Chicago with his *people*. He'll be just fine. And what about you, Miss Bazillionaire? Now that the courts have certified you as Joseph's legal heir, you'll have to learn how to live with the heavy burden of extravagant wealth."

Tallie blushed. "Some of that inheritance is greatly in question. There's talk of the government seizing the island as a military training installation."

"How do you feel about that?" Marlene asked.

"With my background?" She smiled. "I'd be fine with that. If they don't take it, I'll put the island in a trust for the people Joseph moved there, or at least to those who want to stay and who weren't charged with crimes. Livvie and Lei could be in serious trouble for administering drugs to people without consent, and Lei's husband and the entire Brain Trust are facing multiple indictments for conspiracy and a dozen other potential federal crimes."

Marlene winced. "It's still such a mess. Most of them walked away from their lives, leaving their families thinking they were dead. How could they do that?"

"They were desperate people in one way or another. It'll take months, maybe years, to sort this all out, but I'd like them to know they have a place to live and work while the legal process plays out," Tallie said.

Marlene rubbed her prickled arms. "That's very generous of you, sugar, but I wonder if it'll ever feel like Utopia again after everything those people've learned about Joseph's schemes and plans."

"Good point. Malik, the groundskeeper, suggested we open the island up as a vacation destination for travelers if and when the legal issues are settled. Maybe hosting happy visitors would help, but making any idea like that happen could be years down the road. The military has to remove Joseph's weapon cache, for one thing."

"And the rest of that fortune?" Marlene said.

"I'm going to run a trust."

"Oh dear. Another trust? Isn't that how we got into this mess?" Marlene asked.

"Not a brain trust, Marlene. A charitable foundation to fulfill some of Joseph's peace initiatives, like clean water, food programs, educational and occupational training, and medical services."

Jackson hugged Tallie. "That's my girl."

Tallie's father returned in jeans and a flannel shirt. "I'm ready to go."

"Look at you!" Jackson laughed. "Where are you two headed? I thought you were going to dinner."

"We're going to *catch* our dinner." Tallie smiled and winked at her father. "We're heading to the Smokies to fish for trout."

Norris walked up dressed in similar attire and must've noticed the stares from the group. "What? This is appropriate attire for the off-site security specialist. But don't worry. I won't horn in on your first daddy-daughter date. You won't even know I'm there."

Tallie's father chuckled and squeezed her shoulder. "Are you ready?"

"You bet I am. I've waited twenty-one years for this date."

She stepped beside Jackson and rested her head on his shoulder as she surveyed their little band of warriors. Everything had changed in a few weeks, some good. Hopeful. Her life was brim with love and possibilities she dared only dream of before. Her father looked over at her, smiled, and winked, sending a warmth into her that lingered and filled her with security. She was no longer alone. Cai Kaswell had put loving her above career and reputation. She was fully his, a daughter to a man she respected and adored.

And her father wasn't the only man who loved her. She and Jackson were not only back on course but moving forward—together. When she imagined her future, he was in it, right by her side; they were equals who were better together than they were apart.

She caught Marlene straightening her father's collar while the major wagged a finger at her, presumably over her upcoming date with Mak. The past weeks had proven Marlene's, Norris's, and Jackson's loyalty to her and her father, and they were family to Tallie.

A contented sigh escaped her, and Jackson tipped her face up to meet her gaze. "Happy?"

"Excruciatingly. Everything I've ever dreamed of is right here in these people in this room." She leaned over and kissed Jackson goodbye. "See you in a few days?"

"I'll be here," he promised. "I love you."

"I know that now. I absolutely know that, and I love you too." She placed another kiss on his lips that set the room off in a howl.

"Time to go," Marlene said as she checked her watch.

Tallie picked up her rucksack and gave Jackson a whimsical smile as she stepped away.

"Don't rush your return," Jackson said as he lifted his hand to wave goodbye. "Life will get busy when you get back. Relax and enjoy your dream come true. Like you said. You've waited a long time for this."

"I'll savor every minute, but truthfully? I'm almost more excited to see what's ahead."

ABOUT THE AUTHOR

Laurie (L. C.) Lewis is a weather-whining wife, mother, and grandma. She's also crazy about crabs, nesting boxes, twinkle lights, sappy movies, and the sea. It's documented that she's craft-challenged and particularly lethal with a glue gun, so she set her creative juices to writing, which was less likely to burn her fingers.

Born in Baltimore, Laurie will always be a Marylander at heart, but a recent move to a house overlooking Utah Lake makes Utah her new love. Her Maryland years, spent within the exciting and history-rich corridor between Philadelphia, Baltimore, and D.C., made her a history nerd and a political junkie. During Laurie's years as a science-education facilitator, she honed her research skills, eventually turning to writing full time.

Revenge Never Rests is Laurie's fifteenth published novel. She writes in multiple genres, penning her women's fiction and romance novels as Laurie Lewis and her historical fiction novels as L. C. Lewis.

She's a RONE Award winner (*The Dragons of Alsace Farm*) and was twice named a New Apple Literary Award winner in 2017 (*The Dragons of Alsace Farm*). In 2018 she won Best New Fiction (*Love on a Limb*). She is a BRAG Medallion honoree, and she was twice named a Whitney Award and USA Best Book Award finalist.

Laurie loves to hear from her readers, and she invites you to join her VIP Readers' Club or contact her on social media.

VIP Readers' Club: laurielclewis.com/newsletter
Website: laurielclewis.com
Twitter: @laurielclewis
Goodreads: goodreads.com/author/show/1743696.Laurie_L_C_Lewis
Facebook: facebook.com/LaurieLCLewis/
Instagram: @laurielclewis
BookBub https://www.bookbub.com/profile/laurie-lewis